CROWN PRINCE'S CHOSEN BRIDE

BY
KANDY SHEPHERD

All rights reserved including the right of reproduction in whole or in part in any form. This edition is published by arrangement with Harlequin Books S.A.

This is a work of fiction. Names, characters, places, locations and incidents are purely fictional and bear no relationship to any real life individuals, living or dead, or to any actual places, business establishments, locations, events or incidents. Any resemblance is entirely coincidental.

This book is sold subject to the condition that it shall not, by way of trade or otherwise, be lent, resold, hired out or otherwise circulated without the prior consent of the publisher in any form of binding or cover other than that in which it is published and without a similar condition including this condition being imposed on the subsequent purchaser.

® and ™ are trademarks owned and used by the trademark owner and/or its licensee. Trademarks marked with ® are registered with the United Kingdom Patent Office and/or the Office for Harmonisation in the Internal Market and in other countries.

First published in Great Britain 2016
By Mills & Boon, an imprint of HarperCollins Publishers
1 London Bridge Street, London, SE1 9GF

© 2016 Kandy Shepherd

Printed and bound in Spain
by CPI, Barcelona

First Published in Great Britain 2016
By Mills & Boon, an imprint of HarperCollins*Publishers*
1 London Bridge Street, London, SE1 9GF

© 2016 Kandy Carpenter

ISBN: 978-0-263-91968-4

23-0316

Kandy Shepherd swapped a career as a magazine editor for a life writing romance. She lives on a small farm in the Blue Mountains near Sydney, Australia, with her husband, daughter and lots of pets. She believes in love at first sight and real-life romance—they worked for her! Kandy loves to hear from her readers. Visit her at www.kandyshepherd.com.

To Cathleen Ross,
in gratitude for your friendship!

CHAPTER ONE

USING AN OLD-FASHIONED wooden spoon and her favourite vintage-style ceramic bowl, Gemma Harper beat the batter for the cake she was baking to mark the end of her six months' self-imposed exile from dating.

Fittingly, the cake was a mixture of sweet and sour—a rich white chocolate mud cake, flavoured with the sharp contrast of lemon and lime. For Gemma, the six months had been sweet with the absence of relationship angst and tempered by sour moments of loneliness. But she'd come out of it stronger, wiser, determined to break the cycle of choosing the wrong type of man. *The heartbreaking type.*

From now on things would be different, she reminded herself as she gave the batter a particularly vigorous stir. She would not let a handsome face and a set of broad shoulders blind her to character flaws that spelled ultimate doom to happiness. She would curb the impulsiveness that had seen her diving headlong into relationships because she thought she was in love with someone she, in fact, did not really know.

And she was going to be much, *much* tougher. Less forgiving. No more giving 'one last chance' and then another to a cheating, lying heartbreaker, unworthy of her, whose false promises she'd believed.

She was twenty-eight and she wanted to get married and have kids before too many more years sped by.

'No more Ms Bad Judge of Men,' she said out loud.

It was okay to talk to herself. She was alone in the large industrial kitchen at the converted warehouse in inner-city Alexandria, the Sydney suburb that was headquarters to her successful party planning business. Party Queens belonged to her and to her two business partners, Andie Newman and Eliza Dunne. The food was Gemma's domain, Andie was the creative genius and Eliza the business brain.

After several years working as a chef and then as a food editor on magazines, in Party Queens Gemma had found her dream job. Going into partnership with Andie and Eliza was the best decision she'd ever made. And throwing herself headlong into work had been the best thing she could have done to keep her mind off men. She would do anything to keep this business thriving.

Gemma poured the batter into a high, round pan and carefully placed it into a slow oven, where it would cook for one and a half hours. Then she would cover it with coconut frosting and garnish it with fine curls of candied lemon and lime peel. Not only would the cake be a treat for her and her partners to share this afternoon, in celebration of the end of her man-free six months, it was also a trial run for a client's wedding cake.

Carefully, she settled the cake in the centre of the oven and gently closed the oven door.

She turned back to face the island countertop, to find she was no longer alone. A tall, broad-shouldered man stood just inside the door. She gasped, and her hand—encased in a hot-pink oven mitt—went to her heart.

'Who are you and how the heck did you get in here?' she asked, her voice high with sudden panic.

Even through her shock she registered that the intruder was very handsome, with a lean face and light brown hair. *Just her type.* No. *No longer her type*—not after six months of talking herself out of that kind of very good-looking man. Especially if he was a burglar—or worse.

She snatched up a wooden spoon in self-defence. Drips of cake batter slid down her arm, but she scarcely noticed.

The man put up his hands as if to ward off her spoon. 'Tristan Marco. I have a meeting this morning with Eliza

Dunne. She called to tell me she was caught in traffic and gave me the pass code for the door.'

The stranger seemed about her age and spoke with a posh English accent laced with a trace of something else. Something she couldn't quite place. French? German? He didn't look Australian. Something about his biscuit-coloured linen trousers, fine cream cotton shirt and stylish shoes seemed sartorially European.

'You can put down your weapon,' he said, amusement rippling through his voice.

Gemma blushed as she lowered the wooden spoon. What good would a spoon have been against a man taller than six foot? She took a deep breath in an attempt to get her heart rate back to somewhere near normal. 'You gave me quite a shock, walking in on me like that. Why didn't you press the buzzer?'

He walked further into the room so he stood opposite the island counter that separated them. This close she noticed vivid blue eyes framed by dark brows, smooth olive skin, perfect teeth.

'I'm sorry to have frightened you,' he said in that intriguing accent and with an expressive shrug of his broad shoulders. 'Ms Dunne did not tell me anyone else would be here.'

Gemma took off her oven mitts, used one to surreptitiously wipe the batter dribbles from her arm and placed them on the countertop.

'I wasn't frightened. It's just that I'm on my own here and—' *now wasn't* that *a dumb thing to say to a stranger?* '—Eliza will be here very soon.'

'Yes, she said she would not be long,' he said. His smile was both charming and reassuring. 'I'm looking forward to meeting her. We have only spoken on the phone.'

He was gorgeous. Gemma refused to let the dangerous little fluttering of awareness take hold. She had just spent six months talking herself out of any kind of instant attraction. She was not going to make those old mistakes again.

'Can I help you in the meantime?' Gemma asked. 'I'm Gemma Harper—one of Eliza's business partners.'

To be polite, she moved around the countertop to be nearer to him. Realising she was still in her white chef's apron, she went to untie it, then stopped. Might that look as if she was *undressing* in front of this stranger?

She gave herself a mental shake. *Of course it wouldn't.* Had six months without a date made her start thinking like an adolescent? Still, there was no real need to take the apron off.

She offered him her hand in a businesslike gesture that she hoped negated the pink oven mitts and the wielding of the wooden spoon. He took it in his own firm, warm grip for just the right amount of time.

'So you are also a Party Queen?' he asked. The hint of a smile lifted the corners of his mouth.

'Yes, I'm the food director,' she said, wishing not for the first time that they had chosen a more staid name for the business. It had all started as a bit of a lark, but now, eighteen months after they had launched, they were one of the most popular and successful party planning businesses in Sydney. And still being teased about being Party Queens.

'Did you…did you want to see Eliza about booking a party?' she asked cautiously. To her knowledge, the steadfastly single Eliza wasn't dating anyone. But his visit to their headquarters might be personal. Lucky Eliza, if that was the case.

'Yes, I've been planning a reception with her.'

'A reception? You mean a wedding reception?'

The good ones were always taken. She banished the flickering disappointment the thought aroused. This guy was a stranger and a client. His marital status should be of no concern to her. Yet she had to admit there was something about him she found very attractive beyond the obvious appeal of his good looks. Perhaps because he seemed somehow…different.

'No. Not a wedding.' His face seemed to darken. 'When I get married, it will not be *me* arranging the festivities.'

Of course it wouldn't. In her experience it was always the bride. It sometimes took the grooms a while to realise that.

'So, if not a wedding reception, what kind of reception?'

'Perhaps "reception" is not the right word. My English…' He shrugged again.

She did like broad shoulders on a man.

'Your English sounds perfect to me,' she said, her curiosity aroused. 'Do you mean a business reception?'

'Yes and no. I have been speaking to Eliza about holding a party for me to meet Australians connected by business to my family. It is to be held on Friday evening.'

It clicked. 'Of course!' she exclaimed. 'The cocktail party at the Parkview Hotel on Friday night.' It was now Monday, and everything was on track for the upscale event.

'That is correct,' he said.

'I manage the food aspect of our business. We're using the hotel's excellent catering team. I've worked with them on devising the menu. I think you'll be very happy with the food.'

'It all looked in order to me,' he said. 'I believe I am in capable hands.'

Everything fell into place. Tristan Marco was their mystery client. Mysterious because his event had been organised from a distance, by phone and email, in a hurry, and by someone for whom Eliza had been unable to check credit details. The client had solved that problem by paying the entire quoted price upfront. A very substantial price for a no-expenses-spared party at a high-end venue. She,

Eliza and Andie had spent quite some time speculating on what the client would be like.

'You are in the best possible hands with our company,' she reassured him.

He looked at her intently, his blue eyes narrowed. 'Did I speak with you?' he said. 'I am sure I would have remembered your voice.'

She certainly would have remembered *his*.

Gemma shook her head. 'Eliza is our business director. She does most of our client liaison. You are not what we—' She clapped her hand to her mouth. *Put a zip on it, Gemma.*

'Not what you what?' he asked with a quizzical expression.

'Not…not what we expected,' she said. Her voice trailed away, and she looked down in the direction of his well-polished Italian shoes.

'What *did* you expect?'

She sighed and met his gaze full on. There was no getting out of this. She really needed to curb her tendency to blurt things out without thinking. That was why she worked with the food and Eliza and Andie with the clients.

'Well, we expected someone older. Someone not so tall. Someone heavier. Someone perhaps even…bald. With a twirling black moustache. Maybe…maybe someone like Hercule Poirot. You know…the detective in the Agatha Christie movies?'

Someone not so devastatingly handsome.

Thank heaven, he laughed. 'So are you disappointed in what you see?' He stood, arms outspread, as if welcoming her inspection.

Gemma felt suddenly breathless at the intensity of his gaze, at her compulsion to take up his unspoken offer to admire his tall, obviously well-muscled body, his lean, handsome face with those incredibly blue eyes, the full sensual mouth with the top lip slightly narrower then the lower, the way his short brown hair kicked up at the front in a cowlick.

'Not at all,' she said, scarcely able to choke out the words. *Disappointed was* not *the word that sprang to mind.*

'I am glad to hear that,' he said very seriously, his gaze not leaving hers. 'You did not know me, but I knew *exactly* what to expect from Party Queens.'

'You…you did?' she stuttered.

'Party Queens was recommended to me by my friend Jake Marlowe. He told me that each of the three partners was beautiful, talented and very smart.'

'He…he did?' she said, her vocabulary seeming to have escaped her.

Billionaire Jake Marlowe was the business partner of Andie's husband, Dominic. He'd been best man at their wedding two Christmases ago. Who knew he'd taken such an interest in them?

'On the basis of my meeting with you, I can see Jake did not mislead me,' Tristan said.

His formal way of speaking and his charming smile made the compliment sound sincere when it might have sounded sleazy. *Had he even made a slight bow as he spoke?*

She willed herself not to blush again but without success. 'Thank you,' was all she could manage to say.

'Jake spoke very highly of your business,' Tristan said. 'He told me there was no better party-planning company in Sydney.'

'That was kind of him. It's always gratifying to get such good feedback.'

'I did not even talk with another company,' Tristan said with that charming smile.

'Wow! I mean…that's wonderful. I…we're flattered. We won't let you down, I promise you. The hotel is a perfect venue. It overlooks Hyde Park, it's high end, elegant and it prides itself on its exemplary service. I don't think I've ever seen so much marble and glamour in one place.'

She knew she was speaking too fast, but she couldn't seem to help it.

'Yes. The first thing I did was inspect it when I arrived in Sydney. You chose well.' He paused. 'I myself would prefer something more informal, but protocol dictates the event must be formal.'

'The protocol of your family business?' she asked, not quite sure she'd got it right.

He nodded. 'That is correct. It must be upheld even when I am in another country.'

'You're a visitor to Australia?' Another piece of the puzzle fell into place. The phone calls had all come from Queensland, the state to the north of New South Wales. Where Jake Marlowe lived, she now realised.

'Yes,' he said.

She still couldn't place the accent, and it annoyed her. Gemma had studied French, German and Italian—not that she'd had much chance to practise them—and thought she had a good ear.

'What kind of business does your family run?' she asked.

That was another thing the Party Queens had wondered about as they'd discussed their mystery client. *He was still a mystery.*

Tristan was still too bemused by the vision of this cute redhead wearing bright pink oven mitts and wielding a wooden spoon as a weapon to think straight. He had to consider his reply and try not to be distracted by the smear of flour down her right cheek that seemed to point to her beautiful full mouth. While he'd been speaking with her, he'd had to fight the urge to lean across and gently wipe it off.

Should he tell her the truth? Or give the same evasive replies he'd given to others during his incognito trip to Sydney? He'd been here four days, and no one had recognised him…

Visiting Australia had been on his list to do before he turned thirty and had to return home to step up his involvement in 'the business'. He'd spent some time in Queensland with Jake. But for the past few days in Sydney, he had enjoyed his anonymity, relished being just Tristan. No expectations. No explanations. Just a guy nearing thirty, being himself, being independent, having fun. It was a novelty for him to be an everyday guy. Even when he'd been at university in England, the other students had soon sussed him out.

He would have to tell Party Queens the truth about himself and the nature of his reception sooner or later, though. *Let it be later.*

Gemma Harper was lovely—really lovely—with her deep auburn hair, heart-shaped face and the shapely curves that the professional-looking white apron did nothing to disguise. He wanted to enjoy talking with her still cloaked in the anonymity of being just plain Tristan. When she found out his true identity, her attitude would change. It always did.

'Finance. Trade. That kind of thing,' he replied.

'I see,' she said.

He could tell by the slight downturn of her mouth that although she'd made the right polite response, she found his family business dull. More the domain of the portly, bald gentleman she'd imagined him to be. Who could blame her? But he didn't want this delightful woman to find *him* dull.

He looked at the evidence of her cooking on the countertop, smelled something delicious wafting from the oven.

'And chocolate,' he added. 'The world's best chocolate.'

Now her beautiful brown eyes lit up with interest. *He'd played the right card.*

'Chocolate? You're talking about my favourite food group. So you're from Switzerland?'

He shook his head.

'Belgium? France?' she tried.

'Close,' he said. 'My country is Montovia. A small principality that is not far from those countries.'

She paused, her head tilted to one side. 'You're talking about Montovian chocolate?'

'You know it?' he asked, surprised. His country was known more for its financial services and as a tax haven than for its chocolate and cheese—undoubtedly excellent as they were.

She smiled, revealing delightful dimples in each cheek. He caught his breath. *This Party Queen really was a beauty.*

'Of course I do,' she said. 'Montovian chocolate is sublime. Not easy to get here, but I discovered it when I visited Europe. Nibbled on it, that is. I was a backpacker, and it's too expensive to have much more than a nibble. It's... Well, it's the gold standard of chocolate.'

'I would say the platinum standard,' he said, pleased at her reaction.

'Gold. Platinum. It's just marvellous stuff,' she said. 'Are you a *chocolatier*?'

'No,' he said. 'I am more on the...executive side of the business.' That wasn't stretching the truth too far.

'Is that why you're here in Sydney? The reason for your party? Promoting Montovian chocolate?'

'Among other things,' he said. He didn't want to dig himself in too deep with deception.

She nodded. 'Confidential stuff you can't really talk about?'

'That's right,' he said. He didn't actually like to lie. Evade—*yes*. Lie—*no*.

'Don't worry—you'd be surprised at what secrets we have to keep in the party business,' she said. 'We have to be discreet.'

She put her index finger to her lips. He noticed she didn't wear any rings on either hand.

'But the main reason I am in Sydney is for a vacation,' he said, with 100 per cent truthfulness.

'Really? Who would want a vacation from Montovian chocolate? I don't think I'd ever leave home if I lived in Montovia,' she said with another big smile. 'I'm joking, of course,' she hastened to add. 'No matter how much you love your job, a break is always good.'

'Sydney is a marvellous place for a vacation. I am enjoying it here very much,' he said.

And enjoying it even more since he'd met her. Sydney was a city full of beautiful women, but there was something about Gemma Harper that had instantly appealed to him. Her open, friendly manner, the laughter in her eyes, those dimples, the way she'd tried so unsuccessfully to look ferocious as she'd waved that wooden spoon. She was too pretty to ever look scary. Yet according to his friend Jake, all three of the partners were formidably smart businesswomen. Gemma interested him.

'March is the best time here,' she said. 'It's the start of autumn down-under. Still hot, but not too hot. The sea is warm and perfect for swimming. The school holidays are over. The restaurants are not crowded. I hope you're enjoying our lovely city.' She laughed. 'I sound like I'm spouting a travel brochure, don't I? But, seriously, you're lucky to be here at this time of year.'

The harbourside city was everything Tristan had hoped it would be. But he realised now there was one thing missing from his full enjoyment of Sydney—female company.

The life he'd chosen—correction, the life he had had chosen *for* him—meant he often felt lonely.

'You are the lucky one—to live in such a beautiful city on such a magnificent harbour,' he said.

'True. Sydney *is* great, and I love living here,' she said. 'But I'm sure Montovia must be, too. When I think of your chocolate, I picture snow-capped mountains and lakes. Am I right?'

'Yes,' he said. He wanted to tell her more about his home but feared he might trip himself up with an untruth. His experience of life in Montovia was very different from what a tourist might find.

'That was a lucky guess, then,' she said. 'I must confess I don't know anything about your country except for the chocolate.'

'Not many people outside of Europe do, I've discovered,' he said with a shrug.

And that suited him fine in terms of a laid-back vacation. Here in Sydney, half a world away from home, he hadn't been recognised. He liked it that way.

'But perhaps our chocolate will put us on the map down-under.'

'Perhaps after your trip here it will. I think...'

She paused midsentence, frowned. He could almost see the cogs turning.

'The menu for your reception... We'll need to change the desserts to showcase Montovian chocolate. There's still time. I'll get on to it straight away.' She slapped her hand to her mouth. 'Sorry. I jumped the gun there. I meant if you approve, of course.'

'Of course I approve. It's a very good idea. I should have thought of it myself.' Only devising menus was quite out of the range of his experience.

'Excellent. Let me come up with some fabulous chocolate desserts, and I'll pass them by you for approval.'

He was about to tell her not to bother with the approval process when he stopped himself. *He wanted to see her again.* 'Please do that,' he said.

'Eliza shouldn't be too much longer—the traffic can't be that bad. Can I take you into our waiting area? It's not big, but it's more comfortable than standing around here,' she said.

'I am comfortable here,' he said, not liking the idea of her being in a different room from him. 'I like your kitchen.' All stainless steel and large industrial appliances, it still somehow seemed imbued with her warmth and welcome.

Her eyes widened. They were an unusual shade of brown—the colour of cinnamon—and lit up when she smiled.

'Me, too,' she said. 'I have a cake in the oven, and I want to keep an eye on it.'

He inhaled the citrus-scented air. 'It smells very good.'

She glanced at her watch. 'It's a new recipe I'm trying, but I think it will be delicious. I don't know how long you're planning to meet with Eliza for, but the cake won't be ready for another hour or so. Then it has to cool, and then I—'

'I think our meeting will be brief. I have some more sightseeing to do—I've booked a jet boat on the harbour. Perhaps another time I could sample your cake?' He would make certain there would be another time.

'I can see that a cake wouldn't have the same appeal as a jet boat,' she said, with a smile that showed him she did not take offence. 'What else have you seen of Sydney so far?' she asked.

'The usual tourist spots,' he said. 'I've been to the Opera House, Bondi Beach, climbed the Sydney Harbour Bridge.'

'They're all essential. Though I've never found the courage to do the bridge climb. But there's also a Sydney tourists don't get to see. I recommend—'

'Would you show me the Sydney the tourists don't see? I would very much like your company.'

The lovely food director's eyes widened. She hesitated. 'I…I wonder if—'

He was waiting for her reply, when a slender, dark-haired young woman swept into the room. Tristan silently cursed under his breath in his own language at the interruption. She immediately held out her hand to him.

'You must be Mr Marco? I'm so sorry to have kept you waiting—the traffic was a nightmare. I'm Eliza Dunne.'

For a moment he made no acknowledgment of the newcomer's greeting—and then he remembered. He was using Marco as a surname when it was in fact his second given name. He didn't actually have a surname, as such. Not when he was always known simply as Tristan, Crown Prince of Montovia.

CHAPTER TWO

GEMMA CLOSED HER eyes in sheer relief at Eliza's well-timed entrance. *What a lucky escape.* Despite all her resolve not to act on impulse when it came to men, she'd been just about to agree to show Tristan around Sydney.

And that would have been a big mistake.

First, Party Queens had a rule of staff not dating clients. The fact that Andie had broken the rule in spectacular fashion by falling in love with and marrying their billionaire client Dominic Hunt was beside the point. She, Gemma, did not intend to make any exceptions. The business was too important to her for her to make messy mistakes.

But it wasn't just about the company rules. If she'd said yes to Tristan she could have told herself she was simply being hospitable to a foreign visitor—but she would have been lying. And lying to herself about men was a bad habit she was trying to break. She found Tristan way too appealing to pretend that being hospitable was all it would be.

'Thank you for taking care of Mr Marco for me, Gemma,' Eliza said. 'The traffic was crazy—insane.'

'Gemma has looked after me very well,' Tristan said, again with that faint hint of a bow in her direction.

Her heart stepped up a beat at the awareness that shimmered through her.

'She hasn't plied you with cake or muffins or cookies?' asked Eliza with a teasing smile.

'The cake isn't baked yet,' Gemma said. 'But I have cookies and—'

'Perhaps another cake, another time,' Tristan said with a shrug of those broad shoulders, that charming smile. 'And I could give you chocolate in return.'

The shrug. The accent. Those blue, blue eyes. *The Montovian chocolate.*

Yes! her body urged her to shout.

No! urged her common sense.

'Perhaps…' she echoed, the word dwindling away irresolutely.

Thankfully, Eliza diverted Tristan's attention from her as she engaged him in a discussion about final guest numbers for his party.

Gemma was grateful for some breathing space. Some deep breathing to let her get to grips with the pulse-raising presence of this gorgeous man.

'I'll let you guys chat while I check on my cake,' she said as she went back around the countertop.

She slipped into the pink oven mitts and carefully opened the oven door. As she turned the pan around, she inhaled the sweet-sharp aroma of the cake. Over the years she had learned to gauge the progress of her baking by smell. Its scent told her this cake had a way to go. This kind of solid mud cake needed slow, even cooking.

That was what she'd be looking for in a man in future. A slow burn. Not instant flames. No exhilarating infatuation. No hopping into bed too soon. Rather a long, slow getting to know each other before any kind of commitment—physical or otherwise—was made. The old-fashioned word *courtship* sprang to mind.

She'd managed six months on her own. She was in no rush for the next man. There was no urgency. Next time she wanted to get it right.

Still, no matter what she told herself, Gemma was superaware of Tristan's presence in her kitchen. And, even though he seemed engrossed in his conversation with Eliza, the tension in the way he held himself let her know that he was aware of her, too. The knowledge was a secret pleasure she hugged to herself. It was reassuring that she could still attract a hot guy. Even if there was no way she should do anything about it.

She scraped clean her mixing bowl and spoon and put them in the dishwasher while keeping an ear on Tristan and Eliza's conversation about the party on Friday and an eye on Tristan himself. On those broad shoulders tapering to narrow hips, on the long legs she imagined would be lean and hard with muscle.

Catching her eye, he smiled. Her first instinct was to blush, then smile back. For a long moment their gazes held before she reluctantly dragged hers away and went back to the tricky task of finely slicing strips of candied lemon peel.

Okay, she wasn't in dating exile any more. There was no law to say she couldn't flirt just a little. But she had spent six months fine-tuning her antennae to detect potential heartbreak. And there was something about this handsome Montovian that had those antennae waving wildly with a message of caution. They detected a mystery behind his formal way of speaking and courteous good manners. It wasn't what he'd said but what he *hadn't* said.

Then there was the fact Tristan was only here for a few days. To be a good-looking tourist's vacation fling was *not* what she needed in order to launch herself back into the dating pool. She had to be totally on guard, so she wouldn't fall for the first gorgeous guy who strolled into her life.

She'd learned such painful lessons from her relationship with Alistair. It had been love at first sight for both of them—or so she'd thought. Followed by an emotional rollercoaster that had lasted for eighteen months. Too blinded by desire, love—whatever that turbulent mix of emotions had been—she'd only seen the Alistair she'd wanted to see. She had missed all the cues that would have alerted her he wasn't what he'd sworn he was.

She'd heard the rumours before she'd started to date

him. But he'd assured her that he'd kicked his cocaine habit—*and* his reputation as a player. When time after time he'd lapsed, she'd always forgiven him, given him the one more chance he'd begged for. And then another. After all, she'd loved him and he'd loved her—hadn't he?

Then had come the final hurt and humiliation of finding him in the bathroom at a party with a so-called 'mutual friend'. Doing *her* as well as the drugs. Gemma doubted she'd ever be able to scour that image from her eyes.

After that there'd been no more chances, no more Alistair. She'd spent the last six months trying to sort out why she always seemed to fall for the wrong type of man. Her dating history was littered with misfires—though none as heart-wrenchingly painful as Alistair's betrayal.

On her first day back in the dating world she wasn't going to backtrack. Tristan was still a mystery man. He had perhaps not been completely honest about himself and was on vacation from a faraway country. How many more strikes against him could there be?

But, oh, he was handsome.

Eliza had suggested that Tristan follow her into her office. But he turned towards Gemma. 'I would like to speak to Gemma again first, please,' he said, with unmistakable authority.

Eliza sent Gemma a narrow-eyed, speculative glance. 'Sure,' she said to Tristan. 'My office is just around the corner. I'll wait for you there.'

Gemma could hear the sound of her own heart beating in the sudden silence of the room as Eliza left. Her mouth went dry as Tristan came closer to face her over the countertop.

His gaze was very direct. 'So, Gemma, you did not get a chance to answer me—will you show me your home town?'

It took every bit of resolve for her not to run around

to the other side of the countertop and babble, *Of course. How about we start right now?*

Instead she wiped her suddenly clammy hands down the sides of her apron. Took a deep breath to steady her voice. 'I'm sorry, Tristan. But I…I can't.'

He looked taken aback. She got the distinct impression he wasn't used to anyone saying *no* to him.

He frowned. 'You are sure?'

'It wouldn't be…appropriate,' she said.

'Because I am a client?' he asked, his gaze direct on hers.

She shifted from foot to foot, clad in the chef's clogs she wore in the kitchen. 'That's right,' she said. 'I'm sorry, but it's company policy.'

Just for a moment, did disappointment cloud those blue eyes? 'That is a shame. As I said, I would very much enjoy your company.'

'I…well, I would enjoy yours, too. But…uh…rules are rules.'

Such rules *could* be broken—as Andie had proved. But Gemma was determined to stick to her resolve, even if it was already tinged with regret.

His mouth twisted. 'I know all about rules that have to be followed whether one likes it or not,' he said with an edge to his voice. 'I don't like it, but I understand.'

What did he mean by that? Gemma wasn't sure if he was referring to the Party Queens rules or a different set of rules that might apply to him. She sensed there might be a lot she didn't understand about him. And now would never get a chance to.

'Thank you,' she said. 'I'll email the amended dessert menu to you.'

'Dessert menu?'

'Using Montovian chocolate for your party,' she prompted.

'Of course,' he said. 'I will look forward to it. I am sorry I will not be seeing more of Sydney with you.'

'I...I'm sorry, too.' But she would not toss away all that hard work she'd done on her insecurities.

'Now I must let you get back to work while I speak with Eliza,' he said, in what sounded very much like dismissal.

Gemma refused to admire his back view as he left the kitchen. *She liked a nice butt on a man.* For better or for worse, that ship had sailed. And she felt good about her decision. She really did.

But she was on edge as she prepared the coconut frosting by melting white chocolate and beating it with coconut cream. She kept glancing up, in case Tristan came back into the room. Was so distracted she grated the edge of her finger as well as the fine slivers of lemon and lime peel that would give the frosting its bite. But a half-hour later, when his meeting with Eliza concluded, he only briefly acknowledged her as he passed by the doorway to her kitchen.

She gripped her hands so tightly her fingernails cut into her hands. The sudden feeling of loss was totally irrational. She would *not* run after him to say she'd changed her mind.

An hour later, as Gemma was finishing her work on the cake, Eliza popped her head around the door.

'Cake ready?' she asked. 'The smell of it has been driving me crazy.'

'Nearly ready. I've been playing with the candied peel on top and tidying up the frosting,' Gemma said. 'Come and have a look. I think it will be perfect for the Sanderson wedding.'

'Magnificent,' Eliza said. She sneaked a quick taste of the leftover frosting from the bowl. 'Mmm...coconut. Nice touch. You really are a genius when it comes to food.'

Gemma knew her mouth had turned downwards. 'Just not such a genius when it comes to guys.'

Eliza patted her on the shoulder. 'Come on—you've done so well with your sabbatical. Aren't we going to celebrate your freedom to date—I mean to date *wisely*—with this cake?'

Both Gemma and Andie had been totally supportive during her man break. Had proved themselves again and again to be good friends as well as business partners.

Gemma nodded. 'I know...' she said, unable to stop the catch in her voice. It was the right thing to have turned down Tristan's invitation, but that didn't stop a lingering sense of regret, of wondering *what might have been*.

'What's brought on this fit of the gloomies?' Eliza asked. 'Oh, wait—don't tell me. The handsome mystery man—Tristan Marco. He's just your type, isn't he? As soon as I saw him, I thought—'

Gemma put up her hand to stop her. 'In looks, yes, I can't deny that. He's really hot.' She forced a smile. 'Our guesses about him were *so* far off the mark, weren't they?'

'He's about as far away from short, bald and middle-aged as he could be,' Eliza agreed. 'I had to stop myself staring at him for fear he'd think I was incredibly bad mannered.'

'You can imagine how shocked I was when he told me *he* was our client for the Friday night party. But I don't think he told me everything. There's still a lot of the mystery man about him.'

'What do you mean, *still* too much mystery? What did you talk about here in your kitchen?'

Gemma filled Eliza in on her conversation with Tristan, leaving out his invitation for her to show him around Sydney. Eliza would only remind her that dating clients was a no-no. And, besides, she didn't want to talk about it—she'd made her decision.

Eliza nodded. 'He told me much the same thing—although he was quite evasive about the final list of guests.

But what the heck? It's his party, and he can invite anyone he wants to it as long as he sticks with the number we quoted on. We're ahead financially, so it's all good to me.'

'That reminds me,' Gemma said. 'I have to amend the desserts for Friday to include Montovian chocolate. And he needs to approve them.'

'You can discuss the menu change with him on Wednesday.'

Gemma stopped, the blunt palette knife she'd used to apply the frosting still in her hand. 'Wednesday? Why Wednesday?'

'Tristan is on vacation in Sydney. He's asked me to book a private yacht cruise around the harbour on Wednesday. And to organise an elegant, romantic lunch for two to be taken on board.'

A romantic lunch for two?

Gemma let go of the palette knife so it landed with a clatter on the stainless steel benchtop, using the distraction to gather her thoughts. So she'd been right to distrust mystery man Tristan. He'd asked her to show him around Sydney. And at the same time he was making plans for a romantic tryst with another woman on a luxury yacht.

Thank heaven she'd said *no*.

Or had she misread him? Had his interest only been in her knowledge of local hotspots? After a six-month sabbatical, maybe her dating skills were so rusty she'd mistaken his meaning.

Still, she couldn't help feeling annoyed. Not so much at Tristan but at herself, for having let down her guard even if only momentarily. If she'd glimpsed that look of interest in *his* eyes, he would have seen it in *hers*.

'Which boat did you book?' she asked Eliza.

The cooking facilities on the charter yachts available in Sydney Harbour ranged from a basic galley to a full-sized luxury kitchen.

'Because it will be midweek, I managed to get the *Argus* on short notice.'

'Wow! Well done. He should love that.'

'He did. I showed him a choice of boats online, but the *Argus* was the winner hands down.'

'His date should be really impressed,' Gemma said, fighting off an urge to sound snarky.

'I think that was the idea—the lucky lady.'

The *Argus* was a replica of a sixty-foot vintage wooden motor yacht from the nineteen-twenties and the ultimate in luxury. Its hourly hire rate was a mind-boggling amount of dollars. To book it for just two people was a total extravagance. Party Queens had organised a corporate client's event for thirty people on the boat at the start of summer. It was classy, high-tech and had a fully equipped kitchen. Tristan must *really* want to impress his date.

'So I'm guessing if lunch is on the *Argus* we won't be on a tight budget.'

'He told me to "spend what it takes",' said Eliza with a delighted smile. The more dollars for Party Queens, the happier Eliza was.

Gemma gritted her teeth and forced herself to think of Tristan purely as a client, not as an attractive man who'd caught her eye. It would be better if she still thought of him as bald with a pot belly. 'It's short notice, but of course we can do it. Any restrictions on the menu?'

Planning party menus could involve dealing with an overwhelming array of food allergies and intolerances.

'None that he mentioned,' said Eliza.

'That makes things easier.' Gemma thought out loud. 'An elegant on-board lunch for two…I'm thinking seafood—fresh and light. A meal we can prep ahead and our chef can finish off on board. We'll book the waiter today.'

'"Romantic" is the keyword, remember? And he wants the best French champagne—which, of course, I'll organise.' Eliza had an interest in wine as well as in spread-sheets.

'I wonder who his guest is?' Gemma said, hoping she wouldn't betray her personal interest to Eliza.

'Again, he didn't say,' Eliza said.

Gemma couldn't help a stab of envy towards Tristan's date, for whom he was making such an effort to be *romantic*. But he was a client. And she was a professional. If he wanted romantic, she'd give him romantic. In spades.

'But tell me—why will *I* be meeting with Tristan on Wednesday?'

'He wants you to be on board for the duration—to make sure everything is perfect. His words, not mine.'

'What? A lunch for two with a chef and a waiter doesn't need a supervisor, as well. You know how carefully we vet the people who work for us. They can be trusted to deliver the Party Queens' promise.'

Eliza put up her hands in a placatory gesture. 'Relax. I know that. I know the yacht comes with skipper and crew. But Tristan asked for you to be on board, too. He wants you to make sure everything goes well.'

'No!' Gemma said and realised her protest sounded over-the-top. 'I...I mean there's no need for me to be there at all. I'll go over everything with the chef and the waiter to make sure the presentation and service is faultless.'

Eliza shook her head. 'Not good enough. Tristan Marco has specifically requested your presence on board.'

Gemma knew the bottom line was always important to Eliza. She'd made sure their business was a success financially. With a sinking heart Gemma realised there would be no getting out of this. And Eliza was only too quick to confirm that.

'You know how lucrative his party on Friday is for us, Gemma. Tristan is an important client. You really have to do this. Whether you like it or not.'

CHAPTER THREE

ON WEDNESDAY MORNING Gemma made her way along the harbourside walk on the northern shore of Sydney Harbour. Milson's Point and the Art Deco North Sydney Swimming Pool were behind her as she headed towards the wharf at Lavender Bay, where she was to join the *Argus*. As she walked she realised why she felt so out of sorts—she was jealous of Tristan's unknown date. And put out that he had replaced her so quickly.

It wasn't that she was jealous of the other woman's cruise on a magnificent yacht on beautiful Sydney Harbour. Or the superb meal she would be served, thanks to the skill of the Party Queens team. No. What Gemma envied her most for was the pleasure of Tristan's company.

Gemma seethed with a most unprofessional indignation at the thought of having to dance attendance on the couple's romantic rendezvous. There was no justification for her feelings—Tristan had asked to spend time with her and she had turned him down. In fact, her feelings were more than a touch irrational. But still she didn't like the idea of seeing Tristan with another woman.

She did not want to do this.

Why had he insisted on her presence on board? This was a romantic lunch for *two*, for heaven's sake. There was only so much for her to do for a simple three-course meal. She would have too much time to observe Tristan being charming to his date. *And, oh, how charming the man could be.*

If she was forced to watch him kiss that other woman, she might just have to jump off board and brave the sharks and jellyfish to swim to shore.

Suck it up, Gemma, you turned him down.

She forced herself to remember that she was the director of her own company, looking after an important client. To convince herself that there were worse things to do than twiddle her thumbs in the lap of luxury on one of the most beautiful harbours in the world on a perfect sunny day. And to remind herself to paste a convincing smile on her face as she did everything in her power to make her client's day a success.

As she rounded the boardwalk past Luna Park fun fair, she picked up her pace when she noticed the *Argus* had already docked at Lavender Bay. The charter company called it a 'gentleman's cruiser', and the wooden boat's vintage lines made it stand out on a harbour dotted with slick, modern watercraft. She didn't know much about boats, but she liked this one—it looked fabulous, and it had a very well-fitted-out kitchen that was a dream to work in.

The Lavender Bay wharf was on the western side of the Sydney Harbour Bridge, virtually in its shadow, with a view right through to the gleaming white sails of the Opera House on the eastern side. The water was unbelievably blue to match the blue sky. The air was tangy with salt. How could she stay down on a day like this? *She would make the most of it.*

Gemma got her smile ready as she reached the historic old dock. She expected that a crew member would greet her and help her on board. But her heart missed a beat when she saw it was Tristan who stood there. Tristan... in white linen trousers and a white shirt open at the neck to reveal a glimpse of muscular chest, sleeves rolled back to show strong, sinewy forearms. Tristan looking tanned and unbelievably handsome, those blue eyes putting the sky to shame. Her heart seemed almost literally to leap into her throat.

She had never been more attracted to a man.

'Let me help you,' he said in his deep, accented voice as he extended a hand to help her across the gangplank.

She looked at his hand for a long moment, not sure what her reaction would be at actually touching him. But she knew she would need help to get across because she felt suddenly shaky and weak at the knees. She swallowed hard against a painful swell of regret.

What an idiot she'd been to say no *to him.*

Gemma looked as lovely as he remembered, Tristan thought as he held out his hand to her. Even lovelier—which he hadn't thought possible. Her auburn hair fell to her shoulders, glinting copper and gold in the sunlight. Her narrow deep blue cut-off pants and blue-and-white-striped top accentuated her curves in a subtle way he appreciated. But her smile was tentative, and she had hesitated before taking his hand and accepting his help to come on board.

'Gemma, it is so good to see you,' he said while his heart beat a tattoo of exultation that she had come—and he sent out a prayer that she would forgive him for insisting in such an autocratic manner on her presence.

She had her rules—he had his. His rules decreed that spending time with a girl like Gemma could lead nowhere. But he hadn't been able to stop thinking about her. So her rules had had to be bent.

'The Party Queens motto is No Job Too Big or Too Small,' Gemma said as she stepped on board. 'This…this is a very small job.'

He realised he was holding her hand for longer than would be considered polite. That her eyes were flickering away from the intensity of his gaze. But he didn't want to let go of her hand.

'Small…but important.' Incredibly important to him as the clock ticked relentlessly away on his last days of freedom.

She abruptly released her hand from his. Her lush mouth tightened. 'Is it? Then I hope you'll be happy with the menu.'

'Your chef and waiter are already in the kitchen,' he said. 'You have created a superb lunch for us.'

'And your guest for lunch? Is she—?'

At that moment a crew member approached to tell him they were ready to cast off from the dock and start their cruise around the harbour.

Tristan thanked him and turned to Gemma. 'I'm very much looking forward to this,' he said. *To getting to know her.*

'You couldn't have a better day for exploring the harbour,' she said with a wave of her hand that encompassed the impossibly blue waters, the boats trailing frothy white wakes behind them, the blue sky unmarred by clouds.

'The weather is perfect,' he said. 'Did Party Queens organise that for me, too?'

It was a feeble attempt at humour and he knew it. Gemma seemed to know it, too.

But her delightful dimples flirted in her cheeks as she replied, 'We may have cast a good weather spell or two.'

He raised his eyebrows. 'So you have supernatural powers? The Party Queens continue to surprise me.'

'I'd be careful who you're calling a witch,' she said with a deepening of the dimples. 'Andie and Eliza might not like it.'

A witch? She had bewitched him, all right. He had never felt such an instant attraction to a woman. Especially one so deeply unsuitable.

'And you?' In his country's mythology the most powerful witches had red hair and green eyes. This bewitching Australian had eyes the colour of cinnamon—warm and enticing. 'Are *you* a witch, Gemma Harper?' he asked slowly.

She met his gaze directly as they stood facing each other on the deck, the dock now behind them. 'I like to think I'm a witch in the kitchen—or it could be that I just have a highly developed intuition for food. But if you want to think I conjured up these blue skies, go right ahead. All part of the service.'

'So there is no limit to your talents?' he said.

'You're darn right about that,' she said with an upward tilt of her chin.

For a long moment their eyes met. Her heart-shaped face, so new to him, seemed already familiar—possibly because she had not been out of his thoughts since the moment they'd met. He ached to lift his hand and trace the freckles scattered across the bridge of her nose with his finger, then explore the contours of her mouth, her top lip with its perfect, plump bow. *He ached to kiss her.*

But there could be no kissing. Not with this girl, who had captured his interest within seconds of meeting her. Not when there were rules and strictures guiding the way he spent his life. When there were new levels of responsibility he had to step up to when he returned home. He was on a deadline—everything would change when he turned thirty, in three months' time. These next few days in Sydney were the last during which he could call his time his own.

His life had been very different before the accident that had killed his brother. Before the *spare* had suddenly become the *heir*. His carefree and some might even say hedonistic life as the second son had been abruptly curtailed.

There had been unsuitable girlfriends—forbidden to him now. He had taken risks on the racing-car circuit and on horseback, had scaled the mountains that towered over Montovia. Now everything he did came under scrutiny. The Crown took priority over everything. Duty had always governed part of his life. Now it was to be his all.

But he had demanded to be allowed to take this vacation—insisted on this last freedom before he had to buckle under to duty. To responsibility. For the love of his country.

His fascination with Gemma Harper was nowhere on the approved official agenda...

'I'm trying to imagine what other feats of magic you can perform,' he said, attempting to come to terms with the potent spell she had cast on him. The allure of her lush mouth. The warmth of her eyes. The inexplicable longing for her that had led him to planning this day.

He should not be thinking this way about a commoner.

She bit her lip, took a step back from him. 'My magic trick is to make sure your lunch date goes smoothly. But I don't need a fairy's wand for that.' Her dimples disappeared. 'I want everything to be to your satisfaction. Are you happy with the *Argus*?'

Her voice was suddenly stilted, as if she had extracted the laughter and levity from it. *Back to business* was the message. And she was right. A business arrangement. That was all there should be between them.

'It's a very handsome boat,' he said. He was used to millionaire's toys. Took this level of luxury for granted. But that didn't stop him appreciating it. And he couldn't put a price on the spectacular view. 'I'm very happy with it for this purpose.'

'Good. The *Argus* is my favourite of any of the boats we've worked on,' she said. 'I love its wonderful Art Deco style. It's from another era of graciousness.'

'Would you like me to show you around?' he said.

If she said yes, he would make only a cursory inspection of the luxury bedrooms, the grand stateroom. He did not want her to get the wrong idea. Or to torture himself with thoughts of what could never be.

She shook her head. 'No need. I'm familiar with the

layout,' she said. 'We held a corporate party here earlier in the spring. I'd like to catch up with my staff now.'

'Your waiter has already set up for lunch on the deck.'

'I'd like to see how it looks,' she said.

She had a large tan leather bag slung over her shoulder. 'Let me take your bag for you,' he said.

'Thank you, but I'm fine,' she said, clutching on to the strap.

'I insist,' he said. The habits of courtliness and chivalry towards women had been bred into him.

She shrugged. 'Okay.' Reluctantly, she handed it to him.

The weight of her bag surprised him, and he pretended to stagger on the deck. 'What have you got in here? An arsenal of wooden spoons?'

Her eyes widened, and she laughed. 'Of course not.'

'So I don't need to seek out my armour?'

It was tempting to tell her about the suits of medieval armour in the castle he called home. As a boy he'd thought everyone had genuine armour to play with—it hadn't been until he was older that he'd become aware of his uniquely privileged existence. Privileged and restricted.

But he couldn't reveal his identity to her yet. He wanted another day of just being plain Tristan. Just a guy getting to know a girl.

'Of course you don't need armour. Besides, I wasn't actually going to *hit* you with that wooden spoon, you know.'

'You had me worried back in that kitchen,' he teased. He was getting used to speaking English again, relaxing into the flow of words.

'I don't believe that for a second,' she said. 'You're so much bigger than me, and—'

'And what?'

'I…I trusted that you wouldn't hurt me.'

He had to clear his throat. 'I would never hurt you,' he said. And yet he wasn't being honest with her. Inadvertently, he *could* hurt her. But it would not be by intent. *This was just one day.*

'So what's really in the bag?' he asked.

'It's only bits and pieces of my favourite kitchen equipment—just in case I might need them.'

'Just in case the chef can't do his job?' he asked.

'You *did* want me here to supervise,' she said, her laughter gone as he reminded her of why she thought she was on board. 'And supervise I need to. Please. I have to see where we will be serving lunch.'

There was a formal dining area inside the cabin, but Tristan was glad Party Queens had chosen to serve lunch at an informal area with the best view at the fore of the boat. Under shelter from the sun and protected from the breeze. The very professional waiter had already set an elegant table with linen mats, large white plates and gleaming silver.

Gemma nodded in approval when she saw it. Then straightened a piece of cutlery into perfect alignment with another without seeming to be aware she was doing it.

'Our staff have done their usual good job,' she said. 'We'll drop anchor at Store Beach at lunchtime. That will be very *romantic.*'

She stressed the final word with a tight twist of her lips that surprised him.

'I don't know where Store Beach is, but I'm looking forward to seeing it,' he said.

'It's near Manly, which is a beachside suburb—the start of our wonderful northern beaches. Store Beach is a secluded beach accessible only from the water. I'm sure you and your...uh...*date* will like it.' She glanced at her watch. 'In the meantime, it's only ten o'clock. We can set up for morning tea or coffee now, if you'd like?'

'Coffee would be good,' he said. Sydney had surprised

him in many ways—not least of which was with its excellent European-style coffee.

Gemma gave the table setting another tweak and then stepped away from it. 'All that's now lacking is your guest. Are we picking her up from another wharf, or is she already on board?'

'She's already on board,' he said.

'Oh…' she said. 'Is she—?' She turned to look towards the passageway that led to the living area and bedrooms.

'She's not down there,' he said.

'Then where—?'

He sought the correct words. 'She…she's right here,' he said.

'I don't see anyone.' She frowned. 'I don't get it.'

He cleared his throat. '*You* are my guest for lunch, Gemma.'

She stilled. For a long moment she didn't say anything. Tristan shifted from foot to foot. He couldn't tell if she was pleased or annoyed.

'*Me?*' she said finally, in a voice laced with disbelief.

'You said there was a rule about you not spending time outside of work with clients. So I arranged to have time with you while you were officially at work.'

Her shoulders were held hunched and high. 'You…you tricked me. I don't like being tricked.'

'You could call it that—and I apologise for the deception. But there didn't seem to be another way. I had to see you again, Gemma.'

She took a deep intake of breath. 'Why didn't you just ask me?'

'Would you have said "yes"?'

She bowed her head. 'Perhaps not.'

'I will ask you now. Will you be my guest for lunch on board the *Argus*?'

She looked down at the deck.

He reached out his hand and tilted her chin upwards so she faced him. 'Please?'

He could see the emotions dancing across her face. Astonishment. A hint of anger. And could that be relief?

Her shoulders relaxed, and her dimples made a brief appearance in the smoothness of her cheeks. 'I guess as you have me trapped on board I have no choice but to say "yes".'

'Trapped? I don't wish you to feel trapped...' He didn't want to seem arrogant and domineering—job descriptions that came with the role of crown prince. His brother had fulfilled them impeccably. They sat uncomfortably with Tristan. 'Gemma, if this is unacceptable to you, I'll ask the captain to turn back to Lavender Bay. You can get off. Is that what you want?'

She shook her head. 'No. That's not what I want. I...I want to be here with you. In fact, I can't tell you how happy I am there's no other woman. I might have been tempted to throw her overboard.'

Her peal of laughter that followed was delightful, and it made him smile in response.

'Surely you wouldn't do that?'

She looked up at him, her eyes dancing with new confidence. 'You might be surprised at what I'm capable of,' she murmured. 'You don't know me at all, Tristan.'

'I hope to remedy that today,' he said.

Already he knew that this single day he'd permitted himself to share with her would not be enough. He had to anchor his feet to the deck so he didn't swing her into his arms. He must truly be bewitched. Because he couldn't remember when he'd last felt such anticipation at the thought of spending time with a woman.

'Welcome aboard, Gemma,' he said—and had to stop himself from sweeping into a courtly bow.

CHAPTER FOUR

GEMMA COULDN'T STOP SMILING—in relief, anticipation and a slowly bubbling excitement. After all that angst, *she* was Tristan's chosen date for the romantic lunch. *She* was the one he'd gone to so much effort and expense to impress. The thought made her heart skitter with wonder and more than a touch of awe.

She'd joked about casting spells, but *something* had happened back there in her kitchen—some kind of connection between her and Tristan that was quite out of the ordinary. It seemed he had felt it, too. She ignored the warning of the insistent twitching of her antennae. This magical feeling was *not* just warm and fuzzy lust born from Tristan's incredible physical appeal and the fact that she was coming out of a six-month man drought.

Oh, on a sensual level she wanted him, all right—her knees were still shaky just from the touch of his hand gripping hers as he'd helped her across the gangplank. But she didn't want Tristan just as a gorgeous male body to satisfy physical hunger. *It was something so much deeper than that.* Which was all kinds of crazy when he was only going to be around for a short time. And was still as much of a mystery to her as he had been the day they'd met.

For her, this was something more than just physical attraction. But what about him? Was this just a prelude to seduction? Was he a handsome guy with all the right words—spoken in the most charming of accents—looking for a no-strings holiday fling?

She tried to think of all those 'right' reasons for staying away from Tristan but couldn't remember one of them. By tricking her into this lunch with him, he had taken the decision out of her hands. But there was no need to get carried away. This was no big deal. *It was only lunch.* It would be up to her to say *no* if this was a net cast to snare her into a one-night stand.

She reached up and kissed him lightly on the cheek in an effort to make it casual. 'Thank you.'

She was rewarded by the relief in his smile. 'It is absolutely my pleasure,' he said.

'Does Eliza know?' she asked. *Had her friend been in on this deception?*

Tristan shook his head. 'I didn't tell her why I wanted you on board. I sense she's quite protective of you. I didn't want anything to prevent you from coming today.'

Of course Eliza was protective of her. Andie, too. Her friends had been there to pick up the pieces after the Alistair fallout. Eliza had seemed impressed with Tristan, though—impressed with him as a client…maybe not so impressed with him as a candidate for Gemma's first foray back into the dating world. He was still in many ways their Mr Mystery. *But she could find out more about him today.*

'I did protest that I wasn't really needed,' she said, still secretly delighted at the way things had turned out. 'Not when there are a chef and a waiter and a crew on the boat.'

'I'm sure the bonus I added to the Party Queens fee guaranteed your presence on board. She's a shrewd businesswoman, your partner.'

'Yes, she is,' Gemma agreed. No wonder Eliza hadn't objected to Gemma's time being so wastefully spent. How glad she was now that Eliza had insisted she go. But she felt as though the tables had been turned on her, and she wasn't quite sure where she stood.

She looked up at Tristan. Her heart flipped over at how handsome he was, with the sea breeze ruffling his hair, his eyes such a vivid blue against his tan. He looked totally at home on this multi-million-dollar boat, seemingly not impressed by the luxury that surrounded them. She wondered what kind of world he came from. One where money was not in short supply, she guessed.

'I…I'm so pleased about this…this turn of events,' she said. 'Thrilled, in fact. But how do we manage it? I…I feel a bit like Cinderella. One minute I'm in the kitchen, the next minute I'm at the ball.'

He seemed amused by her flight of fancy, and he smiled. What was it about his smile that appealed so much? His perfect teeth? The warmth in his eyes? The way his face creased into lines of good humour?

'I guess you could see it like that…' he said.

'And if I'm Cinderella…I guess *you're* the prince.'

His smile froze, and tension suddenly edged his voice. 'What…what do you mean?'

Gemma felt a sudden chill that was not a sea breeze. It perplexed her. 'Cinderella… The ball… The prince… The pumpkin transformed into a carriage… You know…' she said, gesturing with her hands. 'Don't you have the story of Cinderella in your country?'

'Uh…of course,' he said with an obvious relief that puzzled her. 'Those old fairytales originally came from Europe.'

So she'd unwittingly said the wrong thing? Maybe he thought she had expectations of something more than a day on the harbour. Of getting her claws into him. She really was out of practice. At dating. At flirting. Simply talking with a man who attracted her.

'I meant… Well, I meant that Cinderella meets the prince and you…well, you're as handsome as any fairytale prince and… Never mind.'

She glanced down at her white sneakers, tied with jaunty blue laces. Maybe this wasn't the time to be making a joke about a glass slipper.

Tristan nodded thoughtfully. 'Of course. And I found Cinderella in her kitchen…'

She felt uncomfortable about carrying this any further. He seemed to be making too much effort to join in the story. His English was excellent, but maybe he'd missed the nuances of the analogy. Maybe he had trouble with her Australian accent.

'Yes. And talking of kitchens, I need to talk to the chef and—' She made to turn back towards the door that led inside the cabin.

Tristan reached out and put his hand on her arm to stop her.

'You don't need to do anything but enjoy yourself,' he said, his tone now anything but uncertain. 'I've spoken to your staff. They know that you are my honoured guest.'

He dropped his hand from her arm so she could turn back to face him. 'You said that? You called me your "honoured guest"?' There was something about his formal way of speaking that really appealed to her. His words made her want to preen with pleasure.

'I did—and they seemed pleased,' he said.

Party Queens had a policy of only hiring staff they personally liked. The freelance chef on board today was a guy she'd worked with in her restaurant days. But it was the Australian way to be irreverent… She suspected she might be teased about this sudden switch from staff to guest. Especially having lunch in the company of such an exceptionally good-looking man.

'They were pleased I'm out of their hair?' she asked.

'Pleased for *you*. They obviously hold their boss in high regard.'

'That's nice,' she said, nodding.

Hospitality could be a tense business at times, what with deadlines and temperamental clients and badly behaving guests. It was good to have it affirmed that the staff respected her.

'What about lunch?' she said, indicating the direction of the kitchen. 'The—?'

Tristan waved her objections away. 'Relax, Gemma.' A smile hovered at the corners of his mouth. As if he were only too aware of how difficult she found it to give up control of her job. 'I'm the host. You are my guest. Forget about what's going on in the kitchen. Just enjoy being the guest—not the party planner.'

'This might take some getting used to,' she said with a rueful smile. 'But thank you, yes.'

'Good,' he said.

'I'm not sure of one thing,' she said. 'Do you still want me as your tour guide? If that's the case, I need to be pointing out some sights to you.'

She turned from him, took a few steps to the railing and looked out, the breeze lifting her hair from her face.

'On the right—oh, hang on...don't we say "starboard" on a boat? To *starboard* are the Finger Wharves at Walsh Bay. The configuration is like a hand—you know, with each wharf a finger. The wharves are home to the Sydney Theatre Company. It's a real experience to go to the theatre there and—'

'Stop!'

She turned, to see Tristan with his hand held up in a halt sign. His hands were attractive, large with long elegant fingers. Yes, nice hands were an asset on a man, too. She wondered how they would feel—

She could not go there.

Gemma knew she'd been chattering on too much about the wharves. Gabbling, in fact. But she suddenly felt...*nervous* in Tristan's presence. And chatter had always been her way of distancing herself from an awkward situation.

She spluttered to a halt. 'You don't want to know about

the wharves? Okay, on the left-hand side—I mean the *port* side—is Luna Park and…'

Tristan lowered his hand. Moved closer to her. So close they were just kissing distance apart. She tried not to look at his mouth. That full lower lip…the upper lip slightly narrower. *A sensual mouth was another definite asset in a man.* So was his ability to kiss.

She flushed and put her hand to her forehead. Why was she letting her thoughts run riot on what Tristan would be like to kiss? She took a step back, only to feel the railing press into her back. It was a little scary that she was thinking this way about a man she barely knew.

'There's no need for you to act like a tour guide,' he said. 'The first day I got here I took a guided tour of the harbour.'

'But you asked me to show you the insider's Sydney. The Wharf Theatre is a favourite place of mine and—'

'That was just a ploy,' he said.

Gemma caught her breath. 'A ploy?'

'I had to see you again. I thought there was more chance of you agreeing to show me around than if I straight out asked you to dinner.'

'Oh,' she said, momentarily lost for words. 'Or…or lunch on the harbour?'

Her heart started to thud so hard she thought surely he must hear it—even over the faint thrumming of the boat's motor, the sound of people calling out to each other on the cruiser that was passing them, the squawk of the seagulls wheeling over the harbour wall, where a fisherman had gutted his catch.

'That is correct,' Tristan said.

'So…so you had to find another way?' To think that all the time she'd spent thinking about *him*, he'd been thinking about *her*.

For the first time Gemma detected a crack in Tristan's self-assured confidence. His hands were thrust deep into the pockets of his white trousers. 'I...I had to see if you were as...as wonderful as I remembered,' he said, and his accent was more pronounced.

She loved the way he rolled his r*'s.* Without that accent, without the underlying note of sincerity, his words might have sounded sleazy. But they didn't. They sent a shiver of awareness and anticipation up her spine.

'And...and are you disappointed?'

She wished now that she'd worn something less utilitarian than a T-shirt—even though it was a very smart, fitted T-shirt, with elbow-length sleeves—and sneakers. They were work clothes. Not 'lunching with a hot guy' clothes. Still, if she'd had to dress with the thought of impressing Tristan, she might still be back at her apartment, with the contents of her wardrobe scattered all over the bed.

'Not at all,' he said.

He didn't need to say the words. The appreciation in his eyes said it all. Her hand went to her heart to steady its out-of-control thud.

'Me neither. I mean, I'm not disappointed in *you.*' *Aargh, could she sound any dumber?* 'I thought you were pretty wonderful, too. I... I regretted that I knocked back your request for me to show you around. But...but I had my reasons.'

His dark eyebrows rose. 'Reasons? Not just the company rules?'

'Those, too. When we first started the business, we initiated a "no dating the clients" rule. It made sense.'

'Yet I believe your business partner Andie married a client, so that rule cannot be set in concrete.'

'How did you know that?' She answered her own question, 'Of course—Jake Marlowe.' The best friend of the groom. 'You're right. But Andie was the exception.' Up until now there had been no client who had made *Gemma* want to bend the rules.

'And the other reasons?'

'Personal. I…I came out of a bad relationship more… more than a little wounded.'

'I'm sorry to hear that.' His eyes searched her face. 'And now?'

She took a deep breath. Finally she had that heartbeat under control. 'I've got myself sorted,' she said, not wanting to give any further explanation.

'You don't wear a ring. I assumed you were single.' He paused. '*Are* you single?'

Gemma was a bit taken aback by the directness of his question. 'Very single,' she said. Did that sound too enthusiastic? As if she were making certain he knew she was available?

Gemma curled her hands into fists. She had to stop second guessing everything she said. Tristan had thought she was wonderful in her apron, all flushed from the heat of the oven and without a scrap of make-up. She had to be herself. Not try and please a man by somehow attempting to be what he wanted her to be. She'd learned that from her mother—and it was difficult to unlearn.

Her birth father had died before she was born and her mother, Aileen, had brought Gemma up on her own until she was six. Then her mother had met Dennis.

He had never wanted children but had grudgingly accepted Gemma as part of a package deal when he'd married Aileen. Her mother had trained Gemma to be grateful to her stepfather for having taken her on. To keep him happy by always being a sweet little girl, by forgiving his moody behaviour, his lack of real affection.

Gemma had become not necessarily a *people* pleaser but a man pleaser. She believed that was why she'd put up with Alistair's bad behaviour for so long. It was a habit she was determined to break.

She decided to take charge of the conversation. 'What about you, Tristan? Are you single, too?'

He nodded. 'Yes.'

'Have you ever been married?'

'No,' he said. 'I...I haven't met the right woman. And you?'

'Same. I haven't met the right man.' Boy, had she met some wrong ones. But those days were past. *No more heartbreakers*.

The swell from a passing ferry made her rock unsteadily on her feet as she swayed with the sudden motion of the boat.

Tristan caught her elbow to steady her. 'You okay?' he said.

The action brought him close to her. So close she could feel the strength in his body, smell the fresh scent of him that hinted at sage and woodlands and the mountain country he came from. There was something so *different* about him—almost a sense of *other*. It intrigued her, excited her.

'F-fine, thank you,' she stuttered.

His grip, though momentary, had been firm and warm on her arm, and her reaction to the contact disconcerted her. She found herself trembling a little. Those warning antennae waved so wildly she felt light-headed. She shouldn't be feeling this intense attraction to someone she knew so little about. *It was against her every resolve.*

She took another steadying breath, as deep as she could without looking too obvious. The *Argus* had left the Harbour Bridge behind. 'We're on home territory for me now,' she said, in a determinedly conversational tone. 'Come over to this side and I'll show you.'

'You live around here?' he said as he followed her.

'See over there?' She waved to encompass the park that stretched to the water under the massive supports for the bridge overhead, the double row of small shops, the terraced houses, the multi-million-dollar apartments that sat at the edge of the water. 'You can just see the red-tiled roof of my humble apartment block.'

Tristan walked over to the railing, leaned his elbows on the top, looked straight ahead. Gemma stood beside him, very aware that their shoulders were almost nudging.

'Sydney does not disappoint me,' he said finally.

'I'm glad to hear that,' she said. 'What made you come here on your vacation?'

He shrugged. 'Australia is a place I always wanted to see. So far from Europe. Like the last frontier.'

Again, Gemma sensed he was leaving out more than he was saying. Her self-protection antennae were waving furiously. She had finetuned them in those six months of sabbatical, so determined not to fall into old traps, make old mistakes. Would he share more with her by the end of the day?

'I think you need to travel west of Sydney to see actual last-frontier territory,' she said. 'No kangaroos hopping around the place here.'

'I would like to see kangaroos that aren't in a zoo,' he said. He turned to face her. 'Living in Sydney must be like living in a resort,' he said.

Gemma tried to see the city she'd lived in all her life through his eyes. It wasn't that she took the beauty of the harbour for granted—it was just that she saw it every day. 'I hadn't thought about it like that but, yes, I see what you mean,' she said. Although she'd worked too hard ever to think she was enjoying a resort lifestyle.

'Do you like living here?' he said.

'Of course,' she said. 'Though I haven't actually lived anywhere else to compare. Sometimes I think I'd like to try a new life in another country. If Party Queens hadn't been such a success, I might have looked for a job as a chef in France. But in the meantime Sydney suits me.'

'I envy you in some ways,' he said. 'Your freedom. The lack of stifling tradition.'

She wondered at the note of yearning in his voice.

'There's a lot more to Sydney than these areas, of course,' she said. 'The Blue Mountains are worth seeing.' She stopped herself from offering to show them to him. He didn't want a tour guide. She didn't want to get too involved. *This was just lunch.*

'I would like to see more, but I go back home on Monday afternoon. With the party on Friday, there is not much time.'

'That's a shame,' she said, keeping her voice light and neutral. She knew this—*Tristan*—was only for today... an interlude. But she already had the feeling that a day, a week, a month wouldn't ever be enough time with him.

'I have responsibilities I must return to.' His tone of voice indicated that he might not be 100 per cent happy about that.

'With your family's corporation? Maybe you could consider opening an Australian branch of the business here,' she said.

He looked ahead of him, and she realised he was purposely not meeting her eyes. 'I'm afraid that is not possible—delightful as the thought might be.'

He turned away from the railing and went over to where he had put down her bag. Again, he pretended it was too heavy to carry, though she could see that with his muscles it must be effortless for him.

'Let's stash your bag somewhere safe and see about that coffee.'

'You don't want to see more sights?'

He paused, her bag held by his side. 'Haven't I made it clear, Gemma? Forgive my English if I haven't. I've seen a lot of sights in the time I've been in Australia. In the days I have left the only sight I want to see more of is *you*.'

CHAPTER FIVE

TRISTAN SAT OPPOSITE Gemma at a round table inside the cabin. After his second cup of coffee—strong and black—he leaned back in his chair and sighed his satisfaction.

'Excellent coffee, thank you,' he said. Of all the good coffee he'd enjoyed in Australia, he rated this the highest.

Gemma looked pleased. 'We're very fussy about coffee at Party Queens—single origin, fair trade, the best.'

'It shows,' Tristan said.

He liked Party Queens' meticulous attention to detail. It was one of the reasons he felt confident that his reception on Friday would be everything he wanted it to be—although for reasons of security he hadn't shared with them the real nature of the gathering.

'Not true,' Tristan muttered under his breath in his own language. He could have told Eliza by now. The reason he was holding back on the full facts was that he wanted to delay telling Gemma the truth about himself for as long as possible. Things would not be the same once his anonymity was gone.

'I'm glad you like the coffee. How about the food?' she asked.

Her forehead was pleated with the trace of a frown, and he realised she was anxious about his opinion.

'Excellent,' he pronounced. Truth be told, he'd scarcely noticed it. Who would be interested in food when he could feast his eyes on the beautiful woman in front of him?

To please her, he gave his full attention to the superbly arranged fruit platter that included some of the ripe mangoes he had come to enjoy in Queensland. There was also a selection of bite-sized cookies—both savoury, with cheese, and sweet, studded with nuts—arranged on the bottom tier of a silver stand. On the top tier were small square cakes covered in dark chocolate and an extravagant coating of shredded coconut.

'It all looks very good,' he said.

'I know there's more food than we can possibly eat, but we knew nothing about your lunch date and her tastes in food,' Gemma said.

'In that case I hope you chose food *you* liked,' he said.

'As a matter of fact, I did,' she said, with a delightful display of dimples.

'What is this cake with the coconut?' he asked.

'You haven't seen a lamington before?'

He shook his head.

'If Australia had a national cake it would be the lamington,' she said. 'They say it was created in honour of Lord Lamington, a nineteenth-century governor.'

'So this cake has illustrious beginnings?'

'You could call it a grand start for a humble little cake. In this case they are perhaps more illustrious, as I made them using the finest Montovian chocolate.'

'A Montovian embellishment of an Australian tradition?'

'I suspect our traditions are mere babies compared to yours,' she said with another flash of dimples. 'Would you like to try one?'

Tristan bit into a lamington. 'Delicious.'

Truth be told, he preferred lighter food. He had to sit through so many official dinners, with course after rich course, that he ate healthily when he had the choice. The mangoes were more to his taste. But he would not hurt her feelings by telling her so.

Gemma looked longingly at the rest of the cakes. 'I have the world's sweetest tooth—which is a problem in this job. I have to restrict myself to just little tastes of what we cook, or I'd be the size of a house.'

'You're in very good shape,' he said.

She had a fabulous body. Slim, yet with alluring curves. He found it almost impossible to keep his eyes from straying to it. He would have liked to say more about how attractive he found her, but it would not be appropriate. *Not yet...perhaps not ever.*

She flushed high on her cheekbones. 'Thank you. I wasn't fishing for a compliment.'

'I know that,' he said.

The mere fact that she was so unassuming about her beauty made him want to shower her with compliments. To praise the cuteness of her freckles, her sensational curves. To admit to the way he found himself wanting to make her smile just to see her dimples.

There was so much he found pleasing about her. But he was not in a position to express his interest. Gemma wasn't a vacation-fling kind of girl—he'd realised that the moment he met her. And that was all he could ever offer her.

It was getting more difficult by the minute to keep that at the top of his mind.

'I'll try just half a lamington and then some fruit,' she said.

She sliced one into halves with a knife and slowly nibbled on one half with an expression of bliss, her eyes half closed. As she licked a stray shred of coconut from her lovely bow-shaped top lip, she tilted back her head and gave a little moan of pleasure.

Tristan shifted in his seat, gripped the edge of the table so hard it hurt. It was impossible for his thoughts not to stray to speculation about her appetite for other pleasures, to how she would react to his mouth on hers, his touch...

There was still a small strand of coconut at the corner

of her mouth. He ached to lean across the table, taste the chocolate on her lips, lick away that stray piece of coconut.

She looked at him through eyes still half narrowed with sensual appreciation. 'The Montovian chocolate makes that the best lamington I've ever tasted.'

She should *always* have chocolate from Montovia.

Tristan cleared his throat. He had to keep their conversation going to distract himself. In his hedonistic past he had been immune to the seduction techniques of worldly, sophisticated temptresses, who knew exactly what they were doing as they tried to snare a prince. Yet the unconscious provocation of this lovely girl eating a piece of cake was making him fall apart.

'I believe you're a trained chef?' he said. 'Tell me how that happened.'

'How I became a chef? Do you really need to know that?'

'I know very little about you. I need to know everything.'

'Oh,' she said, delightfully disconcerted, the flush deepening on her creamy skin. 'If that's what you want...'

'It is what I want,' he said, unable to keep the huskiness from his voice. There was so much more he wanted from her, but it was impossible for him to admit to the desire she was arousing in him.

'Okay,' she said. 'I was always interested in food. My mother wasn't really into cooking and was delighted to let me take over the kitchen whenever I wanted.' She helped herself to some grapes, snipping them from the bunch with a tiny pair of silver scissors.

'So you decided to make a career of it?' It wouldn't be an easy life, he imagined. Hard physical work, as well as particular skills required and—

He completely lost his train of thought. Instead he

watched, spellbound, as Gemma popped the fat, purple grapes one by one into her luscious mouth.

Inwardly, he groaned. *This was almost unbearable.*

'Actually, I was all set to be a nutritionist,' she said, seemingly unaware of the torment she was putting him through by the simple act of eating some fruit. 'I started a degree at the University of Newcastle, which is north of Sydney. I stayed up there during the vacations and—'

'Why was that? I went to university in England but came home for at least part of every vacation.'

He'd loved the freedom of living in another country, but home had always been a draw card for him—the security and continuity of the castle, the knowledge of his place in the hierarchy of his country. His parents, who were father and mother to him before they were king and queen.

Gemma pulled a face—which, far from contorting her features, made her look cute. *Had she cast a spell on him?*

'Your home might have been more…welcoming than mine,' she said.

A shadow darkened her warm brown eyes at what was obviously an unpleasant memory. It made him sad for her. His memories of childhood and adolescence were happy. Life at the castle as the 'spare' had been fun—he had had a freedom never granted to his brother. A freedom sorely lost to him now—except for this trip. There had always been some tension between his father and mother, but it had been kept distanced from him. It hadn't been until he'd grown up that he'd discovered the cause of that tension—and why both his parents were so unhappy.

'You were not welcome in your own home?' he asked.

'My mother was always welcoming. My stepfather less so.'

'Was he…abusive?' Tristan tensed, and his hands tightened into fists at the thought of anyone hurting her.

She shook her head. The sunshine slanting in through

the windows picked up amber highlights and copper glints in her hair as it fell around her face. He wanted to reach out and stroke it, see if it felt as fiery as it looked.

'Nothing like that,' she said. 'And he wasn't unkind—just indifferent. He didn't want children, but he fell in love with my mother when I was a little kid and I came as part of the package deal.'

'A "package deal"? That seems a harsh way to describe a child.'

Again he felt a surge of protectiveness for her. It was a feeling new to him—this desire to enfold her in safety and shield her from any harm the world might hurl at her. A girl he had known for only a matter of days...

Her shrug of one slender shoulder was obviously an effort to appear nonchalant about an old hurt, but it was not completely successful. 'He couldn't have one without the other. Apparently he wanted my mother badly—she's very beautiful.'

'As is her daughter.' He searched her face. It was disconcerting, the way she seemed to grow lovelier by the minute.

'Thank you.' She flushed again. 'My mother always told me I had to be grateful to my stepfather for looking after us. *Huh.* Even when I was little I looked after myself. But I did my best to please him—to make my mother happy.' She wrinkled her neat, straight nose. 'Why am I telling you all this? I'm sure you must find it boring.'

'You could never be boring, Gemma,' he said. 'I know that about you already.'

It was true. Whether or not she'd cast some kind of witch's spell over him, he found everything about her fascinating. He wanted nothing more than to find out all about her. Just for today, the rest of his life was on hold. It was just him and Gemma, alone in the curious intimacy of a boat in the middle of Sydney Harbour. Like a regular, everyday date of the kind that would not be possible for him once he was back home.

'Are you sure you want to hear more of my ordinary little story?' she asked, her head tilted to one side.

'Nothing could interest me more.'

She could read out loud the list of ingredients from one of her recipes and he'd hang on every word, watching the expressions flit across her face, her dimples peeking in and out. Although so far there didn't appear to be a lot to smile about in her story.

The good-looking dark-haired waiter came to clear their coffee cups and plates. Gemma looked up and smiled at him as she asked him to leave the fruit. Tristan felt a surge of jealousy—until he realised the waiter was more likely to be interested in *him* rather than *her*. Gemma thanked him and praised the chef.

After the waiter had left, she leaned across the table to Tristan. Her voice was lowered to barely above a whisper. 'It feels weird, having people I know serve me,' she said. 'My instinct is to jump up and help. I'm used to being on the other side of the kitchen door.'

Tristan had been used to people serving him since he was a baby. An army of staff catered to the royal family's every need. He'd long ago got used to the presence of servants in the room—so much that they'd become almost invisible. When he went back he would have a hand-picked private staff of his own to help him assume his new responsibilities as crown prince.

The downside was that there was very little privacy. Since his brother had died every aspect of his life had been under constant, intense scrutiny.

Gemma returned to her story. 'Inevitably, when I was a teenager I clashed with my stepfather. It made my mother unhappy. I was glad to leave home for uni—and I never went back except for fleeting visits.'

'And your father?'

'You mean my birth father?'

'Yes.'

'He died before I was born.' Her voice betrayed no emotion. It was as if she were speaking about a stranger.

'That was a tragedy.'

'For my mother, yes. She was a ski instructor in the French resort of Val d'Isère, taking a gap year. My father was English—also a ski instructor. They fell madly in love, she got pregnant, they got married and soon after he got killed in an avalanche.'

'I'm sorry—that's a terrible story.'

Skiing was one of the risky sports he loved, along with mountaineering and skydiving. The castle staff was doing everything it could to wean him off those adrenaline-pumping pastimes. He knew he had to acquiesce. The continuity of the royal family was paramount. His country had lost one heir to an accident and could not afford to lose him, too.

But he railed against being cosseted. Hated having his independence and choice taken away from him. Sometimes the price of becoming king in future seemed unbearably high. But duty overruled everything. Tragedy had forced fate's hand. He accepted his inheritance and everything that went with it—no matter the cost to him. *He was now the crown prince.*

Gemma made a dismissive gesture with her hands. 'I didn't know my father, so of course I never missed him. But he was the love of my mother's life. She was devastated. Then his posh parents arrived at the resort, looked down their noses at my mother, questioned the legality of my parents' marriage—it *was* totally legit, by the way—and paid her to forget she was ever married and to never make a claim on them. They even tried to bar her from the funeral back in England.' Her voice rose with indignation.

'You sound angry,' he said. But what her father's parents had done was something *his* parents had done when he and his brother were younger. They would have paid any amount of money to rid the family of an unsuitable woman. Someone who might reflect badly on the throne. A commoner. *Someone like Gemma.*

His parents' actions had slammed home the fact that marriage for a Montovian prince had nothing to do with love or passion. It was about tradition and duty and strategic alliance. When he had discovered the deep hypocrisy of his parents' relationship, his cynicism about the institution of marriage—or at least how it existed in Montovia—had been born.

That cynicism had only been reinforced by his brother's marriage to the daughter of a duke. The castle had trumpeted it as a 'love match'. Indeed, Carl had been grateful to have found such a pretty, vivacious bride as Sylvie. Only after the splendid wedding in the cathedral had she revealed her true self—venal and avaricious and greedy for the wealth and status that came with being a Montovian princess. She'd cared more for extravagant jewellery than she had for his brother.

Consequently, Tristan had avoided marriage and any attempts to get him to the altar.

He schooled his face to appear neutral, not to give Gemma any indication of what he was thinking. Her flushed face made it very clear that she would *not* be sympathetic to those kind of regal machinations.

'You're darn right. I get angry on behalf of my poor mother—young and grieving,' she said. 'She wanted to throw the money in their faces, but she was carrying me. She swallowed her pride and took the money—for my sake. I was born in London, then she brought me home to Sydney. She said her biggest revenge for their treatment of her was that they never knew they had a grandchild.'

Tristan frowned. He was part of a royal family with a lineage that stretched back hundreds of years. Blood meant everything. 'How did you feel about that?'

Gemma toyed with the remainder of the grapes. He noticed her hands were nicked with little scars and her nails were cut short and unpolished. There were risks in everything—even cooking.

'Of course, I've always felt curious about my English family,' she said. 'I look nothing like my mother or her side of the family. When I was having disagreements with my stepfather, I'd dream of running away to find my other family. I know who they are. But out of loyalty to my mother I've never made any attempt to contact my Clifford relatives.'

'So your name is really Gemma Clifford?'

She shook her head. 'My stepfather adopted me. Legally I bear his name. And that's okay. For all his faults, he gave me a home and supported me.'

'Until you went to university in Newcastle?'

'Whatever his other faults, he's not mean. He kept on paying me an allowance. But I wanted to be independent—free of him and of having to pretend to be someone I was not simply to please him. I talked my way into a part-time kitchen hand's job at the best restaurant in the area. As luck would have it, the head chef was an incredibly talented young guy. He became a culinary superstar in Europe in the years that followed. Somehow he saw talent in me and offered me an apprenticeship as a chef. I didn't hesitate to ditch my degree and accept—much to my parents' horror. But it was what I really wanted to do.'

'Have you ever regretted it?'

'Not for a minute.'

'It seems a big jump from chef to co-owning Party Queens,' Tristan said.

Gemma offered the remaining grapes to him. When he

refused, she popped some more into her mouth. He waited for her to finish them.

'It's a roundabout story. When my boss left for grander culinary pastures, his replacement wasn't so encouraging of me. I left the Newcastle restaurant and went back to Sydney.'

'To work in restaurants?'

'Yes—some very good ones. But it's still a very male-dominated industry. Most of the top chefs are men. Females like me only too often get relegated to being pastry chefs and are passed over for promotion. I got sick of the bullying in the kitchen. The sexist behaviour. I got the opportunity to work on a glossy women's magazine as an assistant to the food editor and grabbed it. In time I became a food editor myself, and my career took off.'

'That still doesn't explain Party Queens,' he said. 'Seems to me there's a gap there.' He'd trained as a lawyer. He was used to seeing what was missing from an argument, what lay beneath a story.

She leaned across the table and rested on her elbows. 'Are you interviewing me?' Her words were playful, but her eyes were serious.

'Of course not. I'm just interested. You're very successful. I want to know how you got there.'

'I've worked hard—be in no doubt about that. But luck plays a part in it, too.'

'It always does,' he said.

Lucky he had walked in on her in her kitchen. Lucky he'd been born into a royal family. And yet there were days when he resented that lucky accident of birth. Like right here, right now, spending time with this woman, knowing that he could not take this attraction, which to his intense gratification appeared to be mutual, *anywhere*. Because duty to his country required sacrificing his own desires.

'There's bad luck too, of course,' Gemma went on.

'Andie was lifestyle editor on the magazine—she'd trained as an interior designer. Eliza was on the publishing side. We became friends. Then the magazine closed without warning and we were all suddenly without a job.'

'That must have been a blow,' he said. He had never actually worked for an employer, apart from his time as a conscript in the Montovian military. His 'job prospects'— short of an exceedingly unlikely revolution—were assured for life.

Again, Gemma shrugged one slender shoulder. 'It happens in publishing. We rolled with it.'

'I can see that,' he said. He realised how resilient she was. And independent. She got more appealing by the minute.

'People asked us to organise parties for them while we were looking for other jobs—between us we had all the skills. The party bookings grew, and we began to see we had a viable business. That's how Party Queens was born. We never dreamed it would become as successful as it has.'

'I'm impressed. With you and with your business. With all this.' He indicated the *Argus*, the harbour, the meal.

'We aim to please,' she said with that bewitching smile.

He could imagine only too well how she might please him and he her.

But he was not here in Sydney to make impossible promises to a girl next door like Gemma. Nor did he want to seduce her with lies just for momentary physical thrills.

Or to put his own heart at any kind of risk.

This could be for only one day.

CHAPTER SIX

GEMMA COULDN'T REMEMBER when she'd last felt so at ease with a man. So utterly comfortable in his presence. Had she *ever* before felt like this?

But she didn't want to question the *why* of it. Just to enjoy his company while she had the chance.

After she'd polished off all the grapes, she and Tristan had moved back out onto the deck. He hadn't eaten much—no more cake and just some mango. She'd got the impression he was very disciplined in his eating habits—and probably everything else. But getting to know Tristan was still very much a guessing game.

The *Argus* had left the inner harbour behind and set course north for Manly and their lunchtime destination of Store Beach. The sun had moved around since they'd gone inside for coffee, and the crew had moved two vintage steamer-style wooden deckchairs into the shade, positioned to take advantage of the view.

She adjusted the cushions, which were printed with anchor motifs, and settled down into one of them. Tristan was to her right, with a small table between them. But as soon as she'd sat down, she moved to get up again.

'My hat,' she explained. 'I need to get it from my bag. Even though we're in the shade, I could get burned.'

Immediately, Tristan was on his feet. 'Let me get it for you,' he said, ushering her to sit back down.

'There's no need. Please… I can do it,' she protested.

'I insist,' he said in a tone that brooked no further resistance.

Gemma went to protest again, then realised that would sound ungracious. *She wasn't used to being cared for by a man.* 'Thank you,' she conceded. 'It's right at the top of the bag.'

'Next to the rolling pins?' he said.

'But no wooden spoons,' she said with a smile.

Not only would Alistair not have dreamed of fetching her hat for her, he would have demanded she get him a beer while she was up. *Good manners were very appealing in a man.*

Tristan held himself with a mix of upright bearing and athletic grace as he headed back into the cabin. Gemma lay back and watched him through her sunglasses. His back view was every bit as pleasing as his front. Broad shoulders tapered to a wide back and then narrow hips. *There could be no doubt that a good butt was also an asset in a man.*

He looked effortlessly classy in the white linen trousers and the loose white shirt. They were so perfectly cut she wondered if they'd been tailored to fit him. Could you get men's casual clothes made to measure? She knew you could have suits bespoke. Anything was possible if you had enough money, she supposed.

He returned with her hat—a favourite white panama. She reached out to take it from him, but he came to the side of her chair and bent down to put it on her head. His face was very close. She could almost imagine he was bending down to kiss her. If he did, she wouldn't stop him. No…she might even kiss him first. She was thankful her sunglasses masked her eyes, so her expression didn't give her away.

'Nice hat,' he said as he placed it on her head. As he tugged it into place, his hands strayed lightly over her hair, her ears, her throat—just the merest touch, but it was enough to set her trembling.

She forced her voice to sound steady—not to betray how excitingly unnerving she found his nearness. 'I've had this hat for years, and I would be greatly distressed if I lost it.'

Again she caught his scent. She remembered how years

ago in high school she'd dated a perfectly nice boy who'd had everything going for him, but she hadn't liked the way he'd smelled. Not that he'd been unclean or unwashed—it was just his natural scent that had turned her off. But Tristan's fresh scent sent her nerve endings into a flurry of awareness.

Was there *anything* about Tristan she didn't find appealing?

His underlying mystery, that sense of him holding back still had her guard up—but perhaps that mystery was part of his appeal. And it was in her power to find out what made Tristan tick. *Just ask him, Gemma.*

There were many points of interest she could draw his attention to on their way to Manly. But she would not waste time on further guidebook lectures. *The only sight I want to see more of is you,* he'd said.

Did he have any idea of how good those words made her feel?

Her self-esteem had taken a terrible battering from Alistair. Six months had not been enough to fix it fully. Just hours in Tristan's company had her feeling better about herself than she had for a long time. The insistent twitching of her antennae told her that his charming words might be calculated to disarm and seduce. But her deeper instincts sensed sincerity—though for what purpose she was still at a loss.

Enjoy the moment, she told herself, *because that's all you've got with him.*

After Tristan had settled into his deckchair, she turned to him, slipped off her sunglasses. 'Your interview technique is so good you know quite a lot about me. Now it's my turn to discover Tristan.'

He gestured with his hands to indicate emptiness. 'There is not much I can tell you,' he said.

Did he mean that literally?

For all the instant intimacy of the situation, she still sensed those secrets. Her antennae waved gently, to remind her to be wary of men who were not what they seemed.

'Ask me questions—I will see if I can answer them,' he said.

As in, he would see if he was *able* to answer her questions? Or *allowed* to answer them? Or he just plain didn't *want* to answer them?

She chose her first question with care. 'What language do you speak in Montovia?' she asked. 'French? German? I think I can detect both in your accent.'

'We speak Montovian—our own language,' he said. 'We are a small country and it is influenced by the other European countries that surround us.'

'Say something to me in Montovian,' she said. 'I'm interested in languages.'

'I've been told it is not an attractive language, so I am warning you,' he said. 'Even to my ears it sounds quite harsh.'

He turned to her and spoke a few sentences as he gazed into her eyes. She tried to ignore the way his proximity made her heart race.

'I didn't understand a word of that, but your language is not unattractive.' And neither was his voice—deep, masculine, arresting. 'What did you actually say to me?'

'You really want to know?'

'Yes.'

'I said that the beauty of this magnificent harbour could not compare to the beauty of the woman sitting beside me.'

Spoken by anyone else, the words might have sounded corny, over the top. But spoken with Tristan's accent they were swoon worthy.

'Oh,' she said, again lost for words. She felt herself blush—that was the problem with being a creamy-skinned redhead…there was no hiding her reactions. 'Seriously?'

He smiled. 'You'll never know, will you? Unless you learn Montovian—and no one outside of my country learns Montovian.'

'Why not?'

'Because it is only spoken in Montovia. I also speak German, French, Italian and Spanish,' he said.

'I'm seriously impressed,' she said. 'I studied French and Italian at school. Then German at night school before I went to Europe on a backpackers' bus tour. But I never use those languages here, and I fear I've lost what skills I had.'

'You'd pick them up again in the right environment. I was out of the habit of speaking English, but I'm getting better at it every day.' His eyes narrowed in that intense way he had of looking at her, as if he were seeking answers—to what, she didn't know. 'Especially talking to you, Gemma'.

'You've inspired me to study some more so that—'

Only just in time she caught herself from saying, *So that next time I'll surprise you by speaking fluent French.* She was surprised at the sharp twist of pain at the reminder that there would be no next time for her and Tristan.

She finished her sentence, hoping he hadn't noticed the pause. 'So that my skills don't just dwindle away. Did you learn English at school?'

'Yes. I also had a tutor. My parents felt it was essential we spoke good English.'

'"We"? You have brothers and sisters?'

Tristan stared out to sea. 'I have a younger sister. I... I had an older brother. He...he died when his helicopter came down in the mountains a year ago.'

Gemma wasn't sure what to say that wouldn't be a cliché. 'I...I'm so sorry to hear that,' was the best she could manage.

His jaw tightened. 'It was...terrible. His wife and their little boy were with him. My family will never get over it.'

Gemma was too shocked to speak. She went to reach out and put her hand on his arm but decided against it, not sure how welcome her touch would be in this moment of remembered tragedy.

'I carry the loss of my brother with me in my heart. There is not a day that I do not think of him.'

'I'm so sorry,' she said again. She wished she could give him comfort. But they were still essentially strangers.

He took a deep breath. 'But enough of sadness,' he said. He turned to her. 'I don't want to talk about tragic things, Gemma.'

There was a bleakness in his eyes, and his face seemed shadowed. She was an only child. She couldn't imagine how it would feel to lose a sibling—*and* his sibling's family. 'No,' she agreed.

How lucky she'd been in her life not to have suffered tragedy. The loss of her birth father hadn't really touched her, though she suspected her mother still secretly grieved. Gemma *had* had her share of heartbreak, though. She had genuinely loved Alistair, and the way their relationship had ended had scarred her—perhaps irredeemably. It would be difficult to trust again.

A silence fell between them that Gemma didn't know quite how to fill. 'Tell me more about Montovia,' she said eventually. 'Are there magnificent old buildings? Do you have lots of winter sports? Do you have a national costume?'

'Yes to all of that. Montovia is very beautiful and traditional. It has many medieval buildings. There is also a modern administrative capital, where the banks and financial services are situated.'

'And the chocolate?'

'The so-important chocolate? It is made in a charming old factory building near the lake, which is a tourist attraction in its own right.'

I'd love to go there some day.

Her words hung unspoken in the air between them. Never could she utter them. He was a tourist—just passing through before he went back to his own life. And she was a woman guarding her heart against falling for someone impossible.

'That sounds delightful,' she said.

'There is a wonderful chocolate shop and tea room near my home. I used to love to go there when I was a child. So…so did my brother and sister.'

Gemma wondered about his sister, but didn't want to ask. 'Where do you live?' she said instead.

He took another deep breath. It seemed to Gemma that he needed to steady himself against unhappy thoughts. His brother must be entwined in Tristan's every childhood memory.

'I live in the old capital of Montovia—which is also called Montovia.'

'That could get confusing, couldn't it?'

'Everyone knows it. The town of Montovia grew up around the medieval castle and the cathedral and sits on the edge of a lake.'

Gemma sat forward in her chair. 'A castle? You live near a *castle*?'

'But of course. Montovia is ruled by a hereditary monarchy.'

'You mean a king and a queen?'

'Yes.'

'I wasn't expecting that. I assumed Montovia would be a republic—a democracy.'

'It is… We have a hereditary monarchy, but also a representative democracy with an elected parliament—and a legal system, of course.'

'So the king and queen are figureheads?'

He shook his head. 'They are rulers, with the power to dissolve parliament. Although that has never happened.'

'Castles and kings and queens—it sounds like something out of a fairytale.' She was too polite to say it sounded feudalistic. Not when he sounded so passionate, defending a way of life that didn't seem of this century.

'On the contrary, it is very real. Our country is prosperous. Montovians are very patriotic. Each of our subjects—I…uh…I mean the people…would fight to the death to protect their way of life. We have compulsory military service to ensure we are ready in case they should ever have to.'

'You mean conscription?'

'Yes. For all males aged eighteen. Women can volunteer, and many do.'

She shuddered. 'I don't think I would want to do that.'

'They would probably welcome someone like you as a cook.'

He smiled. Was he teasing her?

'But I'd still have to do the military training. I've seen what soldiers have to do—running with big packs on their back, obstacle courses, weapons…' Her voice dwindled away at the sheer horror of even contemplating it.

'Sign up even as a cook and you'd have to do the training. And no wooden spoons as weapons.'

'You'll never let me forget that, will you?'

'Never,' he said, his smile widening into a grin.

Until he went on his way and never gave this girl in Sydney another thought.

Why were they even talking about this? She was unlikely to visit Montovia, let alone sign up for its military.

'Did you serve?' she asked.

'Of course. My time in the army was one of the best times of my life.'

Oh, yes. She could imagine him in uniform. With his

broad shoulders and athletic build. That must be where his bearing came from. Tristan in uniform would be even hotter than Tristan in casual clothes. Or Tristan without any—

Don't go there, Gemma.

But her curiosity about Montovia was piqued. When she went home this evening, she would look up the country and its customs on the internet.

'Did you actually have to go to battle?' she asked.

'I spent time with the peacekeeping forces in eastern Europe. My brother went to Africa. It was good for us to see outside our own protected world.'

'You know, I wasn't really aware that such kingdoms as Montovia still existed.'

'Our royal family has ruled for centuries,' he said— rather stiffly, she thought. 'The people love the royal family of Montovia.'

'Do *you*?' she asked. 'You're not harbouring any secret republican leanings?'

His eyebrows rose, and he looked affronted. 'Never. I am utterly loyal to the king and queen. My country would not be Montovia without the royal family and our customs and traditions.'

Gemma was silent for a long moment. 'It's all so outside of my experience. As a child I led an everyday suburban existence in a middle-class suburb of Sydney. You grew up in a town with a medieval castle ruled by a king and queen. What…what different lives we must lead.'

He steepled his fingers together. 'Yes. Very different.'

Tristan was glad of the interruption when the waiter brought out a tray with the cool drinks they had ordered. *He had to be more careful.* He'd been on tenterhooks while chatting with Gemma for fear that he would inadvertently reveal the truth about himself and his family. There had been a few minor slip-ups, but nothing that couldn't be excused as a mistake with his English.

He drank iced tea as Gemma sipped on diet cola. It was too early for anything stronger.

The longer he maintained this deception, the harder it would become to confess to it. But did that really matter? After the party on Friday night he wouldn't need to be in any further contact with Party Queens. Or with Gemma.

He could leave the reveal until she found out for herself—when he appeared at his party wearing his ceremonial sash and medals. No doubt she would be shocked, would maybe despise him for lying to her. Her opinion should not matter—he would never see her again after the party.

But her opinion of him did matter. *It mattered very much*.

Just now there had been an opportunity for him to explain his role in the royal family of Montovia—but he had not been able to bring himself to take it. He was still hanging on fiercely to the novelty of being just Tristan in Gemma's eyes.

'I haven't finished my interrogation yet,' she said, a playful smile lifting the corners of her mouth.

He liked it that she was unaware of his wealth and status. It must be obvious to her that he was rich. But she seemed more interested in *him* than in what he had. It was refreshing.

'You said you went to university in England?' she asked.

'To Cambridge—to study European law.'

Her finely arched auburn brows rose. 'You're a lawyer?'

'I don't actually practise as a lawyer. I have always worked for...for my family's business. A knowledge of European law is necessary.'

For trade. For treaties. For the delicate negotiations required by a small country that relied in some measure on the goodwill of surrounding countries—but never took that goodwill for granted.

'Is it your father's business?'

'Yes. And it was my grandparents' before that.' Back and back and back, in an unbroken chain of Montovia's hereditary monarchy. It had been set to continue in his brother's hands—not his.

Tristan knew he could not avoid talking about his brother, much as it still hurt. There'd been an extravagance of public mourning for his brother's death—and the death of his little son, whose birth had placed a second male between Tristan and the throne. But with all the concern about his unexpected succession to the position of crown prince, Tristan hadn't really been able to mourn the loss of Carl, his brother and best friend. Not Carl the crown prince. And his sweet little nephew. This trip away had been part of that grieving process. Being with Gemma was helping.

'My brother played a senior role in the...the business. I now have to step up to take his role.'

'And you're not one hundred per cent happy about that, are you?'

'I never anticipated I would have to do it. The job is not my choice.'

Not only had he loved his brother, he had also admired the way Carl had handled the role of crown prince. Tristan had never resented not being the heir. He had never been sure if he had an unquestioning allegiance to the old ways in order not to challenge the archaic rules that restricted the royal family's existence even in the twenty-first century. One onerous rule in particular...

'Will it bring more responsibility?' Gemma asked. 'Will you be more involved in the chocolate side of things?'

For a moment he wasn't sure what she meant. Then he

remembered how he had deliberately implied that chocolate was part of his family's business.

'More the finance and managerial side,' he said. And everything else it took to rule the country.

'I'm sure you will rise to the challenge and do a wonderful job,' she said.

He frowned. 'Why do you say that, Gemma, when we scarcely know each other?'

Her eyes widened. 'Even in this short time I'm convinced of your integrity,' she said. 'I believe you will want to honour your brother's memory by doing the best job you can.'

His integrity. Short of downright lying, he had been nothing but evasive about who he was from the moment they'd met. How would she react when she found out the truth?

The longer he left it, the worse it would be.

He turned to face her. 'Gemma, I—'

Gemma suddenly got up from her deckchair, clutching her hat to her head against a sudden gust of wind. 'We're passing across the Heads.'

'The Heads?'

'It's the entrance from the ocean to Sydney Harbour, guarded by two big headlands—North Head and South Head. But, being exposed to the Pacific Ocean, the sea can get rough here, so prepare for a rocky ride ahead.'

CHAPTER SEVEN

TRISTAN HAD PLANNED with military precision in order to make this day with Gemma happen. But one important detail had escaped his plan.

He cursed his inattention with a blast of favourite curse words. Both relatively sheltered when they'd been conscripted to the military, he and his brother had expanded their vocabulary of new and interesting words with great glee. He had never lost the skill.

Gemma was standing beside him at the bow of the *Argus*. 'Do I detect some choice swearing in Montovian?' she asked with a teasing smile.

'Yes,' he said, still furious with himself.

'Can you translate for me?'

'No,' he said.

'Or tell me what it was all about?'

Exasperated, he waved his hand to encompass the view. 'Look at this place—Store Beach…even more perfect than you said it would be.'

'And there's a problem with that?'

The *Argus* had dropped anchor some one hundred metres from shore. The beach was more what he would call a bay, with a sheltered, curving stretch of golden sand. Eucalypt trees and other indigenous plants grew right down to where the sand started. The water rippled through shades of azure to wash up on the beach in a lacy white froth. The air was tangy with salt and the sharp scent of the eucalypts. It took no stretch of the imagination to feel as if they were on a remote island somewhere far away.

'Not a problem with the beach,' he said. 'It's difficult to believe such a pristine spot could be so close to a major city.'

'That's why we chose Store Beach for your lunch date,' she said. 'And, being midweek, we've got it all to ourselves. So what's the problem?'

'It's hot, the water looks awesome, I want to swim. But I didn't think to bring a swimsuit—or order one for you.'

Her eyebrows rose. 'For me? *Order* a swimsuit for me?'

'Of course. You would not have known to bring one as you thought you would be working. There is a concierge at my hotel—I should have asked her to purchase a choice of swimsuits for you.'

Gemma's brows drew together in a frown. 'Are you serious?'

'But of course.'

'You are, aren't you?' Her voice was underscored with incredulity.

'Is there something wrong with that?'

'Nothing *wrong*, I guess. But it's not the kind of thing an Australian guy would do, that's for sure. None that *I* know, anyway.'

Tristan realised he might sound arrogant, but went ahead anyway. 'It is the kind of thing I would do, and I am annoyed that I did not do so.'

She tilted her head to one side, observing him as if he were an object of curiosity. 'How would you have known my size?'

'I have observed your figure.' He couldn't help but cast an appreciative eye over the curves of her breasts and hips, her trim waist. 'I would have made a very good estimate.'

Immediately, he suspected he might have said the wrong thing. Again he muttered a Montovian curse. Under stress—and the way she was looking at him *was* making him stressed—he found his English wasn't turning out quite the way he wanted it to.

Thankfully, after a stunned silence on her part, Gemma erupted into a peal of delightful laughter. 'Okay…I'm flattered you've made such a close observation of my figure.'

'It's not that I…I didn't mean—'

Her voice was warm with laughter. 'I think I know what you mean.'

'I did not say something…inappropriate?'

'You kinda did—but let's put it down to culture clash.'

'You do not think me…bad mannered? Rude?'

Crass. That was the word he was seeking. It was at the tip of his tongue. He had a master's degree in law from a leading English university. Why were his English language skills deserting him?

It was *her.*

Gemma.

Since the moment she'd come at him with her wooden spoon and pink oven mitts she'd had him—what was the word?—*discombobulated.* He was proud he had found the correct, very difficult English word, but why didn't he feel confident about pronouncing it correctly? The way she made him feel had him disconcerted, disorientated, behaving in ways he knew he should not.

But the way she was smiling up at him, with her dimples and humour in her brown eyes, made him feel something else altogether. *Something that was forbidden for him to feel for a commoner.*

She stretched up on her toes to kiss him lightly on the cheek, as she had done when she'd boarded the boat. This time her lips lingered longer, and she was so close he inhaled her heady scent of vanilla and lemon and a hint of chocolate, felt the warmth of her body. He put his hand to his cheek, where he had felt the soft tenderness of her lips, and held it there for a moment too long.

'I don't think you're at all rude,' she said. 'I think you're charming and funny and generous…and I…I…'

For a long moment her gaze held his, and the flush high on her cheekbones deepened. Tristan held his breath, on tenterhooks over what she might say next. But she took a step back, took a deep, steadying breath—which made her breasts rise enticingly under her snug-fitting top—and said something altogether different from what he'd hoped she might say.

'And I can solve your swimsuit problem for you,' she said.

'You can?'

'First the problem of a swimsuit for me. That impossibly big bag of mine also contains a swimsuit and towel. The North Sydney Olympic Pool is on the way from Lavender Bay wharf to my apartment in Kirribilli. I intended to swim there on my way home—as I often do.'

'That's excellent—so you at least can dive in and swim.'

'So can you.'

'But I—'

'I understand if you don't want to go in salt water in your smart white trousers. Or…or in your underwear.'

Her voice had faltered when she'd mentioned his underwear. A sudden image of her in *her* underwear flashed through his mind—lovely Gemma, swimming in lacy sheer bra and panties, her auburn hair streaming behind her in the water…

He had to clear his throat to speak. 'So what do you suggest?'

'In a closet in the stateroom is a selection of brand-new swimwear for both men and women. Choose a swimsuit and the cost of it will be added to the boat hire invoice.'

'Perfect,' he said. 'You get everything right, don't you, Party Queen Gemma?'

Her expression dimmed. 'Perhaps not everything. But I'll claim this one.'

'Shall we go swimming?' he asked. 'I saw a swimming

platform aft on the boat.' His skin prickled with heat. He should have worn shorts and a T-shirt instead of trying to impress Gemma in his bespoke Italian sportswear. 'I can't wait to get into that water.'

'Me, too. I can't think of anything I would rather do on a beautiful day like this.'

Tristan could think of a number of things he'd like to do with *her* on a beautiful day like this. All of which involved them wearing very few clothes—if any at all.

Gemma changed quickly and went back out onto the deck, near the swimming platform at the back. Tristan had gone into the stateroom to choose a swimsuit and change. She felt inexplicably shy as she waited for him. Although she swam often, she never felt 100 per cent comfortable in a swimsuit. The occupational hazard of a career filled with tempting food made her always think she needed to lose a few pounds to look her best in Lycra.

Her swimsuit was a modest navy racer-back one-piece, with contrast panels of aqua and white down the sides. More practical than glamorous. Not, in fact, the slightest bit seductive. Which was probably as well…

The door from the stateroom opened and Tristan headed towards her. Tristan had confessed to 'observing' her body. She smiled at the thought of his flustered yet flattering words. She straightened her shoulders and sucked in her tummy. And then immediately sucked in a breath as well at the sight of him. He'd looked good in his clothes, but without them—well, *nearly* without them—he was breathtaking in his masculinity.

Wearing stylish swim shorts in a tiny dark-blue-and-purple check and nothing else, he strode towards her with athletic grace and a complete lack of self-consciousness. *He was gorgeous.* Those broad shoulders, the defined muscles of his chest and arms, the classic six-pack belly and long, leanly muscled legs were in perfect proportion. He didn't have much body hair—just a dusting in the right places, set off against smooth golden skin.

He smiled his appreciation of *her* in a swimsuit. His smile and those vivid blue eyes, his handsome, handsome face and the warmth of his expression directed at her, all made her knees so wobbly she had to hold on to the deck railing for support. Her antennae didn't just wave frantically—they set off tiny, shrill alarms.

She realised she was holding her breath, and it came out as a gasp she had to disguise as a cough.

'Are you okay?' Tristan asked.

'F-fine,' she said as soon as she was able to recover her voice. As fine as a red-blooded woman *could* be when faced with a vision of such masculine perfection and trying to pretend she wasn't affected.

The crew had left a stack of red-and-white-striped beach towels in a basket on the deck. Tristan picked one up and handed it to her. 'Your swimsuit is very smart,' he said.

The open admiration in his eyes when he looked at her made her decide she had no cause for concern about what he thought of her shape.

She had to clear her throat. 'So...so is yours.'

Tristan picked up a towel for himself and slung it around his neck. As he did so, Gemma noticed something that marred all that physical perfection—a long, reddish scar that stretched along the top of his shoulder.

Tristan must have noticed the line of her gaze. 'You have observed my battle wound?'

She frowned. 'I thought you said you didn't go to war?'

'I mean my battle wound from the polo field. I came off one of my ponies and smashed my collarbone.'

She wanted to lean over and stroke it but didn't. 'Ouch. That must have hurt.'

'Yes. It did,' he said with understatement.

She didn't know if it was Tristan's way or just the way he spoke English. She wondered how different he might be if she were able to converse with him in fluent Montovian.

'I have a titanium plate and eight pins in it.'

'And your pony?' Gemma wasn't much of a horseback rider, but she knew that what was called a polo 'pony' was actually a very expensive and highly trained thoroughbred horse. Polo was a sport for the very wealthy.

'He was not hurt, thank heaven—he is my favourite pony. We have won many chukkas together.'

'Can you still play polo?'

'I hope to be able to play in the Montovian team this summer.'

She could imagine Tristan in the very tight white breeches and high black boots of a polo player, fearlessly ducking and weaving in perfect unison with a magnificent horse.

'You play polo for your country?'

'I have that honour, yes,' he said.

Again she got that feeling of *otherness*. Not only did he and she come from different countries and cultures, it seemed Tristan came from a different side of the tracks, as well. The posh, extremely wealthy side. Her stepfather was hardly poor, but he was not wealthy in the way she suspected Tristan was wealthy. Dennis was an orthodontist, with several lucrative practices. She could thank him for her perfectly aligned teeth and comfortable middle-class upbringing.

As a single mother, I could never have given you this life, her mother had used to say, reinforcing her instructions for Gemma always to be grateful and acquiescent. *Why couldn't you have married someone who didn't always make me feel in the way?* Gemma had wanted to shout back. But she had loved her mother too much to rebel.

Running a string of polo ponies, hiring a luxury yacht

on Sydney Harbour for just two people, the upcoming no-expenses-spared function on Friday night all seemed to speak of a very healthy income. If she thought about it, Tristan had actually *bought* her company on the boat today—and it had been a very expensive purchase.

But she didn't care about any of that.

She liked Tristan—*really* liked him—and he was far and away the most attractive man she had ever met. It was a waste of time to worry when she just wanted to enjoy his company.

She reached into her outsize bag for her high-protection sunscreen. 'You go in the water. I still have to put on some sun protection,' she said to Tristan.

'I'll wait for you,' he said.

Aware of Tristan's intense gaze, she felt self-conscious smoothing cream over her arms and legs, then twisting and turning to get to the spot on her back she could never quite reach. 'Australia is probably not the best climate for me,' she said. 'I burn, I blister, I freckle...'

'I think your pale skin is lovely,' he said. 'Don't try to tan it.'

'Thank you,' she said. It wasn't a compliment she heard often in a country obsessed with tanning.

'Let me help,' said Tristan. He grabbed the tube of sunscreen before she could protest. 'Turn around.'

She tensed as she heard him fling the towel from around his neck, squeeze cream from the tube. Then relaxed as she felt his hands on her back, slowly massaging in the cream with strong, sure fingers, smoothing it across her shoulders and down her arms in firm, sweeping motions.

The sensation of his hands on her body was utter bliss— she felt as if she was melting under his touch. When his hands slid down her back, they traced the sides of her breasts, and her nipples tightened. His breath fanned her hair, warm and intimate. She closed her eyes and gave herself over to sensation. *To Tristan.*

Her breathing quickened as her body responded to him, and from behind her she heard his breath grow ragged. He rested his hands on her waist. She twisted around, her skin slick with cream, and found herself in the circle of his arms.

For a long, silent moment she looked up into his face— already familiar, dangerously appealing. She knew he would see in her eyes the same mix of yearning and desire and wariness she saw in his: the same longing for something she knew was unwise. She swayed towards him as he lowered his head and splayed her hands against his bare, hard chest, his warm skin. She sighed as his lips touched hers in the lightest of caresses, pressed her mouth against his as she returned his kiss.

He murmured against her mouth. 'Gemma, I—'

Then another voice intruded. 'Gemma, I need to get your opinion on the plating of the yellow-tail kingfish *carpaccio.* Do you want— Oh. *Sorry.* I didn't realise I was interrupting—'

Gemma broke away from Tristan's kiss. Glared over his shoulder to her chef, who had his hands up in surrender as he backed away.

'No need. I'll sort the *carpaccio* out for myself.'

But he had a big grin plastered on his face, and she knew the team at Party Queens would find out very soon that Gemma had been caught kissing the client. She muttered a curse in English—one she was sure Tristan would understand. *She wanted to keep Tristan to herself.*

Tristan's arms remained firmly around her, and she didn't really want to leave them. But when he pulled her towards him again, she resisted. 'It's as well our chef came along,' she said. 'We shouldn't really be starting something we can't continue, should we?'

Tristan cleared his throat, but his voice was husky when he replied. 'You are right—we should not. But that does not stop me wanting to kiss you.'

She took a step back. 'Me neither. I mean I want to kiss *you*, too. But…but you're only here a few days and I—'

I'm in danger of falling for you, even though I hardly know you and I have to protect myself from the kind of pain that could derail me.

'I understand. It would be best for both of us.' He sounded as if he spoke through gritted teeth.

Disappointment flooded through her but also relief that he hadn't pressed for more. After the world of promise in that brief, tender kiss, she might have been tempted to ignore those frantically waving antennae and throw away every self-protective measure and resolve she had made in that lonely six months.

'Yes,' was all she could murmur from a suddenly choked throat.

'What I really need is to get into that cold water,' he said.

'You mean…like a cold shower?'

'Yes,' he said, more grimly than she had heard him speak before.

'Me, too,' she said.

He held out his hand. 'Are you coming with me?'

CHAPTER EIGHT

As TRISTAN SWAM alongside Gemma, seeing her pale limbs and the auburn hair floating around her shoulders reminded him of the Montovian myths of water nymphs. Legend had it that these other-world temptresses in human form inhabited the furthest reaches of the vast lakes of Montovia. They were young, exquisite and shunned human contact.

If a man were to come across such a nymph, he would instantly become besotted, bewitched, obsessed by her. His beautiful nymph would entice him to make love to her until he was too exhausted to swim and he'd drown—still in her embrace—in the deepest, coldest waters. The rare man who survived and found his way home would go mad with grief and spend the rest of his life hunting the shores of the lakes in a desperate effort to find his nymph again.

Montovians were a deeply superstitious people—even the most well educated and sophisticated of them. Tristan shrugged off those ancient myths, but in a small part of his soul they lived on despite his efforts to deny them.

Gemma swam ahead of him with effortless, graceful strokes, ducking beneath the water, turning and twisting her body around. How did he describe how she seemed in the water? *Joyous.* That was the word. She was quite literally in her element, playing in the water like some... well, like a nymph enchantress.

She turned back to face him, her hair slicked back off her face, revealing her fine bone structure, the scattering of freckles across the bridge of her nose. She trod water until he caught up with her.

'Isn't the water wonderful?' she said. 'I would have hated you if I'd had to stay in the kitchen while you cavorted in the sea with that other woman—uh, that other woman who didn't actually exist.'

'You would have "hated" me?' he asked.

'Of course not. I...I... You...'

Again he got the sense that she had struggled with the urge to say something significant—and then changed her mind.

'I'm very thankful to you for making this day happen. It...it's perfect.'

'I also am grateful that you are here with me,' he replied. 'It is a day I will not forget.'

How could he forget Gemma? He would bookmark this time with her in his mind to revisit it in the lonely, difficult days he would face on his return to Montovia.

A great lump of frustration and regret seemed to choke him as he railed against the fate that had led him to this woman when duty dictated he was not able to follow up on the feelings she aroused in him. When he'd been second in line to the throne, he had protested against the age-old rules governing marriage in Montovia. Now he was crown prince, that avenue had been closed to him.

Not for the first time he wished his brother had not gone up in his helicopter that day.

'Do you want to swim to shore?' she asked. 'C'mon— I'll race you.'

She took off in an elegant but powerful freestyle stroke. Tristan was fit and strong, but he had to make an effort to keep up with her.

They reached the beach with her a few strokes ahead. He followed her as they waded through the shallows to the sand, unable to keep his eyes off her. Her sporty swimsuit showed she meant business when she swam. At the same time it clung to every curve and showcased the smooth expanse of her back, her shapely behind, her slender strong legs.

Gemma Harper was a woman who got even more attractive the better he knew her. *And he wanted her.*

She stopped for him to catch up. Her eyes narrowed. 'I hope you didn't let me win on purpose in some chivalrous gesture?'

'No. You are a fast swimmer. It was a fair race.'

He was very competitive in the sports he played. Being bested by a woman was something new, and he respected her skill. But how could a Montovian, raised in a country where the snow-fed lakes were cold even in midsummer, compete with someone who'd grown up in a beachside city like Sydney?

'I used to race at school—but that was a long time ago. Now I swim for fun and exercise. And relaxation.' She looked at him as if she knew very well that he was not used to being beaten. 'You'd probably beat me at skiing.'

'I'm sure you'd challenge me,' he said. 'Weren't both your parents ski instructors?'

'Yes, but I've only ever skied in Australia and New Zealand. Skiing in Europe is on my wish list—if I ever get enough time away from Party Queens to get there, that is.'

Tristan uttered something non-committal in reply instead of the invitation he wished he could make. There was nothing he would like better than to take her skiing with him. Show her the family chalet, share his favourite runs on his favourite mountains, help her unwind après-ski in front of a seductively warm log fire... But next winter, and the chance of sharing it with Gemma, seemed far, far away.

The sand was warm underfoot as he walked along the beach with her, close enough for their shoulders to nudge against each other occasionally. Her skin was cool and smooth against his and he found it difficult to concentrate on anything but her, difficult to clear his mind of how much he wanted her—and could not have her.

He forced himself to look around him. She'd brought him to an idyllic spot. The vegetation that grew up to the sand was full of birdlife. He saw flashes of multi-coloured parrots as they flew through the trees, heard birdsong he couldn't identify.

'How could you say Sydney is not like living in a resort when a place like this is on your doorstep?' he asked.

'I guess you *would* feel like you were on vacation if you lived around here,' she said. She waved her hand at the southern end of the beach. 'Manly, which seems more like a town than a suburb, is just around the bay. You can hire a two-man kayak there and paddle around to here with a picnic. It would be fun to do that sometime.'

But not with him. He would be far away in Montovia, doing his duty, honouring his family and his country. No longer master of his own life. 'That would be fun,' he echoed. He could not bear the thought of her kayaking to this beach with another man.

She sat down on the sand, hugging her knees to her chest. He sat down next to her, his legs stretched out ahead. The sun was warm on his back, but a slight breeze kept him cool.

'Did you wonder why this beach is called Store Beach?' she asked.

'Not really. But I think you are going to tell me.'

'How did you get to know me so quickly?' she asked, her head tilted to one side in the manner he already found endearing.

'Just observant, I guess,' he said. *And because he was so attracted to her.* He wanted to know every little thing about her.

'There must be a tour guide inside me, fighting to get out,' she joked.

'Set her free to tell me all about the beach,' he said. This sea nymph had bewitched him so thoroughly that sitting on a beach listening to the sound of her voice seemed like heaven.

'If you insist,' she said with a sideways smile. 'Behind us, up top, is an isolation hospital known as the Quarantine Station. Stores for the station were landed here. For the early settlers from Europe it was an arduous trip of many months by sailing ship. By the time some of them got here, they had come down with contagious illnesses like smallpox. They were kept here—away from the rest of Sydney. Some got better...many died.'

Tristan shuddered. 'That's a gruesome topic for a sunny day.'

'The Quarantine Station closed after one hundred and fifty years. They hold ghost tours there at night. I went on one—it was really spooky.'

Her story reminded Tristan of what a very long way away from home he was. Even a straightforward flight was twenty-two hours. Any kind of relationship would be difficult to maintain from this distance—even if it were permitted.

'If I had time I would like to go on the ghost tour, but I fear that will not be possible,' he said.

Had he been here as tourist Tristan Marco, executive of a nebulous company that might or might not produce chocolate, he would have added, *Next time I'll do the ghost tour with you.* But he could not in all fairness talk about 'next time' or 'tomorrow.' Not with a woman to whom he couldn't offer any kind of relationship beyond a no-strings fling because she had not been born into the 'right' type of family.

'We should be heading back to the boat for lunch,' she said. 'I'm looking forward to being a guest for the awesome menu I planned. Swimming always makes me hungry.'

He stood up and offered her his hand to help her. She hesitated, then took it and he pulled her to her feet. She stood very close to him. Tristan took a step to bring her even closer. Her hair was still damp from the sea and fell in tendrils around her face. He smoothed a wayward strand from her cheek and tucked it around her ear. He heard her quick intake of breath at his touch before she went very still.

She looked up at him without saying a word. Laughter danced in her eyes and lifted the corners of her lovely mouth. He kept his hand on her shoulder, and she swayed towards him in what he took as an invitation. There was nothing he wanted more than to kiss her. He could not resist a second longer.

He kissed her—first on her adorable dimples, one after the other, as he had longed to do from the get go. Then on her mouth—her exquisitely sensual mouth that felt as wonderful as it looked, warm and welcoming under his. With a little murmur that sent excitement shooting through him, she parted her lips. He deepened the kiss. She tasted of chocolate and salt and her own sweet taste. Her skin was cool and silky against his, her curves pressed enticingly against his body.

All the time he was kissing her Tristan, knew he was doing so under false pretences. He was not used to deception, had always prided himself on his honesty. He wanted more—wanted more than kisses—from this beautiful woman he held in his arms. But he could not deceive her any longer about who he really was—and what the truth meant to them.

Tristan was kissing her—seriously kissing her—and it was even more wonderful than Gemma had anticipated. She had wanted him, wanted *this*, from the time she had first seen him in her kitchen. Her heart thudded in double-quick time, and pleasure thrummed through her body.

But she was shocked at how quickly the kiss turned from something tender into something so passionate that it ignited in her an urgent hunger to be closer to him. Close, closer…as close as she could be.

She had never felt this wondrous sense of connection and certainty. That time was somehow standing still. That she was meant to be here with him. That this was the start of something life-changing.

They explored with lips and tongues. Her thoughts, dazed with desire, started to race in a direction she had not let them until now. *Could* there be a tomorrow for her and Tristan? Why had she thought it so impossible? He wasn't flying back to the moon, after all. Long distance could work. Differences could be overcome.

Stray thoughts flew around her brain, barely coherent, in between the waves of pleasure pulsing through her body.

Tristan gently bit her bottom lip. She let out a little sound of pleasure that was almost a whimper.

He broke away from the kiss, chest heaving as he gasped for breath. She realised he was as shocked as she was at the passion that had erupted between them. Shocked and…and shaken.

Gemma wound her arms around his neck, not wanting him to stop but glad they were on a public beach so that there would be no temptation to sink down on the sand together and go further than kisses. She gave her frantic antennae their marching orders. This. To be with him. It was all she wanted.

'Tristan…' she breathed. 'I feel like I'm in some wonderful dream. I…I don't want this day to end.'

Then she froze as she saw the dismay in his eyes, felt the tension in his body, heard his low groan. She unwound her arms from around his neck, crossed them in front of her chest. She bit her lip to stop her mouth from trembling. Had she totally misread the situation?

'You might not think that when you hear what I have to say to you.' The hoarse words rushed out as if they'd been dammed up inside him and he could not hold on to them any longer.

She couldn't find the words to reply.

'Gemma. We have to talk.'

Did any conversation *ever* go well when it started like that? Why did those four words, grouped together in that way, sound so ominous?

'I'm listening,' she said.

'I have not been completely honest with you.'

Gemma's heart sank to the level of the sand beneath her bare feet. Here it came. He was married. He had a girl-friend back home. Or good old *I'm not looking for commitment.*

Those antennae were now flopped over her forehead, weary and defeated from trying to save her from her own self-defeating behaviour.

She braced herself in readiness.

A pulse throbbed under the smooth olive skin at his temple. 'My family business I told you about…?'

'Yes?' she said, puzzled at the direction he was taking.

'It isn't so much a *business* as such…'

Her stomach clenched. The wealth. The mystery. Her sense that he was being evasive. 'You mean it's a…a crim-inal enterprise? Like the mafia or—?'

He looked so shocked she would have laughed at his expression if she'd had the slightest inclination to laugh. Or even to smile.

'No. Not that. You've got it completely wrong.'

She swallowed against a suddenly dry throat. 'Are you…are you a spy? From your country's intelligence service? If so, I don't know what you're doing with me. I don't know anything. I—'

The shock on his face told her she'd got that wrong, too.

'No, Gemma, nothing like that.'

He paused, as if gathering the strength to speak, and then his words came out in a rush.

'My family is the royal family of Montovia. My parents are the king and queen.'

CHAPTER NINE

GEMMA FELT AS if all the breath had been knocked out of her by a blow to the chest. She stared at him in total disbelief. 'You're kidding me, right?'

'I'm afraid I am not. King Gerard and Queen Truda of Montovia are my parents.'

'And…and you?'

'I am the crown prince—heir to the throne.'

Gemma felt suddenly light-headed and had to take in a few short, shallow breaths to steady herself. Strangely, she didn't doubt him. Those blue eyes burned with sincerity and a desperate appeal for her to believe him.

'A…a prince? A real-life prince? You?'

That little hint of a bow she'd thought she'd detected previously now manifested itself in a full-on bow to her. A formal bow—from a prince who wore swim shorts and had bare feet covered in sand.

'And…and your family business is—?'

'Ruling the country…as we have done for centuries.'

It fitted. Beyond all belief, it fitted. All the little discrepancies in what he'd said fell into place.

'So…what is a prince doing with a party planner?' Hurt shafted her that she'd been so willingly made a fool of. 'Slumming it?'

Despite all her resolutions, she'd slid back into her old ways. Back at the dating starting gates, she'd bolted straight for the same mistake. She'd fallen for a good-looking man who had lied to her from the beginning about who he was. Lied big-time.

She backed away from him on the sand. Stared at him as if he were a total stranger, her hands balled by her sides.

Her disappointment made her want to lash out at him in the most primitive way. But she would not be so uncivilised.

Her voice was cold with suppressed fury, and when she spoke it was as if her words had frozen into shards of ice to stab and wound him. 'You've lied to me from the get go. About who you are—what you are. You lied to get me onto the boat. I don't like liars.'

And she didn't want to hear any more lies.

Frantically, she looked around her. Impenetrable bushland behind her. A long ocean swim to Manly in front of her. And she in a swimsuit and bare feet.

Tristan put out a hand. 'Gemma. I—'

She raised both hands to ward him off. 'Don't touch me,' she spat.

Tristan's face contorted with an emotion she couldn't at first identify. Anger? Anger at *her*?

No—anger at himself.

'Don't say that, Gemma. I...I liked you so much. You did not know who I was. I wanted to get to know you as Tristan, not as Crown Prince Tristan. It was perhaps wrong of me.'

'Isn't honesty one of the customs of your country? Or are princes exempt from telling the truth?'

His jaw clenched. 'Of course not. I'm furious at myself for not telling you the truth earlier. I am truly sorry. But I had to see you again—and I saw no way around it. If you had known the truth, would you have relaxed around me?'

She crossed her arms firmly against her chest. But the sincerity of his words was trickling through her hostility, slowly dripping on the fire of her anger.

'Perhaps not,' said. She would have been freaking out, uncertain of how to behave in front of royalty. As she was now.

'Please. Forgive me. Believe the sincerity of my motives.'

The appeal in his blue eyes seemed genuine. *Or was she kidding herself?* How she wanted to believe him.

'So...no more lies? You promise every word you say to me from now on will be the truth?'

'Yes,' he said.

'Is there any truth in what you've told me about you? About your country? You really *are* a prince?'

'I am Tristan, Crown Prince of Montovia.'

'Prince Tristan...' She slowly breathed out the words, scarcely able to comprehend the truth of it. *Of all the impossible men, she'd had to go and fall for a prince.*

'And everything else you told me?'

'All true.'

'Your brother?'

The pain in his eyes let her know that what he'd told her about his brother's death was only too true.

'Carl was crown prince, heir to the throne, and he trained for it from the day he was born. I was the second in line.'

'The heir and the spare?' she said.

'As the "spare," I had a lot more freedom to live life the way I wanted to. I rebelled against the rules that governed the way we perform our royal duties. Then everything changed.'

'Because of the accident? You said it's your brother's job you are stepping up to in the "family business," didn't you? The job of becoming the next king?'

'That is correct.'

Gemma put her hands to her temples to try and contain the explosion of thoughts. 'This is surreal. I'm talking to a *prince*, here. A guy who's one day going to be king of a country and have absolute power over the lives of millions people.'

'Not so many millions—we are a small country.'

She put down her hands so she could face him. 'But still… You're a prince. One day you'll be a king.'

'When you put it like that, it sounds surreal to me, too. To be the king was always my brother's role.'

Her thoughts still reeled. 'You don't just live *near* the castle, do you?'

'The castle has been home to the royal family for many hundreds of years.'

'And you probably *own* the town of Montovia—and the chocolate shop with the tea room where you went as a little boy?'

'Yes,' he said. 'It has always been so.'

'What about the chocolate?'

'Every business in Montovia is, strictly speaking, our business. But businesses are, of course, owned by individuals. They pay taxes for the privilege. The chocolate has been made by the same family for many years.'

'Was your little nephew a prince, too?'

'He…little Rudolph…*was* a prince. As son of the crown prince, he was next in line to the throne. He was only two when he died with his mother and father.'

'Truly…truly a tragedy for your family.'

'For our country, too. My brother would have been a fine ruler.'

She shook her head, maintained her distance from him. 'It's a lot to take in. How were you allowed to come to Australia on your own if you're the heir? After what happened to your brother?'

'I insisted that I be allowed this time on my own before I take up my new duties. Duties that will, once I return, consume my life.'

'You're a very important person,' she said slowly.

'In Montovia, yes.'

'I would have thought you would be surrounded by bodyguards.'

Tristan looked out to sea and pointed to where a small white cruiser was anchored. 'You might not have noticed, but the *Argus* was discreetly followed by that boat. My two Montovian bodyguards are on it. My parents insisted on me being under their surveillance twenty-four hours a day while I was in a foreign country.'

'You mean there are two guys there who watch you all the time? Did they see us kissing?' She felt nauseous at the thought of being observed for the entire time—both on the boat and on the beach.

'Most likely. I am so used to eyes being on me I do not think about it.'

'You didn't think you could have trusted me with the truth?'

'I did not know you,' he said simply. 'Now I do.'

Their lives were unimaginably different. Not just their country and their culture. He was *royalty*, for heaven's sake.

'I don't have to call you your royal highness, do I?' She couldn't help the edge to her voice.

'To you I am always Tristan.'

'And my curtsying skills aren't up to scratch.'

Pain tightened his face. 'This is why I went incognito. You are already treating me differently now you know I am a prince. Next thing you'll be backing away from me when you leave the room.'

'Technically we're on a beach, but I get your drift. I'm meant to back away from you across the sand?'

'Not now. But when—' he crossed himself rapidly '—when, God forbid, my father passes and I become king, then—'

'I'd have to walk backwards from your presence.'

'Yes. Only in public, of course.'

'This is…this is kind of incomprehensible.' It was all so unbelievable, and yet she found herself believing it. And no matter how she tried, she could not switch off her attraction to him.

A shadow crossed over his face. 'I know,' he said. 'And…and it gets worse.'

'How can it get worse than having to back away out of the presence of a guy my own age? A guy I've made friends with? Sort of friends—considering I don't generally make pals of people who lie to me.'

'Only "friends", Gemma?' he said, his brows lifted above saddened eyes. 'I think we both know it could be so much more than that.'

Tristan stepped forward to close the gap between them. This time she didn't back away. He traced her face lightly with his fingers, across her cheekbones, down her nose, around her lips. She had the disconcerting feeling he was storing up the sight of her face to remember her.

'Yes,' she admitted. 'I…I think I knew that from the get go.'

It was difficult to speak because of the little shivers of pleasure coursing through her at his touch.

'I did also,' he said. 'I have never felt this way. It was… *instant* for me. That was why I had to see you again—no matter what I had to do to have you with me.'

'I told you I could cast spells,' she said with a shaky smile. 'Seriously, I felt it too. Which is why I resisted you. Whether you're a prince or just a regular guy, I don't trust the "instant" thing.'

'The *coup de foudre*? I did not believe it could happen either—certainly not to me.'

She frowned. 'I'm not sure what you mean?'

'The bolt of lightning. The instant attraction out of nowhere. I have had girlfriends, of course, but never before have I felt this…this intensity so quickly.'

She *had* felt it before—which was why she distrusted it. Why did it feel so different this time?

It was him. *Tristan*. He was quite unlike anyone she had ever met.

She braced her feet in the sand. 'So how does it get worse?'

'First I must apologise, Gemma, for luring you onto the boat.'

'Apologise? There's no need for that. I'm having a wonderful day…enjoying being with you. We could do it again tomorrow—I have vacation days due to me. Or I could take you to see kangaroos…maybe even a koala.'

'You would want that?'

'We could try and make this work.' She tried to tone down the desperation in her voice, but she felt he was slipping away from her. 'We live on different sides of the world—not different planets. Though I'm not so sure about how to handle the prince thing. That's assuming you want to date me?' She laughed—a nervous, shaky laugh that came out as more of a squeak. 'I feel more like Cinderella than ever…'

Her voice trailed away as she read the bleak expression in his eyes. This was not going well.

'Gemma, you are so special to me already. Of course I would like to date you—if it were possible. But before you plan to spend more time with me you need to hear this first,' he said. 'To know why I had no right to trick you. You said you would never hate me, but—'

'So tell me,' she said. 'Rip the sticking plaster off in one go.'

'I am not free to choose my own wife. The heir to the throne of Montovia must marry a woman of noble blood. It is forbidden for him to marry a commoner.'

His words hit her like blows. 'A…a "commoner"? I'm not so sure I like being called a commoner. And we're not talking marriage—we hardly know each other.'

'Gemma, if the way I feel about you was allowed to de-velop, it would get serious. *Very* serious.'

He spoke with such conviction she could not help but find his words thrilling. The dangerous, impossible kind of thrilling.

'I…I see,' she said. Until now she hadn't thought be-yond today. 'I believe it would get serious for me, too.' *If she allowed herself to get involved.*

'But it could not lead to marriage for us. Marriage for a crown prince is not about love. It is about tradition. My brother's death changed everything. Brought with it an ur-gency to prepare me for the duties that face me. As crown prince I am expected to marry. I must announce my en-gagement on my thirtieth birthday. A suitable wife has been chosen for me.'

'An arranged marriage? Surely not in this day and age?'

'There is no compulsion for me to marry her. She has been deemed "suitable" if I cannot find an aristocratic wife on my own. And my time is running out.'

Pain seared through her at the thought of him with an-other woman. But one day together, a few kisses, gave her no claim on him.

'When do you turn thirty?'

'On the eighteenth of June.'

She forced her voice to sound even, impartial. 'Three months. Will you go through with it? Marry a stranger?'

'Gemma, I have been brought up believing that my first duty is to my country—above my own desires. As second in line to the throne I might have tried to defy it. I even told my family I would not marry if I could not choose my own bride. But as crown prince, stepping into the shoes of my revered brother, who married the daughter of a duke when he was twenty-six and had a son by the time he was twenty-eight, I have no choice but to marry.'

'But not…never…to someone like me…' Her voice

trailed away as the full impact of what he was saying hit her. She looked down to where she scuffed the sand with her bare toes. She had humiliated herself by suggesting a long-distance relationship.

Tristan placed a gentle finger under her chin so she had to look up at him. 'I am sorry, Gemma. That is the way it has always been in Montovia. Much as I would wish it otherwise.' His mouth twisted bitterly. 'Until I met you I was prepared to accept my fate with grace. Now it will be that much harder.'

'Aren't princess brides a bit short on the ground these days?'

'To be from an aristocratic family is all that is required—she does not need to be actual royalty. In the past it was about political alliances and dowries...'

Nausea brewed deep in the pit of her stomach. Why hadn't he told her this before he'd kissed her? Before she'd let herself start to spin dreams? Dreams as fragile as her finest meringue and as easily smashed.

Sincere as he appeared now, Tristan had deceived her. She would never have allowed herself to let down her guard if she'd known all this.

Like Alistair, he had presented himself as a person different from what he really was. And she, despite all best intentions, had let down her guard and exposed her heart. Tristan had started something he knew he could not continue with. That had been dishonest and unfair.

She could not let him know how much he had hurt her. Had to carry away from this some remaining shreds of dignity. For all his apologies, for all his blue blood, he was no better than any other man who had lied to her.

'I'm sorry, too, Tristan,' she said. 'I...I also felt the *coupe de foudre*. But it was just...physical.' She shrugged in a show of nonchalance. 'We've done nothing to regret. Just...just a few kisses.'

What were a few kisses to a prince? He probably had gorgeous women by the hundred, lining up in the hope of a kiss from him.

'Those kisses meant something to me, Gemma,' he said, his mouth a tight line.

She could not deny his mouth possessing hers had felt both tender and exciting. But... 'The fact is, we've spent not even a day in each other's company. I'm sure we'll both get over it and just remember a...a lovely time on the harbour.'

The breeze that had teased the drying tendrils of her hair had dropped, and the sun beat down hot on her bare shoulders. Yet she started to shiver.

'We should be getting back to the boat,' she said.

She turned and splashed into the water before he could see the tears of disappointment and loss that threatened. She swam her hardest to get to the boat first, not knowing or caring if Tristan was behind her.

Tristan stood on the shore and watched Gemma swim away from him in a froth of white water, her pale arms slicing through the water, her vigorous kicks making very clear her intention to get as far away from him as quickly as possible.

He picked up a piece of driftwood and threw it into the bush with such force that a flock of parrots soared out of a tree, their raucous cries admonishing him for his lack of control. He cursed loud and long. *He had lost Gemma.*

She was halfway to the boat already. He wished he could cast a wide net into the sea and bring her back to him, but he doubted she wanted more of his deceitful company.

In Montovian mythology, when a cunning hunter tried to capture a water nymph and keep her for himself, he'd drag back his net to find it contained not the beautiful woman he coveted but a huge, angry catfish, with rows of razor-sharp teeth, that would set upon him.

The water nymphs held all the cards.

An hour later Gemma had showered and dressed and was sitting opposite Tristan at the stylishly laid table on the sheltered deck of the *Argus*. She pushed the poached lobster salad around her plate with her fork. Usually she felt ravenous after a swim, but her appetite had completely deserted her.

Tristan was just going through the motions of eating, too. His eyes had dulled to a flat shade of blue, and there were lines of strain around his mouth she hadn't noticed before. All the easy camaraderie between them had disintegrated into stilted politeness.

Yet she couldn't bring herself to be angry with him. He seemed as miserable as she was. Even through the depths of her shock and disappointment she knew he had only deceived her because he'd liked her and wanted her to like him for himself. Neither of them had expected the intensity of feeling that had resulted.

She still found it difficult to get her head around his real identity. For heaven's sake, she was having lunch with a *prince*. A prince from a kingdom still run on medieval rules. He was royalty—she was a commoner. *Deemed not worthy of him.* Gemma had grown up in an egalitarian society. The inequality of it grated. She did not believe herself to be *less*.

She made another attempt to eat, but felt self-conscious as she raised her fork to her mouth. Did Tristan's bodyguards have a long-distance lens trained on her?

She slid her plate away from her, pushed her chair back and got up from the table.

'I'm sorry, Tristan, I can't do this.'

With his impeccable manners, he immediately got up,

too. 'You don't like the food?' he said. But his eyes told her he knew exactly what she meant.

'You. Me. What could have been. What can never be. Remember what I said about the sticking plaster?'

'You don't want to prolong the pain,' he said slowly.

Of course he understood. In spite of their differences in status and language and upbringing, he already *got* her.

This was heartbreaking. He was a real-life Prince Charming who wanted her but couldn't have her—not in any honourable way. And she, as Cinderella, had to return to her place in the kitchen.

'I'm going to ask the skipper to take me to the wharf at Manly and drop me off.'

'How will you get home?'

'Bus. Ferry. Taxi. Please don't worry about me. I'm very good at looking after myself.'

She turned away from him and carried with her the stricken expression on his face to haunt her dreams.

CHAPTER TEN

GEMMA STRUGGLED TO hear what Andie was saying to her over the rise and fall of chatter, the clink of glasses, the odd burst of laughter—the soundtrack to another successful Party Queens function. The Friday night cocktail party at the swish Parkview Hotel was in full swing—the reception being held to mark the official visit of Tristan, crown prince of Montovia, to Sydney.

Gemma had explained to her business partners what had happened on the *Argus* and had excluded herself from any further dealings with him. Tristan had finalised the guest list with Eliza on Thursday.

Tristan's guests included business leaders with connections to the Montovian finance industry, the importers and top retailers of the principality's fine chocolate and cheese, senior politicians—both state and federal—even the governor of the state.

If she didn't have to be here to ensure that the food service went as it should for such an important function, she wouldn't have attended.

Her antennae twitched. Okay, so she was lying to herself. How could she resist the chance to see him again? On a strictly 'look, don't touch' basis. Because no matter how often she told herself that she'd had a lucky escape to get out after only a day, before she got emotionally attached, she hadn't been able to stop thinking about him.

Not that it had been an issue. Tristan was being the ideal host and was much in demand from his guests. He hadn't come anywhere near her, either, since the initial formal briefing between Party Queens and its client. She shouldn't have felt hurt, but she did—a deep, private ache to see that after all that angst on the *Argus* it seemed he'd been able to put her behind him so easily.

The secret of his identity was now well and truly out. There was nothing the media loved more than the idea of a handsome young European prince visiting Australia. Especially when he was reported to be 'one of the world's most eligible bachelors.' She knew there were photographers swarming outside the hotel to catch the money shot of Prince Charming.

'What did you say, Andie?' she asked her friend again.

Tall, blonde Andie leaned closer. 'I said you're being very brave. Eliza and I are both proud of you. It must be difficult for you, seeing him like this.'

'Yeah. It is. I'm determined to stay away from him. After all it was only one day—it meant nothing.' One day that had quite possibly been one of the happiest days of her life—until that conversation on Store Beach. 'No big deal, really—unless I make it a big deal.'

'He lied to you. Just remember that,' said Andie.

'But he—' It was on the tip of her tongue to defend Tristan by saying he hadn't out-and-out lied, just skirted around the truth. But it was the same thing. Lying by omission. And she wasn't going to fall back into bad old ways by making excuses for a man who had misled her.

But she couldn't help being aware of Tristan. Just knowing he was here had her on edge. He was on the other side of the room, talking to two older men. He looked every inch the prince in an immaculately tailored tuxedo worn with a blue, gold-edged sash across his chest. Heaven knew what the rows of medals pinned to his shoulder signified—but there were a lot of them. He was the handsome prince from all the fairytales she had loved when she was a kid.

Never had that sense of *other* been stronger.

'Don't worry,' said Andie. 'Eliza and I are going to make darn sure you're never alone with him.'

'Good,' said Gemma, though her craven heart *longed* to be alone with him.

'You didn't do all that work on yourself over six months to throw it away on an impossible crush. What would Dr B think?'

The good thing about having worked on a women's magazine was that the staff had had access to the magazine's agony aunt. Still did. 'Dr B' was a practising clinical psychologist and—pushed along by her friends—Gemma had trooped along to her rooms for a series of consultations. In return for a staff discount, she hadn't minded seeing her heavily disguised questions appearing on the agony aunt's advice page in her new magazine.

Dear Dr B,
I keep falling for love rats who turn out to be not what they said they were—yet I put up with their bad behaviour. How can I break this pattern?

It was Dr B who had helped Gemma identify how her unbalanced relationship with her stepfather had given her an excessive need for approval from men. It was Dr B who had showed her how to develop her own instincts, trust her antennae. And given her coping strategies for when it all got too hard.

'I can deal with this,' she said to Andie. 'You just watch me.'

'While you watch Tristan?'

Gemma started guiltily. 'Is it that obvious? He's just so *gorgeous*, Andie.'

'That he is,' said Andie. 'But he's not for you. If you start to weaken, just think of all that stuff you dug up on the internet about Montovia's Playboy Prince.'

'How could I forget it?'

Gemma sighed. She'd been shocked to the core at discovering his reputation. Yet couldn't reconcile it with the Tristan she knew.

Was she just kidding herself?

She must not slide back into bad old habits. People had warned her about Alistair, but she'd wanted to believe his denials about drugs and other women. Until she'd been proved wrong in the most shockingly painful way.

Andie glanced at her watch. 'I need to call Dominic and check on Hugo,' she said. 'He had a sniffle today and I want to make sure he's okay.'

'As if he *wouldn't* be okay in the care of the world's most doting dad,' Gemma said.

Andie and Dominic's son, Hugo, was fifteen months old now, and the cutest, most endearing little boy. Andie often brought him into the Party Queens office, and Gemma doted on him. One day she wanted a child of her own. She was twenty-eight. That was yet another reason not to waste time on men who were Mr Impossible—or Crown Prince Impossible.

'Where's Eliza?' Andie asked. 'I don't want to leave you by yourself in case that predatory prince swoops on you.'

'No need for name-calling,' said Gemma, though Andie's choice of words made her smile. 'Eliza is over there, talking with the best man at your wedding, Jake Marlowe. He's a good friend of Tristan's.'

'So I believe… Dominic is pleased Jake's in town.'

'From the look of it, I don't know that Eliza would welcome the interruption. She seems to be getting on *very* well with Jake. You go and make your phone call. I'm quite okay here without a minder, I assure you. I'm a big girl.'

Gemma shooed Andie off. She needed to check with the hotel liaison representative about the service at the bar. She thought they could do with another barman on board. For this kind of exclusive party no guest should be left waiting for a drink.

But before she could do so a bodyguard of a different kind materialised by her shoulder. She recognised him immediately as one of the men who had been discreetly shadowing Tristan. She shuddered at the thought that he'd been spying on her and Tristan as they'd kissed on the beach.

'Miss Harper, His Royal Highness the Crown Prince Tristan would like a word with you in the meeting room annexe through that door.' He spoke English, with a coarser version of Tristan's accent.

She looked around. Tristan was nowhere to be seen. From the tone of this burly guy's voice, she didn't dare refuse the request.

Neither did she want to.

Tristan paced the length of the small breakout room and paced back again. Where was Gemma? Would she refuse to see him?

He had noticed her as soon as he'd got to the hotel. Among a crowd of glittering guests she had stood out in the elegant simplicity of a deep blue fitted dress that emphasised her curves and her creamy skin. Her hair was pulled up and away from her face to tumble to her shoulders at the back. She was lovelier than ever.

He had to see her.

He was taking a risk, stepping away from the party like this. His idyllic period of anonymity was over. He was the crown prince once more, with all the unwanted attention that warranted.

The local press seemed particularly voracious. And who knew if one of his invited guests might be feeding some website or other with gossipy Prince Charming titbits? That was one of the nicknames the media had given him. They would particularly be looking out for any shot of him with a woman. They would then speculate about her and make her life hell. That girl could not be Gemma. She did not deserve that.

And then she was there, just footsteps away from him. Her high heels brought her closer to his level. The guard left discreetly, closing the door behind him and leaving Tristan alone with her. Could lightning strike twice in the same place? For he felt again that *coup de foudre*—that instant sensation that this was *his woman*.

His heart gave a physical leap at the expression on her face—pure, unmitigated joy at seeing him. For a moment he thought—hoped—she might fling herself into his arms. Where he would gladly welcome her.

Then the shutters came down, and her expression became one of polite, professional interest.

'You wanted to see me? Is it about the canapés? Or the—?'

'I wanted to see you. Alone. Without all the circus around us. I miss you, Gemma. I haven't been able to stop thinking about you.'

Her face softened. 'There isn't a moment since I left the *Argus* that I haven't thought about *you*.'

Those words, uttered in her sweet, melodious voice, were music to his ears.

He took a step towards her, but she put up her hand in a halt sign.

'But nothing has changed, has it? I'm a commoner and you're a prince. Worse, the Playboy Prince, so it appears.'

Her face crumpled, and he saw what an effort it was for her to maintain her composure.

'I…I didn't think you were like that…the way the press portrayed you.'

The Playboy Prince—how he hated that label. Would he ever escape the reputation earned in those few years of rebellion?

'So you've dug up the dirt on me from the internet?' he said gruffly.

She would only have had to type *Playboy Prince* into a search engine and his name would come up with multiple entries.

'Is it true? All the girlfriends? The parties? The racing cars and speedboats?'

There was a catch in her voice that tore at him.

He gritted his teeth. 'Some of it, yes. But don't believe all you read. My prowess with women is greatly exaggerated.'

'You're never photographed twice with the same woman on your arm—princesses, heiresses, movie stars. All beautiful. All glamorous.'

'And none special.'

No one like Gemma.

'Is that true? I...I don't know what to believe.' Her dress was tied with a bow at the waistline, and she was pleating the fabric of its tail without seeming to realise she was doing so.

'I got a lot of attention as a prince. Opportunities for fun were offered, and I took them. There were not the restraints on me that there were on my brother.'

'If I'd been willing, would I have been just another conquest to you? A Sydney fling?'

'No. Never. You are special to me, Gemma.'

'That sounds like something the Playboy Prince might say. As another ploy.'

There was a cynical twist to her mouth he didn't like.

'Not to you, Gemma. Do not underestimate me.'

She was not convinced.

He cursed under his breath. He wanted her to think well of him. Not as some spoiled, privileged young royal. Which he had shown all the signs of being for some time.

'There was a reason for the way I behaved then,' he

said. 'I was mad about an English girl I'd met at university. She was my first serious girlfriend. But my parents made it clear they did not approve.'

'Because she was a commoner?'

'Yes. If she'd been from a noble family they would have welcomed her. She was attractive, intelligent, talented. My parents—and the crown advisers—were worried that it might get serious. They couldn't allow that to happen. They spoke to her family. No doubt money changed hands. She transferred to a different university. I was angry and upset. She refused to talk to me. I realised then what it meant to have my choice of life partner restricted by ancient decrees.'

'So you rebelled?'

'Not straight away. I still believed in the greater good of the throne. Then I discovered the truth behind my parents' marriage. The hypocrisy. It was an arranged marriage— my father is older than my mother. He has a long-time mistress. My mother discreetly takes lovers.' He remembered how gutted he'd felt at the discovery.

'What a shock that must have been.'

'These days they live separate lives except for state occasions. And yet they were determined to force me along the same unhappy path—for no reason I could see. I was young and hot-headed. I vowed if I couldn't marry the girl I wanted then I wouldn't marry at all.'

She sagged with obvious relief. 'That's understandable.'

'So you believe me?'

Slowly, she nodded. 'In my heart I didn't want to believe the person I was reading about was the person I had found so different, so...*wonderful*.'

'I was unhappy then. I was totally disillusioned. I looked at the marriages in my family. All were shams. Even my brother's marriage was as cynical an arrangement as any other Montovian royal marriage.'

'And now?'

She looked up at him with those warm brown eyes. Up close he saw they had golden flecks in them.

'It is all about duty. Duty before personal desire. All the heroes in our culture put duty first. They sacrifice love to go to war or to make a strategic marriage. That now is my role. Happiness does not come into the equation for me.'

'What would make you happy, Tristan?'

'Right now? To be alone with my beautiful Party Queen. To be allowed to explore what…what we feel for each other. Like an everyday guy and his girl. That would make me happy.' He shrugged. 'But it cannot be.'

There was no such thing as happiness in marriage for Montovian royalty.

This sea nymph had totally bewitched him. He had not been able to stop thinking about her. Coming up with one scheme after another that would let him have her in his life and explore if she might be the one who would finally make him want to marry—and discarding each as utterly impossible.

'I…I would like that, too,' she said. 'To be with you, I mean.'

He took both her hands in his and pulled her to him. She sighed—he could not tell if it was in relief or surrender—and relaxed against him. He put his arms around her and held her close. She laid her head on his shoulder, and he dropped a kiss on her sweetly scented hair.

Then he released her and stepped back. 'We cannot risk being compromised if someone comes in,' he explained. 'The last thing we want is press speculation.'

'I…I didn't realise that your life was under such scrutiny,' she said.

'That is why I wanted to be incognito. We could not have had that day together otherwise. I do not regret keeping the truth from you, Gemma. I do not regret that day. Although I am sorry if I hurt you.'

She had abandoned the obsessive pleating of the bow on her dress. But her hands fluttered nervously. Looking into her face, he now understood what it meant to say that someone had her heart in her eyes.

She felt it, too. That inexplicable compulsion, that connection. His feelings for Gemma might be the most genuine emotions he had ever experienced. Not *love* at first sight. He didn't believe that could happen so quickly. But something powerful and intense. Something so much more than physical attraction.

'We…we could have another day…together,' she said cautiously, as if she were testing his reaction.

'What do you mean?'

'We could have *two* days. I'm offering you that chance. You don't leave until Monday morning. All day Saturday and Sunday stretch out before us.'

She was tempting him almost beyond endurance. 'You would want us to spend the weekend together knowing it could never be more than that? Not because I don't *want* it to be more, but because it would never be allowed?'

'Yes. I do want that. I…I ache to be with you. I don't want to spend a lifetime regretting that I didn't take a chance to be with you. I keep trying to talk sense to myself—tell myself that I hardly know you; that you're leaving. But at some deep, elemental level I feel I *do* know you.' She shook her head. 'I'm not explaining this very well, am I?'

'I understand you very well—for it is how I also feel. But I do not want to hurt you, Gemma.'

'And I certainly don't want to get hurt,' she said. 'Or hurt *you*, for that matter. But I don't want to be riddled with regret.'

'Remember in three months' time I must announce my

engagement to a suitable bride. I cannot even offer to take you as my mistress—that would insult both you and the woman who will become my wife. I will not cheat on her. I will *not* have a marriage like that of my parents.'

'I understand that. Understand and admire you for your honesty and…and moral stance. I'm offering you this time with me, Tristan, with no strings attached. No expectations. Just you and me together. As we will never be allowed to be again.'

He was silent for a moment too long. Common sense, royal protocol—all said he should say no. If the press found out it would be a disaster for her, uncomfortable for him. The Playboy Prince label would be revived. While such a reputation could be laughed off, even admired, for the second or third in line to the throne, it was deeply inappropriate for the crown prince and future king.

Gemma looked up at him. She couldn't mask the longing in her eyes—an emotion Tristan knew must be reflected in his own. Her lovely, lush mouth trembled.

'I should go,' she said in a low, broken voice. 'People will notice we've left the room. There might be talk that the prince is too friendly with the party planner. It…it could get awkward.'

She went to turn away from him.

Everything in Tristan that spoke of duty and denial and loyalty to his country urged him to let her walk away.

But something even stronger urged him not to lose his one chance to be with this woman with whom he felt such a powerful connection. If he didn't say something to stop her, he knew he would never see her again.

He couldn't bear to let her go—no matter the consequences.

Tristan held out his hand to her.

'Stay with me, Gemma,' he said. 'I accept your invitation to spend this time together.'

CHAPTER ELEVEN

NEXT MORNING, in the grey light of dawn, Tristan turned to Gemma, who was at the wheel of her car. 'Where exactly are you taking me?'

'We're heading west to my grandmother's house in the Megalong Valley in the Blue Mountains. She died a few years ago, and she left her cottage to me and my two cousins. We use it as a weekender and for vacations.'

'Is it private?'

'Utterly private. Just what we want.'

He and Gemma had plotted his escape from the hotel in a furtive whispered conversation the previous night, before they had each left the annexe room separately to mingle with his guests. There had been no further contact with each other until this morning.

While it was still dark, she had driven to his hotel in the city and parked her car a distance away. He had evaded his bodyguards and, with his face covered by a hoodie, had met her without incident. They had both laughed in exhilaration as she'd gunned the engine and then floored the accelerator in a squeal of tyres.

'The valley is secluded and rural—less than two hundred people live there,' Gemma said. 'You might as well be ten hours away from Sydney as two. The cottage itself is on forty acres of garden, pasture and untamed bushland. We can be as secluded as we want to be.'

She glanced quickly at him, and he thrilled at the promise in her eyes. This was a relaxed Gemma, who had pulled down all the barriers she'd put up against him. She was warm, giving—and his without reservation for thirty-six hours.

'Just you and me,' he said, his voice husky.

'Yes,' she said, her voice laced with promise. 'Do you think there's any chance your goons—sorry, your body-guards—could find us?'

'I was careful. I left my laptop in my suite and I've switched off my smartphone so it can't be tracked. But I did leave a note to tell them I had gone of my own free will on a final vacation and would be back late Sunday night. The last thing we want them to think is that I've been kid-napped and start a search.'

'Is kidnapping an issue for you?' Her grip visibly tight-ened on the steering wheel.

'It is an issue for anyone with wealth. The royal chil-dren are always very well guarded.'

'I'm not putting you at risk, am I? I…I couldn't bear it if I—'

'Here, the risk is minimal. Please do not concern your-self with that. We are more at risk from the media. But I checked that no one was lurking about at my hotel.'

'Can you imagine the headlines if they did find us? *Playboy Prince in Secluded Love Nest with Sydney Party Planner.*'

Tristan rather liked the concept of a love nest. 'They would most likely call you a *sexy* party planner.'

Gemma made a snort of disgust, then laughed. 'I'll own sexy. Or how about: *Playboy Prince Makes Aussie Con-quest*? They'll want to get the local angle in, I'm sure.'

'You could also be *Mystery Redhead*?' he suggested.

He found he could joke about the headlines the press might make about his life—there had been enough of them in the past. Now he was crown prince he did not want to feature in any more. He appreciated the effort Gemma was making to preserve their privacy.

They made up more outrageous headlines as Gemma drove along the freeway until Sydney was behind them.

'Are you going to unleash your inner tour guide and tell me about the Blue Mountains?' Tristan asked as the road started to climb.

'How did you know I was waiting for my cue?' she said.

'Please, go ahead and tell me all I need to know—plus *more* than I need to know,' he said.

'Now that I've been invited...' she said, with a delightful peal of laughter.

Tristan longed to show her Montovia some day—and pushed aside the melancholy thought that that was never likely to happen. He had thirty-six hours with her stretching ahead of him—bonus hours he had not thought possible. He would focus his thoughts on how he could make them special for her.

'They're called the Blue Mountains because they seem to have a blue haze over them from a distance, caused by the eucalypt oil from the trees,' she said.

'I didn't know that,' he said.

'Don't think of them as mountains like Montovian mountains. Australia is really old, geologically, and the mountains would have been underwater for millions of years. They're quite flat on top but very rugged. There are some charming small towns up there, and it's quite a tourist destination.'

It wasn't that he found what she was saying boring. On the contrary, visiting Australia had long been on his 'to do' list. But Tristan found himself getting drowsy.

For the last three nights he had slept badly, kept awake by thoughts of Gemma and how much he wanted her to be part of his life. Now she was next to him and they were together. Not for long enough, but it was more than he could have dreamed of. For the moment he was content. To drift off to the sound of her voice was a particular kind of joy...

When he awoke, Gemma was skilfully negotiating her car down a series of hairpin bends on a narrow road where the Australian bush grew right to the sides.

'You've woken just in time for our descent into the valley,' she said. 'Hold on—it's quite a twisty ride.'

The road wound through verdant rainforest and huge towering indigenous trees before emerging onto the valley floor. Tristan caught his breath in awe at the sight of a wall of rugged sandstone mountains, tinged red with the morning sun.

'It's magnificent, isn't it?' she said. 'You should see it after heavy rain, when there are waterfalls cascading down.'

The landscape alternated harshness with lush pastures dotted with black and white cattle. There was only the occasional farmhouse.

'Do you wonder why I'm driving so slowly?' Gemma asked.

'Because it's a narrow road?' he ventured.

'Because—ah, here they are. Look!'

A group of kangaroos bounded parallel to the road. Tristan wished he had a camera. His smartphone was switched off, and he didn't dare risk switching it back on.

'You have to be careful in the mornings and evenings not to hit them as they cross the road.' She braked gently. 'Like that—right in front of the car.'

One after the other the kangaroos jumped over a low spot in the fence and crossed the road. Halfway across, the largest one stopped and looked at him.

'He is as curious about me as I am about him,' Tristan whispered, not wanting to scare the creature. 'I really feel like I am in Australia now.'

'I promised you kangaroos in the wild, and I've delivered,' Gemma said with justifiable triumph.

While he could promise her nothing.

* * *

As Gemma showed Tristan around the three-bedroom, one-bathroom cottage, she wondered what he really thought of it. He was, after all, used to living in a castle. The royal castle of Montovia was splendid—as befitted the prosperous principality.

Her internet research had showed her a medieval masterpiece clinging to the side of a mountain and overlooking a huge lake ringed by more snow-topped mountains. Her research had not shown her the private rooms where the family lived, but even if they were only half as extravagant as the public spaces Tristan had grown up in, they would be of almost unimaginable splendour.

And then there was a summer palace, at the other end of the lake. And royal apartments in Paris and Florence.

No doubt wherever he lived, he was waited on hand and foot by servants.

But she would not be intimidated. She was proud of her grandma's house—she and her cousins would probably always call it that, even though it was now their names on the deed of ownership.

She loved how it had been built all those years ago by her grandfather's family, to make the most of the gun-barrel views of the escarpment. To a prince it must seem very humble. But Gemma would never apologise for it.

Tristan stood on the wide deck her grandfather had added to the original cottage. It looked east, to the wall of the escarpment lit by the morning sun, and it was utterly private. No one could see them either from the neighbouring property or from the road.

Tristan put his arm around her to draw her close, and she snuggled in next to him. No more pretence that what they felt was mere friendship. She'd known when she'd invited him to spend his final weekend with her what it would lead to—and it was what she wanted.

Tristan looked at the view for a long time before he spoke. 'It's awe-inspiring to see this ancient landscape all around. And to be able to retreat to this charming house.'

She should have known that Tristan would not look down his princely nose at her beloved cottage.

'I've always loved it here. My grandmother knew what the situation was with my stepfather and made sure I was always welcome whenever I wanted. Sometimes I felt it was more a home than my house in Sydney.'

He turned to look back through the French doors and into the house, with its polished wooden floors and simple furnishings in shades of white.

'Was it like this when your grandmother had it? I think not.'

'Good guess. I loved my grandma, but not so much her taste in decorating. When I inherited with my cousins Jane and John—they're twins—I asked Andie to show us what to do with it to bring it into the twenty-first century. Not only did she suggest stripping it back to the essentials and painting everything we could white, but she used the house as a makeover feature for the magazine. We got lots of free help in return for having the house photographed. We put in a new kitchen and remodelled the bathroom, and now it's just how we want it.'

'The canny Party Queens wave their magic wands again?'

'You could put it like that.'

He pulled her into his arms. 'You're an amazing woman, Gemma Harper. One of many talents.'

'Thank you, Your Highness. And to think we're only just getting to know each other…I have many hidden talents you have yet to discover.'

'I've been keeping *my* talents hidden, too,' he said. 'But for no longer.'

He traced the outline of her mouth with his finger, the

light pressure tantalising in its unexpected sensuality. Her mouth swelled under his touch, and she ached for him to kiss her there. Instead he pressed kisses along the line of her jaw and down to the sensitive hollows of her throat. She closed her eyes, the better to appreciate the sensation. How could something so simple ignite such pleasure?

She tilted back her head for more, but he teased her by planting feather-light kisses on her eyelids, one by one, and then her nose.

'Kiss me properly,' she begged, pressing her aching mouth to his.

He laughed deep in his throat, then deepened the kiss into something harder and infinitely more demanding. She wound her arms around his neck to pull him closer, craving more. Her antennae thrummed softly—not in warning but in approval. She wanted him. She needed him. He was hers. Not forever, she knew that. But for *now*.

This was the first time she had walked into a less-than-ideal relationship with her eyes wide open. It was her choice. With Tristan she had not been coerced or tricked. She just hoped that when the time came she would be able to summon the inner strength to let him go without damage to her heart and soul—and not spend a lifetime in futile longing for him.

But she would not think of that now. Her mind was better occupied with the pleasure of Tristan's mouth, his tongue, his hands skimming her breasts, her hips.

He broke away from the kiss so he could undo the buttons of her shirt. She trembled with pleasure when his fingers touched bare skin. He knew exactly what he was doing, and she thrilled to it.

'I haven't shown you around outside,' she said breathlessly. 'There are horses. I know you like horses. More kangaroos maybe…'

Oh! He'd pulled her shirt open with his teeth. Desire,

fierce and insistent, throbbed through her. She slid his T-shirt over his head, gasped her appreciation of his hard, muscular chest.

He tilted her head back to meet his blue eyes, now dark with passion. 'How many times do I have to tell you? The only sight I'm interested in is you. *All of you.*'

CHAPTER TWELVE

THE SUNLIGHT STREAMING through the bedroom window told Gemma she had slept for several hours and that it must be heading towards noon. She reached out her hand to find the bed empty beside her, the sheets cooling.

But his lingering scent on the pillow—on *her*—was proof Tristan had been there with her. So were the delicious aches in her muscles, her body boneless with satisfaction. She stretched out her naked limbs, luxuriating in the memories of their lovemaking. Was it the fact he was a prince or simply because he was the most wonderful man she had ever met that made Tristan such an awesome lover?

She wouldn't question it. Tristan was Tristan, and she had never been gladder that she'd made the impulsive decision to take what she could of him—despite the pain she knew lay ahead when they would have to say goodbye.

Better thirty-six hours with this man than a lifetime with someone less perfect for her.

Her tummy rumbled to let her know the hour for breakfast was long past and that she'd had very little to eat the night before.

The aroma of freshly brewed coffee wafted to her nostrils, and she could hear noises coming from the kitchen. She sat up immediately—now fully awake. Tristan must be starving, too. How could she have slept and neglected him? *How could she have wasted precious time with him by sleeping?*

She leapt out of bed and burrowed in the top drawer of the chest of drawers, pulled out a silk wrap patterned with splashes of pink and orange and slipped it on. She'd given the wrap to her grandmother on her last birthday and kept it in memory of her.

She rushed out to the kitchen to find Tristan standing in front of the open fridge, wearing just a pair of blue boxer shorts. Her heart skipped a beat at the sight. Could a man be more perfectly formed?

He saw her and smiled a slow smile. The smile was just for her, and memories of their passionate, tender lovemaking came rushing back. The smile told her his memories of her were as happy. They were so good together. He was a generous lover, anticipating her needs, taking her to heights of pleasure she had not dreamed existed. She in turn revelled in pleasing him.

All this she could see in his smile. He opened his arms, and she went straight to them, sighing with pleasure as he pulled her close and slid his hands under the wrap. His chest was warm and hard, and she thrilled at the power of his body. He hadn't shaved, and the overnight growth of his beard was pleasantly rough against her cheek.

For a long moment they stood there, wrapped in each other's arms. She rested her head against his shoulder, felt the steady thud of his heartbeat, breathed in the male scent of him—already so familiar—and knew there was nowhere else she would rather be.

'You should have woken me,' she murmured.

'You looked so peaceful I did not have the heart,' he said. 'After all, you drove all the way here. And I only woke half an hour ago.'

'I…I don't want to waste time sleeping when I could be with you.'

'Which is why I was going to wake you with coffee.'

'A good plan,' she said.

'Hold still,' he said as he wiped under her eye with his finger.

'Panda eyes?' She hadn't removed her mascara the night before in the excitement of planning their escape.

'Just a smear of black,' he said. 'It's good now.'

She found it a curiously intimate gesture—something perhaps only long-time couples did. It was difficult to believe she had only met him on Monday. And would be losing him by the next Monday.

'You've been busy, by the look of it,' she said.

The table was set for a meal. She noticed he had set the forks and spoons face down, as she'd seen in France. The coffee machine hissed steam, and there were coffee mugs on the countertop.

'I hope you don't mind.'

'Of course not. The kitchen is designed for people to help themselves. No one stands on ceremony up here. It's not just me and my cousins who visit. We let friends use it, too.'

'I went outside and picked fresh peaches. The tree is covered in them.'

'You picked tomatoes, too, I see.'

Her grandmother's vegetable garden had been her pride and joy, and Gemma was determined to keep it going.

'Are you hungry?'

'Yes!'

'We could have breakfast, or we could have lunch. Whatever you choose.'

'Maybe brunch? You're going to *cook*?'

'Don't look so surprised.'

'I didn't imagine a prince could cook—or would even know his way around a kitchen.'

'You forget—this prince spent time in the army, where his title did not earn him any privileges. I also studied at university in England, where I shared a kitchen with other students. I chose not to have my own apartment. I wanted to enjoy the student experience like anyone else.'

'What about doing the dishes?' she teased.

'But of course,' he replied in all seriousness. 'Although I cannot say I enjoy that task.'

She pressed a quick kiss to his mouth—his beautiful, sensual mouth which she had now thoroughly explored. He tasted of fresh, ripe peach. 'Relax. The rule in this kitchen is that whoever cooks doesn't have to do the dishes.'

'That is a good rule,' he said in his formal way.

She could not resist another kiss, and then squealed when he held her close and turned it into something deeper, bending her back over his arm in dramatic exaggeration. She laughed as he swooped her back upright.

He seemed so blessedly normal. And yet last night he had worn the ceremonial sash and insignia indicating his exalted place in a hereditary monarchy that stretched back hundreds of years. He'd hobnobbed with the highest strata of Sydney society with aplomb. It was mind-blowing.

'The fridge and pantry are well stocked,' she said. 'It's a long way up the mountain if we run out of something.'

'I have already examined them. Would you like scrambled eggs and bacon with tomatoes? And whole-wheat toast?'

'That sounds like a great idea. It makes a pleasant change for someone to cook for me.'

'You deserve to be cherished,' he said with a possessive arm still around her. 'If only—'

'No "if onlys",' she said with a sudden hitch to her voice. 'We'll go crazy if we go there.'

To be cherished by him was an impossible dream...

She was speared by a sudden shaft of jealousy over his arranged bride. Did that well-born woman have any idea how fortunate she was? Or *was* she so fortunate? To be married to a man in a loveless marriage for political expediency might not make for a happy life. As it appeared had been the case for Tristan's parents.

'So—what to do after brunch?' she asked. 'There are horses on the property that we're permitted to ride. Of course they're not of the same calibre as your polo ponies, but—'

'I do not care what we do, so long as I am with you.'

'Perhaps we could save the horses for tomorrow?' she said. 'Why don't we walk down to the river and I'll show you some of my favourite places? We can swim, if you'd like.'

'I didn't pack my swim shorts.'

'There's no need for swimsuits,' she said. 'The river is on our property, and it's completely private.'

A slow smile spread across his face, and her body tingled in response. Swimming at the river this afternoon might be quite the most exciting it had ever been. She decided to pack a picnic to take with them, so they could stay there for as long as they wanted.

Gemma woke during the night to find Tristan standing by the bedroom window. The only light came from a full moon that sat above the enormous eucalypts that bounded the garden. It seemed every star in the universe twinkled in the dark canopy of the sky.

He was naked, and his body, silvered by the moonlight, looked like a masterpiece carved in marble by a sculptor expert in the depiction of the perfect male form.

Gemma slid out of bed. She was naked, too, and she slid her arms around him from behind, resting her cheek on his back. He might look like silvered marble but he felt warm, and firm, and very much a real man.

'You okay?' she murmured.

He enfolded her hands with his where they rested on his chest.

'I am imagining a different life,' he said, his voice low and husky. 'A life where I am a lawyer, or a businessman working in Sydney. I live in a water-front apartment in Manly with my beautiful party-planner wife.'

She couldn't help an exclamation and was glad he couldn't see her face.

'You know her, of course,' he said, squeezing her hand. 'She and I live a resort life, and she swims every day in the sea. We cross the harbour by ferry to get to work, and I dream of the day I can have my own yacht. On some weekends we come up here, just the two of us, and ride horses together and plan for the day that we…that we—' His voice broke.

He turned to face her. In the dim light of the moon his face was in shadow, but she could see the anguish that contorted his face.

'Gemma, I want it so much.' His voice was hoarse and ragged.

'It…it sounds like a wonderful life,' she said, her own voice less than steady. 'But it's a fantasy. As much a fantasy as that party planner living with you as a princess in a fairytale castle. We…we will only get hurt if we let ourselves imagine it could actually happen.'

'There is…I could abdicate my role as crown prince.'

For a long moment Gemma was too shocked to say anything. 'You say that, but you know you could never step down from your future on the throne. Duty. Honour. Responsibility to the country you love. They're ingrained in you. You couldn't live with that decision. Besides, I wouldn't let you.'

'Sometimes that responsibility feels like a burden. I was not born to it, like my brother.'

'But you *will* rise to it.'

He cradled her face in his hands, looked deep into her eyes, traced the corner of her mouth with his thumb. 'Gemma, you must know how I feel about you—that I am falling in lo—'

'No.' She put her hand over his mouth to stop him. 'Don't go there,' she said. 'You can't say the *L* word until you can follow it with a proposal. And we know that's not going to happen. Not for us. Not for a prince and a party planner. I...I feel it, too. But I couldn't bear it if we put words to it. It would make our parting so much more painful than...than it's already going to be.'

She reached up and pulled his head down to hers, kissed him with all the passion and feeling she could bring to the kiss. Felt her tears rolling down her cheeks.

'This. This is all we can have.'

Tristan held Gemma close as she slept, her head nestled in his shoulder. He breathed in her sweet scent. Already he felt that even blindfolded he would recognise her by her scent.

His physical connection with this special woman was like nothing he had ever experienced. Their bodies were in sync, as though they had made love for a lifetime. He couldn't label what they shared as *sex*—this was truly making *love*.

Being together all day, cooking companionably—even doing the dishes—had brought a sense of intimacy that was new to him. Was this what a *real* marriage could be like? As opposed to the rigid, hypocritical structure of a royal marriage?

What he felt with Gemma was a heady mix of physical pleasure and simple joy in her company. Was that how marriage should be?

There was no role model for a happy marriage in his family. His parents with their separate lives... His brother's loveless union... And from what he remembered of his grandparents, his grandmother had spent more time on the committees of her charitable organisations than she had with his grandfather. Except, of course, when duty called.

Duty. Why did he have to give up his chance of love for *duty*?

Because he didn't have a choice.

He had never felt for another woman what he felt for Gemma. Doubted he ever would. She was right—for self-protection neither of them could put a label on what they felt for each other—but he knew what it was.

She gave a throaty little murmur as she snuggled closer. He dropped a kiss on her bare shoulder.

The full impact of what he would miss out on, what he had to give up for duty, hit him with the impact of a sledgehammer.

Feeling as he did for Gemma, how could he even contemplate becoming betrothed to another woman in three months' time? He could taste the bitterness in his mouth. Another loveless, miserable royal marriage for Montovia.

He stayed awake for hours, his thoughts on an endless loop that always seemed to end with the Montovian concept of honour—sacrificing love for duty—before he eventually slept.

When Tristan awoke it was to find Gemma dropping little kisses over his face and murmuring that breakfast was ready. He had other ideas, and consequently it was midmorning before they got out of bed.

They rode the horses back down to the river. He was pleased at how competent Gemma was in the saddle. Despite their differences in social status, they had a lot in common, liked doing the same things, felt comfortable with each other. *If only...*

He felt a desperate urgency as their remaining time together ticked on—a need to landmark each moment. Their last swim. Their last meal together. The last time they'd share those humble domestic duties.

He was used to being brave, to denying his feelings, but he found this to be a kind of torture.

Gemma had *not* been trained in self-denial. But she was brave up until they'd made love for the last time.

'I can't bear knowing we will never be together like this again,' she said, her voice breaking. 'Knowing that I will never actually see you again, except in the pages of a magazine or on a screen.'

She crumpled into sobs, and there was no consoling her. How could he comfort her when he felt as if his heart was being wrenched out of him and pummelled into oblivion?

Tristan tilted her chin up so he could gaze deep into her eyes, reddened from where she'd tried to scrub away her tears. Her lovely mouth trembled. It was a particular agony to know he was the cause of her pain.

He smoothed her hair, bedraggled and damp with tears, from her face. 'Gemma, I am sorry. I should not have pursued you when I knew this could be the only end for us.'

She cleared her voice of tears. Traced his face with her fingers in a gesture he knew with gut-wrenching certainty was a farewell.

'No. Never say that,' she said. 'I don't regret one moment I've spent with you. I wish it could be different for us. But we went into this with our eyes open. And now... and now I know what it *should* be like between a man and a woman. I had no idea, you see, that it could be like this.'

'Neither did I,' he choked out. Nor what an intolerable burden duty to his beloved country could become.

'So no beating ourselves up,' she said.

But for all her brave words he had to take the wheel of her car and drive back to Sydney. She was too distressed to be safe.

Only too quickly he pulled up the car near his hotel and killed the engine. The unbearable moment of final farewell was upon them.

He gave her the smartphone he had bought to use in Australia so they could easily stay in touch. 'Keep it charged,' he said.

'I won't use it, you know,' she said, not meeting his eyes. 'We have to make a clean break. I'll go crazy otherwise.'

'If that's what you want,' he said, scarcely able to choke out the words with their stabbing finality. But he stuffed the phone into her bag anyway.

'It's the only way,' she said, her voice muffled as she hid her face against his shoulder. 'But…but I'll never forget you and…and I hope you have a good life.'

All the anger and ambivalence he felt towards his role as heir to the throne threatened to overwhelm him. 'Gemma, I want you to know how much I—'

She pushed him away. 'Just go now, Tristan. Please.'

He wanted to be able to say there could be more for them, but he knew he could not. Instead he pulled the hoodie up over his face, got out of the car and walked back to his life as crown prince without looking back.

CHAPTER THIRTEEN

Ten weeks later

GEMMA SAT ON the bed in a guest room at the grand gated Georgian house belonging to her newly discovered English grandparents. She was a long way from home, here in the countryside near Dorchester, in the county of Dorset in the south-west of England.

In her less-than-steady hand she held the smartphone Tristan had insisted on leaving with her on the last day she'd seen him. It was only afterwards that she'd realised why. If she needed to get in touch with him she doubted the castle staff would put through a call to the crown prince from some unknown Australian girl.

The phone had been charging for the last hour.

She had never used it—rather had kept to her resolve never to contact him. That had not been easy in the sad black weeks that had followed the moment when he had stumbled from her car and had not looked back. But she had congratulated herself on how well she had come through the heartbreak of having her prince in her life for such a short time before she'd had to let him go.

The only time she had broken down was when she had flicked through a gossip magazine to be suddenly confronted by an article about the crown prince of Montovia's upcoming birthday celebrations. It had included photos of Tristan taken at the Sydney reception, looking impossibly handsome. A wave of longing for him had hit her with such intensity she'd doubled over with the pain of it.

Would contacting him now mean tearing the scab off a wound better left to heal?

When she thought about her time with him in Sydney—she refused to think of it as a fling—it had begun to take on the qualities of a fondly remembered dream. After this length of time she might reasonably have expected to start dating again. Only she hadn't.

'Don't go thinking of him as your once-in-a-lifetime love,' Andie had warned.

'I never said he was,' Gemma had retorted. 'Just that he *could* have been if things had been different.'

Now, might she have been given another chance with Tristan?

Gemma put down the phone, then picked it up again. Stared at it as if it might give her the answer. Should she or shouldn't she call him?

She longed to tell Tristan about her meeting with the Cliffords. But would he be interested in what she had to say? Would he want to talk to her after all this time? *Would he even remember her?*

She risked humiliation, that was for sure. By now he might be engaged to some princess or a duchess—that girl in Sydney a distant memory.

But might she always regret it if she didn't share with Tristan the unexpected revelation that had come from her decision to seek out her birth father's family?

Just do it, Gemma.

With trembling fingers she switched on the phone and the screen lit up. So the service was still connected. It was meant to be. She *would* call.

But then she was astounded to find a series of recent missed calls and texts of escalating urgency flashing up on the screen. All from Tristan. All asking her to contact him as soon as possible.

Why?

It made it easy to hit Call rather than have to take the actual step of punching out his number.

He answered almost straightaway. Her heart jolted so hard at the sound of his voice she lost *her* voice. She tried to say hi, but only a strangled gasp came out.

'Gemma? Is that you?'

'Yes,' she finally managed to squeak out.

'Where *are* you?' he demanded, as if it had been hours rather than months since they'd last spoken. 'I've called the Party Queens office. I've called both Andie and Eliza, who will not tell me where you are. Are you at the cottage? Are you okay?'

Gemma closed her eyes, the better to relish the sound of his voice, his accent. 'I'm in Dorset.'

She wondered where he was—in some palatial room in his medieval castle? It was difficult to get her head around the thought.

There was a muffled exclamation in Montovian. 'Dorset, England?'

She nodded. Realised that of course he couldn't see her. 'Yes.'

'So close. And I didn't know. What are you doing there?'

'Staying with my grandparents.'

'They…they are not alive. I don't understand…'

She could almost see his frown in his words.

'My birth father's parents.'

'The Clifford family?'

He'd remembered the name. 'Yes.'

What else did he remember? She hadn't forgotten a moment of their time together. Sometimes she revisited it in dreams. Dreams from which she awoke to an overwhelming sense of loss and yearning for a man she'd believed she would never see again—or hear.

'The people who paid your mother off? But they are not known to you…'

She realised she was gripping the phone so tensely her fingers hurt. 'They are now. I came to find them. After all your talk of your birthright and heritage, I wanted to know about mine. I told my mother I could no longer deny my need to know just because my stepfather felt threatened that she'd been married before.'

Her time with Tristan had made her want to take charge of her life and what was important to her.

'Those people—did they welcome you?'

'It seems I look very much like my father,' she said. In fact her grandmother had nearly fainted when Gemma had introduced herself.

'They were kind?'

The concern in his voice made her think Tristan still felt something for her.

'Very kind. It's a long story. One I'd like to share with you, Tristan.' She held her breath, waiting for his answer.

'I would like to hear it. And there is something important I have to tell you.'

'Is that why you were calling me?'

'Yes. I wanted to fly to Australia to see you.'

'You were going to fly all that way? But it's only two weeks until your birthday party.'

'I want to see you. Can you to come to Montovia?'

For a long moment she was too shocked to reply. 'Well, yes, I would like to see Montovia,' she finally choked out. *Tristan.* She just wanted to see Tristan. Here, there, Australia—she didn't care where. 'When?'

'Tomorrow.'

Excitement or trepidation? Which did she feel more? 'I'll look up flights.'

'I will send a private jet,' he said, without hesitation. *Of course he would.*

'And a limousine to pick you up from where you are in Dorset.'

'There's no need. I have a rental car...I can drive—'

'I will send the car.'

When she'd flown to England from Australia she'd had no intention of contacting Tristan. Certainly not of visiting Montovia. The meeting with her grandparents had changed everything.

It wasn't until after she had disconnected the phone that she realised she hadn't asked Tristan what was so important that he'd left all those messages.

The next day the limousine arrived exactly on time and took her to Bristol airport. She was whisked through security and then onto the tarmac.

It wasn't until she began to climb the steps to board the plane that she started to feel nervous. *What the heck was she doing here?*

She'd been determined to take charge of her own life after so many years of acquiescing to men, but then with one word from Tristan—actually, two words: *private* and *jet*—she'd rolled over and gone passive again.

Then he was there, and thoughts of anything else were crowded out of her mind.

Tristan.

He stood at the top of the steps, towering over her. Tall, broad-shouldered, wearing an immaculately tailored business suit in deepest charcoal with a narrow grey tie. His hair was cut much shorter—almost military in style. When she'd last seen him he hadn't shaved for two days and had been wearing blue jeans and a T-shirt. The time before that he'd been wearing nothing at all.

He looked the same, but not the same.

And it was the *not the same* that had her feet seemingly stuck to the steps and her mouth unable to form words of greeting.

He was every bit as handsome as she remembered. But this Tristan appeared older, more serious. A man of wealth and stratospheric status—greeting her on board a private jet that was to fly her to his castle. While she was still very much just Gemma from Sydney.

Gemma looked the same as Tristan had remembered—her hair copper bright, her heart-shaped face pretty, her lovely body discreetly shown off in deep pink trousers and a white jacket. As he watched her, he thought his heart would burst with an explosion of emotion.

He had never lost faith that he would see her again. That faith had paid off now, after all those dark hours between the moment he had said goodbye to her in Sydney and this moment, when he would say hello to her again. Hours during which he had honoured her request not to contact her. Hours when he had worked with all the driven frenzy of the Montovian fisherman searching for his water nymph to find a way they could be together.

But Gemma stood frozen, as though she were uncertain whether to step up or back down. There wasn't a dimple in sight.

Was it fear of flying? Or fear of *him*?

He hadn't said he'd be on the jet to meet her—he'd had to reschedule two meetings with his father and the inner circle of court advisers to make the flight. He hadn't wanted to make a promise he might not have been able to keep. Perhaps she was too shocked at his presence to speak.

He cursed under his breath. Why hadn't he thought to radio through to the chauffeur?

Because he'd been too damn excited at the thought of seeing her so soon to follow through on detail.

Now he wanted to bound down those steps, sweep her into his arms and carry her on board. The dazed look in her cinnamon-coloured eyes made him decide to be more circumspect. What had he expected? That she would fall back into his arms when, for all she knew, the situation hadn't changed between them and he still could not offer her anything more than a tryst?

Tristan urged himself to be patient. He took a step down to her, his arms outstretched in welcome. 'Gemma. I can't believe you're in Europe.'

For a long moment she looked up at him, searching his face. He smiled, unable to hide his joy and relief at seeing her again.

At last her lovely mouth tilted upwards and those longed-for dimples flirted once more in her cheeks. Finally she closed the remaining steps between them.

'Tristan. I can't believe it's you. I… I thought I would never see you again. Your smile…it's still the same.'

That puzzled him. Of course his smile was still the same. Probably a lot warmer and wider than any smile on his face since he'd last seen her. But all he could think about was Gemma. Back in his arms where she belonged.

He held her close for a long moment measured by the beating of her heart against him. He breathed in her essence, her scent heart-rendingly familiar.

Gratitude that everything had worked out surged through him. He didn't know how she had come to be just an hour's flight away from him, but he didn't question it. The need to kiss her was too strong—questions and answers could come later.

He dipped his head to claim her mouth. She kissed him back, at first uncertainly and then with enthusiasm.

'Tristan…' she murmured in that throaty, familiar way.

At last. Now everything was going to be as he wanted it.

CHAPTER FOURTEEN

GEMMA HAD ONLY ever seen the inside of a private jet in movies. Was this a taste of the luxury in which Tristan lived? If so, she guessed it was her first look at his life in Montovia. The armchair-like reclining seats, the sofas, the bathrooms... All slick and sleek, in leather, crystal and finest wool upholstery. The royal Montovian coat of arms—an eagle holding a sword in its beak—was embroidered on the fabrics and etched into crystal glasses. No wonder Tristan had not been overly impressed with the *Argus*—it must have seemed everyday to him.

Once they were in the air the attendant, in a uniform that also bore the royal coat of arms, served a light lunch, but Gemma was too tightly wound to eat. Tristan didn't eat much either. She wanted to tell him her news but didn't know how to introduce the topic. They sat in adjoining seats—close, but not intimate. She wasn't yet ready for intimate.

She was grateful when he asked outright. 'So, tell me about your meeting with your new grandparents.'

'They're not new—I mean they've been there all the time, but they didn't know I existed, of course.'

'They honestly had never checked up on your mother over the years?'

The words spilled out of her. 'Their shock at meeting me appeared genuine. The dimples did it, I think; my grandmother has them too. Eliza had joked that the Cliffords would probably want a DNA test, but they scarcely looked at my birth certificate. They loved their son very much. I think they see me as some kind of unexpected gift. And I... Well, I like them a lot.'

'It must have been exciting for you to finally find out about your father,' he said. 'Did it fill a gap for you?'

'A gap I didn't really know was there,' she said. 'You know I had only ever seen one photo of my father? The Cliffordses' house is full of them. He was very handsome. Apparently, he was somewhat of an endearing bad boy, who dropped out of Oxford and was living as a ski bum when he met my mother. His parents were hoping he'd get it out of his system and come back to the fold, but then he…he died. The revelation that he was married came as a huge shock to them.'

'What about the way they treated your mother?'

'I'm not making any excuses for them. I still think it was despicable. But apparently there's some serious money in the family, and there had been gold-diggers after him before. I told them my mother had no idea about any of that. She was clueless about English class distinctions.'

'For your sake, I am glad it's worked out for you…'

Gemma could sense the unspoken question at the end of his sentence. 'But you want to know why I decided to share my adventure with you.'

'Yes,' he said. 'I know you turned on the smartphone I left you because you decided to get in touch with me. I can only suppose it was because of your meeting with your new family.'

'You're right. But before I tell you I want to ask you something.' She felt her cheeks flush warm. 'It's your birthday in two weeks' time. I…I saw in a magazine that you have a big party planned. Are you…are you engaged to be married? To the girl your parents chose for you? Or anyone else?'

'No,' he said, without hesitation.

She could not help her audible sigh of relief.

Tristan met her gaze. 'What about you? Is there another man in your life?'

'There has been no one since…since you.'

'Good,' he said fiercely, his relief also apparent.

Seeing Tristan again told her why she had felt no interest in dating other men. Their attraction was as strong, as compelling, as overwhelming as it had ever been.

'Before I tell you what happened at my grandparents' house, let me say I come to you with no expectations,' she said. 'I realise when it comes down to it we…well, we've only known each other a week, but—'

Tristan made a sound of impatience that definitely involved Montovian cursing. 'A *week*? I feel I have known you a lifetime, Gemma. I know all I need to know about you.'

He planted a swift kiss on her mouth—enough to thrill her and leave her wanting more. She would have liked to turn to him, pull his head back to hers—but not before she'd had her say.

'You might want to know this, as well,' she said. 'You're speaking to a person who is, in the words of her newly discovered grandmother, "very well bred".'

Tristan frowned. 'I'm not sure what you mean.'

It had taken her a while to get her head around what she'd learned. Now she felt confident of reciting the story, but still her words came out in a rush. As if she still didn't quite believe it.

'It seems that on my grandmother's side I am eighth cousin to Prince William, the Duke of Cambridge, through a common distant ancestor, King George II, and also connected by blood to the Danish royal family. One of the connections was "on the wrong side of the blanket", but apparently that doesn't matter as far as genealogy is concerned.'

'But…but this is astonishing.'

She couldn't blame Tristan for his shocked expression;

she was sure her grandparents had seen the same look on her face.

'I thought so, too,' she said. 'In fact I couldn't believe it could possibly be true. But they showed me the family tree—to which I am now going to be added, on the short little branch that used to end with my father.'

Tristan shook his head in disbelief. 'After all I have done—'

'What do you mean? What have you done?'

'It is not important,' he said with a slight shake of his head. 'Not now.'

The way he'd said that had made it sound as though it *was* important. She would have to ask him about it at another time. Right now she was more concerned at the impact of her own news.

'I…I wanted to ask you if that connection is strong enough for… Well, strong enough to make things between us not so impossible as when I was just a commoner. Not that I'm not a commoner still, really. But as far as bloodlines are concerned—that's what my grandmother calls them—I…I have more of a pedigree than I could ever have imagined.'

He nodded thoughtfully. 'Forgive me, Gemma. This is a lot to take in.'

A chill ran up her spine. Was she too late? 'I'd hoped it might make a difference to…to us. That is if there *is* an "us".'

His dark brows rose, as if she had said something ridiculous. 'As far as I am concerned there was an "us" from the moment you tried to attack me with that wooden spoon.'

She smiled at the reminder. 'You are never, ever going to let me forget that, are you?'

'Not for the rest of our lives,' he said.

She could see it took an effort for him to keep his voice steady.

'Gemma, I've been utterly miserable without you.'

It was still there between them—she could see it in his eyes, hoped he saw it in hers. The attraction that was so much more than physical. If it no longer had to be denied because of the discovery of her heritage, where might it go from here?

Like champagne bubbles bubbling to the top of a glass, excitement fizzed through her.

'Me...me too. Though I've tried very hard to deny it. Kept congratulating myself on how well I'd got over you. I had no hope, you see. I didn't know—none of us did— that the requisite noble blood was flowing in my veins.'

'Stay with me in Montovia, Gemma. Be my guest of honour at the party. Let me woo you as a prince *can* woo the eighth cousin of a prince of this country.'

Again that word *surreal* flashed through her mind. Perhaps this was all meant to be. Maybe she and Tristan were part of some greater plan. Who knew? And Party Queens could manage without her. She hadn't taken a break since the business had started.

'Yes, Tristan,' she said. 'Show me Montovia. I couldn't think of anything better than spending the next few weeks with you.'

She hugged his intention to 'woo' her—what a delight-fully old-fashioned word—to herself like something very precious. Then she wound her arms around his neck and kissed him.

By the time the jet started its descent into Montovia, and the private airfield that served the castle, she and Tristan were more than ready to go further than kisses. She felt they were right back where they'd left off in her grand-mother's cottage. He might be a prince, but more than that he was the man she wanted—wanted more than ever.

And they had two weeks together.

She couldn't remember when she'd felt happier.

Gemma caught her breath in admiration as, on Tristan's command to the pilot, the jet swooped low over the town of old Montovia. In the soft light of late afternoon it looked almost too beautiful to be real.

The medieval castle, with its elaborate towers and turrets, clung to the side of a forest-covered mountain with the ancient town nestled below. The town itself was set on the shore of a lake that stretched as far as she could see, to end in the reflections of another snow-capped mountain range. A medieval cathedral dominated the town with its height and grandeur.

'You can see from here how strategically they built the castle, with the mountains behind, the lake in front, the steep winding road, the town walls,' said Tristan, from where he sat beside her. 'The mountains form a natural barricade and fortification—it would be an exceptional army that could scale them. Especially considering there's snow and ice on the passes most months of the year.'

He kept his hand on her shoulder as he showed her what to look for out of the window. Gemma loved the way he seemed to want to reassure himself she was there, with a touch, a quick kiss, a smile. It was like some kind of wonderful dream that she was here with him after those months of misery. And all because she'd followed up on her curiosity about her father.

'It's good to see you taking your turn as tour guide,' she said. 'There's so much I want to know.'

'Happy to oblige,' he said with his charming smile. 'I love Montovia, and I want you to love it, too.'

For just two weeks? She didn't dare let herself think there could be more...

She reached out to smooth his cowlick back into place— that unruly piece of hair that refused to stay put. It was a small imperfection. He was still beautiful in the way of a virile man.

That inner excitement continued to bubble. Not because of castles and lakes and mountains. But because of Tristan. *She loved him.* No longer did she need to deny it—to herself or anyone else. She loved him—and there was no longer any roadblock on a possible future together.

'The castle was originally a fortress, built in the eleventh century on the ruins of a Roman *castellum*,' he said. 'It was added to over the centuries to become what it is now. The south extension was built not as a fortress but to showcase the wealth and power of the royal family.'

Gemma laughed. 'You know, I didn't see all that strategy stuff at all. I only saw how beautiful the setting is, how picturesque the town, with those charming old houses built around the square. Even from here I can see all the flower boxes and hanging baskets. Do you realise how enchanting cobbled streets are to Australian eyes? And it looks like there's a market being held in the town square today.'

'The farmers from the surrounding cantons bring in their goods, and there's other household stuff for sale, too—wooden carvings, metalwork, pottery. We have a beautiful Christmas market in December.'

'I can't wait to see more of the countryside. And to walk around the town. Am I allowed to? Are you? What about your bodyguards?'

'We are as safe as we will ever be in our own town. We come and go freely. Here the royal family are loved, and strangers are rare except for tourists.'

'Do you mean strangers are not welcome?' A tiny pinprick was threatening to leak the happiness from her bubble.

'Are you asking will you be welcome?'

'I might be wondering about it,' she said, quaking a little. 'What will you tell your family about me?'

'They know all about the beautiful girl I met in Sydney. They know I flew to England to get her today. You will be their guest.'

That surprised her. Why would he have told anyone about his interlude with an unsuitable commoner? And wouldn't she be staying with *him*, not his family?

'Will I be seen as an interloper?'

'You are with me—that automatically makes you not a stranger.'

She noticed a new arrogance to Tristan. He was crown prince of this country. Was he really still the Tristan she had fallen for in Sydney? Or someone else altogether?

'I'm glad to hear that,' she said. She paused. 'There's another thing. A girly thing. I'm worried about my clothes. When I left Sydney I didn't pack for a castle. I've only got two day dresses with me. And nothing in the slightest bit formal. I wasn't expecting to travel.' She looked down at what she was wearing. 'Already this white jacket is looking less than its best. What will your parents think of me?'

Being taken home to meet a boyfriend's parents was traumatic at best. When they were a king and queen, the expectation level went off the scale.

'You are beautiful, Gemma. My mother and father are looking forward to meeting you. They will not even notice your clothes. You look fine in what you are wearing.'

Hmm. *They lived in a castle.* She very much doubted casual clothes would be the order of the day. In Dorset she'd felt totally underdressed even in her newly found grandparents' elegant house. At least she'd managed to pop into Dorchester and buy a dress, simply cut in navy linen.

'I have so many questions. When will I meet your parents? Will…will we be allowed to stay together? Do I—?'

'First, you are invited to dinner tonight, to meet my parents and my sister. Second, you will stay in one of the castle's guest apartments.'

Again there was that imperious tone.

'By myself?'

Her alarm must have shown on her face.

'Don't worry, it is not far from mine.'

'Your apartment?'

'We each have our independent quarters. I am still in the apartment I was given when I turned eighteen. The crown prince's much grander apartment will be mine when its refurbishment is complete. I wanted my new home to be completely different. I could not live there with sad memories of when the rooms were Carl's.'

'Of course…' Her words trailed away.

She shouldn't be surprised that she and Tristan wouldn't be allowed to share a room. Another pinprick pierced that lovely bubble. She hadn't anticipated being left on her own. And she very much feared she would be totally out of her depth.

CHAPTER FIFTEEN

TRISTAN WANTED TO have Gemma to himself for a little longer before he had to introduce her to his family. He also wanted to warn his parents and his sister not to say anything about the work he'd done on what he had privately termed 'Project Water Nymph' in the months since he'd been parted from Gemma.

He sensed in her a reticence he had not expected—he'd been surprised when she'd reminded him she'd only known him for a week. There was no such reticence on his part— he had no doubt that he wanted her in his life. But instinct now told him she might feel pressured if she knew of the efforts he'd gone to in order to instigate change.

Not that he regretted the time he'd spent on the project—it had all been to the good in more ways than one. But news of her noble connections had removed some of that pressure. So long as no one inadvertently said something to her. He wanted her to have more time here before he told her what he'd been doing while she'd been tracking down her English connections.

'Let me show you my favourite part of the castle before I take you to your rooms,' he said. 'It is very old and very simple—not like the rooms where we spend most of our time. I find it peaceful. It is where I go to think.'

'I'd love that,' she said, with what seemed like genuine interest.

'This part of the castle is open to the public in the summer, but not until next month,' he said. 'We will have it to ourselves today.'

He thought she would appreciate the most ancient part of the castle, and he was not disappointed. She exclaimed her amazement at all his favourite places as he led her along the external pathways and stone corridors that hugged the walls of the castle, high above the town.

'This is the remains of the most heavily barricaded fortress,' he explained. 'See the slits in the walls through which arrows were fired? Those arched lookouts came much later.'

Gemma leaned her elbows on the sill of the lookout. 'What a magnificent view across the lake to the mountains! It sounds clichéd, but everywhere I look in your country I see a postcard.'

With her hair burnished by the late-afternoon sun, and framed by the medieval arch, Gemma herself looked like a beautiful picture. To have her here in his home was something he'd thought he'd never see. He wanted to keep her here more than he'd ever wanted anything. This image of Gemma on her first day in Montovia would remain in his mind forever.

He slipped his arms around her from behind. She leaned back against his chest. For a long time they looked at the view in a companionable silence. He was the first to break it. 'To me this has the same kind of natural grandeur as the view from the deck of your grandmother's cottage,' he said.

'You're right,' she said. 'Very different, but awe-inspiring in the same way.'

'I wish we could stay here much longer, but I need to take you to your rooms now so that you can have some time to freshen up before dinner.'

And so that he'd have time to prepare his family for his change in strategy.

If this was a guest apartment, Gemma could only imagine what the royal family's apartments were like. It comprised a suite of elegantly decorated rooms in what she thought was an antique French style. Andie would know exactly how to describe it.

Gemma swallowed hard against a sudden lump in her throat. Andie and Party Queens and Sydney and her everyday life seemed far, far away. She was here purely for Tristan. Without his reassuring presence she felt totally lost and more than a tad terrified. What if she made a fool of herself? It might reflect badly on Tristan, and she *so* didn't want to let him down. She might have been born with noble blood in her veins, but she had been raised as just an ordinary girl in the suburbs.

She remembered the times in Sydney when she had thought about Tristan being *other*. Here, in this grand castle, surrounded by all the trappings of his life, she might as well be on a different planet for all she related to it. Here, *she* was *other*.

A maid had been sent to help her unpack her one pitifully small suitcase. She started to speak to her in Montovian, but at Gemma's lack of response switched to English. The more Gemma heard Montovian spoken, the less comprehensible it seemed. How could she let herself daydream about a future with Tristan in a country where she couldn't even speak the language?

She stood awkwardly by while the maid shook out her hastily packed clothes and woefully minimal toiletries and packed them away in the armoire. Knowing how to deal with servants was totally outside of her experience.

The maid asked Gemma what she wanted to wear to dinner, and when Gemma pointed out the high-street navy dress, she took it away to steam the creases out. By the time Gemma had showered in the superb marble bathroom—thankfully full of luxurious bath products—her dress was back in the bedroom, looking 100 per cent better than it had.

Did you tip the maids? She would have to ask Tristan.

There was so much she needed to ask him, but she didn't want to appear so ignorant he might regret inviting her here.

Her antennae gave a feeble wave, to remind her that Tristan had fallen for her the way she was. He wouldn't expect her to be any different. She would suppress her tremors of terror, watch and learn and ask questions when necessary.

She dressed in the navy sheath dress and the one pair of high-heeled shoes she'd brought with her, a neutral bronze. The outfit had looked fine in an English village, but here it looked drab—the bed was better dressed than she was, with its elegant quilted toile bedcover.

Then she remembered the exquisite pearl necklace her new grandmother had insisted on giving her from her personal jewellery collection. The strand was long, the pearls large and lustrous. It lifted the dress 100 per cent.

As she applied more make-up than she usually would Gemma felt her spirits rise. Darn it, she had royal blood of her own—even if much diluted. She would *not* let herself be intimidated. Despite their own personal problems, the king and queen had raised a wonderful person like Tristan. How could they *not* be nice people?

When Tristan, dressed in a different immaculate dark business suit, came to escort her to dinner, he told her she looked perfect and she more than half believed him.

Feeling more secure with Tristan by her side, Gemma tried not to gawk at the splendour of the family's dining room, with its ornate ceilings and gold trimmings, its finely veined white marble and the crystal chandeliers that hung over the endless dining table. Or at the antique silk-upholstered furniture and priceless china and silver. And these were the private rooms—not the staterooms.

Tristan had grown up with all this as his birthright.

How would she ever fit in? Even though he hadn't actually come out and said it, she knew she was on trial here. Now there was no legal impediment to them having a future together, it was up to her to prove she *could* fit in.

Tristan's parents were seated in an adjoining sitting room in large upholstered chairs—not thrones, thank heaven. His blonde mother, the queen, was attractive and ageless—Gemma suspected some expert work on her face—and was exquisitely groomed. She wore a couture dress and jacket, and outsize diamonds flashed at her ears, throat and wrists. His father had dark greying hair and a moustache, a severe face and was wearing an immaculately tailored dark suit.

Tristan had said they dressed informally for dinner.

Thank heaven she'd changed out of the cotton trousers and the jacket grubby at the cuffs.

Ordinary parents would have risen to greet them. Royal parents obviously did not. Why hadn't Tristan briefed her on what was expected of her? What might be second nature to him was frighteningly alien to her.

Prompted perhaps by some collective memory shared with her noble ancestors, Gemma swept into a deep curtsy and murmured, 'Your Majesties.'

It was the curtsy with which she'd started and ended every ballet class for years when she'd been a kid. She didn't know if it was a suitable curtsy for royalty, but it seemed to do the trick. Tristan beamed, and his mother and father smiled. Gemma almost toppled over in her relief.

'Thank you, my dear,' said his mother as she rose from her chair. 'Welcome.' She had Tristan's blue eyes, faded to a less vivid shade.

The father seemed much less forbidding when he smiled. 'You've come a long way to reach us. Montovia makes you welcome.'

Tristan took her hand in a subtle declaration that they

were a couple, but Gemma doubted his parents needed it. She suspected his mother's shrewd gaze missed nothing.

When Tristan's sister joined them—petite, dark-haired Natalia—Gemma sensed she might have a potential friend at the castle.

'Tristan mentioned you might need to buy some new clothes?' Natalia said. 'I'd love to take you shopping. And of course you'll need something formal for Tristan's party next week.'

Royals no doubt needed to excel at small talk, and any awkwardness was soon dispelled as they sat down at the table. If she hadn't already been in love with Tristan, Gemma would have fallen in love with him all over again as he effortlessly included her in every conversation.

He seemed pleased when she managed a coherent exchange in French with his mother and another in German with his father.

'I needed to fill all my spare time after you left Sydney so I wouldn't mope,' she whispered to him. 'I found some intensive language classes.'

'What do you think about learning Montovian?' he asked.

'I shall have to, won't I?' she said. 'But who will teach me?'

There was a delicious undercurrent running between her and Tristan. She knew why she was here in his country—to see if she would like living in Montovia. But it was a formality, really. If she wanted to be with him, here she would have to stay. Nothing had been declared between them, so there was still that thrilling element of anticipation—that the best was yet to come.

'*I* will teach you, of course,' he said, bringing his head very close to hers so their conversation remained private.

'It seems like a very difficult language. I might need a lot of attention.'

'If attention is what you need, attention is what you shall get,' he said in an undertone. 'Just let me know where I need to focus.'

'I think you might already know where I need attention,' she said.

'Lessons should start tonight, then,' he said, and his eyes narrowed in the way she found incredibly sensuous.

'I *do* like lessons from you,' she murmured. 'All sorts of lessons.'

'I shall come to your room tonight, so we can start straight away,' he said.

She sat up straighter in her antique brocade dining chair. 'Really?'

'You didn't think I was going to let you stay all by yourself in this great rattling castle?'

'I did wonder,' she said.

'I have yearned to be alone with you for close on three months. Protocol might put us in different rooms. That doesn't mean we have to stay there.'

The soup course was served. But Gemma felt so taut with anticipation at the thought of being alone—completely alone—with Tristan she lost her appetite and just pushed the soup around in her bowl.

It was the first of four courses; each course was delicious, if a tad uninspired and on the stodgy side. Gemma wondered who directed the cook, and wondered, if she were to end up staying in Montovia, if she might be able to improve the standard of the menus without treading on any toes.

The thought took her to a sudden realisation—one she had not had time to consider. She knew the only way she would be staying in Montovia was if she and Tristan committed to something permanent.

Finding out the truth about her father's family had precipitated their reunion with such breakneck speed, putting their relationship on a different footing, that she hadn't had time to think about the implications.

If she and Tristan… If she stayed in Montovia she would have to give up Party Queens. In fact she supposed she would have to give up any concept of having her own life. Though there was actually no reason why she couldn't be involved with the business remotely.

She had spent much of the last year working to be herself—not the version of herself that others expected her to be. Without her work, without her friends, without identification with her own nationality, would she be able to cope?

Would being with Tristan be enough?

She needed to talk to Tristan about that.

CHAPTER SIXTEEN

BUT SHE DIDN'T actually have much time alone with Tristan. The next day his parents insisted on taking them to lunch at their mountain chalet, more than an hour and a half's drive away from the castle. The honour was so great there was no way she could suggest she would rather be alone with Tristan.

The chalet was comparatively humble. More like a very large, rustic farmhouse, with gingerbread wood carving and window boxes planted with red geraniums. A hearty meal was served to them by staff dressed in traditional costume—full dirndl skirts for the women and leather shorts and embroidered braces for the men.

'Is this the real Montovia?' she asked Tristan. 'Because if it is, I find it delightful.'

'It is the traditional Montovia,' he said. 'The farmers here still bring their cattle up to these higher pastures in the summer. In winter it is snowed in. People still spend the entire winter in the mountains. Of course, this is a skiing area, and the roads are cleared.'

Would she spend a winter skiing here? Perhaps all her winters?

That evening was taken up with his cousin and his girlfriend joining them for the family dinner. They were very pleasant, but Gemma was surprised at how stilted they were with her. At one point the girlfriend—a doctor about her own age—started to say how grateful she was to Gemma, but her boyfriend cut her off before she could finish the sentence.

Natalia, too, talked about her brother's hard work in

changing some rule or another, before being silenced by a glare from Tristan.

And although they all spoke perfect English, in deference to her, there were occasional bursts of rapid Montovian that left Gemma with the distinct impression that she was being left out of something important. It wasn't a feeling she liked.

She tackled Tristan about it when he came to her room that night.

'Tristan, is there something going on I should know about?'

'What do you mean?' he said, but not before a flash of panic tightened his face.

'I mean, Mr Marco, you made a promise not to lie to me.'

'No one is lying. I mean... *I* am not lying.'

'"No one"?' She couldn't keep the hurt and betrayal from her voice.

'I promise you this is not bad, Gemma.'

'Better tell me, then,' she said, leading him over to the elegant chaise longue, all gilt-edged and spindly legged, but surprisingly comfortable.

Tristan sank down next to her. He should have known his family would let the secret slip. No way did he want Gemma to feel excluded—not when the project had been all about including her.

'Have I told you about the myth of the Montovian water nymph?' he asked.

'No, but it sounds intriguing.'

Tristan filled her in on the myth. He told her how he saw her as *his* sea nymph, with her pale limbs and floating hair enticing him in the water of Sydney Harbour.

'When I got back to Montovia, I was like the fisherman who escaped his nymph's deadly embrace but went mad without her and spent his remaining years searching the lake for her.'

Gemma took his hand. 'I was flailing around by myself, too, equally as miserable.'

He dropped a kiss on her sweet mouth. 'This fisherman did not give up easily. I searched the castle archives through royal decrees and declarations to find the origin of the rule that kept us apart. Along the way I found my purpose.'

'I'm not sure what you mean.' she said.

'Remember, I've been rebelling against this rule since my Playboy Prince days? But I began to realise I'd gone about it the wrong way—perhaps a hangover from being the "spare". I'd been waiting for *someone else* to change the rules.'

He gave an unconsciously arrogant toss of his head.

'So I decided *I* was the crown prince. *I* was the lawyer. *I* was the person who was going to bring the royal family of Montovia kicking and screaming into the twenty-first century. All motivated by the fact I wanted the right to choose my own bride, no matter her status or birth.'

'So this was about *me*?'

'Yes. Other royal families allow marriage to commoners. Why not ours?'

'Be careful who you're calling a commoner,' she said. 'Now I know why I disliked the term so much. My noble blood was protesting.'

Tristan laughed. He loved her gift of lightening up a situation. It would stand her in good stead, living in a society like Montovia's.

'I practically lived in the archives—burrowing down through centuries of documents. My research eventually found that the rule could be changed by royal decree,' he said. 'In other words, it was in the power of the king—my father—to implement a change.'

'You must have been angry he hadn't already done so.'

'I was at first. Then I realised my father genuinely believed he was bound by law. Fact is, he has suffered from its restrictions more than anyone. He has loved his mistress since they were teenagers. She would have been his first choice of bride.'

Gemma slowly shook her head. 'That's so sad. Sad for your father, sad for his mistress and tragic for your mother.'

'It is all that. Until recently I hadn't realised my father's relationship with his mistress stretched back that far. They genuinely love each other. Which made me all the more determined to change the ruling—not just for my sake but for future generations of our family.'

'How did you go about it?'

'I recruited some allies. My sister Natalia who—at the age of twenty-six—has already refused offers of marriage from six eligible, castle-approved suitors.'

'"Suitors". That's such an old-fashioned word,' she mused.

'There is nothing modern about life in the royal castle of Montovia, I can assure you. But things are changing.'

'And you like being that agent of change?'

'I believe my brother would have preserved the old ways. I want to be a different kind of king for my country.'

'That's what you meant by finding your purpose.' She put her hand gently on his cheek, her eyes warm with approval. 'I'm proud of you.'

'Thank you,' he said. 'You met my next recruit tonight—my cousin, who is in love with that lovely doctor he met during their time in the military. Then my mother came on board. She suggested we recruit my father's mistress. It is too late for them, but they want to see change.'

'Your father must have felt outnumbered.'

'Eventually he agreed to give us a fair hearing. We presented a united front. Put forward a considered argument. And we won. The king agreed to issue a new decree.'

'And you did all that—'

'So I could be with my sea nymph.'

For a long, still moment he searched her face, delighted in her slow smile.

'A lesser man might have given up,' she said.

'A lesser man wouldn't have had you to win. If I hadn't met you and been shown a glimpse of what life could be like, I would have given in to what tradition demanded.'

'Instead you came to terms with the role you were forced to step up to, and now Montovia will get a better ruler when the time comes.'

'All that.'

'I wish I'd known what you were doing,' she said.

'To get our hopes up and for them to come to nothing would have been a form of torture. I called you as soon as I got the verdict from the king.'

She frowned. 'What about your arranged bride? Where did she fit into this?'

'I discovered she did not want our marriage any more than I did. She was being pressured by her ambitious father. He was given sufficient reparation that he will not cause trouble.'

'So why didn't you tell me all this when I told you about my grandparents?'

'I did not want you to feel pressured by what I had done. My feelings for you have been serious from the start. I realised you'd need time to get used to the idea.'

She reached up and put her hand on his face. 'Isn't it already serious between us?'

He took her hand and pressed a kiss into her palm. 'I mean committed. It would be a very different life for you in Montovia. You will have to be sure it is what you want.'

'Yes,' she said slowly.

Tristan felt like the fisherman with his net. He wanted to secure Gemma to live with him in his country. But he knew, like the water nymph, she had to make that decision to swim to shore by herself.

CHAPTER SEVENTEEN

ON FRIDAY MORNING Tristan's sister, Natalia, took Gemma shopping to St Pierre, the city that was the modern financial and administrative capital of Montovia.

Gemma would rather have gone with Tristan, but he had asked Natalia to take her, telling them to charge anything she wanted to the royal family's account. No matter the cost.

St Pierre was an intriguing mix of medieval and modern, but Gemma didn't get a chance to look around.

'You can see the city another time,' Natalia said. 'Montovians dress more formally than you're probably used to. The royal family even more so. You need a whole new wardrobe. Montovians expect a princess to look the part.'

'*You* certainly do,' said Gemma admiringly.

Natalia dressed superbly. Gemma hoped she would be able to help her choose what she needed to fit in and do the right thing by Tristan. She suspected the white jacket might never get an airing again.

Natalia looked at her a little oddly. 'I wasn't talking about me. I was talking about you, when you become crown princess.'

Gemma was too stunned to speak for a moment. 'Me? Crown princess?'

'When you and Tristan marry you will become crown princess. Hadn't you given that a thought?'

Natalia spoke as though it were a done deed that Gemma and Tristan would marry.

'It might sound incredibly stupid of me, but no.'

In the space of just a few days she'd been whisked away by private jet and landed in a life she'd never known existed outside the pages of glossy magazines. She hadn't thought any further than being with the man she loved.

Natalia continued. 'You will become Gemma, crown princess of Montovia—the second highest ranking woman in the land after the queen—and you will have all the privileges and obligations that come with that title.'

Gemma's mouth went suddenly dry and her heart started thudding out of control. How could she, a girl from suburban Sydney, become a princess? She found the thought terrifying.

'It's all happened so incredibly quickly,' she said to Natalia. 'All I've focused on is Tristan—him stepping up to the role of crown prince and making it his own. I...I never thought about what it meant for me.'

Panic seemed to grasp her stomach and squeeze it hard. She took some deep breaths to try and steady herself but felt the blood draining from her face.

Natalia had the same shrewd blue eyes as her mother, the queen. 'Come on, let's get you a coffee before we start shopping. But you need to talk about this to Tristan.'

'Yes...' Gemma said, still dazed by the thought. *They had not talked nearly enough.*

Natalie regarded her from the other side of the table in the cafe she had steered Gemma to. She pushed across a plate of knotted sugar cookies. 'Eat one of these.'

Gemma felt a little better after eating the cookie. It seemed it was a traditional Montovian treat. She must get the recipe...

'The most important thing we've got to get sorted is a show-stopping formal gown for next Saturday night,' said Natalie. 'Tristan's birthday is a real milestone for him. My brother has changed the way royal marriages have worked for centuries so you two can be together. All eyes will be on you. We've got to have you looking the part.'

Again, terror gripped Gemma. But Natalia put a comforting hand on her arm.

'There are many who are thankful to you for being a catalyst for change. Me included.'

'That's reassuring,' said Gemma. Although it wasn't. Not really. What about those who *didn't* welcome change—and blamed her for it?

'The more you look like a princess, the more you'll be treated like one,' said Natalia.

Natalia took her into the kind of boutiques where price tags didn't exist. The clothes she chose for Gemma—from big-name designers, formal, sophisticated—emphasised the impression that she was hurtling headfirst into a life she'd never anticipated and was totally unprepared for.

She had to talk to Tristan.

But by the time she got back to the castle, sat through another formal dinner with his family—this time feeling more confident, in a deceptively simple black lace dress and her pearls—she was utterly exhausted.

She tried to force her eyes to stay open and wait for Tristan, but she fell fast asleep in the vast antique-style bed before he arrived.

During the night she became aware of him sleeping beside her, with a possessive arm around her waist, but when she woke in the morning he was gone. And she felt groggy and disorientated from a horrible dream.

In it, she had been clad only in the gauzy French bra and panties Natalia had helped her buy. Faceless soldiers had been dragging her towards a huge, grotesquely carved throne while she shouted that she wasn't dressed yet.

CHAPTER EIGHTEEN

BEING CROWN PRINCE brought with it duties Tristan could not escape. He hated leaving Gemma alone for the morning, but the series of business meetings with his father and the Crown's most senior advisers could not be avoided.

Gemma had still been asleep when he'd left her room. He'd watched her as she'd slept, an arm flung over her head to where her bright hair spilled over the pillow. Her lovely mouth had twitched and her eyelids fluttered, and he'd smiled and wondered what she was dreaming about. He'd felt an overwhelming rush of wonder and gratitude that she was there with him.

Like that fisherman, desperately hunting for his water nymph, the dream of being reunited with Gemma was what had kept him going through those months in the gloomy castle archives. He saw the discovery of her noble blood as confirmation by the fates that making her his bride was meant to be.

He'd gently kissed her and reluctantly left the room.

All throughout the first meeting he'd worried about her being on her own but had felt happier after he'd been able to talk to her on the phone. She'd reassured him that she was dying to explore the old town and had asked him for directions to his childhood favourite chocolate shop and tea room. He'd arranged for his driver to take her down and back. They'd confirmed that she'd meet him back at the castle for lunch.

But now it was lunchtime, and she wasn't in the rose garden, where he'd arranged to meet her. She wasn't answering her phone. His driver confirmed that he had brought her back to the castle. Had she gone back to her room for a nap?

He knocked on the door to her guest apartment. No answer. He pushed it open, fully expecting to find her stretched out on the bed. If so, he would revise his plans so that he could join her on the bed and *then* go out to lunch.

But the bed was empty, the apartment still and quiet. There was a lingering trace of her perfume, but no Gemma. *Where was she?*

A wave of guilt washed over him because he didn't know. He shouldn't have left her on her own. He'd grown up in the labyrinth of the castle. But Gemma was totally unfamiliar with it. She might actually have got lost. Be wandering somewhere, terrified. He regretted now that he'd teased her, telling her that some of the rooms were reputed to be haunted.

As he was planning where to start looking for her, a maid came into the room with a pile of fresh towels in her arms. She dipped a curtsy. Asked if he was looking for his Australian guest. She had just seen Miss Harper in the kitchen garden…

Tristan found Gemma standing facing the view of the lake, the well-tended gardens that supplied fruit and vegetables for the castle behind her. Her shoulders were bowed and she presented a picture of defeat and misery.

What the heck was wrong?

'Gemma?' he called. 'Are you okay?'

As he reached her she turned to face him. He gasped. All colour had drained from her face, so that her freckles stood out in stark contrast, her eyes were red rimmed and even her hair seemed to have lost its sheen. She was dressed elegantly, in linen trousers and a silk top, but somehow the look was dishevelled.

He reached out to her but she stepped back and he let his arms fall by his sides. 'What's happened?'

'I...I can't do this, Tristan.' Her voice was thick and broken.

'Can't do what? I don't know what you mean.'

She waved to encompass the castle and its extensive grounds. 'This. The castle. The life. It's so different. It's so *other*.' She paused. 'That's why I came here.' She indicated the vegetable garden, with its orderly plantings. 'Here it is familiar; here I feel at home. I...I pulled a few weeds from those carrots. I hope you don't mind?'

He wasn't exactly sure what she meant by 'other', but her misery at feeling as if she didn't fit in emanated from her, loud and clear.

'I'm sorry, Gemma. I didn't know you were feeling like this. I shouldn't have left you on your own.'

Her chin tilted upwards. 'I don't need a nursemaid, Tristan. I can look after myself.'

'You're in a foreign country, and you need a guide. Like you were *my* guide when I was in your home country.'

She took a deep, shuddering breath. 'I need so much more than a guide to be able to fit in here,' she said. 'I...I was so glad to be here with you—so excited that we could be together when we thought we never could.'

Was so glad?

'Me, too. Nothing has made me happier,' he said.

'But I didn't think about what it would mean to be a *princess*. A princess worthy of you. I'm a Party Queen—not a real queen in waiting. You need more than...than me...for Montovia.'

'Let me be the judge of that,' he said. 'What's brought this on, Gemma? Has someone scared you?'

Who could feel so threatened by the change of order they might have tried to drive her away? When he found who it was, heads would roll.

Gemma sniffed. 'It started with Natalia, she—'

His sister? He was surprised that she would cause trouble. 'I thought you liked her, that she was helping you?'

'I do. She was. But—'

He listened as she recounted what had happened the day before in St Pierre.

'I felt so…ignorant,' Gemma concluded. 'It hadn't even entered my head that I would be crown princess. And I have no idea of what might be expected of me.'

Mentally, Tristan slammed his hand against the side of his head. Why look for someone to blame when it was himself he should be blaming? He had not prepared her for what was ahead. Because she'd made such a good impression on his family, he had made assumptions he shouldn't have. Once she had swept into that magnificent curtsy, once he had seen the respect with which she interacted with his parents, he'd been guilty of assuming she would be okay.

His gut twisted painfully when he thought about how unhappy she was. And she hadn't felt able to talk to him. The man who loved her.

Tristan spoke through gritted teeth. 'My fault. I should have prepared you. Made it very clear to everyone that—'

'That I'm wearing my princess learner plates?' she said with another sniffle.

He was an intelligent, well-educated man who'd thought he knew this woman. Yet he'd had no idea of what she'd gone through since he'd dumped her into his world and expected her to be able to negotiate it without a map of any kind.

'What else?'

'The maid. I asked her to help me with a few phrases in Montovian, so I could surprise you. She told me her language was so difficult no outsider could ever learn to speak it. Then she rattled off a string of words that of course I

didn't understand and had no chance of repeating. I felt…
I felt helpless and inadequate. If I can't learn the language,
how can I possibly be taken seriously?'

'She loses her job today,' he said, with all the autocracy
a crown prince could muster.

Gemma shook her head. 'Don't do that. She was well-
meaning. She was the wrong person to ask for help. I
should have asked—'

'*Me*. Why didn't you?'

'I…I didn't want to bother you,' she whispered. 'You
have so much on your plate with your new role. I…I'm
used to being independent.' She looked down at her feet,
in their smart new Italian walking shoes.

'I'm sorry, Gemma. I've let you down. I can't tell you
how gutted I am that you are so unhappy.'

She looked up at him, but her eyes were guarded. 'I
was okay until Natalia mentioned something this morning
about when I become queen. She was only talking about
the kind of jewellery I'd need, but I freaked. Becoming
crown princess is scary enough. But *queen*!'

Now Tristan gritted his teeth. He'd let duty rule him
again—to his own personal cost. Those meetings this
morning should have been postponed. He might have lost
Gemma. Might still lose her if he didn't look after her better. And that would be unendurable.

'Anything else to tell me?'

She twisted the edge of her top between her fingers.
'The old man in the chocolate shop. He—'

'He said something inappropriate?' He found it hard to
reconcile that with his memories of the kindly man.

'On the contrary. He told me what a dear little boy you
were, and how he was looking forward to treating *our* children when we brought them in for chocolate.'

'And that was a problem?' Tristan was puzzled at the
way Gemma had taken offence at those genial words.

'Don't you see? *Children*. We've never talked about children. We haven't talked about our future at all. I feel totally unprepared for all this. All I know is that we want to be together. But is it enough?'

He did not hesitate. 'Yes. I have no doubt of that.'

She paused for so long dread crept its way into his heart.

'I…I'm not sure it is. You can do better than me. And I fear that if I try to be someone I'm not—like I spent so much of my life doing—I will lose myself and no longer be the person you fell in love with. You've grown up in this royal life. It's all so shockingly different for me—and more than a little scary. I don't want to make your life a misery because I'm unhappy. Do you understand that?'

'I will do anything in my power to make you happy.' His voice was gruff.

'I've been thinking maybe your ancestors had it right. When your new spouse comes from the same background and understands your way of life, surely that must be an advantage?'

'No,' he said stiffly. 'Any advantage is outweighed by the massive *dis*advantage of a lack of love in such a marriage.'

'I'm not so sure,' she said. 'Tristan, I need time to think this through.'

Tristan balled his hands into fists. He was not going to beg. She knew how he felt—how certain he had always been about her. But perhaps he had been wrong. After all the royal feathers he had ruffled, the conventions he had overturned, maybe Gemma did not have the strength and courage required to be his wife and a royal princess.

'Of course,' he said.

He bowed stiffly in her direction, turned on his heel and strode away from her.

Gemma watched Tristan walk away with that mix of military bearing and athletic grace she found so attractive. It struck her how resolute he looked, in the set of his shoulders, the strength of his stride.

He was walking out of her life.

Her hand went to her heart at the sudden shaft of pain.

What a massive mistake she had just made.

He must think she didn't care. And that couldn't be further from how she felt.

The truth hit her with a force that left her breathless. This wasn't about her not understanding the conventions of being a princess, being nervous of making the wrong kind of curtsy. It was about her fearing that she wasn't good enough for Tristan. Deep down, she was terrified he would discover her inadequacies and no longer want her. This was all about her being afraid of getting hurt. She had behaved like a spineless wimp. A spineless, *stupid* wimp.

Through all the time she'd shared with Tristan, fragmented as it had been, he had been unequivocal about what he felt for her. He had tricked her onto the *Argus* because he had been so taken with her. He had confessed to a *coup de foudre*. He had left her with his phone because he had wanted to stay in touch. *He had changed the law of his country so they could be together.*

It was *she* who had resisted him from the get go—she who had backed off. *She* who had insisted they break all contact. If he hadn't left those messages on the phone, would she have even found the courage to call him?

And now the man who was truly her once-in-a-lifetime love had left her. He was already out of sight.

She had to catch him—had to explain, had to beg for another chance. To prove to him she would be the best of all possible princesses for him.

But he was already gone.

She ran after him. Became hopelessly confused as she hit one dead end after the other. Clawed against a bolted gate in her frustration. Then she remembered the ancient walkway he had taken her to on that first afternoon. The place where he went to think.

She peered up at the battlement walls. Noted the slits through which his ancestors had shot their arrows. Noticed the steps that wound towards the walkway. And picked up her speed.

He was there. Standing in the same arched lookout where she'd stood, admiring that magnificent view of the lake. His hands were clasped behind his back, and he was very still.

It struck her how solitary he seemed in his dark business suit. How *lonely*. Tristan was considered one of the most eligible young men in the world. Handsome, charming, intelligent and kind. Yet all he wanted was her. And she had let him down.

She swore under her breath, realised she'd picked up a Montovian curse word. And that it hadn't been as quiet as she'd thought.

He whipped around. Unguarded, she saw despair on his face—and an anger he wasn't able to mask. Anger at *her*.

'Gemma. How did you find me here?'

What if he wouldn't forgive her?

'I followed my heart,' she said simply.

Without a word Tristan took the few steps to reach her and folded her in his arms. She burrowed against his chest and shuddered her deep, heartfelt relief. *This was where she belonged.*

Then she pulled back from his arms so she could look up into his face. 'Tristan, I'm so sorry. I panicked. Was afraid I'd let you down. I lost sight of what counts—us being together.'

'You can *learn* to be a princess. All the help you need is here. From me. From my sister…my mother. The people who only wish you happiness.'

'I can see that now. You stepped up to be crown prince. I can step up to be crown princess. *I can do it.* But, Tristan, I love you so much and—'

He put his hand over her mouth to silence her. 'Wait. Don't you remember when we were at your grandmother's cottage? You instructed me not to say the L word until I was able to propose.'

'I do remember.' Even then she'd been putting him off. She felt hot colour flush her cheeks. 'When it comes to proposing, is it within the Montovian royal code of conduct for the woman to do the asking?'

'There's nothing I know of that forbids it,' he said.

'Okay, then,' she said. 'I'll do it. Tristan, would you—?'

'Just because you *can* propose, it doesn't mean I want you to. This proposal is mine.'

'I'm willing to cede proposing rights to you,' she said. She spread out her hands in mock defeat.

He took them both in his, looked down into her face. Her heart turned over at the expression in the blue eyes that had so captivated her from the beginning.

'Gemma, I love you. I love you more than you can imagine. 'Will you be my wife, my princess, my queen? Will you marry me, Gemma?'

'Oh, yes, Tristan. *Yes* to wife. *Yes* to princess. *Yes* to queen. There is nothing I want more than to marry you and love you for the rest of my life.'

Tristan kissed her long and sweetly, and she clung to him. How could she ever have thought she could exist without him?

'There's one more thing,' he said.

He reached into his inner pocket and drew out a small velvet box.

She tilted her head to one side. 'I thought…'

'You thought what?'

'Natalia implied that part of the deal at the crown

prince's birthday is that he publicly slips the ring on his betrothed's finger.'

'It has always been the custom. But I'm the Prince of Change, remember? I *had* intended to follow the traditional way. Now I realise that proposing to you in front of an audience of strangers would be too overwhelming for you—and too impersonal. This is a private moment—*our* moment.'

He opened the box and took out an enormous, multicarat cushion-cut diamond ring. She gasped at its splendour.

'I ordered the ring as soon as my father agreed to change the rule about royals marrying outside the nobility. I never gave up hope that you would wear it.'

He picked up her left hand. She noticed his hand was less than steady as he slid the ring onto her third finger.

'I love you, Gemma Harper—soon to be Gemma, crown princess of Montovia.'

'More importantly, soon to be your wife,' she said.

She held up her hand, twisting and turning it so they could admire how the diamond caught the light.

'It's magnificent, and I shall never take it off,' she said. She paused. 'Natalia said it was customary to propose with the prince's grandmother's ring?'

'That's been the custom, yes,' he said. 'But I wanted to start our own tradition, with a ring that has significance only to us. Your ring. Our life. Our way of ruling the country when the time comes.'

'Already I see how I can take my place by your side.'

'*Playboy Prince Meets His Match*?' he said, his voice husky with happiness.

'*Mystery Redhead Finds Her Once-in-a-Lifetime Love*...' she murmured as she lifted her face for his kiss.

CHAPTER NINETEEN

As Gemma swept into the castle ballroom on Tristan's arm, she remembered what Natalia had told her. 'The more you look like a princess, the more you'll be treated like one.'

She knew she looked her best. But was it *princess* best?

The exquisite ballgown in shades of palest pink hugged her shape in a tight bodice, then flared out into tiers of filmy skirts bound with pink silk ribbon. Tiny crystals sewn randomly onto the dress gleamed in the light of the magnificent chandeliers under which guests were assembled to celebrate the crown prince's thirtieth birthday.

The dress was the most beautiful she had ever imagined wearing. She loved the way it swished around her as she walked. Where in Sydney would she wear such a gown? Back home she might devise the *menu* for a grand party like this—she certainly wouldn't be the crown prince's guest of honour. What was that old upstairs/downstairs thing? Through her engagement to Tristan—still unofficial—she had been rapidly elevated to the very top stair.

The dress was modest, its bodice topped with sheer silk chiffon and sleeves. Natalia had advised her that a princess of Montovia was expected to dress stylishly yet modestly. She must never attract attention for the wrong reasons, be the focus of critical press or be seen to reflect badly on the throne.

So many rules to remember. Would she ever be able to relax again?

'You are the most beautiful woman in the room,' Tristan murmured in her ear. 'There will be much envy when I announce you as my chosen bride.'

'As long as I'm the most beautiful woman in your eyes,' she murmured back.

'You will always be that,' he said.

The thing was, she believed him. She felt beautiful when she was with him—whether she was wearing a ball-gown or an apron.

Yet even knowing she looked like a princess in the glorious gown, with her hair upswept and diamonds borrowed from the queen—*she had borrowed jewellery from a queen!*—she still felt her stomach fall to somewhere near the level of her silver stilettoes when she looked into the room. So many people, so many strange faces, so much priceless jewellery.

So many critical eyes on her.

Would they see her as an interloper?

Immediately Tristan stepped closer. 'You're feeling intimidated, aren't you?'

She swallowed hard against a suddenly dry throat. 'Maybe,' she admitted.

In this glittering room, full of glittering people, she didn't know a soul except for Tristan and his family. And she was hardly on a first-name basis with the king and queen.

'Soon these faces will become familiar,' Tristan said. 'Yes, there are courtiers and officials and friends of my parents. But many of these guests are my personal friends—from school, the military, from university. They are so looking forward to meeting you.'

'That's good to hear,' she said, grateful for his consideration. Still, it was unnerving.

Thank heaven she hadn't been subjected to a formal receiving line. That would come at their formal engagement party, when she'd have the right to stand by Tristan's side as his fiancée. This was supposedly a more informal affair. With everyone wearing ballgowns and diamonds. Did Montovians actually *ever* do informal?

'Let me introduce you to someone I think you will like very much,' Tristan said.

He led her to a tall, thin, grey-haired man and his plump, cheery-faced wife. He introduced the couple as Henry and Anneke Blair.

'Henry was my English tutor,' Tristan said.

'And it was a privilege to teach you, Your Highness,' Henry said.

'Your English is perfect,' said Gemma.

'I was born and bred in Surrey, in the UK,' said Henry, with a smile that did not mock her mistake.

'Until he came to Montovia to climb mountains and fell in love with a local girl,' said his wife. 'Now he speaks perfect Montovian, too.'

Henry beamed down affectionately at his wife. So an outsider *could* fit in.

'Gemma is keen to learn Montovian,' said Tristan. 'We were hoping—'

'That I could tutor your lovely fiancée?' said Henry. He smiled at Gemma—a kind, understanding smile. 'It would be my pleasure.'

'And I would like very much to share with you the customs and history of the Montovian people,' said Anneke. 'Sometimes a woman's point of view is required.'

Gemma felt an immense sense of relief. She couldn't hope to fit in here, to gain the people's respect, if she couldn't speak the language and understand their customs. 'I would like lessons every day, please,' she said. 'I want to be fluent as soon as possible. And to understand the way Montovian society works.'

Tristan's smile told her she had said exactly the right thing.

Tristan had been right, Gemma thought an hour later. Already some of the faces in the crowd of birthday celebration guests were familiar. More importantly, she sensed a swell of goodwill towards her. Even among the older guests—whom she might have expected would want to adhere to the old ways—there was a sense that they cared for Tristan and wanted him to be happy. After so much tragedy in the royal family, it seemed the Montovians were hungry for a story with a happy ending and an excuse for gaiety and celebration.

She stood beside Tristan on a podium as he delivered a charming and witty speech about how he had fallen so hard for an Australian girl, he had worked to have the law changed so they could be together, only to find that she was of noble birth after all.

The audience obviously understood his reference to water nymphs better than she did, judging by the laughter. It was even more widespread when he repeated his speech in Montovian. She vowed that by the time his thirty-first birthday came around she would understand his language enough to participate.

She noticed the king had his head close to a tall, middle-aged woman, chatting to her with that air of familiarity only long-time couples had, and realised she must be his mistress. Elsewhere, the queen looked anxious in the company of a much younger dark-haired man. Even from where she stood, Gemma realised the man had a roving eye.

How many unhappy royal marriages had resulted from the old rules?

Then Tristan angled his body towards her as he spoke. 'It is the custom that if a crown prince of Montovia has not married by the age of thirty he is obliged to announce his engagement on the night of his birthday celebration. In fact, as you know, he is supposed to propose to his future bride in front of his assembled guests. I have once again broken with tradition. To me, marriage is about more than tradition and alliances. It is about love and a shared life and bringing children up out of the spotlight. I felt my future wife deserved to hear me ask for her hand in marriage in private.'

In a daze, Gemma realised she was not the only person in the room to blink away tears. Only now did she realise the full depth of what Tristan had achieved in this conservative society in order to ensure they could spend their lives together.

He took her hand in his and turned them back so they both faced the guests. The chandeliers picked up the facets in her diamond ring so it glinted into tiny shards of rainbow.

'May I present to you, my family and friends, my chosen bride: Gemma Harper-Clifford—future crown princess of Montovia.'

There was wild applause from an audience she suspected were usually rather more staid.

Her fiancé murmured to her. 'And, more importantly, my wife and the companion of my heart.'

'*Crown Prince Makes Future Bride Shed Tears of Joy…*' she whispered back, holding tightly to his hand, wanting never to let it go.

EPILOGUE

Three months later

IF TRISTAN HAD had his way, he would have married Gemma in the side chapel of the cathedral the day after he'd proposed to her.

However, his parents had invoked their roles as king and queen to insist that some traditions were sacrosanct and he would break them at his peril.

His mother had actually made mention of the medieval torture room in the dungeon—still intact and fully operational—should her son imagine he could elope or in any other way evade the grand wedding that was expected of him. And Tristan hadn't been 100 per cent certain she was joking.

A royal wedding on the scale that was planned for the joining in holy matrimony of Tristan, crown prince of Montovia, and Gemma Harper-Clifford, formerly of Sydney, Australia, would usually be expected to be a year in the planning.

Tristan had negotiated with all his diplomatic skills and open chequebook to bring down the planning time to three months.

But he had been so impatient with all the rigmarole required to get a wedding of this scale and calibre off the ground that Gemma had quietly taken it all away from him. She'd proceeded to organise the whole thing with remarkable efficiency and grace.

'I am a Party Queen, remember?' she'd said, flushed with a return of her old confidence. 'This is what I *do*. Only may I say it's a heck of a lot easier when the groom's family own both the cathedral where the service is to take place *and* the castle where the reception is to be held. Not to mention having a limitless budget.'

Now he stood at the high altar of the cathedral, dressed in the full ceremonial military uniform of his Montovian regiment, its deep blue tunic adorned with gold braid and fringed epaulettes. Across his chest he wore the gold-trimmed blue sash of the royal family and the heavy rows of medals and insignia of the crown prince.

Beside him stood his friend Jake Marlowe as his best man, two of his male cousins and an old school friend.

Tristan peered towards the entrance to the cathedral, impatient for a glimpse of his bride. She'd also invoked tradition and moved into his parents' apartment for the final three days before the day of their wedding. He had no idea what her dress—ordered on a trip to Paris she'd made with Natalia—would look like.

Seemed she'd also embraced the tradition of being ten minutes late for the ceremony...

Then he heard the joyous sound of ceremonial trumpets heralding the arrival of the bride, and his heart leapt. He was surprised it didn't set his medals jangling.

A tiny flower girl was the first to skip her way down the seemingly endless aisle, scattering white rose petals along the red carpet. Then Gemma's bridesmaids—his sister, Princess Natalia, Party Queens Andie and Eliza and Gemma's cousin Jane—each in gowns of a different pastel shade, glided down.

The trumpets sounded again, and the huge cathedral organ played the traditional wedding march. At last Gemma, flanked by her mother on one side and her Clifford grandfather on the other—both of whom were going to 'give her away'—started her slow, graceful glide down the aisle towards him.

Tristan didn't see the king and queen in the front pew,

nor the hundreds of guests who packed the cathedral, even though the pews were filled with family, friends and invited dignitaries from around the world, right down to the castle servants in the back rows. And the breathtaking flower arrangements might not have existed as far as Tristan was concerned.

All he saw was Gemma.

Her face was covered by a soft, lace-edged veil that fell to her waist at the front and at the back to the floor, to join the elaborate train that stretched for metres behind her, which was attended by six little girls from the cathedral school. Her full-skirted, long-sleeved dress was both magnificent and modest, as was appropriate for a Montovian bride. She wore the diamond tiara worn by all royal brides, and looked every inch the crown princess.

As she got closer he could see her face through the haze of the veil, and he caught his breath at how beautiful she was. Diamonds flashed at her ears—the king and queen's gift to her. And on her wrist was his gift to her—a diamond-studded platinum bracelet, from which hung a tiny platinum version of the wooden spoon she had wielded at their first meeting.

His bride.

The bride he had chosen and changed centuries of tradition for so he could ensure she would become his wife.

Tristan. There he was, waiting for her at the high altar, with the archbishop and the two bishops who would perform the ceremony behind him. She thought her heart would stop when she saw how handsome he looked in his ceremonial uniform. And the love and happiness that made his blue eyes shine bright was for her and only her. It was a particular kind of joy to recognise it.

She had never felt more privileged. Not because she was marrying into a royal family, but because she was joining her life with the man she loved. The *coup de foudre* of love at first sight for the mysterious Mr Marco had had undreamed-of repercussions.

She felt buoyed by goodwill and admiration for the way she was handling her new role in the royal family. And she was surrounded by all the people she loved and who loved her.

There was a gasp from the congregation when she made her vows in fluent Montovian. When Tristan slid the gold band onto her ring finger, and she and the man she adored were pronounced husband and wife, she thought her heart would burst from happiness.

After the service they walked down the aisle as a new royal couple to the joyful pealing of the cathedral bells. They came out onto the top of the steps of the cathedral to a volley of royal cannons being fired—which, Gemma could not help thinking, was something she had never encountered at a wedding before. And might not again until their own children got married.

Below them the town square was packed with thousands of well-wishers, who cheered and threw their hats in the air. *Their subjects.* It might take a while for an egalitarian girl from Australia to truly grasp the fact that she had *subjects*, but Tristan would help her with all the adjustments she would have to make in the years to come. With Tristan by her side, she could face anything.

Tension was building in the crowd below them and in the guests who had spilled out of the cathedral behind them. The first royal kiss of the newly wed prince and his princess was what they wanted.

She looked up at Tristan, saw his beloved face smiling down at her. They kissed.

The crowd erupted, and she was almost blinded by the lights from a multitude of camera flashes. They kissed again, to the almost hysterical delight of the crowd. A third kiss and she was almost deafened by the roar of approval.

Tristan had warned her that lip-readers would be planted in the audience, to see what they might say to each other in this moment. Why not write the headlines for them?

'*Prince Weds Party Planner*?' Tristan whispered.

'*And They Live Happily Ever After...*' she murmured as, together with her husband, she turned to wave to the crowd.

* * * * *

Travis tipped her chin up, drew his thumb along Kate's lower lip.

"I know you need more time. I won't push you. But while you're weighing the pros and cons, don't forget to include this in your calculations."

He lowered his head, giving her time to draw back, feeling the jolt when she didn't. At the first brush of his mouth on hers, hunger too long held in check kicked like an afterburner at full thrust. The heat, the fury burned like a blowtorch.

His palm slid to the nape of her neck. His mouth went from gentle to coaxing. From giving to taking. He circled her waist, drew her into him. They were hip to hip, thigh to thigh, her breasts pressed against his chest, her palms easing over his shoulders.

This was what he needed. What he'd ached for. The feel of her. The taste of her.

* * *

Three Coins in the Fountain:
When you wish upon your heart…

"I DO"...
TAKE TWO!

BY
MERLINE LOVELACE

First Published in Great Britain 2016
By Mills & Boon, an imprint of HarperCollins*Publishers*
1 London Bridge Street, London, SE1 9GF

© 2016 Merline Lovelace

ISBN: 978-0-263-91968-4

23-0316

Our policy is to use papers that are natural, renewable and recyclable products and made from wood grown in sustainable forests.The logging and manufacturing processes conform to the legal environmental regulations of the country of origin.

Printed and bound in Spain
by CPI, Barcelona

A career air force officer, **Merline Lovelace** served at bases all over the world. When she hung up her uniform for the last time, she decided to try her hand at storytelling. Since then, more than twelve million copies of her books have been published in over thirty countries. Check her website at www.merlinelovelace.com or friend Merline on Facebook for news and information about her latest releases.

To my own handsome hero,
who's explored Italy with me from tip to toe.
What great memories we've made, my darling…
with so many more to come!

Chapter One

"C'mon, Kate. We have to do it."

"No, we don't."

Katherine Elizabeth Westbrook—Kate to the two friends tugging her through the crowd lined up at one of Rome's most famous landmarks—dragged her feet. The water spouting from the Trevi Fountain's gloriously baroque sculptures glistened in the late August sunshine, but Kate had no inclination to participate in the time-honored tradition of tossing a coin in the sparkling pool.

"This is too touristy for words."

"No, it's not." Vivacious, auburn-haired Dawn McGill dismissed Kate's protest with an airy wave. "We've talked about doing this for*ever*."

"Remember the first time we watched *Three Coins in the Fountain*?"

That came from Callie Langston, the quiet one of the

unbreakable triumvirate forged more than twenty years
ago, when eight-year-old Kate and her family moved to
the small town of Easthampton, Massachusetts.

Callie's reminder of that long-ago sleepover won a
smile from Kate. "How could I forget?"

They'd been friends for years by then, all three hope-
less romantics and avid movie buffs. In that particular all-night extravaganza, they'd devoured pizza and
Twinkies and a gallon of triple ripple mocha fudge
while bingeing on rented movie classics.

Callie had chosen the 1940 megahit *The Philadel-
phia Story*, which had the three teens drooling over a
debonair Cary Grant. Dawn had opted for Audrey Hep-
burn and Humphrey Bogart in *Sabrina*, a sparkling romance that provoked laughter and tears and a burning
desire to run off to Paris. Kate had gone with the 1954
version of *Three Coins in the Fountain*, starring Doro-
thy McGuire and a dreamy Louis Jourdan as a playboy
Italian prince. The story of three single women finding
love and adventure in Rome made all three girls vow
that one day they, too, would visit the Eternal City and
toss a coin in its famed fountain.

Kate had loved the movie. Then. Back when she
was young and naive and stupid enough to believe in
happy endings.

"The wish won't come true unless all three of us do
it," the irrepressible Dawn insisted.

"That's right," Callie chimed in. "All for one…"

"…and one for all." Kate dredged up another smile.
"Okay, okay! Who's got a coin I can bum?"

"Here."

Dawn thrust a euro into her friend's left hand. It was
dull and tarnished and banded by a rim of brass. Soon

to be replaced, Kate knew from her work at the World Bank, by a newer, shinier model.

Out with the old, in with the new.

Like her life, she thought, although her new was uncertain and her old hurt almost more than she could bear. Her fist closed around the euro while images cut through her mind like shards of jagged glass. Of Travis roaring up to her college dorm on his decrepit but much-loved Harley. Their engagement the day she'd pinned his air force pilot's wings on his uniform. The wedding two years later that Kate and her two friends had planned in such excruciating detail. The much-dreamed-of trip to Italy that she and her husband had been forced to put off repeatedly while he rotated in and out of Afghanistan and Iraq and a dozen other locales he couldn't tell her about.

The irony of it ate at Kate as she remembered the hours she'd spent planning this dream trip. She remembered, too, all the days she'd buried herself in her own work to dull her gnawing worry about her husband. And the long, empty nights she'd tossed and turned and prayed for his safe return from whatever hot spot he'd been sent to this time.

Now here they were. She and Major Travis Westbrook. In Italy! Separated by only a few hours' train ride. The sad part was that Kate hadn't even *known* her soon-to-be ex was operating out of the NATO base near Venice until she'd talked to his mother just before she and Dawn and Callie had left for their Roman Holiday.

Venice might lie only a few hours north of Rome, but the distance between Kate and Travis couldn't be bridged. Not now, not ever. They'd said too many painful goodbyes and spent too much time apart. They'd also grown into different people. Travis, according to the Facebook post his wife had obviously *not* been intended to see, more so than her.

"Make a wish," Dawn urged. "Then toss the coin over your shoulder."

"You don't have to make a wish," Callie corrected in her calm way. "It's implicit in the act. Throwing a coin in the fountain means you'll return to Rome someday."

Kate barely heard her two friends. Fist clenched, eyes squeezed shut, she let her subconscious spew out the anger and hurt that came from deep in her gut.

I wish... I wish... Dammit all to hell! I wish the bitch-whore who bragged on Facebook about having an affair with my husband would develop a world-class case of...whatever!

She flung up her arm and let fly. Not even the water gushing through the fountain's many spigots could drown out the loud thunk as the euro bounced off the basin's rim, or the amusement in the deep drawl that sounded from just behind her.

"You never could throw worth a damn, Katydid."

Her arm froze in the middle of its downward arc. Disbelief jolted through her even as something hot and wild balled in her belly. She couldn't move, couldn't breathe. Her frantic gaze shot to her two friends. Dawn's ferocious scowl was as telling as the mask of icy disapproval that dropped instantly over Callie's face. Kate closed her eyes. Sucked in a shuddering breath. Forced herself to turn slowly, deliberately. Her initial reaction to the first sight of her husband in more than four months was purely instinctive. Bunching her fists, she refused to yield to the all-too-familiar worry over the tired lines webbing his hazel eyes. Refused, as well, to let any trace of anger or hurt seep into her voice.

"Hello, Travis. Your mom must have told you that I finally made it to Rome."

"She did."

Those changeable green-brown eyes drifted over her face and lingered on her mouth. For an incredulous moment Kate thought he might actually try to kiss her. Flashing a warning, she took a half step back.

Dawn and Callie must have read the same intent. They moved simultaneously, one to either side of Kate. Travis's glance moved from Dawn's scowl to Callie's set mouth.

Was that regret that flickered across his face? Or a trace of the amused wariness he'd always insisted he had to pull on like a Kevlar vest when confronted by the trio he'd dubbed the Invincibles? The look came and went so quickly, Kate couldn't tell.

"Rome's a big city." She managed to maintain an even tone, but the effort made her throat cramp. "How did you find us?"

The amusement surfaced. No question about it now. And with it came the crooked grin that had curled her toes inside her black suede boots the first time he'd aimed it her way.

Memories slapped at her again. The gray, blustery November day, the cold wind biting at her cheeks, the icicles hanging like frozen tears from the eaves. Kate and Callie and Dawn had bundled up and were just heading out to the mall when Dawn's older brother pulled into the drive. All three girls had gone goggle-eyed when Aaron introduced the roommate he'd brought home for Thanksgiving.

Although Travis's cheery hello had encompassed the three friends equally, he'd soon cut Kate out of the herd. She'd been a sophomore at Boston College at the time, he a senior at the University of Massachusetts in Amherst. All it took was two dates that magical Thanksgiving vacation. Just two. Then she...

"Finding you wasn't hard."

Her husband's reply jerked her back to the here and now.

"You told me often enough that tossing a coin in the Trevi Fountain topped your to-do list for Rome." He hooked a thumb toward a busy café on the other side of the piazza. "So I staked out a table and waited for you to show."

She hadn't told his mom where she was staying. Hadn't told anyone except her assistant, and David knew better than to divulge her itinerary. Kate wasn't that high up the banking world, but she'd negotiated several multibillion-dollar deals and had recently been featured as one of five up-and-comers on a prominent financial website. Common sense—and her bank's director of security—had advised her to maintain a low profile while traveling abroad. Trust Travis to have tracked her down.

"How long have you been waiting?" she asked with reluctant curiosity.

"Since early morning."

Dawn gave a surprised huff. "You anchored a table in this crowded tourist mecca *all day*? That must have cost a few euros."

"Only enough to feed a family of four for a week. But..." His glance swung back to Kate. "It was worth every euro."

Dammit! How did he do it? A grin, a shared glance, and she was almost ready to forget her angry wish of a few moments ago. Almost.

The bitterness that had spawned it came back, leaving a sour taste in her mouth and a ragged hole in her heart. "You wasted your money, Trav. We said all we needed to when we met with the lawyer."

"Not hardly." The smile left his eyes. "I was served with divorce papers the day after I returned from a classified mission. The meeting with the attorney was set for less than a week later."

"At which point you evoked the Soldiers' and Sailors' Civil Relief Act to delay the proceedings for another ninety days!"

"Only because you—"

He broke off and blew out a slow breath. With a nod that encompassed the elbow-to-elbow tourists cocooning them in a bubble of noise and laughter, he tried again.

"Cm'on, Kate. Let me at least buy you a glass of vino. All of you," he added belatedly.

"You bet your booty all of us," Dawn shot back.

"And only if Kate feels inclined to accept your invitation," Callie put in coolly but no less adamantly.

The Invincibles ride again.

Their united front didn't surprise Travis any more than their fierce protectiveness. He'd known from day one that Kate and her two friends were closer than most sisters. Different personalities, different family backgrounds, but so many shared interests and experiences that they could finish each other's sentences.

And as different as they were physically, each one spelled trouble for the male of the species. With her auburn hair, vivacious personality and lush curves, Dawn drew men like a magnet. Callie was quieter, more reserved, the kind of attentive listener who made men think they were a whole lot smarter than they really were.

But it was Kate who'd sparked his interest that snowy

November day. She'd been bundled into a bulky jacket, her brown eyes barely visible above the scarf muffling the lower half of her face, her curly blond hair streaming from a colorful knit stocking cap.

Her lower half hadn't been as bulked up as the upper half. Her snug jeans had given Travis plenty of opportunity to admire world-class legs above calf-high black suede boots, trim hips and a nice little butt. Yet he'd sensed instantly the whole was so much more than the sum of those enticing parts. Maybe it was the intelligence in those cinnamon-brown eyes. Or the smile when she nudged the scarf down with her chin. Or the way she countered Aaron's teasing with a quick quip.

Whatever it was, by the time Travis headed back to UMass, he was halfway in love and all the way in lust. He'd plunged in the rest of the way in the two years that followed, a hectic time crammed with weekend visits to either his campus or hers and shared summer adventures. Then had come USAF officer training school, followed by the thrill of being accepted for flight school. When Kate flew down to pin on his air force pilot's wings, he'd capped the ceremony with an engagement ring. Between her grad school and his follow-on flight training, it had been another two years before he slid the matching diamond-studded wedding band on her finger.

He'd caught the sparkle of that band when she tossed the coin a few minutes ago. The sight had given him a visceral satisfaction that sliced deep. His rational mind understood a wedding band was merely a symbol. A more primal male instinct viewed it as something more primitive, more possessive. Kate of the laughing brown eyes and lively mind was his mate, his woman, the only one he'd ever wanted to share his life with. And knowing she still wore his ring only intensified Travis's determination to see she didn't take it off.

That would take some doing. He couldn't deny their marriage had hit the skids. He knew his frequent deployments had strained it to the breaking point. Knew, too, that he hadn't sent a strong enough *hands off* signal to the young captain who'd mistaken his interest in her career for something a lot more personal. Travis still kicked himself for not handling that situation with more finesse. Especially since she'd reacted to his rejection by putting a fanciful but too-close-to-the-truth post about her involvement with a certain sexy C-130 pilot on Facebook.

He'd had no excuse for letting the captain get so close in the first place. None that Kate had bought, anyway. And it didn't help that his wife's intelligence and quick smile came packaged with a stubborn streak that would make a Kentucky mule look like a wuss in comparison. She took her time and weighed all factors before making a major decision. Once she did, however, that was it. Period. *Finito.* Done.

Not this time, he swore fiercely. Not this time.

Under Massachusetts law, a divorce didn't become final until three months after issuance of a nisi judgment. That gave Travis exactly two weeks to breach the chasm caused by so many separations and one exercise of monumental stupidity. Determined to win back the wife he still ached for, he issued a challenge he knew she wouldn't refuse.

"Too scared to share a bottle of wine, sweetheart?"

"What do you think?"

The disdainful lift of her brows told him she knew exactly what he was doing, but Travis held his ground.

"What I think," he returned, "is that we should get

out of this crowd and enjoy the really excellent chianti I have waiting."

The raised brows came together in a frown. Catching her lower lip between her teeth, Kate debated for several moments before turning to her friends.

"Why don't you two go on to the Piazza Navona? I'll catch up with you there. Or," she amended with a glance at the shadows creeping down the columned facade behind the fountain, "back at the hotel."

"We shouldn't separate," Callie protested. "Rome's a big city, and a woman alone makes a tempting target."

Travis blinked. Damned if the slender brunette hadn't just impugned his manhood, his combat skills and his ability to fend off pickpockets and mashers.

"She won't be alone," he said drily. "And I think I can promise to keep her out of the line of fire."

"Riiiight." The redhead on Kate's other side bristled. "And we all know what your promises are worth, Westbrook."

Jaw locked, he heroically refrained from suggesting that a woman who'd left two grooms stranded at the altar probably shouldn't sling stones. His wife read the signs, though, and hastily intervened.

"It's okay," Kate told her self-appointed guard dogs. "Travis and I can remain civil long enough to share a glass of wine. Maybe. Go on. I'll see you at the hotel."

The still-aggressive Dawn would have argued the issue, but Callie tugged her arm. The redhead settled for giving Travis a final watch-yourself glare before yielding the field.

"Whew," he murmured as the two women wove through the crowd. "Good thing neither of them was armed. I'd be gut shot right now."

"You're not out of danger yet. I haven't had to resort

to any of the lethal moves you taught me to take down an attacker. There's always that first instance, however."

Travis figured this wasn't the time or place to admit those training sessions had generated some of his most erotic memories. He couldn't count the number of times he'd bedded down in yet another godforsaken dump of an airstrip and treated himself to the mental image of his wife in skintight spandex, sweaty and scowling and determined to wrestle him to the mat.

"I'll try not to become your first victim," he said as she started toward the café.

Without thinking, he put a hand to the small of her back to guide her through the milling crowd. As light as it was, the touch stopped Kate in her tracks. He smothered a curse and removed his hand.

"Sorry. Force of habit."

Kate dipped her chin in a curt nod. One she sincerely hoped gave no clue of the wildly contradictory emotions generated by the courteous and once-welcome gesture.

Swallowing hard, she threaded a path through the crowd. His innate courtesy was one of the character traits she'd treasured in her husband. He'd grown up in a grimy Massachusetts mill town still struggling to emerge from its sweatshop past. Yet his fiercely determined mother had managed to blunt the rough edges he'd had to develop to survive in the gang-ridden town. In the process, she'd instilled an almost Victorian set of manners. A full scholarship to UMass followed by his introduction to the hallowed traditions of the air force officer ranks had added more layers of polish.

And there was another irony, Kate mused as her husband held out a chair for her at one of the rickety tables set under a green-and-white-striped awning. The magna cum laude grad and the thoughtful, courteous gentleman seemed to have no problem coexisting with the gladiator honed by street brawls and the brutal training he'd gone through to become a special operations pilot.

The thought spawned another, one that made her chest hurt as she waited for Travis to claim his seat. Loyalty was another character trait she'd always believed went bone-deep in her husband. He was part of an elite cadre chosen to fly the HC-130J, the latest version of the venerable Hercules transport that performed yeoman service in the Vietnam War. Dubbed the Combat King II, this modern-day, technically sophisticated version of the Herc was the only dedicated personnel recovery platform in the air force inventory. That meant it could fly high over extended distances with air-to-air refueling or go in low and slow to drop, land or recover special operations teams.

Most of the Combat King crew members Kate met over the years were too macho to spout platitudes about the brotherhood of arms or the bonds forged by battle. They didn't have to. The racks of ribbons decorating their service uniforms said it for them. Was it that closeness, the exclusivity of the war fighters' world, that had prompted Travis to take such a personal interest in Captain Diane Chamberlain? He swore it was. Swore he'd only intended to mentor the bright young communications officer.

Kate had ached to believe him. If she hadn't been all too aware of the unwritten rule that what happened when deployed, stayed deployed... If his ambitious protégée hadn't included those graphic details in her Facebook post... If Kate and Trav hadn't already drifted so far apart...

And that, she'd admitted—to him and to herself, when she'd worked through the initial anger and hurt—was the real crux of the matter. Their careers had taken them down such different paths. His from a brand-new pilot with shiny wings to a commander of battle-hardened air crews. Hers from a starting job as a foreign accounts manager at a Bank of America branch to the Washington, DC, headquarters of the World Bank.

Now here they were. Four years of tumultuous courtship and five years of marriage later. Near strangers sharing a tiny table in the city they'd always planned to explore together. As Travis tipped wine from the waiting bottle into dark green glasses, Kate let her gaze drift from the gloriously baroque Trevi Fountain to the tall earth-toned hotels and residences ringing the piazza's other three sides.

"I can't believe we're really in Rome," she murmured.

"Took us long enough to get here."

The rueful acknowledgment drew her gaze from the vibrant scene to her husband. She searched his face, seeing again the weariness etched into the white squint lines at the corners of his eyes. Seeing, too, the scatter of silver in the dark chestnut hair he always kept regulation short.

She couldn't help herself. Before she even realized what she was doing, she reached across the tiny table and feathered a finger along his temple. "Is this gray I see?"

"It is. Helluva note when heredity and the job conspire to make you an old man at thirty-two."

Her gaze dropped to the muscled shoulders molded by his blue Oxford shirt. Its open collar showcased the strong column of his neck, the rolled-up sleeves his tanned forearms. Withdrawing her hand, she sat back and accepted the wine he passed her with a reluctant smile.

"You're not totally decrepit yet, Major Westbrook."

"You, either, Ms. Westbrook. Does it violate the ground rules of our truce if I say that you look damned good for a senior investment accounts officer?"

"Make that executive investments accounts officer. I was promoted two months ago."

"Who died?"

The long-standing joke drew a chuckle. It was a more or less accepted axiom in the banking community that a manager only moved up when a superior keeled over at his or her desk.

Thankfully Kate hadn't had to step over any corpses to reach her present position. Her undergraduate degree in business management from Boston College and a master's in international finance and economic policy from Columbia had given her an edge in the race to the top. That and the fact that she'd begun her career at Bank of America. With BOA's diversity of services and global reach, she'd been able to snag positions of increasing responsibility each time Travis transferred to a new base.

"No one that I know of," she answered.

"Good to hear." Mugging an expression of profound relief, he lifted his glass. "Here's to the World Bank's smartest and best-looking executive investments accounts officer."

She clinked her glass to his, surprised and secretly grateful for the easy banter. She still hadn't quite recovered from the shock of his unexpected appearance in Rome. Although...

She swirled the chianti inside her mouth for a moment, ostensibly to savor the rich, robust flavors of blueberry and clove. Not so ostensibly to deliver a swift mental kick.

She should have at least *considered* the possibility Travis would track her down. Especially since they'd planned and canceled a trip to Italy so many times that it, too, became a long-standing joke. Then an annoyance. Then one more casualty of their crumbling marriage.

"So how are you liking Washington?"

She let the wine slide down her throat and answered carefully. "So far, so good."

Long, agonizing hours had gone into her decision to accept the job at the World Bank. Travis had agreed it was a fantastic opportunity, too good to pass up. He'd also acknowledged that they'd put his career ahead of hers up to that point. What neither of them could admit was that her move to DC had signaled the beginning of the end.

Even then they'd tried to make it work. He'd flown in between deployments for short visits. She'd zipped down to Florida for the ceremony awarding him the Silver Star—despite the fact his plane had taken hits from intense antiaircraft fire, Travis and his crew had managed a daring extraction of a navy SEAL team pinned down and about to be overrun. An air force general and a navy admiral had both been present at the ceremony. Each had commented on how proud Kate must be of her husband.

She was! So proud she often choked up when she tried to describe what he did to outsiders. Pride was cold comfort, though, when he grabbed his go kit and took off for another short-notice rotation to Afghanistan or Somalia or some other war-ravaged, disease-stricken area of operations.

Then there were the ops he couldn't tell her about. Highly classified and often even more dangerous. Like, she guessed a moment later, the present one. She got her first clue when he glossed over her question about how long he'd be in Italy.

"We're not sure. Could be another month, could be more. What about you? How long are you staying?"

"I fly home on the twentieth."

He cocked his head. "Two days after our divorce becomes final."

"Dawn and Callie thought it would be easier to... That is, I wanted to..." She played with her glass, swirling the dark red chianti, and dug deep for a smile. "I couldn't think of a better distraction than touring Italy with the two of them."

"How about touring it with me?"

Her hand jerked, almost slopping wine over the edge of the glass. "What?"

"I owe you this trip, Kate. Let me make good on that debt."

"You can't be serious!"

"Yeah, I am."

Stunned, she shook her head. "We're too far down the road, Trav. We can't backtrack now."

"True." He leaned forward into a slanting beam of sunlight, so close and intent she could see the gold flecks in his hazel eyes. "But we *can* take some time to see if there's enough left to try a different track."

"That's crazy. All we'll do is open ourselves up to more hurt when we say goodbye."

"No, Kate, we won't. Despite Dawn's snide comment a few minutes ago, I hold to my word." Reaching across the table, he curled a knuckle under her chin. "When and if we say goodbye, I promise you won't regret this time together."

Chapter Two

"Kate!" Dismay chased across Dawn's expressive face. "Tell me you're not actually going to traipse off with the man!"

"I said I'd consider it."

"But…but…"

"I know," Kate admitted with a grimace. "The whole idea of this trip was to help me remember there's a big, wide world out there that doesn't have to include Travis Westbrook."

"Now you want to narrow it down again?"

"Maybe. For a week. Or not. I don't know."

The less-than-coherent reply had Dawn swiveling on the crimson brocade sofa lavishly trimmed with gold rope. It was one of two plush sofas in the sitting room of their suite at the five-star Rome Cavalieri. A member of the Waldorf chain, the hotel sat perched on fifteen acres of private parkland overlooking the Eternal City.

With its elegant decor, breath-stealing view of St. Peter's Basilica in the near distance and shuttle service to the heart of Rome, the Cavalieri provided a home base of unparalleled luxury and convenience. The stunning vista framed by the doors of their suite's balcony was the last thing on the minds of anyone at the moment, however.

Ignoring the city lights twinkling like fireflies in the purple twilight, Dawn made an urgent appeal. "Talk to her, Callie. Remind her how many times she and Travis tried to bridge the gap. When he was home long enough to do any bridging, that is."

"She doesn't need reminding. She knows the count better than we do. And God knows you and I haven't scored any better in the love-and-marriage game."

Dawn scrunched her nose at the unwelcome reminder while Callie searched their friend's face. "Which way are you leaning? Yea or nay?"

Sighing, Kate unclipped her hair and raked a hand through the sun-streaked blond spirals. She kept intending to get the shoulder-length curls cut, maybe have them tamed into a sleek bob. Another manifestation of the new Kate Westbrook, like the tailored suits she'd invested in for her move to the World Bank and the two-bedroom condo she'd rented in DC.

"I keep swinging back and forth," she admitted. "My head says it would be a monumental mistake. If I think of it in terms of a return on investment, I can't see how a few days together will alter the long-term viability of our marriage. Not unless we introduce some new variables into the equation."

"Forget equations and investment returns," Callie urged. "Don't think like a banker. Think like a wife who has to decide whether she wants to give her husband one last chance. It's that simple."

"No, it isn't! You and Dawn figure into the equation, too. I can't desert you at the very start of our vacation."

"Sure you can. Granted, it won't be anywhere near as much fun without you. I suspect we'll manage to keep ourselves entertained, though."

"But I planned our itinerary in such detail." Of all the iterations of this trip Kate had devised over the years, this was the most elaborate. "I've laid out all the train schedules, subway maps, museum hours, hotel locations."

"Dawn and I are big girls. We can get ourselves from point A to point B. Can't we?"

"I guess."

With that reluctant concession, Dawn shoved off the sofa and skirted a coffee table topped with what seemed like an acre of black marble to plop down beside Kate. Tucking one leg under her, she reached for Kate's hand and threaded their fingers.

"Much as I hate to admit it, Callie's right. Rambling around Italy won't be nearly as much fun without you. But she'll get us where we need to go, and I'll do my damnedest to hook us up with a couple of studly Fabios. So don't factor us into your equation. All you have to do is decide whether you want to give Travis another chance to break your heart."

"Oh, well, when you put it that way…"

"Dawn, for heaven's sake!"

With an exasperated laugh, Callie joined them on the sofa. Wiggling her bottom, she wedged in on Kate's other side and grasped her free hand.

They'd huddled together like this so many times as young girls to watch TV or giggle over the silliness of boys. As teens, to whisper secrets and weave dreams.

As women, to share their joys and heartaches. More heartache in the past few years, it seemed, than joy.

"It sounds to me as though your head and your heart are pulling you in opposite directions," Callie said quietly. "So my advice, girlfriend, is to go with your gut."

When the three women went down to dinner, Travis was seated at a table in the Cavalieri's gorgeously landscaped outdoor restaurant. Hurricane lamps flickered, the tables were draped in snowy linen and tall-stemmed crystal goblets gleamed. The floodlit dome of St. Peter's Basilica looming against a star-studded sky a mile or so away took the setting out of the realm of sophisticated and straight into magical.

Kate suspected her husband would have preferred she deliver her answer to his outrageous proposal in private. Callie and Dawn had made no attempt to conceal their animosity at the Trevi Fountain, and Travis had to know they would be even less thrilled over the possibility Kate might abandon them. No special ops pilot would ever turn tail and run in the face of the enemy, however. Whatever her decision, he would take his licks.

Pushing his chair back, he rose as a hostess escorted the three women to the table. He'd topped his jeans and blue Oxford shirt with the gray suede sport coat that Kate knew packed easily and wore well. All he needed was a salon tan and a leather shoulder satchel slung over the back of his chair to fit right in with the casually sophisticated European males in the restaurant.

Kate, too, had dressed for the occasion in the caramel-colored slacks and matching hip-length jacket she'd bought especially for this trip. Made of a slinky, packable knit, the outfit could be dressed up with the black silk camisole she now wore or down with a cotton tank and chunky wooden necklace. The appreciative gleam in her husband's eyes as he seated her said he approved of her new purchase.

No surprise there, she thought ruefully as he and the hostess seated Callie and Dawn. Travis had pretty much approved of anything and everything Kate pulled on, from cutoffs and baggy T-shirts to tailored business suits to the strapless, backless gown in screaming red she'd bought for one of their formal military functions. He'd approved of that sinful creation even more, she remembered with a jolt low in her belly, when he'd discovered how easy it was to remove.

Oh, God! Burying her suddenly tight fists in her lap, she was asking herself for the twentieth time if she really wanted to put them both through all the hurt again when Travis reclaimed his seat.

"Almost like old times," he said with a cautious smile.

"Which times?" Dawn oozed honey-coated acid. "Before or after you got up close and cuddly with your little captain?"

Callie winced. Kate's nails dug deeper into her palms. Travis folded his elbows on the table and took the knife thrust head-on.

"Okay, I know Kate shared that Facebook business with you two. I'm sure she also shared my pathetic defense. I'll state it once more, for the record. And only once."

His eyes as hard and flat as agates, he held Dawn's glare.

"I *did* spend time with Captain Chamberlain talking goals and career paths. More than I should have, obviously. I did *not*, however, touch, kiss or otherwise indicate I wanted to have sex with her. Nor did I have any idea she'd posted those pictures of me sweaty and stripped to the waist."

Fairness compelled Kate to intervene before blood was spilled. "They were taken during a volleyball match between aircrews. Travis sent me the uncropped versions later, after..."

She lifted a hand, let it drop. No need to bring all the ugliness into this starlit night. She'd got past it. Mostly.

"After the crap hit the fan," he finished when she didn't. "Now do you think you can sheathe your claws long enough for us to have dinner, Dawn?"

"I can try. But I'm not making any promises."

Surprisingly, the snarky reply took some of the stiffness out of his shoulders.

"Actually," he said gruffly, "I asked Kate to let me buy the three of you dinner for a specific purpose. I want to thank you, Dawn. And you, Callie. You stood shoulder to shoulder with her all these months. I'm more grateful than I can say she had you to turn to."

Dawn blinked, and even Callie was surprised into a semithaw. "It hasn't been easy for you, either," she replied. "We know that. And we want you to know we're good with whatever Kate's decided to do for the rest of her stay in Italy."

"Yeah, well, I want to talk about that, too."

Their server arrived at that point to take their drink orders. The women opted for the Italian classic Bellini, Travis for a scotch rocks. He waited for the server to retreat before laying his cards on the table.

"I know I'm putting a major dent in your plans by asking Kate to spend this time with me. I'd like to make up for it by proposing an alternative to your itinerary, too."

Kate had to bite back an instinctive protest. All her

work, all the timetables and reservations and prepaid museum passes stored in her iPhone, appeared to be going up in a puff of smoke right before her eyes.

"As Kate may have mentioned, I'm on temporary assignment to the NATO base up near Venice. I'm working with a project involving several of our closest allies, one of whom is an Italian Special Ops pilot."

"So?"

Dawn wasn't giving an inch. Travis took her belligerence in stride and continued. "So Carlo's family owns a villa in Tuscany. He says it's within easy driving distance of Florence and Siena and on the fast train line to Milan and Venice. He also says the villa is currently vacant but fully staffed. It's yours if you want to make it your home base for the next week or so."

"Sounds wonderful," Dawn admitted, surprised out of her hostility by the generous offer, "but the hotel here in Rome was our big splurge. We can't afford to spring for a fully staffed villa."

Actually, *she* could. Since Kate regularly advised her on various mutual funds and investments, she knew precisely how much her friend raked in each year as a graphic designer for a Fortune 500 health-and-fitness firm in Boston. She might come across as bubbly and carefree, but she was damned good at her job and had invested wisely.

Callie was a different story, however. She'd walked away from her job as a children's ombudsman with the Massachusetts Office of the Child Advocate just weeks before this Roman holiday. After watching how the heartbreak of the cases she had to adjudicate shredded her emotions, both Dawn and Kate had cheered the decision. They'd also offered to pay her share of expenses for the trip, which she'd adamantly refused.

Still, they suspected she'd had to dip into her savings, and neither wanted her to dig deeper.

Then Travis made it clear she wouldn't have to. "Actually, there would be no charge. Carlo commands one of Italy's crack special ops units. He and I took part in a joint mission some months back, and he now thinks he owes me."

"For what?" Dawn wanted to know.

"Nothing worth writing home about."

Although he dodged the question with a careless shrug, a familiar pressure built in Kate's chest. The American media gave scant coverage to forces from other countries engaged in the war on terror, but she knew troops from dozens of different nations were engaged in the life-and-death struggle. They, like Travis and his crews, put their lives on the line every day.

If this Italian major thought her husband owed him, the joint mission they'd participated in had to have been hairy as hell. Kate's chest squeezed again as she tried *not* to imagine the scenario.

Their server arrived at that point with the three Bellinis and a crystal tumbler of scotch. When she'd served the drinks, Travis picked up where he'd left off.

"So what do you think? Want to spend an all-expense-paid week in Tuscany?"

"That depends on what Kate's decided."

Three questioning faces turned her way. She looked at them blankly for a moment while she tried to factor this unexpected bonus for her friends into an equation made even more complicated by the stress of knowing Travis and this Italian commando had shared what she guessed had been a life-and-death situation. Torn, she took Callie's advice and went with her gut.

"I think you should take this guy… What's his name?"

"Carlo."

"I think you should take Carlo up on his offer." Her gaze turned to her husband. "And I'll take you up on yours."

Dinner went reasonably well after that. The tantalizing prospect of a week in a Tuscan villa with a full staff to see to her needs blunted the sharpest edges of Dawn's antagonism. Kate knew the fiery redhead would snatch up the sword again in a heartbeat, though. So would Callie. Kate would have loved them for that no-questions-asked, just-let-us-at-him support even if the three of them weren't already bonded by so many years of BFF-hood. She loved Travis, too, for setting them up so comfortably.

The insidious thought sneaked in before she could block it.

Damn! Had he preplanned this whole maneuver—leveraged whatever debt this guy Carlo owed him to preempt Kate's nagging guilt over abandoning her friends? Was he that focused, that determined to achieve his objective?

Oh, yeah. Absolutely. Major Travis Westbrook never skimmed down a runway and lifted off without extensive preflight planning. Nor would he hesitate to deploy all available countermeasures to deflect or defeat enemy fire. Still, Kate had to admit he'd orchestrated a pretty impressive op plan for separating his primary target from its outer defenses.

Travis texted Carlo between drinks and dinner to let him know Ms. Dawn McGill and Ms. Callie Langston would arrive at his family's villa the day after tomorrow, assuming it was still available. The Italian Air Force officer texted back confirming availability. The same text provided both directions and the code for the front gate.

Travis shot them to Callie's and Dawn's cell phones before the four of them settled in for a truly remarkable meal. Abandoning any inclination to count either carbs or calories, Kate ordered a grilled-peach-and-buffalo-mozzarella salad followed by a main course of lobster ravioli in a sinfully rich cream sauce.

She would have quit at that point if Dawn hadn't talked her into sharing a spun-sugar-and-limoncello confection that depicted an iconic scene from Michelangelo's Sistine Chapel ceiling. She felt almost sacrilegious forking into the portrayal of Adam's hand reaching up to touch God's. After the first taste, though, she and Dawn attacked the edible art with the same fervor as the Visigoths who'd sacked Rome in 410 AD.

It was almost 10:00 p.m. when their server cleared the table and poured the last of the sweet, sparkling *asti spumante* Travis had ordered to accompany dessert. Another countermeasure, Kate guessed, to prevent a final round of hostile fire from either Dawn or Callie. If so, it didn't work.

When Kate indicated she wanted to talk to Travis for a few moments, her friends waged a short but spirited battle to pay for their share of dinner. Defeated, they pushed away from the table. If Travis thought he'd bought a reprieve with the astronomically expensive dinner, he soon learned otherwise. Dawn took only a few steps, turned back and aimed her forefinger like a cocked Beretta.

"Do *not* forget, Westbrook. Callie and I are only a phone call away. All Kate has to do is hit speed dial, and we're there."

"Good to know that hasn't changed in all the years I've known the Invincibles."

His obvious sincerity angled Dawn's chin down a notch. Just one. The mulish set to her mouth, however, suggested she wasn't ready to quit the field until Callie bumped her hip.

"He got the message. Time for us to make an exit."

"I guess I deserved that," Travis commented as the two women wove their way through the candlelit tables.

"Actually, they let you off easy. You don't want to know the various surgical procedures Dawn performed on you in absentia."

"Most, I would guess, done with a rusty pocket-knife."

"In her more generous moments. Other times she went to work with a hacksaw."

"Ouch."

His exaggerated shudder earned him a faint smile. He had to fight the urge to follow it up by reaching across the table and folding her hand in his.

"I meant what I said earlier," he told her instead.

"About?"

"About being grateful to them. They were there for you when you needed them."

When he *couldn't* be.

Facing his wife across the table, Travis acknowledged that he'd abrogated his role as a husband too many times. When the Bank of America promoted Kate in recognition of her adroit handling of foreign investments during the recession that panicked markets around the world, he'd been swatting mosquitoes at a remote airstrip in Kenya. And just months ago, while she'd agonized over whether to accept the offer from the World Bank and move to DC, he'd been freezing his ass off at a classified location he still couldn't talk about. Time now, he vowed silently, to realign his priorities and reclaim a place in her life.

Assuming she would let him. He'd cracked the door open by getting her to spend this time with him, but the determined expression that now settled over her face suggested he'd have his work cut out to push it open all the way.

"What did you want to talk about?" he asked her.

"We need to discuss the ROE."

"Are we speaking your language or mine?"

ROE in her world stood for *return on equity*, a formula that assessed a company's efficiency at generating profits for its stockholders. In his, *ROE* stood for the rules of engagement outlining the type of force that could be employed in various situations.

"In this instance, they represent the same thing. We need a set of parameters that define what we should and shouldn't do during this time together."

Travis didn't much like the sound of that. "I figured we would play it by ear."

"Right. Like you did with the villa? Tell me you just pulled that idea out of the air."

"Okay, I might have scoped out a few possible courses of action…"

"Exactly. And if I remember the principles of war correctly, the purpose of a course of action is to achieve an objective."

She didn't add *at all costs*, but the implication hung heavy on the air. His brows snapping together, Travis shook his head.

"We're not at war, Kate. At least I hope to hell we're not."

"No, we're not. Now. And I want to keep it that way."

"All right," he conceded, not particularly happy with the direction this conversation was taking. "Let's hear your ROE."

She raised a hand and ticked them off with a decisiveness that told him she didn't intend to negotiate. "One, separate bedrooms. Two, we share all expenses. Three, we decide on the itinerary together. Four, no changes unless by mutual consent. Five, no surprises of any size, shape or dimension."

He took a moment. "Okay."

"That was too easy," Kate said, frowning. "What am I missing?"

"Nothing."

"Do you want to add to the list?"

"I think you've covered the essentials."

Her frown deepened. "This won't work if we're not honest with each other, Trav."

"I am being honest. I can live with those ROE. As long as *you* understand I intend to focus most of my energy on number four."

Focus, hell. He intended to use every weapon at his disposal to make it happen.

"That's my sole objective, Katydid. Gaining your consent…to changes in bedrooms, expenses, itinerary and—oh, yeah—our pending divorce."

"Well." She sat back, her brown eyes wide. "That's certainly honest enough."

"Good." He pushed back his chair, figuring he'd better make tracks before she added to their list of rules. "Why don't you text me a proposed itinerary? I'll look at it tonight and we can negotiate if necessary. Just be sure to factor in some driving time. I want you to see Italy the way it should be seen."

"I, uh… Fine."

The blunt declaration left Kate feeling flustered as they crossed the Cavalieri's elegant lobby to the elevators. Travis didn't touch her this time, not even a gentlemanly hand on her elbow, and she was furious with herself for missing that small courtesy. So furious she jabbed the elevator button before she could miss more than his touch. Like the feel of his breath tickling her ear. The whisper of her name when he…

The elevator doors pinged open. Kate almost jumped in with a promise to zap him a proposed agenda within an hour.

Dawn and Callie were still up and open to further discussion on plans for the remainder of their time in Italy. Snatching up her notebook filled with maps and detailed descriptions of major tourist attractions, Kate worked up an alternate itinerary for them based out of the Tuscan villa. Then she went to work on one for her and Travis.

Driving time. He'd said to factor in driving time. So…

Lips pursed, Kate studied her heavily annotated map of Italy. Since driving in Rome was a nightmare, Kate decided she and Travis should depart the city in the morning, tour the countryside and save Rome for the end of the trip…assuming they were still together at that point. The uncertainty of that churned in her belly as she emailed the proposed itinerary to Travis's phone.

He emailed back while she was still studying her map. The flight plan looked good. No negotiations or changes necessary. He'd pick her up at eight thirty.

* * *

Kate fully expected to lie awake the rest of the night riddled by doubts. She slid between the satiny sheets, still mulling over Travis's stated intention to do whatever he could to change her mind about their future. But almost as soon as her head touched the pillow, the combination of rich food, several glasses of wine and mental exhaustion following hours of wildly conflicting emotions put her out.

The alarm she'd set on her iPhone went off at 7:00 a.m., but the happy marimba barely penetrated. Fumbling for the phone, she hit the snooze button. Twice. So when she finally came fully awake, she glanced at the time, let out a yelp and scrambled to get showered, dressed and packed.

Luckily, she'd packed light for the trip. All three of them had. Just one tote and roll-on each. The absence of heavy luggage made traveling so much easier but restricted choices. Kate had opted for two pairs of jeans, one pair of khaki twill slacks, tanks and Ts in various colors, a lightweight cotton sundress, and her slinky, caramel-colored pants and jacket. Since she would spend the day driving, she decided on jeans and a cap-sleeved black T paired with the chunky wooden necklace.

Callie was up when Kate dashed out of her bedroom, but Dawn hadn't seen the light of day yet. Noting the tote and roll-on, Callie smiled.

"No second thoughts?"

"God, yes! Second, third and fourth. But… Well…"

"You don't have to explain. Just keep safe, Kate, and keep us posted on how things go."

"I will."

The doubts hit with a vengeance while she waited in the Cavalieri's lobby. The break with Travis had been agony enough four months ago. She had to be certifiable to court that kind of pain again.

She swiped her palms down the sides of her jeans and tried to settle her nerves by admiring the magnificent triptych that dominated the wall above the reception desk. The Cavalieri's website boasted that it was home to one of the greatest private collections in the world. The hotel's art historian even offered private tours of the old masters, rare tapestries and priceless antiques that included, among other things, a crib commissioned by Napoleon for his baby son.

At the moment, Kate was too revved to appreciate the art displayed in niches and on pedestals. Last night she'd thought she'd been so precise, so clearheaded and unemotional by laying out those ground rules. Then Travis had to turn them—and her—upside down with his statement of intent.

And that nickname. Katydid. He'd tagged her with it one hot summer evening when they'd spread a blanket under the stars and listened to the quivering whir of grasshoppers feasting on fresh-cut grass. Only he could call her an insect and make it feel like the soft stroke of a palm against her skin. And only he could blot out every one of those zillion stars with a single kiss.

Oh, God! What was she doing?

She tightened her grip on the roll-on, almost ready to scurry back to her room, when she caught a flash from the corner of one eye. Turning, she spotted her husband at the wheel of the convertible that pulled up at the front entrance. It was low, sporty, hibiscus red, and it gleamed with chrome. It also, she saw when she exited the automatic doors, displayed a distinctive logo on its sloping hood. Like the bellman and parking attendant, she was riveted by the medallion depicting a rampant black stallion silhouetted against a field of yellow.

"Is this a Ferrari?"

"It is," Travis confirmed as he waved off the parking attendant who hurried forward. Rounding the hood, he took Kate's case and stashed it in the trunk. "Compliments of Carlo."

"Free use of a villa *and* a Ferrari? He owes you that much?"

"He doesn't owe me anything. He just thinks he does."

Shadowy images of what must have gone down to rack up such a large debt, real or imagined, made Kate swallow. Hard. Trying to blank her mind to the possible circumstances, she folded herself into the cloud-soft black leather of the passenger seat.

"It's got a retractable hardtop," Travis said as he slid behind the wheel. "If the wind is too much, let me know and I'll put it up."

She nodded, still trying to force her thoughts away from downed aircraft and skies ablaze with tracers from enemy fire. Her husband didn't help by sharing a bit of historical trivia.

"Did you know Ferrari derived his logo from the insignia of a World War I Italian ace?"

"Why am I not surprised?" Kate said drily. "The symbol for such a lean, mean muscle machine could only have come from a flier."

"Damn straight." Grinning, Travis keyed the ignition and steered past a parade of taxis waiting to pick up departing guests. "Count Francesco Baracca was cavalry before he took to the air, so he painted a prancing black stallion on the sides of his plane. Baracca racked up so many kills he became a national hero, and when

Ferrari met the count's mother some years later, she suggested he paint the same symbol on his racing car for good luck."

"The ace didn't object to having his personal symbol co-opted?"

"He probably wouldn't have, but we'll never know. He went down in flames just a few months before the end of the war."

Both the dancing stallion and the sleek vehicle it decorated lost their dazzle in Kate's eyes. "Some good-luck charm," she muttered. "I hope your pal Carlo hasn't stenciled it on his plane."

"No, the aircraft in his unit sport their own very distinctive nose art. The wing's name in Italian is the Seventeenth Stormo Incursori, if that gives you any clue."

When she shook her head, his grin widened.

"It translates literally to 'a flock of raiders.' Not so literally to 'watch your asses, bad guys.'"

"Of course it does. Do they fly the K-2, too?"

K-2 was their shorthand for the Combat King II. The latest model of the HC-130 was still relatively new to the USAF inventory and dedicated to special ops.

"They do," Travis confirmed. "Just got 'em in this year. Carlo and his crew were still doing a shakedown when we got tagged for that joint op."

Kate dug in her purse for a fat plastic hair clip, thinking that her husband and his Italian counterpart had forged quite a bond. It might be of recent origin, but it sounded almost as deep and unbreakable as the one between her, Dawn and Callie.

"I'd like to meet this new friend of yours sometime," she commented as she anchored her hair back with the clip.

"I'd like that, too." He cut her a quick glance. "Want

to amend our itinerary to include the base at Aviano? And maybe Venice?"

"I…uh…"

For pity's sake! They hadn't even left the Cavalieri's landscaped grounds and were already making changes to the agenda. But the lure of Venice proved almost as powerful as the desire to meet this new friend of her husband's.

"Okay by me."

"Great."

When they reached the bottom of the long, curving drive, Travis downshifted and hit the brake. His hand rested casually on the Ferrari's burled walnut gearshift knob while its engine purred like a well-fed feline.

"This baby can go from zero to sixty in three-point-five seconds," he confided as they waited for the cross street to clear. "Once we shake free of Rome, we'll open her up."

Chapter Three

Despite the Ferrari's impressive prowess, it took Kate and Travis all day to make what would ordinarily be a three-hour drive from Rome to Florence.

They left the autostrada about two hours north of Rome and made a leisurely side trip through the Chianti region, with several stops to sample wine and olive oil. After a light lunch in the historic center of Siena, they followed a winding country road to the fortified hilltop town of San Gimignano.

Its seven towers dated from the Middle Ages. Square and unyielding, they stood like sentinels against a sky puffy with white clouds. The town center was closed to nonlocal traffic, so they parked in a lot outside the main gate and explored the winding medieval streets on foot. By then it was late afternoon. A creamy gelato carried them until dinner, which they ate in a restaurant built into one of San Gimignano's ancient walls. The

view from the restaurant's terrace of undulating vineyards and red-tiled farms guarded by tall cypresses was
a landscape painter's dream.

They hit the outskirts of Florence as a sky brilliant
with purple and gold and red was darkening into night.
With typical efficiency, Kate had called ahead to change
the reservations she'd previously made at a small boutique hotel perched on a bank of the Arno River just a
short distance from the famous Ponte Vecchio.

She felt pleasantly tired from the long day. Not tired
enough, however, to banish the awkwardness and un-
avoidable hurt of checking into two separate rooms.
She was the one who'd insisted, she reminded herself
fiercely as they took the elevator to the second floor.

Still, she felt as though a fist had locked around her
heart and was squeezing hard when she paused outside
the door to her room. Key in one hand and the handle
of her roller bag in the other, she covered the hurt with
a smile.

"Thanks for today, Trav. I...I had fun."

"Me, too, Katydid."

They'd both been so careful. No casual physical contact, no sensitive subjects, no reminders of how many
times they'd planned this trip. Now all she could think
of was how much she ached to kick off her shoes and
curl up beside him on a comfy sofa to review the day's
adventures.

Her memories of Italy, she realized suddenly, would
always carry this bittersweet flavor. She had to turn
away before the tears prickling her eyes welled up.

"I'm more tired than I realized," she lied, shoving the
key in the lock. "I'll see you in the morning."

When the door closed behind her, Travis stared at

the white-painted wood panel. He was gripping his own key card so fiercely the edges cut into his palm.

He'd known this trip would be hard. Had fully anticipated spending most of the day with his insides balled in a knot. Turned out he'd grossly underestimated the degree of difficulty. It took everything he had to refrain from rapping on that door, folding his wife in his arms and kissing away the sadness that had flickered across her face for the briefest instant.

A low, vicious oath did little to relieve his frustration. Slinging his carryall onto the bed in his room didn't help, either. Not when all he could think about, all he could see, was Kate's long, slender body stretched out on the brocaded coverlet, her skin bathed in moonlight and her eyes languorous after a bout of serious sex.

"Dammit all to hell!"

He stalked to the minibar and ripped the cap off a plastic bottle of scotch. Glass in hand, he stood at the window and gazed unseeing at the floodlit dome of Florence's famous *duomo*, just visible above the jumble of buildings in the heart of the city.

When he headed down to the hotel's breakfast room the next morning, he was feeling the aftereffects of a restless night. Kate was already there, coffee cup in hand and a fistful of brochures fanned on the table in front of her.

Grunting, Travis squinted to block the glare from the picture windows framing the Ponte Vecchio. Despite the early hour, tourists were already streaming onto the medieval stone bridge that spanned the Arno River. The bridge was topped with multistory shops, just as it had been centuries ago, but shopkeepers now hawked gold instead of scalded chickens and haunches of raw meat dangling from iron hooks. Since the bridge no doubt topped Kate's list of must-see sights, Travis gave fervent thanks they wouldn't have to battle with the flies and smells of an open-air market like those he'd visited in Africa and Asia.

She looked up at his approach. The faint shadows under her eyes gave him a small, totally selfish dart of satisfaction. Apparently her night hadn't been any more restful than his.

The rest of her looked good, though. Too good. He pulled out a chair, wondering how the hell he was going to get through another day without dropping a kiss on the soft skin left bare by the honey-colored curls she'd clipped up and off her neck.

"Good morning."

Her polite greeting only increased his irritation. What was he? Some casual acquaintance? His response came out short and a little gruff.

"Mornin'."

"Uh-oh." Cradling her cup in both hands, she eyed him over the rim. "Rough night?"

"I've had better." He debated for a moment and decided there was no point pretending to be noble. "Took a while to get to sleep. The combination of warm scotch and a cold shower finally did the trick."

"Took me a while, too," she admitted with obvious reluctance. She looked down at her half-empty cup, then up again. "Maybe this isn't such a good idea, Trav."

"What?" He helped himself from the carafe on the table. "You? Me? Sleeping in separate beds? Dumbest idea since pet rocks."

She set her cup down with a clink. "What I *meant* was you. Me. Thinking we could patch our marriage together by playing tourist."

"Okay, hang on a sec."

He needed a jolt of caffeine for this. Preferably main-lined straight to a major vein. He settled for taking it hot and black and bitter. Fortified, he met her challenge head-on.

"First, I'm not playing at anything. I'm dead serious. I love you. Always have. Always will. Second, I don't—"

"Wait! Stop! Back up."

The crease that suddenly grooved her brow annoyed him no end.

"Cm'on, Kate. Despite that Facebook stupidity, you know...you *have* to know you're the only woman I've ever wanted to spend my life with."

When the groove dug deeper, the thought Travis had kept buried in the dark recesses of his mind slithered out of its hole like a venomous snake in search of something to feed on.

"Unless..." He reached deep, fought savagely for calm. "Have you found someone else? Someone you want to spend yours with?"

"No! God!"

"You can tell me. I'll understand." His jaw worked. "I won't like it, but I'll understand."

"Oh, for pity's sake! Do you think I'd dump Dawn and Callie and take off with you if I had another man waiting in the wings?"

Breathing deep, he lopped off the snake's head and booted its carcass into the netherworld. "So what's the bottom line here, Kate? Why *did* you dump Callie and Dawn?"

"Bottom line?"

She caught her lower lip between her teeth. He waited, certain the painful honesty he saw in her brown eyes signaled the end. If it did, he swore with a vow that cut sharp and deep, he would back off. Accept the damned divorce. Let her get on with her life.

"I love you, too," she said quietly. "Always have. Always will. But we've both learned the hard way that love isn't always enough. I guess I wanted... I *needed*... one last shot at bridging the gap between what is and what could be."

His chest unfroze. His heart started beating again. His lungs pumped enough air to fuel an instant decision.

"We need to reopen negotiations."

Instantly wary, she held up both palms. "No way. I'm not ready for—"

"The itinerary," he cut in. "Are you up for another side trip?"

"Depends. Where do you want to go?"

"Let me make a call. Then I'll give you the details."

He tossed his napkin on the table and found a quiet corner in the hall outside the breakfast room. Digging his cell phone out of his jeans pocket, he used his thumb to skim his list of contacts and found the one he wanted. A few seconds later, the call went through the international circuits.

"Ellis."

"It's Westbrook."

Brian Ellis was president and CEO of Ellis Aeronautical Systems, the prime contractor on the highly classified modification to the Combat King's avionics that Travis and his Italian counterpart were currently testing. Ellis had flown over to Italy for a progress review and the final test flights.

A former aviator himself, Ellis had struck a chord with both Travis and Carlo. Over beers a few nights ago, he'd let drop that his corporation was in the process of subcontracting with Lockheed for a multinational, multimillion-dollar contract for an upgrade to the jet engine's electronic injection system. He'd also mentioned that he'd scheduled a visit with one of the other major players in the proposed upgrade.

"You still heading down to Modena this afternoon?" he asked Ellis.

"I am. Assuming Mrs. Wells can manage Tommy."

"Oh. Right."

Travis had almost forgotten that Ellis had brought his six-year-old son to Europe. The plan, the CEO had explained drily, was to spend some quality time with his son before school started while exposing him to as much history as his young mind could absorb.

Travis admired the busy executive for wanting to spend time with his son. But he'd had to grin when Ellis confided that the little stinker had already escaped his nanny twice during those hours his father couldn't be with him. The boy knew better than to leave the hotel on his own, his exasperated father related, and he'd wreaked enough havoc within its centuries-old walls to make it questionable whether they'd be allowed back.

"What's your schedule in Modena?" Travis asked.

"The meet and greet at the headquarters is set for one, followed by a tour of their engine manufacturing facility."

"I need ten minutes. How about we catch you before the meet and greet?"

"Who's we?"

He shot a glance through the double doors of the breakfast room. The sunlight pouring through the windows made a golden nimbus of Kate's hair. With her creamy skin and classic features, she could have posed for one of the Renaissance masters whose paintings filled Florence's museums.

Before he could answer, Ellis connected the dots. "You dog! You convinced your wife to take you back?"

"I'm working on it."

"Then by all means, let's get together in Modena."

"Great. See you a little before one."

Pocketing the phone, he strolled back to his curious wife. "If you don't mind putting Florence on hold for another day, there's someone I want you to meet."

"The phantom Carlo?"

"No, a guy named Brian Ellis. He and Carlo and I… Well…"

"I know, I know. You can't talk about it."

"Ellis is visiting the Maserati factory in Modena this afternoon. It's just north of Bologna, about a hundred klicks from here, autostrada all the way. We could get there and back in time to watch the sun set over the Arno."

Kate arched a brow. "First a Ferrari, now a factory full of Maseratis. You're coming up in the world, Westbrook."

"Could be," he muttered under his breath as he reclaimed both his seat and his coffee. "Most definitely could be."

Kate didn't catch the low comment. His mention of Bologna had triggered something in her memory cells. The city hadn't made her must-see list. Not surprising, with everything Rome and Florence and Milan had to offer a first-time visitor, but it might be worth a short visit.

"You order breakfast," she instructed Travis, "while I check out what else there is to see in Bologna and Modena besides Maseratis."

A bunch, she discovered after a quick search on her iPhone. The city of Bologna dated back more than three thousand years. With its central location smack-dab in the middle of the Italian boot, it had survived and flourished under subsequent waves of Etruscans, Celts, Romans and medieval lords.

"Bologna's home to the oldest university in the world," she informed Travis, "founded in 1088."

"Beats UMass by about eight hundred years."

"It's also famous for its arched walkways," she read. "They run for more than thirty-eight kilometers, connecting the largest historical city center in Italy. The porticoes are actually included on the UNESCO World Heritage list of significant historical, cultural or geographical landmarks."

"Who knew?" Travis commented with a grin.

Certainly not Kate. Fascinated, she Googled away while he ordered an omelet for himself, a fresh fruit cup and a toasted bagel for her.

The order stilled her flying fingers. He knew her so well, she thought with a gulp. Her breakfast routine. Her love affair with classical music, which he'd struggled so valiantly—and unsuccessfully—to share. He also sympathized with her ferocious battle to keep the ten pounds she'd gained since their first meeting from inching up to fifteen, twenty. Not that he'd minded the extra padding. That time in Vegas, when he'd peeled off her bra and panties and slicked his tongue over...

Whoa! This wasn't the time *or* the place to think about where his tongue had gone. Heart hammering, Kate went back to working the phone's tiny keyboard.

"Aha!"

"Aha?" Travis echoed, shooting up a brow. "Does that carry the same connotation as 'gadzooks'?"

"I wouldn't know. I don't read comic books, like some people do."

"More than some. Google 'manga' and see how far back that cultural tradition goes."

"Do you want to hear this or not?"

He surrendered gracefully. "Yes, ma'am."

"Bologna is home to Cassa di Molino, one of Italy's largest banks. It was organized back in the 1800s by a commission of wealthy patrons to manage the city's poorhouses. The commission also encouraged better-off citizens to save by offering them a safe place to deposit funds they could draw on in emergencies or old age."

Her fiscal interests fully engaged, Kate skimmed the article describing the minimum deposit—not less than six scudi—and loans tailored to craftsmen and merchants to stimulate the local economy.

"Back then the bank allocated all profits to helping young entrepreneurs, depositors who fell on hard times and women with no dowries."

"I'm guessing it's not as philanthropic these days."

Ignoring the sardonic comment, she worked her thumbs. "And I think… Yes! Here he is, Antonio Gallo. The bank's new president."

She angled the phone to display a photo of a distinguished gentleman with a genial smile and a full head of silver hair.

"I met him at a conference last year. He mentioned then that he was being considered for a senior position. I didn't remember where until just now, when you mentioned Bologna."

"Sounds like a useful contact."

"Very useful."

"Since we're heading in that direction anyway, why

don't you call and see if he's available for a courtesy call?"

She hesitated for only a second or two. She hadn't factored any business calls into her vacation schedule. Then again, neither had she planned a visit to Bologna. As Travis indicated, however, this was too good an opportunity to let slip.

So much for their carefully reconstructed agenda, she thought, as she Googled the number for the headquarters of Cassa di Molino. After speaking to several underlings, she reached Signore Gallo's executive assistant, who advised that his boss's schedule was quite full but a short visit at 11:20 a.m. might be possible if he juggled some other appointments. Could he call Signorina Westbrook back to confirm? And in the interim, perhaps she might email a short bio?

"Certainly."

She gave him her contact information, then zinged off a copy of the bio she kept stored in her iCloud documents file.

"We're tentatively set for eleven twenty. Can we make that?"

He checked his watch. "Shouldn't be a problem if we hit the road within the next half hour."

"I need to change. Can you get my bagel to go?"

"Sure. Or…"

"What?"

"Rather than drive up and back, we could check out here and go on to Venice after our meetings. Stop over in Florence on the return leg."

He was right. It didn't make a lot of sense to drive a hundred kilometers north, come back, then retrace the route a few days later on the way to Venice and Aviano.

Conceding defeat, Kate mentally shredded their much-amended and totally useless itinerary.

"Sounds like a plan," she agreed.

"You go change and pack. I'll get our breakfast to go, throw my stuff together and meet you in the lobby."

Upstairs, she hurriedly sorted through her limited wardrobe. The slinky caramel-colored pantsuit she'd worn for dinner at the Cavalieri was her most viable option. It would do for a business meeting if she dressed it down.

The chunky wooden necklace she'd brought to wear with the cotton tanks and sweaters was a little *too* down, though. What she needed was a scarf, she decided. One that could perform the double duty of adding a touch of sophistication to her wardrobe and keeping her hair from whipping free of the plastic clip during the drive. Remembering the many street vendors she'd seen set up close to the hotel last evening, she shimmied out of her jeans and into the knit slacks.

Signore Gallo's assistant called to confirm the appointment as she was pulling on a pearly tank. Flinging an emergency makeup repair kit into her purse, she hurried down to the lobby. Travis was already there, holding his leather carryall and a cardboard tray with two to-go cups and a bag she assumed contained their breakfast. He was wearing the gray suede sport coat and jeans again but had paired them with a very European-looking black crewneck.

"I need a scarf," she told him a little breathlessly. "I'll duck out and buy one while they're bringing the car around."

Most of the street vendors were still setting up, but she found one vendor who offered quite a selection of scarves. They ran the gamut from a neon yellow square imprinted with a kaleidoscope of the city's most famous landmarks to a red banner featuring a blinged-up version of Michelangelo's *David*. She was tempted, really tempted, but decided against walking into Cassa di Molino sporting a naked, sparkling *David*.

She settled instead for a silky oblong with an ocher-hued palace set amid a garden bursting with spring blooms and moss-covered fountains. The scarf was long enough to wrap securely around her head and neck yet still leave the ends to flutter like colorful wings when they hit the autostrada.

Kate tried to pump Travis for more information about Brian Ellis during the drive, but aside from sharing the interesting fact that the man had brought his young son to Italy, her husband seemed reticent to go into much detail about the reason for this spur-of-the-moment meeting. Shelving her curiosity, she gave herself over to the enjoyment of the sunlit morning and the rolling vista of small towns and hills covered with vineyards.

With step-by-step directions from MapQuest, Travis navigated the narrow, twisting streets of Bologna's historic center and got them to the Cassa di Molino twenty minutes ahead of their appointment. Barely enough time, as it turned out, to find a parking place. Dodging heavy traffic and a web of one-way streets, they completely circled the block before they noticed the *Riservato Mrs. Westbrook* sign. It was right at the entrance to the magnificent pink-and-white marble palazzo that housed the bank.

A receptionist just inside the cavernous lobby called Signore Gallo's assistant. He came down a few moments later and introduced himself as Maximo Salvatore. Kate tried, she really tried, not to gawk as he led them up a grand staircase graced by wrought-iron railings as beautifully crafted as the paintings and statues gracing the upper level.

Proud of both his heritage and his institution, Maximo had to show them a library with an elaborately stuccoed ceiling, several salons hung with portraits and damask tapestries, and the two antique safes that had secured the hard-earned scudi of the bank's first depositors. He was about to usher them into the president's suite of offices when Kate spotted a discreet sign for restrooms.

"I need to make some emergency repairs," she told the two men. "I'll just be a moment."

"But of course," Maximo said courteously. "We shall await you here."

The ladies' room was small but as beautifully decorated as the rest of the bank. It was also occupied by a woman with both palms planted on the marble sink. Her head was bowed, her shoulders shaking.

"Oh!" Kate started to back out. *"Scusi."*

The woman whipped her head around. She was older than Kate by some years, her dark brown hair streaked with gray. Tears spilled from her red-rimmed eyes and left glistening tracks on her cheeks. Kate hesitated, caught between chagrin for invading her privacy and an instinctive urge to offer comfort.

"Can I help you?"

The older woman answered in an obviously embarrassed spate of Italian.

"I'm sorry," Kate responded. "I don't… Uh… *Non parlo italiano.*"

That produced another mortified river of words, accompanied this time by an agitated wiggle of her hands. Kate got the message and said nothing further as the woman swiped a wet paper towel across her cheeks and hurried out.

Kate used the facilities, then made the necessary repairs to her own hair and face. She debated mentioning the brief encounter to Maximo but decided against it. Women, especially those in the rarefied upper levels of international banking, had to stick together. Whatever was troubling the older woman, she obviously hadn't wanted witnesses to her tears.

Pushing the episode to the back of her mind, Kate summoned a smile and rejoined the men. Maximo ushered her and Travis through an outer office with five gilt-edged desks, three of them empty at the moment. It also boasted an entire wall of portraits of appropriately somber bankers staring down at them from elaborately carved frames.

The inner sanctum was paneled in gleaming golden oak. Tall windows draped in rose-and-gold damask filled the office with light. The silver-haired gentleman who rounded a desk the size of a soccer field was every bit as gracious as Kate remembered from their brief meeting at the conference.

Signore Gallo welcomed her enthusiastically, professed himself delighted to meet her husband and accepted her congratulations on his new position as president of the prestigious bank with a deprecating shrug.

"An honor such as this comes if one survives long enough in this demanding and so exhausting profession, yes? As it will to you, Signora Westbrook."

"Perhaps. If *I* survive long enough."

"Of course you will. You are… How do you say it? A rising star. One had only to read your profile in *Wall Street Journal* to know you are on your way to the top."

He caught the look of surprise on her husband's face

and lifted a bushy white brow. "Your wife did not tell you she was identified as one of the young superstars, someone to watch in the field of international investments? No, I can see she did not. You should be most proud of her, Major Westbrook."

"I am. More proud than she knows."

"*Bene, bene.* So. You must tell me. Are you in Italy on business or pleasure?"

Travis left it to Kate to answer. "Some of both, actually. My husband is on temporary duty at Aviano Air Base and I, er, flew over for a visit."

She wasn't lying. Not technically. Travis *was* at Aviano, and she *had* flown over for a visit. Just not with him.

"And you came to our beautiful city of Bologna!" Signore Gallo exclaimed in delight. "There is much to see here and much to do."

"Unfortunately, we just have time for a short visit. We're on our way to Modena, then Venice."

A discreet signal from his assistant reminded the genial banker that his time, too, was limited.

Expressing profuse regrets that he had to terminate their visit, Gallo got to his feet. When Kate and Travis rose, as well, the banker took both of her hands in his.

"You must come to visit again, signora. I should very much like to discuss the recent changes to the liquidity index promulgated by the US Securities and Exchange Commission with you."

"I'd like that, too, but…"

"Yes, yes, you are on vacation. I understand, and I don't wish to impose on your precious time. But may I have Maximo call you in a day or two? Perhaps we can arrange something."

Buoyed by the visit and feeling smug after Gallo's

effusive compliments, Kate exchanged air-kisses with Cassa di Molino's president before preceding Travis and Maximo out of the sumptuous inner office.

Two steps into the outer office, her startled gaze locked with that of the well-dressed matron seated behind one of the desks. The woman gulped and telegraphed an unmistakable appeal from eyes still showing a faint trace of red.

Kate responded to the mute plea with a friendly, impersonal nod and let Maximo escort her and Travis down to the lobby. She fully intended to tell her husband about the brief encounter, but he distracted her with a demand for more details about this *Wall Street Journal* profile. That discussion was cut short by the intense concentration required to exit the city center.

To make matters worse, an accident just a few blocks from the bank blocked the narrow streets and enveloped them in a traffic snarl of gargantuan proportions. As a result, they pulled into the parking lot of Maserati's gleaming steel-and-glass headquarters in Modena just minutes before they were supposed to connect with Brian Ellis.

And five minutes after meeting the supercharged aerospace executive, the last thing on Kate's mind was a chance encounter in the ladies' room of Cassa di Molino.

Chapter Four

"You're going to work for Ellis Aeronautical Systems? As VP for test and evaluation?"

Kate's incredulous gaze bounced from her husband to the executive in what she guessed was a two-thousand-dollar suit and back again. "Starting the first of the year?"

They were ensconced in a small conference room on the top floor of the steel-and-glass tower housing Maserati's headquarters. Its solid wall of windows overlooked the curving, glass-fronted building that showcased the world-famous manufacturer's latest automotive offerings.

Sunlight slanted through the windows' mini-blinds and painted Travis's face in alternating stripes of shadow and sincerity as he responded to her shocked question. "It isn't a done deal yet."

"Not from lack of trying on my part," Ellis admitted with a wry smile.

He was a big man. Not heavy, but tall and broad shouldered, with ice-blue eyes above a nose that sported a slight dent in the bridge.

"Your husband's a legend among the special ops community, Ms. Westbrook. Not just because of the rows of ribbons on his dress uniform. They speak to his airmanship and courage under fire. Add in his hours in the cockpit, and we're talking a level of experience few can match. I know I don't have to tell you he's racked up twice as many combat hours as other C-130 pilots with his years in service."

"No," Kate agreed tightly, "you don't. But..."

She swiveled her ultramodern chrome-and-leather sling chair to face her husband. Now that her first stunned surprise had ebbed, other emotions flooded in. Chief among them was doubt that he could jettison a career he loved without a mountain of regret. And guilt that he would even consider it. And a sudden, swamping hope they might carve out a future together after all. Those jumbled emotions were followed almost instantly by a spurt of indignation that he would spring this on her here, in front of a total stranger, with no warning.

"How long have you been considering this?" she asked with an edge to her voice.

"Brian made the offer a few days ago, but I didn't even consider taking him up on it until last night."

When they'd adjourned to separate bedrooms. He didn't say it. He didn't have to. Kate could fill in the blanks.

"And before I do accept it," he said instead, "I want you to hear exactly what the offer entails."

Ellis's keen blue eyes assessed Kate's face. "We

usually try to woo the spouse as well as a prospective executive-level hire, Ms. Westbrook. We recognize a position like this is a team effort. If we were meeting at our corporate headquarters, we'd do this more graciously."

"Call me Kate. And I don't need to be wooed with expensive dinners and visits to corporate headquarters."

"Then I'll skip the hype and cut straight to the basics."

Any other time she would have admired the polished manner so at odds with those wrestler's shoulders. Now all she could think about was the fact that Travis was actually considering turning his whole world around. *Their* whole world.

"We're a Fortune 500 company specializing in the research, design and manufacture of advanced aircraft avionics. About half our contracts are with the Department of Defense, the rest with other agencies in the States and abroad. Our headquarters are in Bethesda, Maryland, which is convenient, considering our primary interface is with Lockheed and Northrop Grumman, both located nearby."

Kate's heart gave a little bump. Bethesda was only thirty minutes from where she worked in downtown DC.

"Our main manufacturing and test facility is in Texas. As VP for test and evaluation, Travis would have to spend a fair amount of time there and at the plants of our various subcontractors."

Last Kate had heard, there were no land mines and IEDs blowing off limbs in Texas. No rocket-propelled grenades slamming into communications centers and crew quarters. No surface-to-air missiles arcing through the sky to take out low-flying aircraft. Every third

Texan might tote a gun, but most of them weren't out to kill men and women wearing a uniform with a US flag.

"Your husband and I are still negotiating a total salary and benefits package," Ellis told her, "but I realize it'll have to be sweet to entice him to leave the military at this midpoint in his career. Big decision, I know."

"Very big," she echoed, still trying to take this all in.

"Given your financial background, I'm not surprised he wants your input before we finalize any deal." His smile suggested that he anticipated some spirited salary negotiations. "That's about as basic as I can get. Do you have any questions for me?"

"Dozens," she admitted, "but none that need asking until I talk to Travis."

"Understood. Well, I'd better head to my meeting." When they got to their feet, Ellis enfolded her hand in his. "It's good to meet you, Kate. I've heard a lot about you."

She certainly couldn't say the same.

"Travis mentioned he was going to try and entice you up for a visit to the base at Aviano," the executive said. "Maybe I'll see you there or at the hotel in Venice. Although," he added, his smile turning rueful, "I'd better warn you that I come prepackaged with a hyperactive six-year-old. He's already tumbled into the Grand Canal once. I'd like to believe that'll be his only swim, but I'm not putting any money on it. Or that he won't take some unsuspecting bystander with him."

She had to laugh at his sardonic expression and couldn't help thinking that he and Travis would be a good fit. They were both so down-to-earth, yet supremely confident in themselves and their abilities. When Ellis departed, however, the look she turned on her husband wasn't exactly complimentary.

Folding her arms, she skewered him with an ice-pick stare. "Why in hell did you let me walk into this cold?"

"Two reasons. First, I wanted your no-frills, no-holds-barred gut reaction."

"Oh, you'll get that."

"Second…"

She waited, foot tapping, until he finished more slowly.

"I guess I needed to hear the offer again before I let myself believe it might happen."

She dropped her arms, her throat suddenly tight. "Do you *want* it to happen, Trav?"

"Only if you do."

The answer cut straight to the tangled knot of their marriage. Kate had always known he'd quit the service in a heartbeat if she asked him to. For that reason, she *couldn't* ask him to.

"We were at the bar in the hotel," he related. "Brian and Carlo and me. The project we're working on passed a major milestone earlier that day and we were having a few beers to celebrate. Brian let drop that the executive who runs his test-and-evaluation division is retiring and asked if I knew anyone with my kind of expertise and number of hours in the cockpit to replace him. I don't know who was more shocked—him, Carlo or me—when I said I might be interested in the job."

Travis had heard the words come out of his mouth and been as stunned as the two men he'd come to know so well in recent weeks. Yet as soon as his brain had processed the audio signals, he'd recognized their unshakable truth. If trading his air force flight suit for one with an EAS patch on it would win Kate back, he'd make the change today.

"So what do you think?" he asked her. "Again, your first, no-frills, no-holds-barred gut reaction?"

"I won't lie," she admitted slowly, reluctantly. "My head, my heart, my gut all leaped for joy."

He started for her, elation pumping through his veins. The hand she slapped against his chest to stop him made only a tiny dent in his fierce joy.

"Wait, Trav! This is too big a decision to make without talking it over. Let's…let's use this time together to make sure it's what you really want."

"I'm sure. Now."

"Well, I'm not." Her brown eyes showed an agony of doubt. "The military's been your whole life up to now."

"Wrong." He laid his hand over hers, felt the warmth of her palm against his sternum. "You came first, Katy-did. Before the uniform, before the wings, before the head rush and stomach-twisting responsibilities of being part of a crew. I let those get in the way the past few years. That won't happen again."

The doubt was still there in her eyes, swimming in a pool of indecision. He needed to back off, Travis conceded. Give her a few days to accept what was now a done deal in his mind.

"Okay," he said with a sense of rightness he hadn't felt in longer than he could remember, "we'll head up to Venice. Let Ellis's proposal percolate for a day or two."

And then, he vowed, they would conduct a virtual burning of the divorce decree before he took his wife to bed.

They left the Ferrari in a patrolled section of the parking garage on Tronchetto Island and took a water taxi across the broad, slate-gray waters of the bay. The wind whipped Kate's hair free of both her clip and colorful head scarf. She didn't even notice as the vaporetto skimmed the choppy waters.

The driver throttled back to enter the Grand Canal. Venice's busy central waterway hummed with water taxis, gondolas filled with tourists snapping picture after picture, and the flat-bottomed scows that transported goods throughout the city. Kate stood braced against the vaporetto's deck, her upper body exposed by its open hatch, her face alive with the delight of viewing one of the world's great treasures for the first time.

Travis had driven up and back from Aviano often enough to take the distinctive fusion of Byzantine, Moorish and Roman architecture in stride. Viewing it through his wife's eyes, though, gave him a renewed appreciation of the arched bridges, domed churches and tall, narrow houses with laundry strung across their windows.

As they curved past the Grand Canal's first bend and headed for the Rialto Bridge, the houses became wider, grander...including the one the vaporetto driver nosed up to. Painted a deep terra-cotta red, it boasted a colonnade of white marble pillars topped by three stories of intricately arched windows.

"This is our hotel?" Kate asked, her eyes wide as Travis helped her out of the boat and onto a marble landing slick with water that lapped from the canal.

"It is."

"Travis!" Her gaze roamed the fifteenth-century exterior. "This has got to cost a fortune!"

"Not as much as it would have if Carlo didn't have an in with the owner. I think they're cousins or something."

"Wow," she murmured as the vaporetto driver handed up their cases. "Your friend and his family certainly live well."

"So it would seem. I don't know the whole story,

though. Carlo doesn't talk about his background, and I'm not about to pry. All I know is that he prefers his air force rank of *maggiore* to the one he inherited."

"Which is?"

"Prince of Lombard and Marino."

"What?" Disbelief and incredulity chased across her expressive face. "Have you stumbled into some alternate universe? One populated with Ferraris and Maseratis, Italian princes and CEOs of Fortune 500 companies?"

"I've asked myself that same question the past few weeks," Travis admitted as a uniformed bellman popped out of a door at the rear of the landing.

"Buonasera. Benvenuti a Palazzo Alleghri.*"

"Thanks."

Switching seamlessly to English, the bellman gestured to a marble staircase. "The lobby is just up those stairs, signore. If you will check in, I'll have your bags carried to your room."

The stairs led to a black-and-white-tiled loggia dominated by gilt-edged mirrors, six-foot-tall vases bursting with flowers and a statue of a muscular Roman goddess in flowing marble robes.

"Ah, yes," the receptionist said when Travis gave his name and a credit card. "Maggiore *e* Signora Westbrook. As *il principe* requested, we've put you in the blue suite. I think you will find it very comfortable."

Comfortable didn't come close to describing the luxurious set of rooms. The source of the suite's name was immediately apparent in the shimmering ultramarine brocade drapes in the sitting room. The same fabric covered the upholstered chairs and was picked up in the broad stripes of an Empire-style sofa with one rolled arm and gleaming gilt trim. A Murano glass chandelier in a rainbow of colors hung from an elaborately carved ceiling medallion, and the antique marble-topped bombé chest that served as a sideboard could have graced a medieval prince's palace.

Which it probably had, Kate thought as she paused in the arched entry to the bedroom to gape at its opulence. More rich brocade, more handblown glass, more sumptuously carved plasterwork…and a massive bed of silver-painted wood with four flat-topped posts entwined in gold-leaf vines. She was still taking in the suite's splendor when the bellman arrived with their luggage. He placed their two small pieces on the bench at the foot of the bed before turning to ask if they cared to dine on the rooftop terrace.

"The view is one such as you will see nowhere else."

Kate looked to Travis, who endorsed the recommendation. "He's right. Once you see Venice in the moonlight, you'll forget that coin you tossed in the Trevi Fountain and always come back here instead of Rome."

"You think?"

"I know."

"Then the terrace it is."

"*Bene*. What time shall I tell the concierge to reserve your table?"

Since they'd eaten breakfast on the run and skipped lunch, they opted for an early dinner.

"I shall see to it."

Silence descended after the bellman's departure. Travis lingered at the foot of the bed; Kate stood by the windows. Her hair was a wind-tossed tangle from the drive and vaporetto ride. Her expression reflected none of the enchantment she'd displayed earlier.

He had a good idea why and gestured to the four-poster. "Sorry about the one bed. I can bunk on the sofa in the other room."

She nodded, but the troubled look didn't leave her eyes.

"We don't have to stay here, Kate. Or in Venice, for that matter. Aviano's only an hour away. My hotel outside the base doesn't have anywhere near the view or elegance, but…"

"It's not the palazzo." She carved a vague circle in the air. "It's everything. This trip. Ellis. His job offer. Your prince. Us. I feel as though I've jumped on a speeding train and don't have a clue where it's heading."

"And that's bad?"

"Unsettling."

Good, Travis thought fiercely. Unsettled was good. He'd take uncertainty any day over her previous insistence they'd grown too far apart to find their way back. And just to inject a little more doubt…

He crossed the room and brushed a knuckle down her cheek. Her eyes widened, but she didn't flinch, didn't draw back.

"Maybe our approach to life was too deliberate the first time around, Katydid. Looking back, we laid it out like a playbook. You would finish your undergraduate degree. I would go through flight school. We'd get engaged, get married, work our way up the chain, take on more challenges, more responsibilities. Start a family only when we were ready."

"That *was* the plan," she agreed, sighing as he made another light pass over her cheek. "What we didn't take into account was how those challenges and responsibilities would force us into such separate worlds. You gone so much, me turning more and more to work to fill the void."

She hesitated but had to tackle the subject that had become increasingly painful for them both. "It wouldn't have been smart or right or fair to bring a baby into that void and expect him or her to fill it."

"So we throw that plan out the window," Travis said with rigidly subdued violence. "Start new. Here. Now. That's why I wanted you to meet Ellis. Why I'm ready to hand in my papers as soon as I return to the base and complete this project." He tipped her chin up, drew his thumb along her lower lip. "I know you need more time. I won't push you. But while you're weighing the pros and cons, don't forget to include this in your calculations."

He lowered his head, giving her time to draw back, feeling the jolt when she didn't. At the first brush of his mouth on hers, hunger too long held in check kicked like an afterburner at full thrust. The heat, the fury burned like a blowtorch.

His palm slid to her nape. His mouth went from gentle to coaxing. From giving to taking. He circled her waist, drew her into him. They were hip to hip, thigh to thigh, her breasts pressed against his chest, her palms easing over his shoulders.

This was what he needed. What he'd ached for. The feel of her. The taste of her. The pleasure was sharp, knifing and so welcome he had to tap his last reserve of willpower before he could raise his head.

When her lids lifted, the smoky desire in her eyes almost snapped his last thread of restraint. He was a breath away from scooping her up and depositing her on that shimmering blue bedspread when she huffed out a husky laugh.

"Well, looks like there's one aspect of our relationship we won't have to restart."

"You sure?" He waggled his brows. "That was a pretty small sample. Maybe we should run another test."

Her laugh was more natural this time, although she didn't quite meet his eyes as she eased out of his arms.

"No time for another test if we're going to make an early dinner. As much as I enjoy swanking around in a Ferrari convertible, I need to soak the road and wind out of my pores. It may take a while," she warned. "Do you want the shower first?"

"You go ahead." He paused for a beat. "Give a shout if you need me to scrub your back. I'm pretty good at it, if you recall."

He was, Kate admitted as she dug out her cosmetic case and clean underwear. Very good! Really excellent, in fact, at scrubbing her back, her front and everywhere in between. They must have slopped an ocean of soapy water onto the tiles in the bathroom of their first apartment.

The erotic mental image took on a more vivid texture with her nerves still skittering from the feel of his mouth and body against hers. Just the sight of the claw-foot tub set in solitary splendor on a raised dais brought the heat rushing back. She sat on the tub's edge, set the old-fashioned black plug and twirled the gilt-edged taps. Steam rose almost instantly from the gushing spout, as hot and vaporous as Kate's memories.

It was only after she'd added floral-scented bath salts and adjusted the temperature that all-too-familiar guilt edged out the memories. Guilt that her pride in her husband's service to his country didn't compensate for empty days and lonely nights. Guilt that she couldn't adjust to the long rotations and short-notice deployments with the same seeming ease as other wives in his unit. Guilt that her gnawing loneliness only added to the stress Travis carried into every op.

Now he was ready to leave the military. Walk away

from a job he loved and the comrades in arms who understood the dangers and frustrations and challenges he faced every day. The men and women who spoke the same language and shared the same highs and lows.

As Kate stripped down and slid into the frothy bubbles, her rational self reared up to do battle with the ever-present guilt. Theirs wasn't the only marriage to crack under the pressure. The divorce rate in the air force was the highest in more than two decades. It ran even higher for special ops. Separations, stress and the high risk of the job all took their toll.

And dammit, she shouldn't feel so guilty at the prospect of Travis walking away from that close-knit special ops community. Judging by the interaction between him and Brian Ellis earlier this afternoon, her husband might well find the same satisfaction, the same camaraderie, outside the military as he did in it.

Buoyed by the thought, she grabbed the puffy sponge supplied by the hotel and dunked it in the still-fragrant froth. A thorough scrubbing left her skin tingling and her thoughts free to dwell on something other than the guilt she'd carried for so long.

Like the kiss Travis had laid on her a few moments ago. And the feel of his shoulders bunching under her palms. And her almost suffocating need to glide her palms over that smooth, hard muscle again. Tonight. After a candlelit dinner on the terrace, with the grand palazzi and glistening canals of Venice.

Oh, hell! Who needs candlelight and canals?

Travis was willing to risk all to save their marriage. Could she do any less?

The decision came without conscious thought, so sudden and sure it brought her out of the tub draped in a slick sheen of bubbles. Plucking a towel from the rack, she wrapped it around her. With only a fleeting prayer of thanks that she'd continued on the pill, she left a trail of wet footprints all the way through the bedroom.

Travis was in the sitting room, his shoes kicked off and ankles crossed on a hassock as he surfed channels on the sixty-inch flat-screen TV. Kate caught snippets of Italian, German and Japanese before she cleared her throat.

The ostentatious "ahem" brought his head around. The sight of her towel-draped body froze his thumb on the remote. The channel stuck on an Asian newscaster with a mellifluous voice describing what looked like a typhoon forming in the South Pacific. The swirling turbulence on-screen matched the chaotic thump of Kate's heart.

"You were right," she said, her pulse pounding.

The remote hovered midair. Caution threaded his voice. "About?"

"The sample was too small. We should run another test."

She almost laughed at his look of blank confusion. It took him a few seconds to make the connection to their kiss right before she'd retreated to the bathroom.

Then his feet hit the floor, the remote hit the hassock and he was out of the chair in one fluid move.

Chapter Five

Travis had vowed to give Kate the romantic Italian interlude she'd always dreamed of. He'd constructed contingency plans for every possible variation, from exploring the hustle and history of Rome to roaming sun-kissed Tuscan vineyards to braving Naples's teeming streets and feasting on the city's famous margherita pizza. Each contingency included the admittedly tenuous hope that they would make slow, delicious love every night they were together.

Slow and delicious didn't so much as pop into his head as he came out of his chair. All he could think of, all he could focus on, was his near-naked wife. The sheen of damp flesh above and below her towel sent his self-control into a frantic free fall. Her wet hair made him hurt with the need to bury his fists and his face in the tangled, silky mass. He was across the room in two strides. Had her backed against the wall in two more.

"I don't know what size sample you had in mind," he got out in a low growl, "but I suggest we start here."

His mouth covered hers, hard and hungry. When he moved to her throat and nipped at the taut cords, his blood was hammering like a pile driver. He inhaled the scent clinging to her wet skin while he feasted on her.

"Then we'll work down to here..."

He tugged the towel free, let it drop in a soggy pile at their feet. Cupping her breast, he teased the nipple with his thumb until it stiffened, then dipped to take the dusky peak in his mouth.

"Oh, Travis." Kate's spine arched. Her fingers dug into his shoulders. "It's been so long."

He grunted a fervent agreement and shifted his attention to her other breast. Head back, neck arched, she let him take his fill until her skin flushed and her breath came in short pants. Wedging an elbow against his chest, she pushed him back a few inches. His heart damned near stopped until she gasped out an urgent demand.

"You need...to get out...of those clothes."

He didn't make it all the way to naked. Her feverish hands shoved down his jeans and shorts, but he barely got one leg free before she wrapped a fist around his already rampant sex. Her fingers were hot, tight, eager. His were every bit as greedy, parting her thighs, exploring her slick folds, matching her stroke for stroke until her brown eyes went wild and stormy.

"Now, Trav. Now!"

He didn't need any further urging. Cupping her bottom, he raised her a few inches, bent a knee and positioned himself. Some last shred of sanity screamed at him to ease in. Slowly. Slowly. Wait for her to open. Take him in. Bring him home.

Every muscle in his body quivered, every tendon strained. Then she hooked a calf around his thigh and ground her hips down on his. Somehow he managed to hang on long enough to pull out, thrust in. Then he shot her into the stratosphere with him.

Kate wasn't sure what pierced her haze of sensual delight. Her first guess was the scratchy itch of textured plaster against her butt. Then again, it might have been the bony hips pinning hers to the wall or the hard chest mashing her breasts. One thing about Travis Westbrook, she thought ruefully as the last waves of pleasure dissipated. There wasn't an ounce of soft or cushiony anywhere on the man.

He'd dropped his forehead to hers. Another pressure point. She tried to adjust by angling her head and body a few degrees. The wiggle only dug his hips deeper into hers. He was still inside her, she realized belatedly, although how long that condition would last was questionable.

"Travis."

"Unnngh."

"I'm going to have permanent marks on my back and butt."

His head lifted. "Huh?"

"My butt. My back. The wall."

"Oh." His hazel eyes went from semidazed to almost clear. "Right."

He eased away a few inches, taking her with him, and hefted her higher while somehow managing to kick free of the jeans still tangled around one foot. She swung up her right leg and caught her left to form a tight vise around his waist as he started for the bedroom. She clung to him, breathing in the sharp tang of his skin.

The scent of him, the feel of him against her, rekindled her sluggish senses. By the time they reached the bed, she'd come alive again. Travis, however, barely got the bolster yanked down and Kate deposited on the sheets before he shed his shirt and shoes and collapsed in a boneless heap beside her. He lay sprawled on his back, long limbed and loose and wearing an expression she could only describe as goofy.

Kate rolled onto her side and propped up on an elbow. As though it had a will of its own, her hand touched and explored and revived memories she'd tried so hard to suppress. The smooth curve of his shoulders, the barrel of his ribs, the ropy muscles of his thighs were as familiar as the nicks and dents he'd collected during a very active boyhood and vigorous manhood.

He'd added a new one, she saw with a hollow sensation in the pit of her stomach. As she feathered a fingertip over the still-angry scar on his hip, the old fear grabbed her by the throat. She had to swallow hard before she could ask.

"How did you get this?"

He didn't open his eyes or alter his lazy sprawl. "Lousy intel."

"I need more than that."

"We flew into a forward airstrip that wasn't as secure as the locals swore it was. Rebels overran the field, and we had to get out of Dodge in a hurry." He pried up one eyelid and angled a look at his hip. The chagrin in his voice tipped into disgust. "It was only a flesh wound, not much worse than a mosquito bite, but I bled all over the damned cockpit before we got back in the air."

She felt caught in the vise of her worst nightmare. She'd dreamed it so many times, with so many variations, and always in terrifying Technicolor. Perimeter forces under assault and falling back. Armed rebels swarming some unimproved dirt landing strip. Travis and his crew scrambling aboard, engines roaring to full power, props spitting up clouds of dust, bullets pinging off the fuselage.

She wanted him out of that. So badly *she* hurt with it. But not unless he wanted it, too. She pushed up higher, her voice suddenly tight and urgent.

"Be honest with me, Trav. Would you really be happy working with Brian Ellis?"

He rolled onto a hip. He had both eyes open now. She saw the light from the windows reflected in their dark pupils, and absolute certainty in their hazel depths.

"Yes, Katydid, I would."

"Then do it. Accept the offer. For me. *Please.*"

He didn't blink, didn't question her abrupt change of mind and didn't hesitate. "Consider it accepted."

With a small sob, she fell forward and buried her face in the warm skin of his neck. Joy flooded her, riding a crest of sheer relief. A distant corner of her mind warned that guilt would return later, but at that moment her heart had no room for anything but happiness.

"I'll call Brian tomorrow. And Colonel Hamilton," he added. "I'd better tell the old man personally before he gets word via the grapevine."

"Yeah, you'd better."

Kate had got to know the colonel and his wife, socially and otherwise. Carol Hamilton served as mentor and confidante to spouses who faced the challenge of coping with sick kids and lost dogs and the frequent short-notice deployments of their husbands and wives. The vivacious brunette took those responsibilities as seriously as her husband did his.

Although Colonel Hamilton would probably cut off

his right arm before admitting to any favorites, Kate knew he considered Travis one of the best and brightest officers in his command. He would *not* be happy to hear Major Westbrook had decided to hang up his air force uniform.

Travis didn't seem particularly daunted at the prospect. His shoulder muscles bunching under Kate's cheek, he slid a hand through her hair and tipped her head back.

"I'll put in the official request for separation from the air force as soon as I get back to Aviano. But not for you, Kate. For us."

When he lowered his head, his kiss smothered the doubt and loneliness and worry she'd lived with for so long. She knew flying was in his blood. Knew he would still strap himself into a cockpit and probably court more than his share of risks as Ellis Aeronautical Systems' VP for test operations. But he wouldn't be dodging surface-to-air missiles or taking off in a hail of bullets.

Or would he?

She jerked her head back, her eyes wide with dismay. His filled with instant wariness.

"What?"

"This big modification you said EAS was working on with Lockheed. Will it require flying into hostile airspace to test it?"

"Maybe. I can't talk specifics at this point. I'm not cleared into the program and don't know anything about it."

"Okay. All right." She chewed the inside of her cheek and fought for calm. "Here's the deal. I need to know what EAS's VP for test and evaluation does. Specifically. I want statistics. Probabilities, if you can't give me hard data. Or at least an estimate of the risk factors involved in testing the kind of aeronautical equipment EAS develops."

He didn't pretend to misunderstand where she was going but did his best to deflect her aim. "For God's sake, Kate. I'll be overseeing a small army of engineers, test pilots, mechanics and technicians. If I log enough hours in the air every month to maintain my FAA certification, it'll be a miracle."

"I don't care," she said stubbornly. "I want to crunch the numbers. And don't hand me the usual BS about the data being classified."

She expected him to protest that it wasn't bull. She didn't expect him to burst out laughing.

"I don't see what's so amusing."

"You don't, huh?"

Still laughing, he took her with him as he fell back on the sheets. They landed in a tangle of arms and legs, chins bumping.

"How about the fact that we're naked and in bed together for the first time in more weeks than I want to count and all you want to do is crunch numbers?"

"Well…" She felt him hardening under her, and her body responded instinctively. Heat boiled low in her belly; her breath turned thick. "That's not *all* I want to crunch."

"Do tell. Or better yet, show."

"I will," she promised. Hiking a leg over his hips, she rolled upright again. "I most definitely will. But I want those numbers."

Travis would have promised her anything at that point. Spreadsheets crammed with EAS test data, diamond ankle bracelets, a cruise to the South Pacific, the yappy toy poodle she'd almost talked herself into some years back. At the time he'd cringed at the possibility one of his crew might spot him walking a white rat with pink bows and toenails on the end of a leash. Now he wouldn't hesitate to parade the critter up and down the flight line if that was what it took to get Kate back.

His mind and body soared. He had her in his arms, in his bed, in his life. He'd keep her there, whatever it took. And damned if this wasn't the perfect start. She looked like a sea siren with her still-damp hair in wild tangles and a seductively wicked smile on her lips as she straddled him. He was determined to take it slow this time. He wanted to watch her skin flush with desire, see her back arch and her head go back as her pleasure mounted.

Only after she'd climaxed in long, tight spasms did he grip her hips and let himself join her.

By the time she surfaced for the second time, a different but almost as compelling hunger gripped Kate. It made itself heard with an insistent rumble from the vicinity of her stomach.

"I need pasta," she moaned. "Lots of pasta!"

"I think that can be arranged."

Recovering far faster than Kate, Travis rolled out of bed with the lithe agility that had landed him a basketball scholarship to UMass.

"We missed our reservation for dinner on the roof, but there's a great little trattoria only a few minutes' walk from here. Not fancy, but really good food."

"I'm in!"

While he grabbed a quick shower, she cleaned up, made a valiant effort with her hair before dressing in khaki slacks and a bright red tank. She'd reached for her purse and was about to sling it over her shoulder when she decided to check her iPhone for messages.

She had a bunch. Scrolling through the long list, she found five from work, one from Cassa di Molino and two from Dawn. The last came with an italicized subject header. *CALL ME!*

Alarmed, Kate hit the re-call button. A dozen gory possibilities blazed through her mind while the phone buzzed. She was a bundle of nerves when Dawn finally answered with a breathless *"Pronto."*

"It's me. I just saw your message. What's wrong?"

"Nothing. Just the opposite, in fact. You should see this villa! It's like something out of *Lifestyles of the Italian Rich and Famous*."

Sagging in relief, Kate dropped onto the rumpled covers as Dawn continued. "It's so over-the-top luxurious, Callie's nervous as hell. She thinks we'll be presented with a bill when we leave that we won't be able to pay and we'll end up in debtors' prison."

"Debtors' prison went out in the late 1800s," Kate countered, but she understood Callie's worry given the fact that her friend was currently unemployed.

"How the heck can an Italian Air Force major afford a place like this?" Dawn wanted to know.

"According to Travis, *maggiore* is only one of Carlo's titles. He's also a prince."

"Prince? Like in royalty or rock star?"

"Royalty."

"Holy crap! Just like in the *Three Coins in the Fountain* movie. Is he as yummy as Louis Jourdan?"

"I didn't ask Travis for a physical description."

"What's his full name? I'll look him up on the internet."

Kate searched her mind. "I'm coming up blank on the last name, but I think he's prince of Lombard and..." She scrunched her forehead. "And someplace else."

"Hold on! I have to tell Callie this!"

Kate waited while Dawn related the news that their absent landlord was a real, live prince. Then Callie took the phone to discuss a far more important issue.

"How's it going with you and Travis?"

"Good." A pause, a sigh and a sappy smile. "Better than good."

"Want to share some details?"

"I will. Tomorrow, I promise."

"You sound happy, Kate."

The soft observation brought tears to her eyes. She blinked them away but couldn't deny the joy behind them.

"I am. And I've got so much to tell you and Dawn. But we're just getting ready to go out and grab something to eat. I'll call you tomorrow."

"You'd better! Ciao for now."

"Ciao."

Travis was waiting when she hurried out of the bedroom. Slinging her purse strap over her shoulder, she issued a hurried apology. "Sorry. I had to return an urgent call from Dawn."

"Is she okay?"

"She is. Mostly she just wanted to rhapsodize about Carlo's villa. She was also as surprised as I was to hear you're hobnobbing with royalty."

He answered with a shrug and the highest accolade he could bestow on a comrade in arms. "Prince or not, he's solid. You ready?"

When they stepped out into night, she discovered that Venice in the moonlight was even more magical than in the bright light of day. The shimmering waters of the Grand Canal reflected a fat, glowing moon and the floodlit facades of its grand palazzi. The tall, narrow dwellings along the smaller side canals lost their slightly decrepit air of peeling plaster and displayed instead necklaces of brightly lit windows.

With the ease of long habit, Travis slipped an arm around Kate's waist and kept her close as they wove through tourists and locals out to enjoy a late dinner. Two turns, several twisting streets and three bridges later, they reached a tiny square bordered on three sides by residences, several of which featured business establishments on the ground floor.

The Trattoria di Pesce was one of these establishments. A string of lightbulbs cast halos over its half dozen outdoor tables. Large plate-glass windows showed an interior with rows of wooden booths dominated by shelves displaying red, black and green pasta in glass jars of every conceivable size and shape. At the very rear was a cutaway providing a glimpse of a kitchen with long strands of noodles hanging from wooden poles.

"Trust me," Travis said as they made for the trattoria. "This place serves the best crab tagliatelle in town."

"I'll take your word for... Oh!" Kate stopped dead. "Listen!"

Head cocked, she drank in the deep, rich notes of a cello. Spinning on one heel, she followed the dark, sensuous notes to the church that formed the fourth side of the square. Its doors stood open, spilling light and the cello's deep tones. Moments later, other strings added their voices. A violin, a viola, another violin, then the cello again.

"I think that's a Rossini sonata," she murmured in delight.

"If you say so." Eyes narrowed in the dim light, Travis squinted at a poster in a glass case beside the church's open doors. "If I'm translating this right, it says students from Venice's classical conservatory are performing here tonight." He paused, gave the poster another squint and squared his shoulders. "The concert is free to the public. Do you want to slip inside and listen?"

If Kate wasn't already falling in love with her husband all over again, the heroic offer would push her over the edge. She and Travis shared so many passions. Walks in the pristine stillness of a fresh snowfall. Butter dripping from their chins while they pigged out on steamed lobster. The noise and mayhem when the Boston Bruins took to the ice. A mutual dedication to their work.

Classical music, however, was *not* one of their shared interests. In all their years together, Kate had dragged her reluctant fiancé and then husband to a total of three symphony concerts. After the first, he'd lied like hell in an unsuccessful attempt to convince her he'd enjoyed the experience. After the second, he'd admitted he wasn't quite there yet. Halfway through the third, his chin dropped to his chest and his snores took on the booming resonance of a tympanic roll. Kate had been forced to elbow him in the ribs throughout the rest of the concert to keep other members of the audience from zinging exasperated looks his way.

After that disaster, they'd worked out a comfortable compromise for their tastes in music. She would screw in her earbuds, he would plug his in and they'd hum along to different beats. Live performances were limited to entertainers they both liked. So the thought that he would brave yet another round of bruised ribs to attend a performance of chamber music made her heart sing along with the four-stringed instruments.

"Why not enjoy the best of both worlds?" she suggested, gesturing to the trattoria. "If we sit outside, we can listen *and* eat."

"Okay by me. But," he added as they recrossed the tiny square, "don't think I don't recognize the ulterior motive here. You're hoping a plate of crab pasta will keep me awake."

"Not hoping," she countered. "Praying!"

She needn't have worried. They lucked out and got one of the outside tables. Just enough of the sonata floated across the square to enchant Kate and form easily ignorable background noise for Travis. They ordered a liter of the house *vino bianco* and sipped the light, fruity white while they studied the menu. It was simple, handwritten and all in Italian. Travis did his best to translate the four items offered.

"Those are tagliatelle," he said, nodding to the broad flat noodles draped over wooden dowels at the rear of the restaurant. "Homemade and the specialty of the house. They're served with various seafoods and sauces."

The gray-haired, stoop-shouldered server who'd delivered their wine filled in the gaps. Employing limited English and swooping hand gestures, he expanded on the menu. Travis went with spider-crab tagliatelle in a cream sauce. Kate opted for the porcini-mushrooms-and-scallops marinara. Their dinners came with cucumber salads and a basket of crusty bread perfect for sopping up olive oil and balsamic vinegar.

The string quartet's performance ended halfway through the meal, which Travis wouldn't have noticed if not for the burst of applause and subsequent emptying of the church.

"That was nice," he commented in a magnanimous concession to a music form that still made him all squinty eyed and sleepy.

"Very nice," Kate agreed solemnly.

They lingered over a shared tiramisu before strolling back through the serpentine streets. Most of the gondolas had been docked and shrouded for the night, but a few water taxis still navigated the Grand Canal. The wooden boats moved slowly, their engines throttled back in deference to the late hour. Iridescent ripples from their wake lapped at the marble steps and landing sites of the palazzi lining this portion of Venice's main waterway.

Like the other palaces, Palazzo Alleghri's exterior was bathed in the light of the moon and discreetly placed floods. Its white columns seemed to rise directly from the shimmering water of the canal, while its tiers of arched windows shed a calm, welcoming glow.

Kate was feeling anything but calm, however. She'd departed the trattoria encased in a bubble of happiness and epicurean satisfaction. Those emotions quickly took a backseat to the pure joy of knowing she would sleep in the same bed as her husband tonight. But with each step closer to their hotel, her joy took on a sharp, shivery edge of anticipation that had everything to do with the bed and nothing to do with sleep.

Three times in one night wasn't their record, but it was enough to make Kate purr when she finally snuggled against Travis's side. Mere moments later, she was dead to the world.

Travis lay beside her, breathing in the scent of their lovemaking, feeling the gentle rise and fall of the breast pressed against his ribs. When he was sure she was out for the count, he glanced at the illuminated dial of the watch he'd left on the nightstand. It was just past midnight here, a little past 6:00 p.m. at his home base back in Florida. If his boss wasn't flying or attending yet another high-level conference on the employment of special ops assets, he might still be at his desk.

Moving carefully, Travis slid his arm from under Kate's head and eased out of bed. Although he'd acted blasé about telling the old man that he'd decided to leave the air force, the prospect sat like a dead weight in his gut. Best to get it done and over with.

Since this wasn't the kind of call he could make naked, he pulled on his jeans and took his cell phone into the other room. He almost hoped Hamilton's exec would say he was gone for a day or in DC or even down with the flu. No such luck.

The colonel was in his office, at his desk and in a blistering mood. "I hope to hell you're calling to tell me you're about to wrap up that project at Aviano."

"Not exactly."

"Well, get it in gear. I need you here, dammit."

Travis had faced armed hostiles with steadier nerves than he felt at this moment. Unconsciously, he squared his shoulders. "I wanted to tell you I'm putting in a request to separate from active duty."

"The hell you say!"

"I've received a job offer, a good one, and I'm going to accept it."

The silence that followed was long, stark and brutal. Hamilton finally broke it with a terse question.

"Will this job get you and Kate back together?"

Travis wasn't surprised Hamilton knew about the split. Crews talked; secrets leaked; rumors spread. More to the point, the colonel's wife kept a finger on the pulse of every family in his command.

"I'm hoping so, sir."

There was no silence this time, no hesitation. The

response came fast and straight from the gut of a man who thought his wife was womanhood incarnate.

"Then do it. I sure as hell would."

Travis breathed easy for the first time since picking up the phone. He could feel the relief—and guilt—rolling off him in waves when the colonel barked a final order before cutting the connection.

"Just make sure you haul your ass back here before you separate, Westbrook. You've got a few things to wrap up at this end, too."

Chapter Six

Kate woke to a day that seemed tinted gold around the edges. The bedroom's heavy drapes shut out most of the light, but a few thin rays sneaked through. Enough to brighten the gilt trim on the chandelier and the gold-leaf vines twining up the bed's four flat-topped posts. Stretching sinuously, she was admiring the intricate woodwork when her husband strolled in.

He'd already showered, shaved and dressed. He'd also obviously ordered from room service. She eyed the silver tray he was carrying avidly.

"Please tell me that's coffee."

"Coffee and *pagnottini*."

"Which is?"

"Sort of a sweet roll stuffed with raisins."

Wiggling upright, she tucked the sheet under her armpits and scooted over to make room for the tray while he tore off a bite for her to sample. It was sweet and yeasty and good. *Really* good!

"Carlo got Brian and me hooked on these little suckers," Travis explained as she savored the delicious morsel. "Wasn't hard to do, since he has them delivered fresh each morning. I'm guessing they come from the same bakery that supplies this hotel."

"Carlo certainly lives the good life," Kate commented. "When do I get to meet this new friend of yours?"

"Well, I thought we could spend today sightseeing in Venice and drive up to the base tomorrow."

Where he would put in an application to separate from the air force. The thought filled her with a pounding eagerness.

"That works for me!"

He tore off another bit of roll and popped it into her mouth. "I called Colonel Hamilton last night, after you fell asleep."

She swallowed the half-chewed lump, felt it stick in her throat. Breathing hard, she got it down before asking hesitantly, "And?"

"I told him I'm putting in my papers."

Her heart thumped painfully. "And?"

"And I'm putting in my papers."

She let that sink in for a few precious seconds. "Did he try to talk you out of it?"

"Actually, he didn't. Just said he'd do the same, given the circumstances."

She should have felt nothing but relief that Travis had taken the first step in what she knew had to be an excruciating process. Stupidly, what she felt was indignant.

"I'm glad he took it so well," she muttered, tearing off another chunk of pastry. "I mean, why should he care if you walk? You've only racked up more combat hours than any other pilot in wing."

"I expect he'll peel a strip off my hide when I get back to base. But until then…"

She didn't mistake either his smile or his meaning. Her indignation on his behalf fading, she finished the thought. "Until then we enjoy ourselves."

"Exactly."

"Just what did you have in mind, flyboy?"

"Well, for starters, I was thinking we could blow off sightseeing and spend the day in bed."

He added incentive by dipping down to drop a kiss on the slope of one breast. Kate gave the proposal the due diligence it deserved before reluctantly shaking her head.

"As tempting as that sounds, I need more than coffee and a sweet roll before we pick up where we left off last night."

She also needed another soak in that decadent clawfoot tub. Travis had stretched muscles last night that hadn't been stretched in too long.

"Let's have breakfast in that rooftop restaurant we didn't get to last night. We can decide where to go from there."

"All right." He conceded the point with feigned reluctance, as if Kate wasn't very well aware he required a man-sized breakfast to jump-start every day. "But you'd better get it in gear. This is the height of tourist season. Lines form early and long."

She snatched another pagni-whatever from the silver basket and balanced it with her coffee as she rolled out of bed. That left no hands for the sheet, which peeled down over her hips. Travis's appreciative wolf whistle followed her into the bathroom.

The realization that it was going to happen, that their lives were really going to take an entirely new direction, filled Kate with as much effervescence as the perfumed bubbles.

She was still high when she made the promised call to Dawn and Callie. Her friends put her on speakerphone, so they both heard the news that Travis was separating from the air force to take a job with Ellis Aeronautical Systems. Their reactions ranged from a disbelieving snort (Dawn) to a careful question (Callie).

"Are you sure that's what you want?"

"Absolutely."

"How about Travis? Is that what he wants?"

"It must be, since he called his boss last night. We're going up to the base at Aviano tomorrow. Travis will put in his papers then."

"What about this big project he's working on?"

Kate hadn't asked him but could reply with absolute confidence. "He'll stay and finish it."

"How long will that take?"

"I have no idea. He can't really…"

"…talk about it," her friends chorused.

Chuckling, Kate redirected the conversation. "How long are you guys planning to wallow in decadent luxury?"

"As long as we can!"

Callie tempered Dawn's emphatic reply. "Another few days. Why?"

"I know Venice wasn't on our original itinerary, but it's too incredible for words. So is the hotel we're staying in. It's owned by one of Carlo's cousins…"

"Carlo, aka the prince?"

"One and the same."

"I've *got* to meet this guy," Dawn exclaimed.

"Me, too," Kate said. "But back to Venice and the hotel. According to Travis, they gave us a very reasonable rate. I could try to get the same for you if you want to jump a train and zip over for the weekend."

"I doubt Trav would appreciate us barging in," Callie commented.

"Oh, I don't think he would mind *too* much." Her lips curved. "We're making up for lost time. Come if you want to."

"We'll think about it."

The most important contact completed, Kate scrolled through her messages again and made a return call to the bank in Bologna. Signore Gallo's assistant, Maximo, wasn't in, but he'd left a message with his secretary.

"Signore Gallo would very much like to chat with you about changes to the liquidity index."

The secretary's voice and heavy accent sounded familiar, but it took Kate a moment to connect them to the woman she'd surprised in the ladies' room at the bank, fighting tears. The odd encounter stuck in her mind as the secretary extended an invitation.

"Would it be possible for you and your husband to join him for lunch in our executive dining room on Monday? At one o'clock, if that's convenient."

"I think we can work that. If not, I'll call back and let you know."

"Grazie."

She relayed the gist of both calls to Travis as they took the elevator to the hotel's rooftop restaurant for a late breakfast.

"If you don't mind, I'd like to make another stop at the bank in Bologna. Signore Gallo's invited us to lunch. It should work out perfectly with our revised itinerary."

"Which version?" he asked with a grin.

"The one that has us in Venice today, Aviano tomorrow and wherever for the weekend. We could head back to Florence on Monday, with a stop in Bologna on the way."

"Works for me."

"I, uh, also told Callie and Dawn that we would check to see if there were any rooms available here at the hotel in case they wanted to zip over and see Venice this weekend."

To her surprise and secret relief, Travis took the invitation in stride. "Be great if they decide to come."

"You don't mind?"

"No, sweetheart, I don't." The elevator door pinged open, but he held it with one hand and tipped her chin with the other.

"You three have been best pals for as long as I've known you. I'd be happy to squire the Invincibles around Venice during the day." His voice dropped to a husky murmur. "As long as the nights are ours."

Shivers of delight dancing along her nerves, she echoed his earlier agreement. "Works for me."

But just in case, Travis thought as the hostess showed them to a table overlooking the Grand Canal, he might see what Brian had laid on for the weekend. Carlo, too. Never hurt to have a little diversionary tactic available when and if one became necessary.

In the meantime, he intended to sit back and enjoy his wife's delight in Venice, a city he'd come to know and appreciate these past weeks. Not that he'd experienced it in such sumptuous surroundings before.

Carlo kept insisting he owed Travis for covering his ass during a raid to rescue a captured Italian news crew. If so, the playboy prince had more than repaid the debt. Just watching Kate's face as she took in the restaurant's fairy-tale atmosphere tipped the scales in Carlo's favor.

Even Travis had to admit the restaurant would rank

at the top of anyone's most-romantic list. Sunbeams filtered through vine-covered trellises, the buffet was fit for a king—correction, for a Venetian doge—and their table gave them a superb view of the vaporetti and gondolas gliding over the canal directly below.

The extravagant buffet also offered guests a choice of wine, mimosas, Bloody Marys or Bellinis. Although the latter was more of a cocktail than a morning eye-opener, it went with the setting.

"You know the Bellini was invented here," Travis commented as Kate opted for the combination of sparkling wine and peach nectar served in a tall crystal flute.

"I know. At Harry's Bar, where Ernest Hemingway and Sinclair Lewis and a bunch of other literary greats hung out in the 1930s and '40s." When their waiter delivered her drink, she held it up to the light to admire the pale pink hue. "Wonder why it's called a Bellini."

Their server was only too happy to supply the answer. "It is named for one of our greatest painters, signora. When Giuseppe Cipriani, who owns Harry's Bar, combines sweet peach nectar with the wine, he says the color is the same as that of a saint's robe in a famous painting by Giovanni Bellini. So he names his creation in honor of this great artist."

Tucking his tray under his arm, the man beamed with local pride. "If you wish to see this painting, it hangs in the Doge's Palace. You plan to visit the palace, yes?"

"We do. Sometime later today, hopefully."

"It becomes very crowded," he said, echoing Travis's earlier warning. "But the hotel can arrange a tour so you do not have to stand in long lines. Shall I call down to the concierge and see what times may be available?"

"That would be wonderful."

She smiled her thanks but hooked a skeptical brow when the waiter departed. "The lines in Venice can't be any longer than the ones in Rome."

"Guess again. The major tourist sights in Rome are spread out. Here, they're pretty much concentrated around St. Mark's Square and the Rialto Bridge."

Kate acknowledged the point but remained dubious until the hotel's private vaporetto delivered them to St. Mark's Square for a one o'clock VIP tour of the pink-and-white Palazzo Ducale. The Doge's Palace had served as the residence of the supreme ruler of the Venetian republic since the eleventh century.

"Oh my god! I don't believe this crowd."

Grasping Travis's hand, Kate stepped off the boat's gleaming gunwale onto the pier and descended into a teeming sea of humanity. Tourists of every age and nationality jammed the square. The lines that snaked toward the entrance of the cathedral and the palace were epic.

Yet somehow the cheerful throng only added to Venice's nowhere-else-in-the-world ambience. There was no pushing, no shoving, and hundreds of kiosks lined the broad walkway in front of the palazzo. Their colorful offerings ranged from inexpensive carnival masks to gondoliers' straw boaters to lace parasols and every conceivable variation of I Love Venice T-shirts.

Their concierge had worked magic. Either that or the name of the hotel he worked for did the trick. Kate felt guilty bypassing the long lines at the Doge's Palace. Not guilty enough to forfeit their VIP tickets, however.

The palace was as magnificent as the guidebooks advertised. Okay, maybe a little overwhelming. It contained so many opulent rooms filled with so many priceless masterpieces that Kate went into overload two-thirds of the way through the tour. She was as relieved as Travis when they escaped into the bright afternoon sunshine...and thoroughly enchanted when he guided her through the crowd to an outside table at a restaurant in St. Mark's Square.

The restaurant was one of several housed in the elegant arcade that surrounded the square on three sides. Each restaurant featured regimented rows of outdoor tables with different-colored chairs. To Kate's delight, each also offered its own orchestra mounted on a platform under gaily striped awnings. The orchestras took turns entertaining the tourists thronging the square as well as the customers willing to pay astronomical menu prices in exchange for a table.

Kate's residency in Washington, DC, had exposed her to the world of outrageously expensive dinners and drinks. Still, she blinked at prices on the tasseled menu. She was mentally converting the cost of a glass of red wine from euros to dollars for the third time when Travis's cell phone buzzed.

"It's Brian Ellis," he announced after a glance at the digital display. "I left him a message earlier, asking for a return call."

"You're going to tell him you want the VP job?"

"I am."

"Make sure he understands it's contingent on giving me a better understanding of what you'll be doing. I want statistics," she hissed as he hit the answer button. "Risk factors."

"Christ, I thought you were kidding. What? No, not you, Brian." He shot Kate a fulminating glance. "I was talking to my wife. Turns out she wants a little more information about the duties of Ellis Aeronautical's VP for

test and evaluation before we sign on the dotted line."
He listened for a moment, then nodded. "Sure, we can
do that. What time? Okay, we'll be there."

He cut the connection and filled in the blanks.

"Brian says he'll be happy to provide any info you
want and suggests we join him for drinks and dinner
at his hotel this evening around seven."

"Okay." She tried to gauge his expression and came
up short. "Are you torqued that I want more detail about
what you'll be doing? I understand you might be. It's
just…"

The waiter appeared at that moment to take their orders. While Travis ordered a glass of red and a small
pastry for each of them, Kate listened absently to their
orchestra's haunting rendition of the theme from *Somewhere in Time* and tried to order her jumbled thoughts.

"It's just that so much of what you do in special ops
is classified," she said when they were as alone as they
could be sitting elbow to elbow with tourists from a
half dozen nations. "When you left on a mission, most
of the time you couldn't tell me where you were going
or who'd be shooting at you. It's not easy to live with
that kind of fear and uncertainty."

"I get that, Kate." Reaching across the small table, he
covered her hands with his. "And I wish I could promise
you'll never have to live with either again. Problem is,
we can mitigate risk but there's no way to completely
avoid it. All we can do is counter its impact with as much
happiness as we can cram into our lives."

He was right. She knew he was right. But she still
wanted some data.

That stubborn determination lasted right up until
their vaporetto nosed up to the private dock of Ellis's

hotel a little before seven that evening. Like the Palazzo Alleghri, the Gritti Palace had once been home to a nobleman of wealth and elegant taste—His Serene Highness Andrea Gritti, a sixteenth-century doge of Venice, according to the bronze plaque at the canal-side entrance.

The scene that greeted Kate and Travis when they entered the hotel, however, was anything but serene. A small army of black-clad employees had gathered in the lobby. Their expressions reflected deep worry as a team of medics wheeled a gurney out of the elevator. Brian Ellis strode along beside the gurney, looking every bit as grim.

Chapter Seven

"Brian!"

Ellis jerked his head around, spotted the new arrivals and signaled to the medics to wait.

As Travis and Kate rushed across the lobby, he had the awful thought that something might have happened to the executive's young son. When Ellis shifted to greet them, however, he saw the figure on the padded gurney was that of a woman who looked to be in her late forties or early fifties. Thankfully, she had her eyes open and appeared cognizant of her surroundings.

"What happened?"

"Mrs. Wells tripped." Ellis laid a comforting hand on the woman's shoulder. "We're hoping her ankle is just sprained, not broken."

"I can't believe I was so clumsy," the woman said with a grimace. "You can't imagine how many times I've warned Tommy to watch where he was going!"

"We're on our way to the hospital," Ellis related. "I'm sorry I didn't have time to call you and cancel dinner."

"Don't give that a second thought."

"Is there anything we can do to help?" Kate asked, turning a sympathetic smile on the other woman. "I'd be happy to come with you if you'd like some female companionship at the hospital."

"Thank you, dear, but I know Brian will take excellent care of me." She bit her lower lip. "I'm more worried about Tommy. My silly accident scared him."

"He'll be fine," Ellis assured her calmly, then gave Kate and Travis an explanation. "The hotel has sent an assistant manager up to keep him company until we get back."

He exuded an air of cool confidence, but Travis knew he had to be as concerned as his son's nanny. There was no guessing how long they would have to remain at the hospital for X-rays and medical consults. Travis was about to offer their services as a babysitter when Kate beat him to it.

"Why don't we stay with him? I realize he doesn't know us, but if you call up and tell him you work with Travis, we won't be total strangers."

Ellis didn't bother with any polite I-don't-want-to-impose-on-you protests. Relief evident in his blue eyes, he nodded. "Thanks. I'll do that."

Asking the medics to wait one more moment, he strode to the hotel employees gathered by the desk. He spoke a few words to a distinguished-looking gentleman in a black suit and silver-striped tie, then picked up the house phone and asked for his suite.

"This is Brian Ellis," he told whoever answered. "I appreciate you stepping in to look after my son, but I'm sending some friends up to stay with him until I get back. Yes. Yes, that's right. May I speak to Tommy, please?"

Kate had to admire his calm as he waited for his son to take the phone. Ellis was obviously used to dealing with crises, even those that involved people close to him. This glimpse of the man behind the CEO put a slightly different spin on the fact that Travis would be working with him.

"Hey, buddy, it's Dad. No, we're not at the hospital yet. I'll call you when we get there and know what the story is. In the meantime, I've asked some friends to hang with you while I'm gone. Remember me telling you about Major Westbrook? The C-130 pilot who's testing some new avionics for me at Aviano? He and his wife are on their way up to our suite, okay? Good. Mrs. Wells and I might be a while, so you behave. That means *no* more trying to swim in the canal and *no* bombing passersby with water balloons."

Kate's brow rose at the instructions, even higher at the one that followed.

"And no pestering Major Westbrook to take you up for a joyride, bud. I've still got the shakes from the last time you took the stick."

Travis was grinning when Ellis hung up. "He sounds like my kind of kid."

"Yeah, well, we'll see how you feel about that when I get back," the kid's dad drawled. "We're in suite 220. Here's my key card, and thanks again for doing this."

"No problem. Take care of Mrs. Wells and don't worry about anything here. We'll hold the fort."

Kate wished the older woman a speedy recovery and accompanied Travis to the elevator. "Those were interesting instructions Brian issued," she commented. "Think we're up to this task?"

"His kid's only six. I've got twenty-five years and probably close to a hundred and fifty pounds on him. Worst case, I'll pin him to the floor while you hog-tie him with the bedsheets."

Kate laughed, but after hearing some of young Tom's exploits, she couldn't help wondering what kind of mischievous imp they'd be spending the next few hours with.

His temporary babysitter answered their knock and let them into a suite that was larger and even more palatial than their rooms at the Palazzo Alleghri. She could get used to all these gilt-edged antiques and handblown chandeliers, Kate thought as they crossed an intricately inlaid parquet floor to greet their charge.

His hair was a lighter brown than his dad's, and his eyes would have been just as bright a blue if they weren't so worried. When the assistant manager made her exit, the boy's first concern was for his nanny.

"Is Mrs. Wells gonna be okay?"

"We don't know," Travis answered truthfully. "She didn't look like she was doing too bad when we saw her downstairs, but your dad said they'll have to x-ray her ankle."

"She's always telling me to not leave my stuff lying around where someone could trip over it, and I didn't. I didn't!"

His cornflower blue eyes took on a bright sheen as he pointed to a raised dining area. The generous space contained a table with seating for eight and a massive cabinet displaying an array of exquisite Venetian goblets, each one a work of art.

"It was that step," Tommy said, his voice quavering. "We ordered some sp'ghetti for dinner 'cause Dad wasn't gonna be here. Mrs. Wells went to clear my puzzles off the table and missed that step."

Kate picked up on the subtext instantly. "You haven't had dinner? I bet you're starved."

His lip quivered. "Kinda."

"Why don't I check on that order? And if it's okay with you, I'll make it spaghetti for three. We haven't had dinner, either."

The three of them managed to consume an entire loaf of garlic bread, colorful caprese salads, heaping bowls of the Gritti Palace's incomparable spaghetti Bolognese, and—for Travis and Tommy—two servings of gelato.

Obviously still on his best behavior, Brian's son insisted on helping clear the table before he assumed an air of cherubic innocence. "Didya ever play 'Space Zombie'?"

He directed the question to both adults. Travis shook his head, but Kate seemed to recall a spirited match with a young cousin some years ago.

"I think so. It's been a while, though."

The angelic facade cracked, disclosing an expression of Machiavellian delight. "It's on the hotel's kid channel. Mrs. Wells 'n' me started a game, but she gave up at level three. We could pick it up there, if you want."

"Okay."

Shooting Travis a glance that said she knew darn well she was being set up, Kate sat next to her challenger on the luxuriously appointed sofa. Tommy's thumbs worked at warp speed, and mere moments later they were engaged in a life-and-death galactic struggle. When her spaceship exploded for the fifth and final time, Kate groaned and offered Travis her controls.

"Tommy's too good for me. You take him on."

Gleeful shouts and hoots punctuated the next thirty or forty minutes. Kate tucked her legs under her and hid a smile as her husband did battle with his youthful alter ego.

He and Tommy could have been hatched from the same egg. They were both so exultant when they scored. Neither gave an inch, although it didn't take long for Travis to realize he was out of his league. He was going down in flames for the third time when the house phone jangled.

Kate was closest to the phone and took the call. As she listened to Brian Ellis's terse report, her smile slipped. "Oh, no! I'm so sorry to hear that."

Her murmur registered instantly with the two males planted in front of the big-screen TV. One assumed a careful expression. The other's face crumpled.

"Yes," Kate said, her glance zinging to Tommy. "I'll tell him. And no, we don't mind at all."

She hung up and broke the bad news. "It looks like Mrs. Wells really did some damage. Her ankle is broken in several places, and the X-rays show floating bone fragments, so she'll have to have surgery."

"Is she gonna die?" Stark fear erupted in Tommy's eyes. "Like my mom?"

Dear God! Kate shot Travis a swift look. She had no idea what had happened to Brian Ellis's wife. But Kate didn't want to offer her son platitudes and assurances he wouldn't believe.

Travis got the message and moved quickly to put a personal spin on the disaster. "I broke my ankle once, too," he told the frightened boy. "When I was playing basketball in high school. Came down hard the wrong way and felt it pop right there on the court."

"Did you have surg'ry?"

"Sure did. The docs had to realign the bones and put screws in to hold them stable while the breaks healed.

Then I got a cast and had to hobble around on crutches for a month or so afterward."

"But…" Tommy gulped, tears brimming. "But you weren't old, like Mrs. Wells. Old people don't get well fast. She said so herself."

"That's true. Mrs. Wells isn't *that* old, though. Not like, uh…" Travis stumbled for a moment to come up with a character the six-year-old could relate to. "Not like Harry Potter's professor at the Hogwarts academy."

"Professor Dumbledore?" Tommy wasn't convinced but made a reluctant concession. "I guess not."

"Your dad said he wanted to stay with Mrs. Wells until they decided the best way to handle the surgery," Kate told the boy. "So Travis and I will hang with you awhile longer, okay?"

"Okay."

Hoping to distract him, Travis gestured to the TV. "Want to finish our battle? I might be able to come up with a few desperate moves yet."

"No." The reply was small and still shaky, but there was no mistaking the noble sacrifice behind his next remark. "I'd better take my bath."

He paused, and some of his incipient panic gave way to an almost imperceptible craftiness. "Mrs. Wells makes me go to bed at nine. But I can usually watch TV until ten."

"Usually?" Travis echoed, hiding a smile.

"Sometimes."

"Well, this might be one of those times. Let's get you in the tub, champ. Then we'll see if there's anything worth watching on TV."

With the resilience of the young, Tommy perked up instantly. "The kids' channel has lots of movies. I've seen *Frozen* bunches of times but I can watch it again."

* * *

Kate's phone buzzed while Tommy was torpedoing an array of tub toys under Travis's watchful eye.

"We've decided to take you up on your offer to see Venice," Callie told her. "If you think we can get a room at the hotel, we'll jump a train tomorrow morning… unless you've changed your mind."

"Or Travis changed it for her," Dawn groused in the background.

Dawn wasn't going to forgive Travis anytime soon, Kate acknowledged with a smile. Her friends were mighty, and they were fierce. For maybe the thousandth time since third grade, she realized how lucky she was to have them in her life.

"We'd love to have you join us," she began. "But—"

"Ha!" Dawn exclaimed. "Told you so!"

"—we've run into a small crisis here," Kate continued. "Brian Ellis, the man who offered Travis the VP job, brought his young son and the boy's nanny to Italy with him. The nanny tripped a few hours ago and bunged up her ankle. She's at the hospital now and it looks like she'll have to have surgery, so Travis and I volunteered to sit with the boy in the interim. I'm not sure how long our services might be required."

"We can help," Callie said with her usual warm-hearted generosity. "We'll take an early train to Venice."

"Do come, but you don't have to do babysitting duty. Travis and I have it covered."

And doing pretty well with it, too, if the high-pitched giggles emanating from the bathroom were any indication. With a sudden, piercing ache, Kate imagined Travis waging bathtub battles with their son. Or hunkering down to have tea with their little girl and her favorite dolls. Or…

"Let me check to see if there's a room available at our hotel," she said, swallowing the lump in her throat. "I'll call you back."

She was poking in her purse for the card with the hotel's number on it when the house phone rang. It was Brian Ellis this time, and he started with a gruff apology.

"I'm so sorry to impose on you and Travis like this."

"We don't mind. Honestly. How's Mrs. Wells?"

"Resting more comfortably now that they've pumped some painkillers into her. Her surgery is scheduled for early tomorrow morning."

Kate could imagine all the strings he'd had to pull to make it happen so quickly.

"She'll be in a cast and on crutches for at least a month," he related, "and may need physical therapy after that. So she's decided to fly home as soon as the docs give her a green light and recuperate with her sister in California."

"When do you think she'll be able to leave Italy?"

"If the surgery goes well tomorrow, she should be okay to travel on Sunday. I've put my private jet on standby." He paused for several beats. "Tommy's mom died during surgery to remove a brain tumor. He was only a baby, too young to remember the specifics. But he's asked about it enough times that he may freak out over all this."

His terse account put the pain Kate had experienced since her break with Travis into sharp perspective. Her husband was right, she thought with a crimp in her heart. There *were* no guarantees. And certainly no ways to completely eliminate risk, whether it came from war, earthquakes or brain tumors.

"Tommy did get a little upset when I told him Mrs. Wells would need surgery," she admitted. "He seems okay now. Travis is supervising his bath at the moment.

Then we thought we might tune in to a movie on the kids' channel, if that's all right?"

"Fine with me. My guess is he'll dragoon you into watching *Frozen*. He's only seen it fifteen or twenty times. Letty—Mrs. Wells—threatened to quit if she had to watch it again."

"I can't speak for Travis, but it'll be the first time for me. So don't worry, okay? Stay with Letty as long as she needs you. We're fine here. And we'll be glad to watch Tommy for you tomorrow," she added, "so you can be at the hospital during the surgery."

"You better check with your husband on that," Ellis said ruefully. "I got the impression he'd planned a romantic interlude with you in Venice. I doubt those plans included riding herd on my lively offspring."

"We're nothing if not flexible," Kate tossed back.

She smiled to herself, thinking how this whole Italian experience had already taken more unexpected turns and twists than she could have imagined.

"And I have reinforcements coming if they're needed. The two friends I'm traveling with called a few minutes ago. They're staying at Carlo's villa in Tuscany but decided to take the train over to Venice for the weekend if I can get them a room at our hotel."

"If not, they could stay there at the Gritti."

Kate glanced around the magnificent suite and didn't even *want* to think how much it must cost a night. "The Gritti might be a little out of their price range."

"No, they would be my guests. Letty's suite is just down the hall from ours," Ellis explained. "Whenever we travel, I always make sure she has her own sanctuary to retreat to in the evenings. She needs one," he said drily, "after a day with Tommy. I'm going to bring whatever she needs to the hospital in the morning. Then

I'll have the hotel staff pack the rest of her things for the flight home. So her suite will be empty. Your friends are welcome to use it this weekend, or longer if they like. It's booked for the duration of our stay."

"That's very generous."

"It's the least I can do after dragooning you into service."

"Let me check with our hotel first. If they don't have anything, we may take you up on that offer."

Or, Kate thought, if the room rate at the Palazzo Alleghri was as exorbitant as she suspected, despite Travis's assurances they were getting a break.

"Whatever works," Ellis said. "I should be back in a couple of hours. I'm just waiting on the surgeon. He's on his way in to discuss tomorrow's procedure with me."

Of course he was. Mere mortals didn't see their surgeons until moments before the anesthetist slapped a mask over their face. Mrs. Wells and her employer obviously occupied a different universe.

"And Kate...?"

"Yes?"

"Thank you. I won't forget this."

"I'm just glad we can help."

She hung up, reflecting yet again on the remarkable acquaintances Travis had made during his stint in Italy. They might not all wear the same uniform, but they sure seemed to have grown as tight as any band of brothers.

A call to the Palazzo Alleghri confirmed that they did indeed have another suite available. And they would be most happy to let Maggiore Westbrook's friends have it at the discounted rate.

"Which is?"

The answer almost stopped her banker's heart. Gulping, she said she would consult with her friends and call back in the next five minutes if they wanted to take the suite.

She hung up with absolutely no intention of calling back. Dawn might be able to swing half of the Palazzo Alleghri's exorbitant rate, but Kate wouldn't even consider allowing Callie to dig deeper into her savings. Instead, she relayed the alternative proposal.

"Have I got a deal for you," she said when Dawn answered.

"Hang on. Let me put you on speaker. Okay, shoot."

"Brian Ellis—the man whose son we're watching—is arranging a private jet to fly the injured nanny back to the States on Sunday."

"A private jet?" Dawn gave a low whistle. "Your hubby seems to be running with a whole different crowd these days."

"No kidding! But back to Ellis. He's taking what the nanny needs to the hospital tomorrow morning and having the rest of her things packed for the flight home. So her suite will be empty, and when I mentioned you guys were coming to Venice, he offered you the use of it as a thank-you to me for watching his son."

"I don't know." That came from Callie. "First this villa, now a hotel suite. I feel as though we're taking advantage of Travis's friends."

"It's your call. But Ellis sounded genuinely sincere." Kate skimmed a glance around the suite. "And trust me, you haven't lived until you've bunked down in an honest-to-goodness doge's palace."

"We'll take it!" Dawn said, overriding Callie's reservations. "I, for one, could get used to living in opulence."

* * *

Kate told Travis about Ellis's generous offer while Tommy fired up the ginormous flat-screen TV in the sitting room.

"Callie was reluctant to accept it," she related, curling up next to her husband on a sofa backed by plump, fringed cushions. "She thinks we're taking advantage of your new pals."

"Well, yeah, we are. But you and I know friendship's a two-way street. You have to give, but you also have to accept each other's gifts graciously."

"True."

Very true, she mused, leaning against the familiar comfort of Travis's shoulder. He toyed idly with a strand of her hair while keeping a close eye on Tommy as he skimmed the movie channels. The boy zipped past the half dozen adult channels, thank goodness, but paused at a shoot-'em-up action drama that promised blood and gore.

"Keep moving," Travis drawled.

As his father had predicted, Tommy opted for a repeat showing of *Frozen*. Halfway through, however, he went out like a light and didn't so much as stir when Travis scooped him up and carried him to bed.

"Whew," Kate murmured when Travis rejoined her on the cushion-strewn sofa. "We managed to make it through the evening with no water balloons or other flying projectiles. Think we'll be as lucky tomorrow?"

"Doubtful." He tucked her against him. "But we don't have to play watchdog tomorrow, Kate. Brian knows how many hoops I had to jump through to get this time with you. He could hire someone to—"

"Yeah, right," she interrupted with a snort. "Like you would bail on a friend in need? Or I would let you?"

"Ah, Katydid." He shifted her in his arms. "That fierce loyalty is just one of the reasons I love you."

"Care to elaborate on the others?"

"Later," he murmured with a smile that did stupid things to her insides. "After we get back to our hotel."

Chapter Eight

It was after midnight when Brian Ellis called from the lobby to let them know he was on his way up.

"That was considerate of him," Kate commented wryly as she scrambled to straighten various items of clothing that had somehow got all twisted and bunched.

"Like I said," Travis replied with a twinkle in his hazel eyes, "he knows the hoops I had to jump through to get this time with you."

Kate's tugging and twisting stilled. She wanted her husband out of the military, but she didn't want him leaving under a cloud. "You're not missing any critical tests or milestones, are you?"

"Carlo is covering what needs to be covered."

"Travis! Please tell me this leave of absence isn't going to get you in trouble."

"If it does, it's nothing I can't handle."

Kate's heart sank. Great! Just great! As if the fact

that she was forcing her husband to choose between her and the career he loved didn't make her feel guilty enough.

She was still squirming at the thought when Ellis rapped on the door. Travis let him in and offered to return his key card.

"I can get another key at the desk. You'd better keep that one…if you're *sure* you don't mind staying with Tommy the Terrible during Letty's surgery."

"We're sure, and he wasn't terrible at all."

"Ha!" his loving father replied. "Don't let that angelic exterior fool you. He's always on his best behavior with strangers. But in the immortal words of Scarlett O'Hara, tomorrow is another day."

Travis laughed, and Kate picked up on that cue. "Speaking of tomorrow, my friends decided to zip over to Venice for the weekend. If *you're* sure you don't mind them taking temporary occupancy of Letty's suite."

"Lord, no! Now I won't feel so guilty about interrupting your Venetian interlude."

"Did you talk to the surgeon?" Travis wanted to know.

"I did. I also had my people do a thorough scrub of his credentials. From all reports, he's tops in his field."

"What time is the surgery?"

"Ten a.m. I need to get to the hospital by eight," Ellis said apologetically. "I want to be there when they prep Letty."

"No problem," Travis assured him. "How about we show up here at seven?"

"Let's make it seven thirty. I'll arrange for a vaporetto to pick you up, then take me directly to the hospital." He raked a hand through his short brown hair.

"It's been a long day. I could use a drink. How about you two?"

To Kate's relief, Travis took a pass. She was feeling as whipped as Brian Ellis now looked. With his tie loosened and whiskers beginning to bristle his cheeks and chin, the executive was showing the effects of the traumatic evening.

He insisted on sending them back to the Palazzo Alleghri in the Gritti's luxurious private vaporetto. Due to the late hour, the oak-paneled motorboat glided almost silently through the canals. Although light still spilled from a few cafés and trattorias, the residences lining the waterway were shuttered and dark. Gondolas shrouded with canvas bobbed in their moorings, and even the floodlights illuminating Venice's distinctive landmarks had been turned off.

Kate drowsed in Travis's arms for most of the short ride, but when the door to their suite clicked shut behind them, she came wide awake. The strenuous activities that followed wiped her out, however. So much that she groaned and dragged the sheet over her head when the phone beside their bed buzzed a wake-up call at six thirty the next morning.

Afterward, Kate could only blame her lack of sleep for forgetting Brian's prophetic warning. Not until she and Travis arrived at the Gritti Palace did she discover that tomorrow was indeed another day.

"There's still time for you to back out," an obviously exasperated Ellis warned when he opened the door.

"You take care of Mrs. Wells. Kate and I will hold down the home front," Travis assured him with what they both later agreed was totally misplaced confidence.

Ellis threw a dubious glance at the pint-size figure planted on the sofa. His arms were crossed over the snarling dinosaur on his T-shirt and a mutinous expression sat on his face.

"Go," Travis insisted.

Yielding, Ellis hefted the small suitcase sitting next to the door. "I've asked the hotel to pack the rest of Letty's things and move them into our suite," he told Kate. "They'll clean the rooms and have them ready for your friends by noon."

"Great. Last word was they planned to arrive around three this afternoon."

"Okay." He shot his son another glance. "I'll call you as soon as Letty's out of surgery and tell you how it went, bud."

His only reply was a scowl.

With his soft brown hair and angelic blue eyes, the boy looked like an advertisement for Cute Kids Inc. But the real Tommy the Terrible emerged almost before the door clicked shut behind his father.

The first crisis involved breakfast. No, he didn't want to go down to the restaurant. No, he didn't want anything on the room service menu. The oatmeal was too mushy. The cereal didn't contain one single raisin, and they did something funny to their scrambled eggs.

"Okay," Travis answered with commendable patience. "What *do* you want?"

"Nothing."

"Suit yourself. But Kate and I haven't eaten." He threw her a conspiratorial glance. "How do blueberry pancakes and a cheese omelet sound?"

"Wonderful. Order a side of bacon, too. I'm starving. And orange juice," she added with a quick look at the pouting youngster.

"And coffee," Travis muttered. "We're going to need coffee."

Mulishly stubborn, Tommy refused juice and bacon but did force down a half glass of milk, a stack of pancakes and several helpings of thick-sliced Italian toast oozing butter and strawberry jam. While they ate, Kate tried to coax him out of his unhappy mood. He was scared, she knew. No doubt thinking of the mother he could barely remember. She tried to soothe those fears by suggesting a walk to St. Mark's Square to feed the pigeons.

His blue eyes lit up briefly. Too briefly. Then the sullen mask dropped over his face again. "Mrs. Wells says the pigeons are dirty. 'N' they poop on your head."

"Okay. What about jumping a vaporetto and heading over to the Lido? One of my guidebooks said there's a beautiful beach. We could swim and—"

"We have a pool right here at the hotel."

"Well…" Desperate, she powered up her iPhone and searched for kids' activities in Venice. "Have you taken the elevator to the top of the Campanile?"

"What's that?"

"The tower across from the cathedral in St. Mark's Square."

"The big one?"

She didn't trust the expression that flitted across his face. With a distinct frisson of alarm, she nixed that idea.

"This says the lines for the Campanile elevators are a mile long and there's no timed entry. But there are timed tickets for St. Mark's Cathedral. Want me to see if we can get in?"

"Is the cathedral where those big horses are?"

"Yes."

"Mrs. Wells 'n' me saw them when we were out walking, but she said she was too old to climb the steps up to where they are. You could climb them, though. You 'n' Major Westbrook 'n' me."

Kate turned a helpless look on Travis. His shoulders lifted in a you-got-us-into-this-one shrug.

"Let me see if there are three tickets available today."

There were, but only at 2:15 and 5:20. Even with timed entry, the website warned, guests should expect to encounter lines. Kate repeated the warning to the two males at the table. Travis left the decision to Tommy, who made a face but said he guessed he could stand in line…for a little while.

Not reassured by the grudging admission, Kate grabbed the earlier entry slots. To fill the time until then, she suggested they check out the ship models at the Castello's naval museum and have a pizza lunch at a trattoria before heading for the cathedral. Tommy made a show of reluctance but agreed with the proposed itinerary.

When they were ready to leave the hotel, Kate penned a quick note to leave at the desk for Callie and Dawn while Tommy retrieved a ball cap and backpack from his room.

Travis eyed the backpack suspiciously. "You're not toting any balloons or water bottles in that, are you?"

"No, sir." His voice rang with indignation. "Dad said not to drop any more, 'n' I *always* do what he tells me to."

Travis didn't dispute that profoundly questionable statement, but his eyes danced as he ushered Tommy and Kate out into the wild vortex that was Venice at the height of tourist season.

* * *

By the time they returned to the Gritti in midafternoon, Travis was seriously rethinking this whole business of being a parent. He and Kate had always planned to have kids—someday. The topic had come up with less and less frequency in the past few years, but it had still been there, part of his vision for their future. Now he was having second thoughts.

He felt almost as whipped as he had after completing his brutal three-week survival, escape, resistance and evasion training. The SERE course was intended to prepare military members who might be trapped behind enemy lines for the worst. Damned if Tommy the Terrible hadn't tested almost every one of Travis's hard-learned survival skills!

True, the sweltering August heat constituted as much of a problem as the crowds. Kate had kept a viselike grip on one of Tommy's hands, Travis the other. They didn't let the kid off the leash for more than two or three milliseconds, yet he somehow managed to melt into the throng at the ship museum. They found him several heart-stopping moments later with his feet planted wide in the well of a life-size model of a fifteenth-century gondola, pretending to pole his way through rough seas.

At that point a disapproving museum attendant had suggested they depart the premises. Chastened, Tommy behaved himself at lunch, although he put away more pizza than Travis would have believed possible for someone his size. Unfortunately, Brian called while they were at the pizzeria to relay the news that Mrs. Wells's surgery was taking longer than expected. Matters went south from that point.

In quick sequence, Tommy let them know that he was *not* happy about having to stand in line for gelato, the men's room, or to retrieve their tickets to St. Mark's Cathedral. Travis responded with dwindling patience to each of those sullen complaints. The terrifying minutes on the balcony of St. Mark's, however, took at least a year off his life.

It started when they claimed their tickets and a brochure that contained a brief history of the four iconic bronze horses mounted on the balcony directly above the cathedral's main entrance. Tommy seemed interested when Travis related the historical background. That the sculptures were probably Greek in origin. That they'd once adorned the hippodrome in Constantinople and were looted by Venetian forces when they sacked the city during the Fourth Crusade.

His mistake, Travis realized too late, was relating the interesting fact that the Venetians had severed the horses' heads to transport the massive war trophies from Constantinople. Once in Venice, they'd soldered the heads back on and fashioned jeweled collars to hide the seam. Naturally, any kid as lively and inquisitive as Tommy Ellis would want to see the decapitation site for himself. And to do that he would have to hoist himself up on the balcony ledge.

Kate had spotted him first. Screeching, she'd grabbed his dinosaur T-shirt and hauled him off the ledge. When he had both feet planted back on the balcony, Travis did a mental ten count. Then another ten. He was about to go for thirty when Brian called. After relating the welcome news that the surgery had gone well and Tommy's nanny was in recovery, Ellis had asked to speak to his son.

The change in the kid was instant. His face lit up like one of the megawatt flares the Combat King dispensed to deflect oncoming missiles. But despite Tommy's dramatic upsurge in spirits, Travis felt as though he'd been put through a meat grinder by the time they returned to the Gritti.

The message waiting at the desk didn't do much to lighten his mood. Kate gave an excited hoot when she learned that Callie and Dawn had arrived a little over an hour ago. She couldn't wait to schmooze with her pals and bring them up to date on all the happenings since they'd parted company in Rome. Travis couldn't wait to down an early but well-deserved scotch.

Kate's friends rang the bell of the Ellis suite less than fifteen minutes later. Eager to see them, Kate set aside the wine Travis had just poured for her and hurried to the door.

"Look at you," Dawn murmured, searching her face with the keen eyes of long friendship. "You're glowing, dammit." She gave an exaggerated sigh. "If that's what taking a belated honeymoon does for you, maybe I shouldn't have left two grooms standing at the altar."

"Well…"

"Never mind. I'll get it right one of these days."

She breezed in on that rueful admission. Callie gave Kate a fierce hug and followed.

Scotch in hand, Travis rose to greet them. His smile carried that faint tinge of wariness he'd adopted since the two women had declared open season on him. "How was Tuscany?"

"Incredible." Dawn's glance swept the opulent suite. "These new pals of yours certainly live well."

"They do. Can I get you a drink?"

"A red wine would be great."

"You got it. Callie?"

"I'm good for now, thanks."

While he attended to things at the antique cabinet

that housed the bar, Callie greeted the fifth person in the room. He was slumped in a corner of the sofa, regarding the newcomers with a mix of curiosity and shyness.

"Hi. I'm Callie."

"I'm Tommy Ellis."

"Nice to meet you, Tommy. Is that a diplodocus on your shirt?"

His eyes went wide. "You know 'bout dinosaurs?"

"I do. I studied them in school."

"I didn't know girls studied stuff like that."

Callie hid a smile. "Some of us do."

"I've got a book with pictures of tyrannosauruses and pterodactyls 'n' stuff. Wanna see it?"

"Sure."

Perked up by the attention, he bounced off the sofa and showed the way to his room.

"Cute kid," Dawn commented as Travis delivered her a crystal goblet of deep, shimmering brunello. "How's his nanny doing?"

"Last report said she came through the surgery fine and should be able to fly home on Sunday, as planned," he related.

"Kate told us about the private jet." She took a sip of the wine, her green eyes knifing into him over the rim of her goblet. "She also told us this guy Ellis offered you a job. Are you going to take it?"

"That's the plan."

"About damned time you pulled your head out of your ass and got your priorities right, Westbrook."

"Thanks, McGill," Travis drawled. "I was just waiting for your stamp of approval to seal the deal."

Hastily, Kate intervened. "Sheathe the swords, you two. How about we take our drinks out on the terrace? I want to hear more about Tuscany."

After the blistering heat of the day, the terrace was
an oasis of shade and soft, sweet fragrance. Planters
ringed the stone balustrade, filled with red geraniums
that brightened so many Venetian window boxes. At
the far end, a lion's head fountain bubbled happily into
a marble basin.

None of these feasts for the senses could compete
with the color and sheer vitality of the canal, however.
Thoroughly delighted, Dawn leaned her elbows on the
wide balustrade to admire the water ballet below. She
leaned over farther, then had to jerk her hand upright to
keep the wine from slopping out of her glass.

"Oops, almost got me a gondolier."

"Better not!" The warning came from Tommy, who'd
just come out with Callie. "We're not s'posed to toss
anything over the rail. Dad said so. After the hotel manager complained," he added with reluctant honesty.

"Why'd he complain?"

"Water balloons," Travis supplied solemnly.

"Uh-oh."

"It's those stupid hats." The six-year-old's nose
scrunched in disgust. "If they're gonna wear straw hats
with ribbons 'n' stuff, I think they should 'spect to get
water bombed."

Dawn looked much struck by the observation. "You're
right. Those hats are stupid. And such easy targets," she
added with a glance at the boats gliding by below.

"Christ, don't encourage him."

Dawn responded to Travis's muttered plea by making a face, then moved to the wrought iron beside the
fountain. "Sit here with me, Tommy. I want to hear more
of your adventures in Venice."

When he settled next to her, the gurgling fountain

drowned out their conversation. The cheerful splash also covered Callie's quiet comment to Kate and Travis.

"He's an extremely bright child. But very concerned about the woman who's been looking after him. I gather she's been with the family for some years."

"Pretty much most of Tommy's life," Kate replied. "Brian said his mother died when he was little more than a baby."

"The father seems to have done a good job with the boy. Tommy's bright and engaging and interacts well with adults."

"He is and he does, although I have to admit he kept us on our toes today."

"I expect he keeps his father on his toes, too," Callie guessed. "Even considering the fact that Ellis can afford to hire live-in help, it's not easy being a single parent. Even tougher when that parent is male. Only 17 percent of single parents in the US are men. As a result, they don't have as many support systems to help them deal with the emotional roller coaster of raising a child on their own."

"Kate and I took a brief ride on that roller coaster this afternoon," Travis related drily. "I haven't looked in the mirror, but I suspect it turned my hair white."

"Pure snow," Callie said, laughing, and gently changed the subject. "Tell me about this new job. Kate says you'll be based out of Washington. What does the job entail, or is that classified?"

"Not completely."

While Travis sketched the bare-bones details of what he would be doing as VP for test operations, Kate thought about Callie's assessment of Tommy. She wasn't surprised her friend had picked up on the boy's worries so quickly. Given her years with the Massachusetts child advocate office, Callie's antennae were finely tuned.

Too finely tuned. The pain and despair she'd had to deal with daily had left their mark on both her heart and her health. She'd lost weight in the past year, Kate thought, her gaze on her friend's prominent cheekbones. So much weight that she and Dawn had begun to worry about the quieter one of their threesome. A primary, if unstated, goal of this trip had been to fatten Callie up on pasta and cannoli.

They'd also wanted to help her forget whatever tragedy had caused her to walk away from her job last month. She never discussed her cases, even with them. Her work was governed by confidentiality laws every bit as strict as those Travis operated under.

Privately, Kate thought part of the problem was that Callie had no one in her life to balance the heartache she'd encountered in her job. Unlike Dawn, who attracted and discarded men with cheerful regularity, Callie approached relationships the way she did everything else, carefully and cautiously. So far none of the men she'd dated—including the half dozen or so Travis had fixed her up with—had made it past her reserved exterior to tap into the passion Kate and Dawn knew she possessed.

She needed someone older, they'd decided. Someone who shared her core values about work and family and friendship. Someone...

Like Brian Ellis.

Almost as soon as the thought hit, Kate dismissed it. The heartache she herself had gone through with Travis these past months had pretty much shattered her naive belief in a perfect match.

They'd complemented each other in almost every

way. Both hardworking, both career oriented, both reasonably intelligent. And so hungry for each other! In those joyously happy first years, neither of them could have even imagined they could cause each other such hurt.

Still… Her glance drifted to Tommy and back again. Be interesting to see if Callie assessed the father as favorably as she had the son.

Chapter Nine

The five of them stayed out on the terrace for another hour. Basking in the attention of the newcomers, Tommy remained on his best behavior. His face lit up, though, when his dad called.

Travis answered the house phone, then passed the instrument to the boy. "Your dad's on his way back to the hotel. He wants to know if you'd like to go to the hospital with him after dinner to visit Mrs. Wells."

Abandoning his manners, Tommy snatched the phone. "Does she want me to come? Really? I miss her, too." His happy glance landed on the geraniums. "I'm gonna pick her some flowers. She likes flowers." He listened a moment, his lips pooching. "But these are pretty red ones. What? O-kaay. I promise."

Heaving a much put-upon sigh, he passed the phone back to Travis. "He wants to talk to you."

Travis took the phone and confirmed that Kate's

friends had arrived and were comfortably settled. "We're all sitting out on your terrace, having drinks and admiring the view."

"I owe you for this," Ellis told him. "But I feel guilty as hell about cutting into your time with Kate. I know you had to hink your flight schedule big-time to get this leave."

"Don't worry about it. Kate and I are glad to help."

"Yeah, well, I may have to hink my schedule, too. I'd planned to stay in Italy through Billy Bob. But with Mrs. Wells out of action, I have to rethink those plans."

Billy Bob was their private code for the final and most critical flight test for the classified modification Ellis Aeronautical Systems had designed for Combat King II. The outcome could mean millions for EAS, possibly billions—Travis wasn't privy to the company's closely held contract negotiations. Not yet, anyway. But he knew EAS's CEO wouldn't have carved this big chunk of time out of his schedule if his company didn't have major bucks riding on the outcome.

"Let's talk about the schedule when you get back to the hotel," he suggested.

He'd kept his reply light. Innocuous. Yet as soon as he disconnected, he found himself the object of three pairs of eyes. Kate's questioning brown, Callie's deep lavender and Dawn's sharp, clear green. Even Tommy had picked up on the subtext.

"Are Dad 'n' me flying home with Mrs. Wells?"

"Maybe."

Emotions washed across the boy's expressive face. Relief, guilt, disappointment...all easily interpreted by the four adults.

"You don't want to go home?" Callie asked.

"Uh-huh, I do. Mostly."

"But?" she probed gently.

"We were s'posed to go to Rome after Venice. I was gonna have my picture taken with a gladiator at the Coliseum. Maybe get a sword 'n' everything."

"Maybe you and your dad should talk about that when you go to see Mrs. Wells after dinner."

"Speaking of which," Dawn put in, "what's the plan? If we're going to eat out, I need to spiffy up."

Kate and Callie shared a quick grin. Even unspiffed, Dawn could bring strong men to their knees. At this particular moment her hair spilled over her shoulders in a careless river of dark red, her I Love Rome T clung to her full breasts and her jeans might have been painted on.

"Why don't we just hit a trattoria for dinner?" Kate suggested. "Travis took me to a fabulous one last night. Very casual."

When Brian Ellis arrived a few moments later, he certainly appeared to agree with Kate's assessment that Dawn didn't need spiffing.

He greeted Callie with a warm smile and countered her thanks for letting them use Mrs. Wells's rooms with the comment that it was small payment for the favor Kate and Travis had done him. But his reaction to Dawn was more visceral and instantly apparent. The handshake was firm, the smile stayed in place, but he did that quick double take Dawn always sparked in the male of the species.

Uh-oh, Kate thought. This could be trouble. As much as she loved her friend, she cringed at the distinct possibility Dawn might wreak her usual love-'em-and-leave-'em havoc on Brian Ellis. The man had lost his wife. He was raising a young son, managing a megacorporation. Anything other than a light flirtation could prove a recipe for disaster.

Hard on the heels of that thought came a healthy side order of guilt. Fiercely, Kate reminded herself that her loyalty lay—and would *always* lie—with Dawn. Ellis was an adult. He could take care of himself.

Still, Kate wasn't surprised when he asked about their plans for dinner, then countered her suggested trattoria with a generous offer. "Why don't you let Tommy and me treat you folks to dinner here at the Gritti? Their indoor restaurant is too formal for us," he said with a conspiratorial wink in his son's direction, "but we enjoy eating out on the terrace."

"You'd like it," the boy assured them. "The chef bakes a special kind of mac 'n' cheese just for me. It's really good!"

Dawn shot him a quick smile. "Sounds great. I'm in."

The others agreed and they were soon settled at a table almost within arm's reach of the water traffic gliding by. Spray misters mounted on tall poles dispersed the last heat of the day and bathed diners in cool comfort. Based on Tommy's enthusiastic recommendation, they all ordered his special dish. The mac and cheese turned out to be a truly glorious combination of penne pasta, crumbled Italian sausage, portobello mushrooms, creamy *pomodoro* sauce and four different Italian cheeses baked in individual ramekins.

During the meal Kate surreptitiously assessed Ellis's interaction with her two friends. After that initial double take, the executive divided his attention between his guests. He was easy with both Dawn and Callie and gave only a hint of the issues he was dealing with when Tommy wanted to know if they were flying home on Sunday with Mrs. Wells.

"I think so, bud. I'll have to fly right back to Venice, though, so I called Monika Sorenson. You remember the au pair who stayed with us when Mrs. Wells went out to visit her sister in California last year?"

"I remember." The boy's nose wrinkled. "She eats those stinky fish in gucky yellow stuff."

"Marinated smelts," Ellis explained to the others, a smile in his blue eyes. "Monika tried to introduce Tommy to some of her native Scandinavian dishes. Without noticeable success, as you can guess by his reaction. Anyway," he continued, addressing his son, "Monika's fall classes at the University of Virginia don't start for a week. She said she could come stay with you, so I'll fly home with you and Mrs. Wells on Sunday, get you both settled, then—" his glance flicked briefly to Travis "—fly back to finish up at the base. Okay, bud?"

"Okay." Tommy accepted the change of plans with only a grudging poke at the remains of his pasta. "But I really wanted to go to Rome 'n' see the gladiators."

"Next trip," Ellis promised, pushing back his chair. "We'd better head to the hospital and see Mrs. Wells before it gets too late. The rest of you please stay and have dessert. And thanks again for today," he said to Travis and Kate. "Tommy and I really appreciate it. Don't we?"

Recalled to his manners, the boy expressed his thanks with a smile for Kate and a manly handshake with Travis. He was so polite, so well behaved, that Kate might have imagined the sullen, unhappy child of the morning and early afternoon.

Travis had the same thought. He watched the two thread their way through the tables and shook his head. "Hard to believe that's the same kid who got us evicted from the ship museum."

"Then tried to check out the severed horses' heads," Kate recalled with a shudder.

"Evicted?" Dawn echoed. "Severed horses' heads? You're going to expound on those provocative comments, aren't you?"

Kate would have lingered at the table and shared the details of the day's adventures, but Travis had other ideas.

"How about we relate our Tommy adventures tomorrow? I had planned to surprise Kate with an evening gondola ride. When we volunteered for babysitting duty, I figured I'd have to cancel the reservation, but we've still got time to make it." He pushed away from the table. "I'll check with the concierge here at the Gritti to see if they can add two more passengers."

"Sounds like fun," Callie said, rising as well, "but something you and Kate should enjoy together. I'll take a pass."

Her gaze cut across the table and telegraphed an unmistakable message.

"Looks like I will, too," Dawn drawled.

Travis flashed them both a grateful look. Carlo had described the nighttime gondola ride as a small procession of lamp-lit boats accompanied by one containing a singer and several accompanists. It was, according to the *maggiore*, one of the most romantic gifts a man could give his wife during their time in Venice. Outside the bedroom, of course.

And after spending the previous evening and all day today with Tommy, Travis wanted this time with Kate. Only with Kate. An urge she teased him about as they made their way back to the Palazzo Alleghri.

"You didn't try very hard to convince Dawn and Callie to join us."

"Probably because I didn't want them to join us."

"Mmm, I got that impression."

He stopped on one of the little bridges that crossed a side canal. Buildings towered on either side of the bridge, wrapping them in shade, while the competing scents of flowers and dank water tinted the air.

"You know I like—" He stopped, corrected himself. "You know I love your pals."

"Yes," she said softly, "I know."

"But I love you more, Katydid." He buried his hands in her hair and tipped her face to his. "I never realized how much until I came so close to losing you."

This, Kate knew instantly, was a moment she would hold in her heart forever. Travis, with the five o'clock shadow on his cheeks and chin and those white squint lines at the corners of his eyes. Colorful laundry hanging from a clothesline draped window to window on the building behind him. The amused grins on the faces of the two young backpacking tourists who edged past them on the narrow bridge.

"I love you, too." Desperate to imprint every sensory detail, she placed her palms against his chest and felt the strong, steady beat of his heart. "I've spent all these weeks...all these months...trying to figure out how I could live without you."

And years worrying about him when he left on yet another classified mission. Panicking every time she caught the tail end of a news flash about a suicide bomber or attack in Afghanistan or Yemen or Somalia. Feeling her throat go tight when someone on the ultra-private special ops spouses' network she subscribed to became a new widow or widower.

"The stupid thing is," she admitted softly, "there's no real way to prepare for having your heart ripped out.

Except maybe to cram in as much joy and happiness as possible when you can, while you can."

"Seems to me we did a pretty good job of cramming our first three or four years together."

"We did," she agreed, flooded with memories. "Oh, God, we did!"

"That's not to say we can't squeeze in more." Bending, he brushed her mouth with his. "Starting tonight, *cara mia.*"

The moonlight gondola ride more than lived up to their expectations. An astonishingly talented accordion player accompanied the curly-haired tenor. Barrel-chested and exuberant, the would-be Pavarotti filled the air with a soaring mix of operatic and pop classics. Tourists and residents alike stopped to gawk as their small fleet of gondolas glided by.

In Travis's opinion, however, the hours that followed blasted the moonlight sonata out of the water. The moment he and Kate hit their suite, they shoved the aquamarine duvet to the foot of the bed and explored the dips and valleys of each other's bodies as though this was the very first time. They savored every tantalizing taste, every kiss and slow, erotic stroke. As their pleasure mounted, so did their hunger.

Gasping now, Kate arched her back. Travis burned with the need to bury himself inside her but locked his jaw, eased down her sweat-slick body and spread her knees. His palms raised her tight-clenched bottom. His mouth found her hot, wet center. A groan ripping from far back in her throat, Kate rode the waves of pleasure his tongue whipped up.

It was long, languorous moments before she could work up enough energy to return the favor. When she took him in her mouth, his taste was hot and salty and achingly familiar.

Only later, when they both sprawled naked and blissfully satiated, did the thoughts she'd entertained earlier that afternoon drift into her lethargic mind.

"Trav?"

His muffled grunt signified either imminent death by pleasure or slowly returning consciousness. Kate chose to interpret it as the latter. Propping up on an elbow, she stared down at the face bathed in the moonlight slipping through the drapes they hadn't taken the time to close completely.

"Trav, are you awake?"

"No."

"I was thinking..."

Opening his eyes, he regarded her warily. "About?"

"Callie."

"Huh?"

Undeterred by the blank response, she used a forefinger to make little swirls in his chest hair. "And Brian Ellis."

"Callie and Brian?" Travis struggled to make the connection. "Did I miss something tonight?"

"No."

"Then what...?"

"I couldn't help thinking they're perfect for each other." Kate made another twirl in the soft, crinkly chest hair. "Callie's so good with kids. Personally *and* professionally. She's also warm and generous and..."

"And a woman who knows her own mind," Travis reminded her, fully conscious now. "Did you pick up any vibe she was attracted to Brian? Or vice versa?"

"Well...no."

Just the opposite, in fact. The only spark Kate had

registered was that brief flash when Ellis's glance settled on Dawn.

"But think about it," she urged her skeptical husband. "It's like some sort of cosmic alignment. Callie's currently unemployed. She and Tommy connected instantly via dinosaurs. Ellis needs someone to watch his son for the next few weeks and…"

"And he and Callie are both mature, intelligent beings," Travis finished. "They don't need you pushing them into your personal version of a cosmic union."

"I'm not pushing."

"Sure sounds like it to me."

Irritated, she twirled harder than she realized.

"Hey!" His hand clamped over hers. "Easy there, champ."

"Sorry."

She couldn't tell him about her instinctive dismay when Brian had spotted Dawn and done that double take. Or her sharp stab of guilt for thinking her love-'em-and-leave-'em friend might toss Ellis aside with the same carelessness she did the other men who went all stupid over her. Kate owed her loyalty to her friend, not some stranger she'd met for the first time just a few days ago.

She would never, *ever* disparage Dawn to anyone, Brian Ellis included. But there was no reason Kate couldn't drop a few hints about Callie's warmth and compassion and training as a child advocate. Or enlist her husband's help in said campaign.

Being the stubborn, hardheaded male that he was, however, Travis would agree to share his insider's knowledge of Callie Langston only if Ellis asked about her… and if Callie agreed to let Travis act as an intermediary.

"You know she won't agree to that!"

"Yes, I do." Rolling her over, he pinned his wife to rumpled sheets. "Which is why this discussion is moot. And why, Ms. Westbrook, I respectfully decline to take part in any extramarital matchmaking. I've got my hands full managing my own."

Despite his firm intention to steer clear of potential third-party matchups, Travis got sucked in the very next morning.

As usual, he woke before Kate and found a voice mail from Brian on his iPhone, requesting a return call. Tugging on his jeans, he padded barefoot to the sitting room so as not to disturb his still-unconscious wife.

"Yo, Brian. What's up? Mrs. Wells okay?"

"She was when Tommy and I left her last night."

"Still planning to fly home with her tomorrow?"

"Actually, that's why I called you. Turns out she's going to need fairly extensive rehab. Her sister wants her to fly straight to California and stay with her during rehab. Which brings me to the point of this call. How well do you know Kate's friends?"

"Almost as well as I do her." He scrubbed a hand over a bristly jaw as his mind winged back through the years. "I call 'em the Invincibles. They've been tight since the second or third grade. When I married Kate, I knew I was getting a package deal. Why?"

"Tommy and I bumped into the dark-haired one. Callie, isn't it?"

"Right, Callie."

"We ran into her in the lobby when we came back from the hospital. She was heading out to explore Venice on her own. I convinced her that even though this city is safer than most, it still wasn't smart to wander around on her own late at night. Took some effort," he added drily. "The woman comes across as cool and serene, but she's got a stubborn streak on her."

Travis thought of the Callie he'd known for so many years. Quiet. Calm. Indomitable. "I would say she's not so much stubborn as self-sufficient."

"I yield to your better knowledge. Anyway, I talked her into going back upstairs and joining me for a nightcap after I put Tommy to bed."

Well, damned if Kate hadn't pegged the situation after all! Or maybe not. The exasperated edge to Brian's next comment suggested the nightcap didn't go well.

"Callie showed up with the other one. The redhead with the cat's eyes and killer body."

Uh-oh. Travis had heard similar sentiments from other males of his acquaintance. There could be trouble ahead. Big trouble.

"That pretty much describes Dawn," he said carefully, "on the outside."

"What about the inside? Is she steady? Reliable?"

He smothered another curse. Talk about a loaded question. He knew damned well that none of the men Dawn had unceremoniously dumped over the years would consider her either steady *or* reliable. He also knew that he himself still ranked pretty close to the bottom of her favorite-person list after the heartache Kate had gone through these past months.

Yet despite the lethal sniper fire Dawn still aimed his way, Travis respected the hell out of her for her fierce loyalty to his wife. He also respected the formidable intelligence too often overlooked by the men she attracted like flies, most of whom never saw past that killer body...including those two losers she'd been engaged to.

"Dawn McGill and I don't always agree," Travis ad-

mitted, "but she's one of two women my wife would
trust with her life. And in that regard, I'd say Kate's
instincts are 100 percent true."

"Good to know. But should I trust her with my six-
year-old son?"

"Come again?"

"It's crazy," Ellis said, sounding even more exasperated. "I still can't figure out exactly how it happened.
One minute, Callie's asking about the flight tomorrow
and whether I needed any help with Tommy or Mrs.
Wells. The next, this fiery-haired sex goddess offers
to hang with my son so we don't have to cut short our
stay in Italy. What's even crazier is that I'm actually
considering the idea."

Just in time, Travis swallowed his instinctive *you
gotta be kidding!* Three seconds' consideration produced a more rational response.

"Dawn and Tommy seemed to hit it off pretty well
yesterday evening."

"Yeah, I saw that. And I know how much Tom wants
to stay in Italy with me. He's a trooper, though. He'll
head home with minimal pouting. But if there's a way
I can keep him here…"

"Okay, maybe it'll make you feel more comfortable
if I tell you Dawn grew up with three older brothers.
I roomed with the youngest in college. Aaron used to
brag about what a tough little tomboy his baby sister
was. Always climbing trees and insisting she could bait
her own hook."

"She's still baiting the hook," Brian muttered.

"What?"

"Nothing. What about her work? She's employed,
isn't she?"

"She is."

"So how can she put her job on hold to extend her stay in Italy for an additional week or two?"

Travis made another pass at his whiskery chin. "I'm not up on all ins and outs of Dawn's job. All I know is that she does graphic design for some big health-food company in Boston. She's damned good at it, too, according to Kate. My guess is it may be something she can do long-distance."

"Maybe." Ellis blew out an audible breath. "Look, I trust your judgment. Yours and Kate's. I don't take risks where my son is concerned, however, so I've asked my people to run a background check on Ms. McGill. Financials, employment history, criminal record, the works."

"Makes sense. In your position, I'd do the same."

Travis hung up a few moments later, hoping like hell he was in the room when Dawn found out Ellis was rooting around in her private life. No way he wanted to miss that fireworks display!

Chapter Ten

Travis still had a grin plastered across his face when he walked back into the bedroom and found his wife stretching sinuously amid the rumpled sheets. He stood in the doorway for a moment to admire the view.

Her hair spilled across the pillow in a tangle of tawny gold, and the sparse light sneaking through the drapes tinted her skin to pale cream. Then the sheets slid lower, and Travis's blood went south with them. He glanced up from her dark-tipped breasts to find her surveying him with a lazy smile.

"What time is it?"

"A little after eight."

"I suppose I should get up," she said with another languorous stretch. "Unless…?"

The sultry invitation hung on the air. Travis told himself he should grab a quick shower before he climbed back in bed with her. Brush his teeth. Shave off these morning bristles. At the very least, call room service for coffee and the *pagnottini* she'd scarfed down so enthusiastically yesterday.

Coffee and rolls could wait, he decided as he tugged down his zipper. And he'd just have to make sure his whiskers didn't scrape off any of that soft, creamy skin. His good intentions detonated, however, when he stepped out of his jeans.

"Now that," she purred, "is a sight worth waking up for."

The throaty murmur hit with the force of a rocket-propelled grenade. Hunger for her grabbed Travis by the throat and sent him across the room in swift strides. As he yanked the sheet the rest of the way down and rolled his wife into his arms, he realized that what he'd said last night was so friggin' true. He'd never really understood how much he needed this woman in his life until he'd almost lost her.

Despite his best intentions, Travis scraped off several layers of Kate's epidermis before they finally collapsed in a sweaty tangle of arms and legs. She laughed off the irritation on her cheeks, chin and breasts but threatened payback for the angry red patch on her thigh.

He soothed the sore spot with a kiss before flopping onto his back beside her. Only then did his brain unscramble enough to tell her about Brian's call. The news that Dawn had volunteered to supervise Tommy the Terrible for the next week or so snapped Kate's brows into an instant frown.

"I know," he said. "I had to breathe deep when Brian asked if she was steady and reliable."

The frown disappeared. Fire ignited in her brown eyes. Rising onto her elbows like an avenging Valkyrie, she skewered him with a metaphorical sword. "What did you tell him?"

"Whoa! Throttle back, Katydid."

"What did you tell him, Westbrook?"

"That you would trust her and Callie with your life."

"And?"

"And *I* trust your instincts."

Mollified, she dropped back down. Travis could almost hear the wheels clanking as she tried to make sense of this turn of events and couldn't resist yanking her chain.

"Remind me. What was that you said last night? Something about how perfect Callie would be for Ellis?"

She punched him in the upper arm. Hard enough to hurt, dammit.

"Hey!" He rubbed his biceps. "Don't take this out on me. If you don't think it's a good idea, talk to Dawn."

She mulled that over for a moment and shook her head. "I can't."

"Why not?"

"I understand why Dawn bonded with Tommy," she said slowly. "He's a mirror image of her when she was young. Adventurous, inventive and utterly fearless."

"She's still pretty fearless," Travis drawled. "I've got the scars to prove it."

"Okay, but she's also...um..."

"Reckless?"

"Maybe a little impulsive."

"Flighty?"

"Discerning."

"How about commitment-phobic?"

"You'd run scared, too," Kate retorted, "if your parents used you as a pawn in a divorce so vicious it sucked every shred of joy from your soul and ripped your family apart."

"Okay, okay. I get that. What I don't get is whether you think it's a good idea for Dawn to assume nanny duties."

A pregnant silence followed.

"I don't know," she finally admitted. "I like Brian. I'd hate to see him end up as another notch on Dawn's belt. On the other hand, he's a big boy. And he's not walking into the situation blind. He's got us to vouch for her."

"Not just us."

"What do you mean?"

"He's having his people run a background check. Employment history, financial, criminal activities."

"You're kidding!" Kate popped up, her face flushed with indignation. "That's a total invasion of her privacy!"

"Wouldn't you want to run a background check before we left our son in someone's care?"

"No! Okay, yes. But…" She shoved back the covers and snatched up Travis's discarded shirt. "This is Dawn we're talking about!"

"What's the big deal? She hasn't embezzled a couple of million or buried any dead bodies in the backyard lately, has she? Kate?"

She turned away, but not before he caught a glimpse of the guilt that flickered across her face.

"Holy Christ!" Rolling out of bed, he pulled on his jeans and stopped her before she could retreat to the bathroom. "What's she done?"

She shook her head, not quite meeting his eyes.

"For God's sake, you can tell me."

"No, actually, I can't."

"We're talking about a six-year-old here," he said

grimly. "The son of the man I'll be working with. If you're privy to something that could impact Tommy's health or safety, you need to let me or Brian know."

Her chin snapped up. "First, I'm talking about the woman who's been as close as a sister to me for over twenty years. Second, Dawn would never do *anything* that might impact a child's health or safety. Which you should damned well know," she finished fiercely, "considering the fact that she's your friend, too."

She stomped past him, hit the bathroom and shut the door with an emphatic thud. Travis stood where he was, his jaw working. Two minutes ago he'd been sprawled in mindless bliss beside an equally relaxed and happy wife. Now he was staring at a door panel decorated with a painted hunting scene and wondering what the hell Ellis's people might find in Dawn's background that would put Kate in a panic.

This, he decided grimly, called for coffee. And *pagnottini*. A whole basket of *pagnottini*.

Kate emerged from the bathroom, wrapped in one of the hotel's luxurious robes. She'd pinned her hair up and swiped on some lip gloss. She'd also recovered from the shock of learning that Ellis was having Dawn investigated.

His people wouldn't find anything. They couldn't.

Settling beside Travis on the sofa, she accepted a cup of coffee and downed a much-needed infusion of caffeine before tackling the elephant in the room. "I'm sorry I got a little huffy a while ago. And I'm sorry my reaction to that business about a background check worried you. I give you my word—Dawn has done nothing that could adversely impact Tommy in any way, shape or form."

The carefully prepared speech didn't appear to satisfy her husband. Frowning, he studied her with troubled eyes. "We've never kept secrets from each other. Not that I know of, anyway. Makes me wonder what else you won't tell me."

"And that," she retorted, "comes from the man who doesn't tell me 90 percent of what he does every day."

"That's different. It's work."

"How do you know this isn't?"

The reply surprised him. His frown eased, and curiosity took its place. "Okay, now my imagination's engaged."

"Travis…"

"What would a graphic designer at one of the world's largest health-food firms want to hide?" He tapped his chin in theatrical deliberation. "She photoshopped four ounces off one of their models? Artificially corrected the color on a Monster drink ad? Or," he mused, turning more serious, "helped disguise the fact that a vitamin supplement was steroid based?"

"No. No. No. And I refuse to respond to further inquisition."

"Cm'on, Kate. You can't just leave me hanging. Give me a hint."

"No."

To reinforce the point, she popped part of a bun in her mouth. Only after she'd savored its yeasty sweetness for several moments did she reopen communications.

"You were going to take me up to the base yesterday, before we volunteered to watch Tommy. Why don't we go today?"

"We could do that. But this is Saturday. The base will be on skeleton manning."

"I've driven onto a few air force bases," Kate reminded him. "Deserted and otherwise."

"Yeah, you have." The skin at the corners of his eyes crinkled. "Remember the day we arrived at Hurlburt the first time?"

"Like I could forget?"

Kate didn't have to fake a shudder. She'd studied dozens of articles and websites in preparation for their move to the Florida Panhandle. They'd all touted the glorious sunshine, the sugar-sand beaches, the sparkling emerald waters.

For obvious reasons, the glowing chamber of commerce articles neglected to mention the hurricanes that slammed into the Gulf Coast with frightening frequency. Including the one that hit while she and Travis were on the road. It barely reached category two, but its eighty-mile-an-hour winds and angry storm surge had made a believer out of her. That and the fact that the air base had battened down all hatches. Metal storm shutters were rolled down, streets were deserted and runways had been emptied of aircraft, flown out of harm's way.

"Tell you what," Travis said. "I'll see if Carlo's flying today. If he is...and you're real sweet to him...he might introduce you to some of his *men*. They're tough. Really tough."

Which, Kate knew, was pretty much the highest accolade her husband could bestow. Anxious to meet the prince who'd exhibited such generous hospitality to her and her friends, she downed the rest of her sweet roll while attempting to translate her husband's brief phone conversation. She wasn't as familiar with NATO acronyms as she was with USAF terminology, but she was pretty sure *AAOC* stood for Allied Air Operations Center, and NATO 07 was probably the prince's call sign.

"Roger that, Aviano. Thanks." Travis cut the connection and pushed off the sofa. "Carlo should touch down about 1100. I've asked the AAOC to let him know I want to meet with him after his mission debrief. I'll go shower and shave. In the meantime, you could call down to the desk and have a vaporetto ready to pick us up in thirty minutes."

Kate made the call as requested and was about to signal for the operator again and ask to be connected to the Gritti when the phone buzzed under her hand. Startled, she lifted the receiver again.

"Pronto?"

"It's me. Sorry to call so early." Dawn didn't sound particularly apologetic. Then again, she rarely did. "I wanted to tell you I'm making a change in my vacations plans."

"Good change?" Kate asked cautiously. "Or bad?"

"Good. I think. Oh, hell, I don't know. It's all kind of spur-of-the-moment."

"With you, it usually is."

"True," her friend admitted, laughing. "Anyway, I've decided to extend my stay in Italy and stand in for Tommy Ellis's nanny."

"Brian called Travis earlier," Kate told her. "He said you'd made the offer. He didn't mention it was a done deal, though."

"It wasn't, until a few minutes ago. Ellis and I just talked. Evidently he's decided I'm not a psychopath or registered sex offender."

And Kate knew the underlying basis for that decision. She started to tell Dawn about the background investigation. Just as quickly, she changed her mind. Ellis's people had obviously forwarded a positive report or he wouldn't have taken Dawn up on her offer. And she certainly sounded enthused about playing nanny. Why throw a wrench in the works at this point?

"What about Callie?" Kate asked instead. "What's she going to do if we both desert her?"

"I've pretty much convinced her to stay in Venice with me, at least until it's time to fly home next week. I suspect she knows I might need backup with this baby-sitting gig."

"I suspect she does," Kate drawled.

But her mind was racing. Her first thought was that Callie and Brian Ellis might connect. Kate still thought they seemed so right for each other, and nothing Dawn had said yesterday or this morning suggested she harbored any particular interest in Tommy's father.

Her second thought took a completely different direction—the antics of a lively six-year-old would fill Dawn's days. Maybe, just maybe, a sexy Italian prince could fill Callie's.

She'd already Googled Carlo Luigi Francesco di Lorenzo, prince of Lombard and Marino. Although his family's antecedents dated back to the seventh century, their ancient principalities had long since been incorporated into other, more modern states. As a result, Carlo's royal title was now purely ceremonial.

Not that the empty title seemed to matter to the paparazzi. They brushed aside the fact that the di Lorenzos had lost most of their domains down through the centuries and focused instead on their business instincts. The family had invested heavily in various agricultural and industrial enterprises over the years. One tabloid suggested the di Lorenzos now sat on one of the largest fortunes in Europe.

The articles Kate had read about the current prince were no less enthusiastic. They portrayed him as a slightly older but no less adventurous version of Britain's Prince Harry. Not surprising, since both men had opted for military careers despite their vast personal wealth and social obligations, at least until Harry resigned his commission last year. The articles also indicated that Prince Carlo thoroughly enjoyed the company of beautiful women but had stated repeatedly that he was in no hurry to marry and settle down.

The photos accompanying the stories weren't particularly flattering to the playboy prince. He looked short compared to the women he was photographed with. Then again, most of those svelte, impossibly glamorous companions were supermodels and starlets. But Kate thought he also looked a little overweight in his flight suit. When she'd commented on that to Travis, he'd shrugged and said Carlo wouldn't be a major in the Stormo Incursori unless he was fit enough to chew nails and spit rivets.

More curious than ever about her husband's new friend, Kate dressed casually for the drive up to the NATO base in jeans and a coral tank, accented with the colorful scarf she'd purchased in Florence. Travis also wore jeans, and his black cotton crewneck clung to his pecs and abs in ways that turned more than one female head in the lobby.

He hooked on his mirrored sunglasses for the vaporetto ride to the parking garage, where they reclaimed the Ferrari. The VIP parking attendant handed over the keys with obvious reluctance and a last, loving pat on the sports car's fender.

"You want the top up or down?" Travis asked when they'd settled into the body-hugging leather seats.

"Down. Definitely down."

While he engaged the system that folded the top into

its storage compartment, Kate caught her hair back with the scarf. Mere moments later they were on their way.

The route took them north from Venice through rolling hills, small villages and acre after acre of vineyards. The purple smudge of the Dolomites rose in the distance. A branch of the Italian Alps, the mountains grew taller and craggier with each passing kilometer. Kate skimmed the guide to Italy on her iPhone during the drive to familiarize herself with the cultural, historical and gastronomic specialties of the area.

Although it was just midmorning, she had to sample the delicacies. She asked Travis to stop at one of the tasting rooms that lined the road so they could taste different vintages of prosecco—the sparkling white wine made from grapes grown only in that area. Delighted with its bubbly effervescence, Kate recomputed the cost per bottle listed on a slate above the counter from euros to dollars.

"This is as good as any champagne I've had," she commented to the young woman who poured the samples. "Why is it so much cheaper?"

"It is how the wine is processed, signora. French champagne is made the traditional way, yes? It is fermented in bottles, which must be turned and cleared of sediment by hand. This is very time-consuming and...how do you say—with many people?"

"Labor-intensive."

"Just so! For prosecco, the secondary fermentation is done in big tanks. The process requires not so many people."

"Let's buy a few bottles to take back with us," Kate suggested. "Dawn's partial to champagne. She'll love this."

"And she'll probably need it after a day with Tommy the Terrible," Travis drawled.

They decided to drive into the hillside town of Conegliano for an early lunch. The lower, more modern part of the town offered plenty of cafés and restaurants, but a short flight of steps took them to the historic center. Revived by an endive salad and risotto with cuttlefish served in a creamy black sauce, Kate consulted her trusty digital guidebook again and led Travis to see the frescoes covering the exterior and interior of the Scuola dei Battuti.

"'*Battuti* is derived from the Italian word for *beaters*,'" she read aloud. "'It refers to the religious lay order that once occupied the building and was known for its brutal self-flagellation rituals.'"

Travis eyed the frescoes and had no comment.

Once back in the Ferrari, they steered straight toward the Dolomites. Thirty minutes later they reached Aviano Air Base, the sprawling installation in the shadow of the snowcapped mountains. The Italian Air Force ran the base and served as hosts to the Thirty-First Tactical Fighter Wing, the only US fighter wing south of the Alps. It also hosted numerous ground and even naval units from a dozen different NATO countries. With its close proximity to hot spots in North Africa and the Middle East, Kate guessed the crews based at or staging out of Aviano had racked up a sobering number of combat sorties in recent years.

Security was tight, and it took a few moments for Travis to get her signed in at the main entrance to the base. From there they drove through a complex of housing, administrative and support buildings all painted in the military's standard tan and brown. Or in this case, tan and a sort of terra-cotta reminiscent of the tile roofs that capped so many Italian buildings.

When Kate and Travis had reported to their first duty station, she'd commented on the blah colors. He'd explained they were designed to blend in with the terrain. She didn't doubt the monochromatic scheme had served its purpose thirty or even twenty years ago, but suspected today's highly sophisticated satellite imagery probably displayed every structure in ultra-clear three-dimensional detail, right down to the ruffles on the kitchen curtains in family housing.

Drab as the colors were, however, they seemed to welcome her home. So did the signs pointing to the base exchange and billeting office and fitness center. Even the flight line had a familiar feel, with hangars and revetments sheltering aircraft of all shapes and sizes and the tang of aviation fuel permeating the warm August air.

What weren't as familiar were the markings on the various aircraft, at least the ones Kate could spot from the car. She recognized the sleek, lethal-looking US F-16 fighter jets with *AV* on the tail, which designated Aviano as their home base. But there were also small executive jets, jumbo transports, a buzz of helicopters and several odd-looking aircraft she'd never seen before.

"Where's your bird?" she asked, searching the ramp for the squat, four-engine turbo-prop Hercules, the workhorse of US and NATO Special Ops.

"Safely tucked away during the day."

Which meant they only flew after dark, using night-vision goggles. Kate knew her husband was fully qualified on NVGs. He and the crews he flew with had to be, since their missions often involved inserting or extracting a team under cover of darkness at unimproved airstrips deep in hostile territory. The fact that the crews were fully qualified didn't mitigate the danger, though. If anything, the pucker factor increased exponentially with NVGs.

With her husband's life on the line, Kate had made it a point to study the risk associated with the increasing use of NVGs in military aviation. One analysis found that 43 percent of class A accidents due to spatial disorientation occurred during NVG flights. Another concluded that NVG operations increased the risk of spatial disorientation by almost five times.

The fact that this supersecret modification Ellis's company had developed for the special ops 130s involved night flying brought her old fears flooding back. Suddenly, the familiar surroundings of a busy air force base didn't seem nearly as welcoming or comfortable. Nor could she feel quite the same excitement about Travis's prospective new job. Not if it put him back in the cockpit, racking up hours under the same—or even more— dangerous conditions.

She was struggling with that sobering thought when they pulled up to a two-story building. A sign in English, Italian and French indicated it served as the NATO Joint Special Operations Center. Just inside the JSOC was a reception desk. Travis fished in his wallet for a green proximity access badge that contained his photo and several lines of bar code. After scanning it at the desk, he requested a visitor's badge for Kate. Once she'd produced the requested two forms of ID and looked into a camera's unblinking eye, she was issued a temporary pass. Travis clipped it to the neck of her tank top and guided her to a small visitors' lounge.

"Hang loose for a few moments. I'll check to see if Carlo has finished his debrief."

A set of double doors controlled access to the rest of the building. Travis waved his proxi badge a few inches from the scanner mounted beside the doors and disappeared. While he was gone, Kate took advantage of the unisex bathroom to comb her wind-tossed hair and reapply some lip gloss. She was back in the reception area, waiting, when the doors to the controlled area swished open.

Travis reappeared, accompanied by two men in flight suits. One was almost as tall as Travis. The other was shorter, stockier and brimming with energy.

"Ciao, Caterina!"

Carlo di Lorenzo, prince of Lombard and Marino, swept across the reception area. His dark eyes were merry above the black handlebar mustache that bristled from cheek to cheek.

"I cannot tell you how happy I am to finally meet the beautiful wife Travis speaks of so often!"

Chapter Eleven

Kate wasn't exactly up on the protocol for greeting Italian royalty. The prince solved her dilemma by extending his hand as he strode toward her. She offered hers, anticipating a polite shake. Instead he caught it in a warm clasp, bowed at the waist and raised it to his lips. At the last second, though, he angled her wrist so his lips grazed her palm. The kiss was warm, moist and disconcertingly intimate.

Startled, Kate blinked down at the merest hint of a bald spot showing through his curly black hair and almost jerked her hand free. But when he raised his head, the mischief dancing in his dark eyes invited her to share in what he obviously considered a great joke.

"You did not exaggerate," he said over his shoulder to Travis. "She is indeed *bellissima*."

Bellissima or not, Kate gave her hand a deliberate tug. The prince released it with a dramatic sigh. "Why is it always my misfortune to fall instantly in love with other men's wives?"

"Beats the hell out of me," Travis drawled. "Now stop pawing the woman and introduce her to your shadow."

Their bantering wiped out most of Kate's surprise at the prince's too-personal kiss. When she turned to the man who'd accompanied the prince, though, the angry red scar slashing the left side of his face almost threw her off balance again. She couldn't *not* look at it, since it carved a jagged line from his cheek to his chin. But after that first instinctive glance, she locked her eyes on his. Smoky gray and keenly intelligent, they acknowledged her swift recovery as the prince made introductions.

"Caterina, please allow me to present Joe Russo, who refuses to allow me to address him as Giuseppe. He and his men watch my back while I am here at Aviano. Even," he said with another exaggerated sigh, "when I would much prefer they discreetly disappear for a few hours."

"It's a pleasure to meet you, Signora Westbrook."

Like the man he guarded, Russo was zipped into an air force flight suit. Unlike his boss's, however, it molded a lean, muscular frame. Also unlike the prince's, Russo's uniform bore no rank, no flag, no identifying insignia of any kind. Nor did his deep voice give any clue to his nationality. Kate thought she detected a faint accent buried in there somewhere but couldn't pin it down to a country or even a continent.

"You must tell me how your friends enjoyed Tuscany," the prince said, reclaiming her attention.

"Enormously! I can't thank you enough for putting your villa at their disposal."

"I'm sorry they couldn't stay longer. I had thought to fly down to Siena this weekend and perhaps show them the city. From what Travis has told me, they are almost as charming and beautiful as you. And," he added with a sly smile, "I understand that one of them, a redhead, I think he said, can be a very lively companion."

Kate shot her husband a nasty look over the prince's head. Travis held up both hands in a gesture of surrender. "Sorry. Carlo's a master at interrogation techniques."

Of course he was. Special ops had elevated extracting information from reluctant sources into an art form.

"Let me guess," she retorted. "This particular interrogation was conducted after a mission debrief. At a local bar. With several bottles of beer to loosen tongues."

"But no, Caterina." The prince actually managed to appear hurt. "It was at my quarters, with several bottles of wine from my family's vineyard. Which brings me back to your friend. She's in Venice now, isn't she?"

So much for the fantasies Kate had woven earlier this morning about hooking Callie up with the prince. He appeared to be as interested in Dawn sight unseen as Brian Ellis had been at first sight. Burying the thought that both men stood to get burned, Kate answered with a brisk "She is."

"Then perhaps I shall have a drive down to Venice later this afternoon. What do you say, Joe? Are you up for a little R & R?"

"Always. Just give me time to get some men in place and conduct a sweep."

"Of course. Now, Caterina, would you care to meet my crew?"

"If it's okay," she said with a dubious glance at the heavy doors.

"We've finished our debrief. All classified materials are locked securely away."

"Then yes, I'd very much like to meet your crew."

"Bene!" With a gallant gesture, he ushered her to the access point and waved his badge at the scanner.

"Aviano is not our primary operating locale, you understand. Normally we are based at Furbara, outside Rome, which is home to Italy's Special Forces Operations Command. Our detachment here is small, but we are mighty." A smug smile creased his face, burying his upper lip under the thick mustache. "Did Travis tell you the Seventeenth Raiders have logged almost as many combat hours in Afghanistan and Iraq as their British and American counterparts?"

"He neglected that small detail."

"And the mission three months ago? Did he tell you about that?"

"No."

"It was bad," Carlo recounted, his face turning grim as he escorted her down a tiled hallway. "Very bad. A special mission to rescue a news crew taken hostage by Boko Haram."

"I didn't know the US participated in that rescue."

It shouldn't have surprised her. An online article she'd read recently claimed that in 2014 US Special Forces had conducted ops in more than 133 countries— almost 70 percent of the nations in the world. Given the clandestine nature, most Americans had no idea of either their scope or their danger.

Travis replied with a shrug and his usual reticence. "It was a multinational op."

The prince was more expansive. "The African jungle is a bitch... *Scusami!* A bear to operate in. The airstrip we flew into was little more than a hacked-out field, and the rebels were more heavily armed than our intel had indicated. They overran the airfield, and we had to use all our firepower to hold them off so the ground team could scramble aboard with the rescued newsmen." He hooked a thumb over his shoulder at his bodyguard. "Joe earned his pay that day. Your husband, too, Caterina. I would be monkey bait if not for them."

That explained the loan of the Ferrari and the Tuscan villa, Kate thought as they made their way down the hall lined with dramatic black-and-white photos of helicopters and various fixed-wing aircraft in action.

"We learned much on that particular op, Travis and I. That's why we are together again, here at Aviano, to test the modification Brian's company has developed for our aircraft. But enough of such grim matters," the prince said with a dismissive wave. "Prepare to meet my crew, the meanest and ugliest in the sky."

Kate didn't question the "mean" part, but the copilot, combat systems officer and two loadmasters Carlo introduced her to were anything but ugly. One of the loadmasters, in fact, could have modeled for Michelangelo's *David*. His hair was short and curly, his features classically Italian, and his smile could make angels sigh.

As with most NATO crews, they were fluent in English and French as well as their native Italian. They were also not the least bit inhibited when it came to recounting what Kate suspected were highly embellished tales. They couldn't talk classified missions, of course, but their accounts of some of the humanitarian missions they'd participated in left Kate helpless with laughter. The one where they'd rescued an *extremely* unhappy bull from raging floodwaters was her favorite. Then there was the time they'd received the wrong coordinates for an airdrop and sent several members of a ranger squad parachuting through the roof of a bordello. Evidently it was several hours before the rangers finally made it to their designated recovery zone.

The prince played a central role in each hilarious account. And with each tale, Kate's impressions of Carlo di Lorenzo took on new and varying hues. There was the generous friend who'd gone all out to aid Travis in his campaign to reconnect with his wife, the playboy prince depicted in the media, the short, stumpy fireplug who was light-years away from the stereotypical image of a hotshot special ops combat pilot. And now the squadron leader who commanded the bone-deep respect of his men.

Even the enigmatic Joe Russo seemed to hold him in high regard. The bodyguard stood off to one side, arms crossed over his chest and a small smile tugging at his lips as he listened to the ribald accounts.

By now Kate had figured out that Russo's unmarked flight suit slotted him into one of three categories. He could belong to the Italian counterpart of the US Delta Force. They, too, wore no identifying national insignia so—at least according to Travis—the government could deny all knowledge of their existence if one of their highly classified ops went bad.

Or Russo and his team might be civilians, astronomically paid security forces employed by companies like the one formerly known as Blackwater. The prince could be paying Joe's parent company megabucks for a more ruthless level of protection than that provided by conventional forces.

Or Russo and his men could be operating on their own. True mercenaries who hired their guns out to the highest bidder and...

An unexpected arrival interrupted her musings. To the delight of the assembled gathering, Brian Ellis appeared in the doorway.

"I got run out of Dodge," he related with a shame-faced grin. "After I checked on Mrs. Wells this morning and finalized arrangements for her flight home tomorrow, my son announced that he and his new nanny had plans that didn't include me."

"Did they include Callie?" Kate wanted to know.

"No. She said she was going to take in a museum. The Peggy Guggenheim Collection, I think it was."

"An excellent choice," the prince commented. "The Guggenheim Collection is one of the best in the world of works by twentieth-century European and American artists. You must see it while you are in Venice, Caterina."

Kate nodded, her mind pinwheeling with thoughts of Dawn on her own with the lively six-year-old. Resolutely, she put them aside. Despite her friend's occasionally flippant approach to life and love, she was rock solid in every way that counted.

"Actually," Ellis was saying to the prince, "I drove up hoping to catch the debrief from your flight this morning."

"We've just finished, but we would be happy to share the results with you. And with you, Travis, if your charming wife would excuse us for a few moments."

"Sure." She guessed it would take longer than a few moments but didn't want to stand in the way of anything that might get Travis home sooner than he anticipated. "I'll wait in the reception area."

"Or," her husband suggested, "you could take the car and swing by the base exchange in case you need to stock up on shampoo or stuff."

Kate started to reply that the luxury hotels where they'd been staying kept her well supplied with stuff, but she couldn't resist the idea of getting behind the wheel of the Ferrari.

"You don't mind trusting me with your car?" she asked the prince.

His Adam's apple took a quick bob, but he responded with a gallant "Of course not."

She hid a grin at his barely disguised chauvinism and claimed the keys from Travis.

"Just be back by four. Don't forget I need to swing by the force-support squadron."

The quiet reminder put a bump in her pulse. *Force support* was an umbrella term for the unit that provided such varied services as billeting, child development centers, recreational facilities, education programs, the base honor guard and the office that managed military and civilian personnel matters. With a few clicks of a keyboard, an airman or sergeant working in the military personnel branch would submit the request to terminate Travis's military career.

"You sure force support is open on Saturdays?"

Stupid question, Kate realized as soon as it was out of her mouth. With the Thirty-First Fighter Wing flying around-the-clock sorties against ISIS in Syria and other hot spots, its support units would maintain at least a skeleton crew 24/7.

"I called before we left Venice and made an appointment," Travis confirmed. He took a moment, drew a breath and turned to the prince. "Brian knows, so I guess I should tell you, too. I'm putting in a request to separate from active duty as soon as we complete this project."

Shock made Carlo's mouth go slack under his mustache. "But...but you cannot!"

"Yeah, I can. I've already talked to my boss back in the States. It's a done deal."

"So undo it," the prince urged. "You have the best

hands on the stick, the coolest head of any NATO pilot I've flown with. You will make colonel well ahead of your peers. General! Surely you don't want to give up those stars."

"Some things are a whole lot more important than rank."

"Pah! You say that now but…"

"It's done, Carlo."

The finality of the reply cut through the air like a blade. The prince clamped his mouth shut but shot a quick glance at Kate. Although he didn't say anything, she felt the weight of his unspoken disapproval as Brian Ellis stepped into the breach.

"You're looking at EAS's new VP for test operations and evaluations, Carlo. I can't tell you how excited I am to have someone with Travis's experience joining our team. Especially if tests validate the project we're currently working on and the mod goes into full development."

The prince took the less-than-subtle hint and snapped back to business. "We're almost there. Joe, will you escort Signora Westbrook out?"

Signora Westbrook, Kate noted. Not *Caterina*.

After saying goodbye to the members of Carlo's crew, she left with Joe Russo. They retraced their steps down the tiled corridor in silence for a few moments. Then curiosity got the better of her.

"How long have you been with the prince?"

"A little over three months."

"Are you and your men military or civilian or what?"

"What."

The reply was cool and unruffled, but an expression Kate couldn't quite define flitted across his face. Even more curious, she tried another probe.

"So where's home?"

He angled her a glance, his gray eyes as unreadable as smoke. "No place you've ever heard of."

Oooo-kay. She could take a hint when it smacked her in the face. Might as well forget about asking if he was married, had kids, or preferred black-cherry gelato over her personal fave, limoncello and cream.

He escorted her into the reception area and signed her out of the building. Then Kate exited into the bright August afternoon. After the air-conditioned chill inside, the sunshine felt good on her skin. She leaned against the Ferrari's fender to absorb the warmth and the view of the mountains in the distance. Gradually her gaze dropped from the mountains to the hangars spaced at defensive intervals along the runway. She was wondering which of them housed the specially modified transport Travis and the prince were testing when two sleek, single-seat fighter jets taxied out for takeoff.

Once in position, the F-16s waited for clearance from the tower. Moments later their engines revved to a louder pitch. Suddenly the first jet shot down the runway. A second after takeoff, its afterburner kicked in with a thunderous boom and the jet went vertical. The second fighter followed, splitting the air with another thunderclap. Head tilted, eyes shaded against the sun with one hand, Kate watched them soar almost straight up.

The number cruncher in her couldn't help wondering how the latest accident stats for these high-flying, supersonic fighter jets compared to that of her husband's transport. Even with all its offensive and defensive systems, the Combat King too often went in low and slow. Exposed to deadly ground fire, it...

No! She wouldn't go there. Not anymore, dammit! Nor would Travis, thank God.

But the guilt she still hadn't been able to shake nagged at her as she slid into the Ferrari's driver seat and started the engine. She'd met so many other military spouses over the years, men and women who measured their loneliness and worry for their mates against a fierce pride in their service. Kate had felt that same pride. She still did!

Nor did she consider herself a self-centered bitch for wanting her husband to trade his military job for one with fewer absences and opportunities to get shot out of the sky. No, her guilt lay in the fact that she was forcing him to choose between her and a career she knew he loved.

She steered across the base, careful to keep to the twenty-five-mile-per-hour speed limit, as the questions tumbled through her head. Would Travis eventually resent being caught in that vise? Would this decision tarnish the years ahead? Was it worth the risk?

Yes!

That answer came fast and unequivocal. When measured against all the other uncertainties in life, that was one risk Kate could live with.

Feeling better after the stern inner pep talk, she followed the signs for the base exchange. Her military dependent ID gained her entrance into a mall containing a fast-food court, florist, optometrist, dry cleaner and barbershop, as well as the vast, Walmart-like main store. To her delight, the mall also contained a row of colorful kiosks that offered a selection of local products ranging from olive oil and cheeses to Venetian masks and blown-glass jewelry.

One kiosk in particular grabbed her attention. It featured Italian-themed toys and crafts for kids, including an assortment of plastic helmets, swords and shields. Kate shuddered at the thought of Tommy rigged out in the cape and red-plumed helmet of a Roman centurion, swishing a plastic sword in a hotel suite filled with expensive antiques. The fanged leopard helmet and gladiator's trident produced the same reaction.

Hoping a three-dimensional puzzle might engage both his attention and energy, she debated between a model of Rome's Coliseum, Pisa's famous leaning tower and a Venetian gondola. She decided on the leaning tower and had just handed over her Visa card when a trio of uniformed officers strolled toward the kiosk. Two men, one woman, all dressed in ABUs—the splotchy gray-green, slate-blue and brown air force version of battle uniform. It was worn with pant legs tucked into sage-green combat boots and subdued patches and rank insignia on the overblouse.

Kate's idle glance landed first on the man on the left. His rank indicated he was a major, and she was pretty sure the badge above his name tape was that of a communications officer. Then her gaze shifted to the woman walking beside him.

Without warning, everything seemed to fade away. The busy mall, the clatter of boots, the snick of her credit card being swiped. All she could hear, all she could feel, was her pounding heart. She recognized the captain instantly. She should. She'd stared at the picture the woman had posted on her Facebook page so long it was burned into her psyche.

"Sign here, please."

Kate couldn't move. Couldn't breathe. The three officers were only a few feet away now, talking among themselves.

"Ma'am?"

Why hadn't Travis told her Captain Chamberlain

was here, at Aviano? How could he keep something like that…?

"Ma'am? Are you all right?"

The vendor's anxious question snagged the attention of the officers. They slowed, angled toward the kiosk. The major started to say something but quickly realized his companion was the one caught in the crosshairs of Kate's unrelenting stare.

The captain picked up on the same thing. With a questioning look, the slender brunette stepped closer. "Can I help you?"

Kate found her breath and her balance. "No, thanks. You've already done enough."

Confusion blanked the other woman's face. It was perfectly made up, Kate noted dispassionately. Delicately penciled brows, mascaraed lashes, a touch of blush to accent her high cheekbones. A distinctly feminine counterpoint to ABUs and combat boots.

"I'm sorry," she said, frowning. "Do I know you?"

"I'm Kate Westbrook."

The captain's nostrils flared as she drew in a swift breath. Hot color flooding her pink-tinted cheeks, she floundered for a response to that blunt statement.

"I…uh…"

Her embarrassment was so obvious and so complete that Kate actually took pity on her. "It's okay," she said, astonished to discover she really meant it. "Travis told me what happened. He blames himself."

Almost as much as I blamed you!

She kept the thought to herself while the young officer hesitated, still floundering. With a visible effort, she tried to pull herself together.

"Look, I'm sorry if… Well…" She bit her lip, then

threw her two companions a quick look. "I'll catch up with you, okay?"

"Yeah, sure."

They moved off, leaving Kate alone with the kiosk attendant and the woman who'd caused her so much heartache. Standing here, seeing the captain's acute embarrassment, the last shreds of that pain fell away.

"It's okay," Kate said again, more gently this time. "Really. Travis and I have put that incident behind us."

The captain nodded but couldn't quite disguise her thoughts when she asked, "He's here? At Aviano?"

"For a short time. You?"

"My unit's redeploying. We touched down a few hours ago. We'll RON here tonight and fly out in the morning."

She didn't say where they were headed. For security reasons, she probably couldn't.

Kate's reply came straight from her heart. "Stay safe."

Chapter Twelve

Kate drove back across the base feeling like a felon released after a long, ugly incarceration. For reasons she hadn't yet had time to figure out, the encounter with the woman who'd caused her so much anguish seemed to have opened the cell doors. Every shred of anger and lingering resentment she'd had toward Captain Diane Chamberlain was gone. So were the doubts and the guilt Kate had struggled with less than an hour ago.

For the first time in longer than she could remember, excitement about the future bubbled through her veins. She savored the sizzle, the sheer joy of it as she parked the Ferrari outside the JSOC building and waited for Travis with her face turned to the sun.

He exited a few moments later. Although he slipped on his mirrored sunglasses against the bright afternoon sunlight, her first impression was that he looked and moved as if he was as jazzed as she felt.

"Good feedback?" she asked when he approached.

"Excellent! We may wrap this sucker up sooner than anticipated. No, you go ahead and drive," he said when she started to open the car door. "The headquarters building is just a few blocks away." He folded his long frame into the low-slung sports car and hooked his seat belt. "Turn left out of the parking lot."

She followed the instructions, enjoying the muted growl of the thousand or so horses under the Ferrari's hood and the cool breeze lifting the ends of her hair.

"You look happy," Travis commented. "What'd you do, buy out the BX?"

Kate considered telling him that she'd come face-to-face with the captain. Just as quickly, she tossed the idea. The encounter didn't matter. The *captain* didn't matter.

"Not quite, but I did buy a three-dimensional puzzle of the Leaning Tower of Pisa for Tommy. I thought it might engage his attention for a few hours."

Travis snorted. "Thirty minutes, maybe. The kid has the attention span of a flea with ADD."

"Ha! Your mom probably said the same thing about you when you were his age. She's told me the only thing that drained your energy and kept her sane was that you shot hoops for three or four hours a day, *every* day."

Those sweat-soaked hours on the weed-grown asphalt court a few blocks from his home had done more than drain his energy. Kate's mother-in-law was convinced they'd saved Travis from the decaying mill town he'd grown up in. Without them, he wouldn't have won a basketball scholarship to UMass or escaped the gang he'd started to run with.

The scholarship had been his mother's salvation, too. All during high school and college, Travis had worked at least one part-time job. Two when the basketball season didn't curtail his extracurricular activities. After he'd graduated from UMass, reported to pilot training and asked Kate to marry him, she'd begun contributing to the kitty, too. Her mother-in-law was now happily ensconced in a two-bedroom condo in an upscale suburb. She'd made a slew of new friends and, until her son's marriage had stalled out, had been eagerly awaiting her first grandchild.

Which swung Kate's thoughts back to Tommy the Terrible. "How do you think Dawn's managing with Brian's son?"

"My bet is they're doing fine. They *both* have the attention span of a—"

"Watch it!"

"They must be doing okay, or Brian wouldn't have driven up here. And let's not forget Callie's there to help."

Kate wanted to protest that Dawn was perfectly capable of looking after the boy without the assistance of an experienced child advocate. The memory of Tommy climbing onto the ledge of St. Mark's Cathedral killed that thought dead, though.

"Turn here."

Following Travis's instruction, she took a right and spotted the sign for the Thirty-First Fighter Wing headquarters. The parking lot was almost a quarter full—another indication of the wing's around-the-clock operation, like the two F-16s Kate had watched take off earlier. She pulled into a slot close to the front entrance and killed the engine.

"Do you want me to go in with you?"

"You might as well sit here and enjoy the view. Since

I called ahead, they'll have the paperwork ready. This should only take a few minutes."

"Travis, wait." She reached across the console and snagged his arm. His biceps was smooth and taut to the touch, his skin warmed by the sun. "Please! Tell me what's in your gut right now, this instant. Do you want to do this?"

"Yes."

"Really, truly, honestly?"

"Really, truly, honestly." He leaned closer and grazed her lips with his. "The last ten years have been all about me, Katydid. The next fifty or sixty will be about *us*."

As predicted, he was in and out of the headquarters in less than twenty minutes.

Kate had exited the car and leaned her hips against the hood. Arms folded, she watched anxiously as he emerged and slipped on his sunglasses. She couldn't see his eyes, but the rest of him looked pretty relaxed. And so damned sexy!

Her avid gaze took in the broad shoulders under his black crewneck. The jeans molding his muscled thighs. The sure, confident stride. Excitement percolated through her veins again, and she muttered a distinctly unladylike curse that she had to wait for the hour-long drive back to Venice to get her hands on him.

Or longer. When Travis accepted the keys she held out and settled into the driver's seat, he suggested they host a predinner gathering at their suite at the Palazzo Alleghri.

"Carlo called while I was inside," he said as he put the car in gear. "He wanted to confirm that he's heading down to Venice this evening and is hoping for an introduction to dazzling Dawn."

Dazzling was one of many adjectives Travis used to describe the more volatile of Kate's two friends. She didn't mistake it for a compliment, however.

"What did you tell him?"

"That we'd try to get everyone together at our place around seven."

"Does everyone include Brian and Tommy?"

"Of course. Brian was still at the JSOC, so Carlo said he'd pass the word."

"You don't think that might be a little awkward?"

"Nah. The kid's a handful, but he's basically okay."

Kate hadn't been referring to Tommy. Nor could she articulate why the thought of putting Dawn in the same room with both Brian and the prince made her feel just a little uneasy. It could have been that flicker of pure male interest in Ellis's eyes when he'd first met Dawn, which she'd shown no signs of returning. Or Kate's own somewhat mixed reaction to Carlo after he'd planted that disconcertingly intimate kiss on her palm. Then there was Callie, who seemed to have been left completely out of the equation.

But Travis had already extended the invitation, so Kate dug out her phone. "I'll call Dawn and Callie and see if that works for them."

It did, Dawn confirmed. "Brian called right before you did," she reported breathlessly. "He's going to swing by the hospital on the way back." She paused, sucked air. "He wants to check on Mrs. Wells, so he'll be a little late."

"How's it going with you three? And why are you out of breath?"

"It's going great, and I'm out of breath because I had to scramble out from under the bed to catch the phone."

"Why were you under the bed, or should I even ask?"

"We're playing hide-and-seek. You wouldn't *believe* the places that little stinker can squeeze into."

"Is Callie playing, too?"

"She went back to our suite to... Hey! No fair, Thomas. You can't tag me. I had come out of hiding to answer the phone. No, it is *not* your turn." Another laugh, this one of pure amusement. "You should see the faces this kid can make. Like the one he's showing me now. Oh, Tommy. That's gross! What if your eyelids get stuck like that?"

With hoots of childish glee sounding in the background, Dawn came back on the line. "As I was saying before I was so rudely interrupted, Brian's going to be late. So I'll feed the brat. Then Callie and I will put him in lockstep and escort him to your hotel."

"Okay. See you around seven."

Kate thumbed the off button and sat staring at the phone for a moment.

"Everything all right?" Travis asked.

"Sounds like it. It also sounds as though Dawn might be having more fun than Tommy."

Her husband took the high ground and wisely refrained from commenting. Still bemused by the brief conversation, Kate shoved her phone in her purse and settled in to enjoy the drive back to Venice.

It was almost six by the time a vaporetto deposited them on the landing of Palazzo Alleghri. Wind whipped and sun chapped, Kate detoured on her way to the shower just long enough to consult the room service menu and choose a selection of munchies for their impromptu cocktail party. Fruit, cheese and antipasto for the adults. A fancy—and very expensive!—version of pizza rolls for Tommy.

While she called the order in, Travis iced down the bottles of sparkling prosecco they'd purchased on the drive up to Aviano.

"Better have them bring up some extra glasses," he suggested.

She added the glasses and several varieties of fruit juice for Tommy, then made a dash for the bathroom, shedding her clothes as she went. She wouldn't have time to wash and blow-dry her hair, she decided as she twisted the knobs for the shower's ultramodern cross jets, but she could...

The press of a very warm, very hard body against her exposed bottom produced a reluctant protest. "We don't have time to play, Trav."

"Who said anything about playing?" He pressed closer. "I just figured we could save time by scrubbing each other's backs."

"And while you scrub, I'm supposed to ignore what's poking my rear?"

"Nothing says we can't make this an economy of effort."

She gave a disbelieving snort, but the feel of him ready and eager killed any further protest.

So when Travis nudged her into the spray, she didn't make any noises about the time or the party or the need to keep her hair dry. She just leaned forward and planted her palms against the tiles. And as fast as that, she was ready.

Her belly went tight. Her vaginal muscles tightened. Anticipation combined with the dancing water to send eager thrills racing over every inch of her skin. Suddenly she was too impatient to wait even a few moments while Travis soaped her back.

"'Scuse me." Wiggling her hips, she pushed against his groin. "I thought we were going to economize here."

"So we were."

The hand holding the soap and washcloth snaked around her waist. The other found her center. Blind pleasure shot through Kate as he parted her folds and applied an exquisite pressure. Then he was inside her, lifting her, filling her. She thrust back, grinding her bottom into his belly, squeezing him tight and hard.

Travis spread his legs for better balance on the terrazzo tile while his breath burned hot in his lungs. He was damned if he was going to rush this. He wanted to imprint the sight of water cascading over his wife's shoulders, running down her back, slicking her hips where they joined with his. She wasn't making it easy, though. With every wiggle, every backward thrust, he could feel the pressure building.

Gritting his teeth, he dropped the soap and put his hands on her hips to control the pace. She wasn't having any of that.

"We're not coming in low and slow this time."

She jerked away, and the abrupt separation left Travis feeling pretty much the way he had the first time he'd crashed and burned in the simulator—as if his lungs had flattened and the rest of his insides had gone to rubber.

Thankfully, the hunger stamped on her face told him this ride wasn't over. Blinking the water out of her eyes, she stabbed a finger at the shower's built-in seat.

"Sit!"

The tiled ledge was wide enough to support him comfortably. And low enough for Kate to straddle his hips without resorting to serious contortions.

"This is better," he admitted as she took him inside

her again. Angling his head, he rasped his tongue over a stiff, hard nipple. "Much better!"

He got in only that one lick before she locked her mouth on his and picked up where they'd left off several gallons of water ago. Her hips pumped, her thighs squeezed and Travis gave up all attempts to control her *or* himself.

The shower jets hadn't been off for more than a few moments when the suite's doorbell chimed. Travis was still toweling himself down, but Kate had wrapped herself in one of the hotel's plush robes to attack her wet tangles with her hairbrush.

"I'll get it."

She scurried out of the bedroom and crossed the sitting room, working the brush while hoping to heck that was room service at the door and not one of their guests.

Actually, it was neither. Or at least not one of the guests she'd been expecting. The brush stilled as she smiled a flustered greeting.

"Hi, Joe. Sorry, we're, uh, running a little late." She peered around him at the empty hall. "Carlo's not with you?"

"He's taking care of some business downstairs. I came up to conduct a quick security sweep."

"Huh?"

"Standard procedures." Amused by her goggle-eyed surprise, he held up what looked like an ordinary cell phone with an extended antenna. "Just a check for hidden cameras, scoping out emergency exits, the usual stuff. Mind if I do a walk-through?"

"Oh. No, of course not. Come in."

She trailed after him as he aimed the antenna in a slow arc over the sitting and dining areas. It occurred to Kate that if the suite *did* contain any hidden cameras, someone had sure got an eyeful the past few days.

Travis emerged at that point, fully dressed except for his bare feet, and nodded to Carlo's shadow. "Hey, Joe. The bedroom and bathroom are all yours."

"Thanks."

"Does he do this every place Carlo goes?" Kate asked as Russo disappeared into the other room.

"Pretty much. Kidnappings almost dropped off the scope after Italy passed a law freezing the assets of a victim's family so they can't pay a ransom. But individuals with Carlo's wealth and high profile are still prime targets for blackmail or extortion or even industrial espionage. Joe's just making sure that whatever his boss says or does here doesn't get doctored by some clever film editor and put us all in an awkward situation."

"But...didn't you tell me his cousin owned this hotel?"

"I did, and your point is?"

She was still grappling with the idea of not being able to trust your own cousin when Russo reappeared.

"All clear. I'll get out of your hair."

"Can't you stay and have a drink with us?"

"I'm still on duty."

"The minibar's well stocked with soda and Pellegrino. And there," she said hopefully when the doorbell chimed again, "is room service. If you can't drink, Joe, you can eat. Please join us."

"Well..."

"Good. Now I'll let you two gentlemen handle the setup while I get dressed."

She beat a hasty retreat to the bedroom. The hairbrush got tossed on the vanity. The plush robe joined the discarded towels dotting the bathroom floor. Grabbing a pair of clean, lace-trimmed hipsters, Kate had one foot in when the bedroom door opened again.

Her first thought was her husband. Her second, a curious six-year-old. With a small squeak, she hopped behind the shield of the bathroom wall.

"Travis?"

"Nope," Dawn sang out as she crossed the bedroom. "*C'est moi.* So where did you find that hottie out there in the— Whoa! What happened here?"

She came to a dead stop, taking in the damp towels, the discarded robe, the puddles of water. When her gaze shifted to the woman caught with her hipsters midway up one thigh, her mouth curved in a smirk.

"Never mind. I've got the picture."

Kate shoved her second leg into the panties. "Forget the picture. Hand me that bra and help me do something with my hair."

"Why mess with it?" Dawn dangled the scrap of lace from her upturned palm. "That just-did-my-husband-in-the-shower style looks good on you."

Kate hooked on the bra and snatched up the brush. "Here. Work some magic, and fast."

"I bet that's not what Travis said."

"Dawnnnnnn."

"Okay, okay. Sit!"

Kate couldn't help herself. "Actually, that's what *I* said."

Eyes dancing, she indicated the shower seat with a jerk of her chin. Dawn followed her lead, saw the abandoned soap and washcloth, and started laughing. Kate held out for all of four or five seconds before she joined in.

They were both still giggling when Callie walked in. "Is this a private party?"

"It was, when the water was running," Kate said, giggling harder.

"And she and Travis got naked."

"And he used the soap to—"

Callie held up a hand. "Stop! I've—"

"Got the picture," Kate and Dawn chorused simultaneously.

Helpless with laughter now, they collapsed. Kate put her back to the smooth tiles and simply slid down until her butt hit the damp floor. Dawn folded her legs and sank with the grace of a ballerina.

Callie shook her head but couldn't hold out against their combined silliness. Drifting down, she joined them. "You two are nuts. You know that, don't you?"

"Is that so?" Dawn poked her in the arm. "So why is Miss Priss 'n' Boots here on the floor with us?"

"Because you look so happy. Especially Kate." A soft smile lit Callie's violet eyes. "It's been a while since you laughed like that."

"I know. I am happy. And oddly enough, I owe at least part of this feeling to the bitch-whore."

Callie and Dawn exchanged startled looks.

"Do you know what she's talking about?"

"Don't have a clue."

They swung back to Kate.

"Okay, girl, talk."

"I met her. Today, up at the base."

Dawn's face went hard. "That son of a bitch Travis! He didn't tell you she was there?"

"He doesn't know. And she's not at Aviano. Her unit's in transit, she couldn't say to where, but they touched down this morning and leave again tomorrow."

"And you believe her?"

"Yes."

Dawn wasn't convinced, but Callie laid a restraining hand on her arm. "Why did meeting the captain make such a difference, Kate?"

"It's hard to explain." She lifted a hand, let it drop. "As brief as the encounter was, it seemed freeing to me. I let go of the anger, the hurt, the guilt I've been dragging around like a damned anchor for so long."

"*You* had nothing to feel guilty about!"

"Oh, Dawn, it wasn't all one-sided. Breakups never are. You know that."

Her friend tipped her chin, and red rushed into her cheeks. Smothering a curse, Kate regretted the reminder of Dawn's near marriages. But before she could apologize, the bedroom door opened and Travis walked in.

He got as far as the foot of the bed before he spotted them in the bathroom, sitting knee to knee on the wet tiles. He stopped short, his brows rising as he surveyed Kate's bra and panties, Dawn's flushed face, and Callie's serene indifference to the wet splotch spreading across her rear, compliments of the towel she'd hunkered down on.

"Is this a private party," he drawled, taking in the scene, "or can the rest of us join you?"

Kate looked at Dawn. Dawn looked at Callie. Their lips trembled. Their eyes brimmed with laughter. It burst from all three of them at the same instant, an uninhibited celebration of friendship and flat-out hilarity.

Chapter Thirteen

The cocktail party was a great success.

As Kate had hoped, the pizza rolls and three-dimensional puzzle totally absorbed Tommy. Not just him, she noted with amusement. Travis's engineering degree and passion for all things mechanical drew him like a moth to the table where Tommy had laid out the puzzle pieces. Travis exercised admirable restraint, however, and confined his input into the construction process to observation and the occasional casual suggestion that a certain piece might fit better somewhere else.

Kate thoroughly enjoyed the tableau they presented—Travis with his dark hair and square jaw leaning over Tommy of the angel-blue eyes and impish grin while the impossibly angled structure rose inch by inch in front of them.

Despite his fascination with the puzzle, Travis didn't neglect his duties as host. He kept everyone supplied with food and drink and contributed to the lively conversation that ranged from Dawn's humiliating defeat at hide-and-seek to Callie's visit to the Guggenheim Museum to Carlo's upcoming participation in a speedboat race in Lake Geneva, Switzerland.

Carlo had claimed a seat on the sofa next to Dawn. Kate and Callie sat across the coffee table from them, while Travis divided his attention between the adults and Tommy. Joe Russo stood a little apart, listening more than participating. If the prince had been surprised to find his bodyguard included in the convivial group, he didn't show it.

Brian Ellis arrived thirty minutes into the gathering with a positive report on Mrs. Wells's condition and assurances for Tommy that he would have a chance to say goodbye before his nanny left for California.

"We'll go to the hospital first thing in the morning," he promised, ruffling his son's hair. "I told her we'd ride in the boat with her to the airport, too. If you're *very* careful and don't try to do wheelies, she may even let you try out her motorized wheelchair."

The boy had been solemn eyed up to the mention of wheelies. Kate could almost see the possibilities whirling through his fertile mind as he showed his dad the construction project. With Tommy busily reengaged, Brian loosened his tie, accepted a glass of prosecco with a grateful smile and joined the two on the oversize sofa.

"Everything go okay this afternoon?" he asked Dawn. "Or do I really want to know?"

"We had fun."

"They took turns hiding from each other," Carlo elaborated, stretching his arm across the back of the sofa. "Dawn was just telling us how long she had to

search before she found Tommaso tucked behind a suitcase on the top shelf of your closet."

Casually, so casually, the prince's fingers brushed the
curve of Dawn's shoulder. The shoulder nearest Brian,
Kate noted.

"The top shelf is one of his favorite hiding places,"
Tommaso's father admitted with an affectionate glance
at his son. "Scared the bejesus out of me the first time
I found him there."

"What I want to know is how the heck he got up
there," Dawn groused, making a face at the grinning
six-year-old. "Your little stinker won't tell me."

"You can't tell her, either, Dad! That's just 'tween
us guys."

Brian lifted his glass in a salute to male secrets and
asked Callie about her afternoon. She expanded a little
on her visit to the Guggenheim, then described taking
a good hour to find her way back to the hotel.

Carlo's white teeth gleamed below the black ruff of
his mustache. "Getting lost is required of all first-time
visitors to Venice. But now that you have fulfilled that
basic requirement, there are parts of the city that most
tourists never find their way to. Glorious works of art
in obscure little churches. Rooftop terraces with views
that will steal your breath. Sunsets over the Lido. You
must let me show you some of these hidden gems. You
and your so charming friend."

His dark eyes glinting, he let his fingers graze over
Dawn's shoulder again. The move was more blatant
this time and provoked markedly different reactions.

Dawn slanted the prince an amused glance. Callie's
response to Carlo's invitation was polite, but cool. Travis looked away and scratched the side of his nose. And
when Kate got up to refill the cheese plate, she caught

a glimpse of a very cynical expression flitting across Joe's face.

Brian showed the least reaction. Downing another sip of his wine, he engaged Callie in a lively discussion of Venice's lack of a direct route to *any* point on the tourist map. Her natural reserve melted under his gentle teasing, and the animation that came into her face seemed to snag the attention of more than one of the males present.

When Dawn decided to help Kate, though, she recaptured their instant notice by pushing off the sofa with sinuous grace and smoothing her filmy top over her hips. Carlo, Brian and Joe all followed the downward sweep of her palms. Even Tommy looked up, broke into a smile and called her over to check his progress.

Travis, bless him, was too used to Kate's friends to spare Dawn more than a quick glance. He got up, as well, to refill wineglasses, but Brian turned down a refill.

"Thanks, but Tom and I better head back to our place. We have to get to the hospital early tomorrow morning," he added when his son protested. "We're accompanying Mrs. Wells to the airport, remember?"

"Oh, yeah. But my puzzle…"

Travis was ready with a solution. Retrieving the box they'd transported the prosecco in, he tore off one of the lid flaps. "Here. Let's slide this piece under the tower, then place it inside the box. The unassembled pieces can go back in their original carton."

Everyone held their breath during the delicate maneuver, but the half-constructed tower made a safe transition to the wine box. While Tommy and Travis gathered the rest of the pieces, Brian used the house phone to call down to the desk for a water taxi.

With only a little prompting from his dad, the boy

thanked Travis and Kate again for the puzzle and said good-night to Callie, the prince and Joe Russo before beaming a smile at his substitute nanny.

"See ya tomorrow, Dawn."

"See ya, dude."

The Ellises' departure turned the others' thoughts to dinner, and Carlo immediately took charge. "You must allow me to take you to my favorite place to dine in Venice. I'll just make a call, yes, and have them ready a table for us."

Callie tried to bow out, but the prince wouldn't hear of it. "No, you must come. It's an experience you'll not soon forget."

His call made, Joe got on *his* phone and sent one of his men ahead to do a sweep. While that was in progress, Dawn gestured to her snug white ankle slacks and filmy top.

"Do we need to change?"

"But no, *cara.*" Carlo's reply was low and warm, his glance a caress. "You are perfect just as you are."

"Careful, Your Highness. Flattery will get you everywhere."

A thoroughly delighted Carlo tucked her arm into his side. "It's hardly flattery when one speaks only the truth. But let's have dinner, shall we, and see where more such truth leads."

The two of them should have looked like everyone's stereotype of a rich man with his latest toy—the tall, voluptuous redhead clinging to the arm of a stocky fireplug of a man some six or eight inches shorter. But Dawn's bubbling personality took the prince's obvious admiration out of the realm of the ridiculous and made it completely understandable.

Still, Kate and Callie shared a quick been-there, done-that glance as they gathered their purses and left.

The next four hours turned out to be a total delight. The prince was obviously smitten with Dawn but included both Kate and Callie in his exaggerated gallantries. And the restaurant he took them to was something out of a dream.

Their vaporetto drew up at the landing of what looked like a private palace. Flaming torches illuminated the elaborate facade. A footman in silks, lace and a powdered wig escorted them up a flight of stairs to a marble-floored foyer lit by hundreds of candles. Joe had them wait there while he conferred with the associate he'd sent ahead. A tall, lanky African-American with a Texas twang, the associate gave the green light.

Carlo didn't press when Joe declined to join them for dinner, leading Kate to think the two men probably preferred not to cross the line between personal and business. Then the footman escorted them into a small private dining room that was right out of fifteenth-century Venice. Candles flickered in tall stands. The table was dark, elaborately carved and set with gold plates. Handblown glass goblets in six different sizes added brilliant, gem-like colors to the table, while delicate notes from a lute and harpsichord drifted from hidden speakers.

Like the footman, the servers who swept in with crystal flagons of wine wore silks and lace and powdered wigs. They presented no menus. Instead, the guests feasted on a meal that proceeded course by stately course. Like the servers and the place settings, each course replicated epicurean masterpieces from the height of the Venetian empire.

It was almost 1:00 a.m. when they finally rolled out of the dining room. Joe must have been alerted by the servers. He met them at the stairs that led down to the landing and assisted them into the vaporetto he had waiting.

As they wound through the moonlit canals, Carlo suggested another stop. "You must let me take you to the Club Blu. The jazz is the best you'll hear this side of the Atlantic."

"Thank you, but I'll pass," Callie said firmly. "After that wonderful dinner and all the hours I walked today, I'm calling it a night."

Carlo made a gallant attempt to change her mind. Ditto Kate's and Travis's, but it was obvious to all concerned that the prince wasn't disappointed to have Dawn to himself.

Callie got off first at the Gritti Palace. Kate and Travis disembarked next at the Palazzo Alleghri. They lingered on the landing, watching as the vaporetto glided away. Dawn and the prince lounged shoulder to shoulder in the rear compartment, Joe standing up front next to the driver.

Travis broke the small silence they left in their wake. "Any bets as to when we'll see Ms. McGill again?"

Kate chose not to place a wager.

To her surprise, Dawn buzzed Kate's cell phone while she and Travis were at breakfast. After the monster meal last night, they'd opted for coffee and a basket of rolls consumed in lazy leisure on their balcony overlooking the Grand Canal.

"You're up early," Kate said by way of greeting.

"Things to do, people to see, places to go," Dawn chirped, sounding bright and cheerful and un-hungover.

"Are you still flying home from Rome with Callie on Wednesday?"

"That's the plan."

And Travis would follow as soon as he wrapped his special project. Until he did, Kate intended to keep *very* busy. They'd already discussed recombining households. Travis didn't care where they lived as long as they were together, so she planned to see if her upscale DC condo complex had a larger unit available. If they did, she would move and get the new place ready for dual occupancy. If not, she'd have to scout out another complex or start looking at homes.

Busy reviewing her mental to-do, it took a second or two for Kate to wonder what had prompted Dawn's question. Several reasons jumped into her mind, including the possibility that her impulsive friend had made some spur-of-the-moment arrangements with the prince.

"Why?" she asked cautiously. "Have you changed your mind about extending your stay in Italy to look after Tommy the Terrible?"

"No. Why would I?"

"Well, you and Carlo seemed to be getting pretty chummy last night."

"We had a great time. He's a sweet little pooh bear, isn't he?"

Kate blinked, but decided not to suggest a major in Italy's elite special ops unit might wince at that characterization.

"If you say so. So what's up?"

"I talked to Brian before he and Tommy left for the hospital this morning. Since you and Callie don't have to check in for your flight until Wednesday afternoon, she's planning to take the early train down to Rome that morning. I thought Tommy and I might go with her. We'd see you two off at the airport, then head into town so the kid can do his gladiator thing at the Coliseum, then zip back up to Venice that evening."

Kate couldn't help remembering the moments of sheer terror she'd experienced when Tommy had climbed up on the ledge at St. Mark's and shuddered to think of the trouble he might get into in Rome.

"Was Brian okay with that?"

"He was, when I told him I would strong-arm Travis into going to the Coliseum with us. I know the Ferrari's only a two-seater, so he'll have to leave it at the airport and train into the city with us. Think he might be up for that?"

"Hang on. I'll let you ask him."

She passed Travis the phone and grinned while he listed at least a dozen different reasons why turning Thomas Ellis loose on Rome was a terrible idea. He eventually caved, though, as Kate knew he would.

"Don't look so put-upon," she said when he disconnected. "Dawn's always had your number. Under that tough, macho exterior she knows you're as soft a touch as her new pooh bear."

Travis's face went blank for a moment, then lit with unholy glee. "That's how she referred to Carlo? Her pooh bear?"

"Her sweet little pooh bear, to be exact."

"Good God! Wait until that works its way back to his crew."

Which it would, Kate guessed, aided by an oh-so-casual comment or two from Travis. She wasn't wrong. Looking positively diabolical at the prospect, he reached for her hand and ejected her from her chair. "We've only got this one day left in Venice. Let's get out and enjoy it."

* * *

They did. So much that the rest of the time flew by and Kate regretted that she and Travis weren't extending their stay in Venice until Wednesday, as Callie and Dawn were.

But she'd agreed to have lunch with Signore Gallo in Bologna. So early the next morning, she slipped into her caramel-colored knit pants. She left the matching jacket off this time. Instead, she paired the pants with a short-sleeved black top and the necklace Travis had insisted on buying during their yesterday's foray to the shops lining the Rialto Bridge. A swirl of turquoise, black and twenty-four-karat gold, the Murano glass heart dangling in the center was as big as a fist and cost more than Kate cared to think about.

Packed and ready to hit the road, she and Travis checked out of the Palazzo Alleghri and took a vaporetto to the car park, where they reclaimed the Ferrari. Travis had timed the drive so they would arrive in Bologna with a comfortable margin before their one o'clock appointment. Since they knew the bank's location and were confident Signore Gallo's efficient assistant would reserve a parking space again, they spent the extra time exploring Bologna's historic center.

They strolled into the bank a few minutes before one. Maximo was waiting for them and once again escorted them up the wide, curving staircase. As before, Kate asked him and Travis to wait a moment while she ducked into the ladies' room to freshen her makeup.

She encountered no sobbing occupant with arms braced on the sides of the sink this time. But she recognized the woman when she and the two men entered the bank president's outer office. The secretary returned Kate's smile with a hesitant one of her own and quickly obeyed Maximo's instruction to advise their boss that his guests had arrived.

The leonine Signore Gallo emerged from his office wreathed in smiles and fervent hopes that Kate and Travis had enjoyed their time in Venice. Mere moments later, the three of them were ensconced in an executive dining room paneled in dark oak and lined with more portraits of the bank's medieval founders.

The consummate host, Signore Gallo engaged Travis in the conversation by keeping it light and nonfiscal through the appetizers and pasta course. The heavy stuff came with the veal *picatta*. Bravely, Travis soldiered through a lengthy discussion of the liquidity index and analysis of the latest stats concerning high-volume bond market issuance.

They lost him over coffee, tiramisu and long-term yields. Although Kate and Signore Gallo were enthusiastic over the fact that low-level volatility appeared to coincide with a rapid growth of cross-border banking, Travis looked as though his eyes might roll back in his head at any moment. Kate took pity on him and was about to thank Signore Gallo for a wonderful lunch when the banker extended an unexpected and completely astounding offer.

"I must confess I'm quite impressed with your work at the World Bank, Signora Westbrook. You've come so far, so fast."

Not hard to do, Kate thought ruefully, when you lost the husband who constituted your entire universe and put your whole heart and soul into your job instead.

"If you will permit me," Gallo continued, "I should like to propose you for membership in the IBA. A vacancy on our junior associates' committee just occurred, and we are anxious to fill it."

Kate's jaw dropped. Literally and figuratively. The blandly labeled International Bankers' Association was, in fact, an exclusive and *extremely* chauvinistic gentlemen's club. Membership was limited to a dozen or so heads of banking consortiums with assets and investments totaling trillions of dollars. The IBA's junior associates' subcommittee was almost as exclusive. As far as Kate knew, no woman had ever been admitted to its ranks. That Signore Gallo would propose her for membership was beyond incredible.

"I'm stunned. I don't know what to say."

He responded with an understanding nod. "It's a great honor for someone as young as you to be put up for membership. And a great responsibility. But everything I read about you reinforces the opinion I've formed in our brief acquaintance. You'll be required to attend quarterly meetings in Bern, of course, but the IBA will cover all travel expenses. So a simple yes is all I need at this point to forward your name to the nominating committee."

Yes! Yes, yes, yes!

Kate was a half breath away from shouting an agreement when her business sense kicked in. How stupid would she be to agree to something this momentous without taking time to weigh the pros and cons?

And chief among those cons, she realized belatedly, would be the required attendance at IBA's quarterly meetings. Including travel time, she could expect to spend days, if not weeks, in Switzerland every three months.

Travis must have weighed the same pros and cons. His grin had stretched wide and proud when Signore Gallo first extended the invitation. It had pretty much disappeared now.

"I can't tell you how honored I am," Kate responded. "May I think about this and get back to you?"

Signore Gallo stared at her with undisguised astonishment. Not surprising, since she was probably the
first woman to be invited into the centuries-old, all-
male enclave.

"Of course," he said after an uncomfortable moment.
"The vacancy will be filled quickly, however. Please let
me know your decision as soon as possible."

"I will," she promised.

Once again Maximo appeared to escort her and Travis out of Cassa di Molino. When he guided them past
the bank president's outer offices, Kate searched for
the woman from the ladies' room, but the dark-haired
secretary wasn't at her desk.

Kate and Travis said goodbye to Maximo at the tall
bronze doors guarding the entrance and stepped out
into the bruising August sunshine. Heat slammed into
her. Convinced the temperature had climbed ten or fifteen degrees during their extended lunch, she flung up
a hand to block the shimmering, exhaust-fueled haze.

Which was why she didn't pick up on the drama oc-
curring across the street as quickly as Travis did. She
was still squinting through the exhaust fumes when she
heard his smothered curse. Sensed him go rigid beside
her. Caught a blur of movement as he burst into action.

Zigzagging across four lanes of traffic, he dodged
a furiously honking driver and aimed for two figures
locked in a desperate struggle. Kate was still standing
openmouthed on the opposite side of the street when the
two combatants turned to meet the unexpected attack.
One, she saw with a shock, was the older woman from
the bank. The other was a younger, wiry man wearing
a striped soccer shirt and a look of vicious desperation.

Travis hit the male with a flying tackle. The woman

staggered back. A fist pressed to her bruised, bleeding mouth, she shouted something in Italian. Horrified, Kate picked up only one word.

Pistola.

"Travis!"

Heedless of traffic, she charged into the street.

"He's got a gun!"

She had to jump back to avoid being flattened by an oncoming bus. It was still rumbling by when a sharp crack split the hot, heavy air.

Chapter Fourteen

Kate's heart stopped dead in her chest. In the second or two it took for the bus to rumble by, she tried to convince herself that crack she'd heard was the sound of a backfire.

Please, let it be backfire!

A second, then a third sharp retort blasted that hope. Almost scorched by the searing exhaust from the tailpipe, she slapped a palm against the rear of the bus and cut around it.

The tableau on the sidewalk seemed to unfold before her horrified eyes like a video played in ultra slo-mo. The soccer-shirted punk was flat on the pavement. Travis had the kid's gun hand pinned to the sidewalk with one fist. His other was up and back and starting a vicious downward arc when the older woman threw herself at the two writhing combatants.

"No!" Her eyes wild, she grabbed Travis's wrist with both hands. *"E mio figlio!"*

Kate didn't try to translate the frantic cry. Her every thought, her entire being, was centered on the crimson splotch on Travis's shoulder. It blossomed even bigger and darker in the few desperate heartbeats it took her to reach the woman hanging on to him with clawing hands.

"E mio figlio! E mio figlio!"

Kate leaped at the dark-haired secretary, fully prepared to pulverize both her and the young tough with the gun. Travis kept his death grip on the punk's gun hand, but the unleashed energy went out of his upraised arm. He seemed to sag, his head down and his shoulders sloping. The momentary weakness combined with the spreading red stain struck terror into Kate's heart.

"Get off him!"

With a viciousness she didn't know she possessed, she grabbed the older woman's hair and yanked. The secretary yelped in pain and put both hands up to her temples. Remorseless, Kate hauled her away from the two men.

Only then did she realize a crowd had gathered. Other hands reached out to grab the older woman, to wrest the gun from the punk's hand, to help Travis roll off him and into a loose slump. Voices pounded at Kate. Questions bombarded her from all directions. Someone was shouting an urgent report into a cell phone.

The carabinieri who arrived on scene took Kate's name and disjointed statement and didn't protest when she insisted on climbing into the ambulance called to transport Travis to the hospital.

He was still in surgery when two other police officers arrived in the waiting room of the sprawling Saint Ursula-Malpighi University Hospital. They checked with the charge nurse and was told the bullet had passed through the victim's shoulder, causing as yet undetermined damage to muscle and the network of nerves running from his neck to his armpit. So Kate was less than sympathetic when the police sergeant confirmed what she'd already figured out for herself.

"The one who shoots your husband, he is the woman's son."

The lean, hard-eyed sergeant wore an olive-drab uniform crossed with a patent leather Sam Browne belt. Like Kate, he evinced little sympathy for the shooter.

"We know him well. He's... How do you say? Small-time. Too small to pay for the filth he pumps into his veins. He broke into his mother's house when she refuses to give him money." The sergeant's mouth twisted. "She also refuses to press charges."

Kate wasn't as forgiving. "Well, we will! This time," she vowed fiercely, "he's going down."

The sergeant nodded, took down her account of the event and promised he would have a translated copy ready for her signature when he returned to take Travis's.

"And these," he said, holding up a set of keys, "we recovered from the street. We've matched them to the car parked in the visitor's space at the bank, but this car is not yours."

Kate recognized the pawing black stallion on the key ring's medallion. "No, it belongs to a friend of ours. Maggiore Carlo di Lorenzo. He loaned it to my husband."

"So we have ascertained," the sergeant said, passing her the keys. "You have powerful friends, signora."

Kate nodded and dropped the keys in her pocket. Mere moments after the carabinieri departed, Signore Gallo and his assistant hurried into the surgical waiting area.

"Signora Westbrook!" The silver-maned bank executive grasped both of Kate's hands. "I cannot tell you how distressed we are that this should have happened."

"Signora Constanza is one of our most valued employees," Maximo put in. "She's been with Cassa di Molino for more than twenty years. But that son of hers. Pah!"

"The boy was such a bright child," Gallo said, shaking his head mournfully. "So happy. Gabriella—Signora Constanza—would bring him to the bank and we all delighted in his quick, eager mind." He sighed, and his expression folded into sorrowful lines. "Then came the drugs."

"Signore Gallo paid for him to go through rehab," Maximo related indignantly. "Not once, but twice! And still the *bastardo* bleeds his mother dry with desperate tales of how his suppliers will break his arm or shoot him in the knee or cut his throat. Better for Gabriella that they had!"

"Enough, Maximo. Let us focus instead on how we may assist Signora Westbrook in this unfortunate situation. Shall we arrange a place for you to stay while your husband recovers? A car and driver, perhaps, since you are unfamiliar with our city?"

"I have a car, but it's still parked in the visitor's space at the bank."

"Ah, yes. The red Ferrari. If you give me the keys, we shall deliver it here."

"Thank you."

"It is the least we can…"

He broke off, his glance whipping to the woman in surgical scrubs who pushed through the swinging doors. She removed her cap and released a short sweep of rich chestnut hair as her gaze landed on Kate.

"I am Dottore Bennati. You are Signora Westbrook?"

"Yes. How's my husband?"

"We have done debridement and *innesto di pelle*."

The surgeon searched for the medical terms in English and looked relieved when Signore Gallo offered to translate.

"She says they removed some damaged tissue and repaired an artery here." The banker tapped a spot close to his shoulder joint. "Luckily, the bullet was small caliber and did not fragment. It is too early to tell if it caused nerve damage, however."

"But my husband will be okay?"

"He will," Gallo confirmed after a brief colloquy with the ER doc. "Whether he will regain full use of his arm, however, must depend on the nerves."

Kate was so relieved by the first half of his comment that the second barely registered. "When can I see him?"

"Very soon," the banker translated. "He is in recovery now."

While Kate waited to see her husband, Signore Gallo assured her that Saint Ursula's School of Medicine and Surgery was the best in Italy and that Travis would recover speedily here. After repeating his offer of assistance, he and Maximo made sure Kate had their business cards and would call if she needed anything, anything at all.

The surgical recovery unit contained eight glassed-in cubicles in a neat semicircle around a central monitoring station. The gleaming floors and what looked like state-of-the-art equipment reassured Kate almost as much as Travis's wobbly smile when she entered his cubicle.

"Heya, Katydid."

His voice was thick, the words slurred. Kate dropped her purse on a chair and carefully threaded her hand through IV lines to take his.

"Heya, handsome. How do you feel?"

"Woozy, but flying high." He slicked his tongue across his lips and frowned in an obvious effort to clear the fog. "That kid? Wh-what happened to him?"

"He's in police custody."

"The woman?"

"She's his mother. He was trying to shake her down for drug money."

"Young…punk."

Kate's sentiments exactly, although she didn't voice them, as Travis's lids had drifted down. She sat there, his hand clasped loosely in hers, and tried not to relive those moments of sheer terror outside the bank.

An hour later Travis was moved to a single room overlooking a small garden. She stood by the window, waiting while the floor staff got him settled, took his vitals and adjusted his various drips and monitors. They were still entering information into a small, portable computer on a wheeled stand when Callie and Dawn arrived.

Callie eased past the nurses and wrapped an arm around Kate's shoulders before giving Travis a warm smile. "You don't look too bad for someone who got on the wrong side of a bullet."

Dawn just shook her head. "I thought you macho special ops types *knew* better than to get on the wrong side of a bullet."

"We do, most of the time. How did you two get here so quickly?"

"Carlo drove us. Carlo and Joe. Carlo had a night flight this evening, so they were just getting ready to head back to the base when Kate called."

"They'll be up in a minute," Callie related. "Joe's

parking the car, and Carlo detoured to speak to your surgeon."

The prince and his bodyguard arrived within moments of each other. Both were in flight suits, Carlo's with his velcroed name tag, wings and distinctive patches, Joe's with no markings at all. The prince repeated Signore Gallo's assurances that Saint Ursula's surgical unit was one of the top three in Italy and added that he'd personally verified Dr. Bennati's credentials.

"She is chairman of the department as well as surgeon in chief," he informed Travis. "You're lucky she was in the operating theater when they brought you in. And lucky, too," he added with a wiggle of his brows, "to have such a beautiful woman cutting on you, yes?"

His chauvinism was as cheerful as it was unabashed, although he attempted a quick recovery.

"But not as beautiful as the so lovely Dawn and Callie and Caterina."

"It's getting thick in here," Dawn commented drily. "And crowded. So these two so lovely ladies will wait in the lounge."

"It's a coffee bar," Callie told Kate. "Shall I bring you a cup?"

"No, I'll come down in a bit and get some."

She waited until she was sure Travis was comfortable with his visitors before slipping out to join her friends.

"What'd you do with Tommy?" she asked Dawn between much-needed sips.

"I called Brian right after you called us. He was already at the base but made immediate arrangements for one of the hotel staff to stay with Tom until he got back. He said they'd drive down to Bologna, too."

Kate wasn't sure Travis was up to a visit from both father and son. She also wondered what kind of memories of Italy Tommy would take home after so many visits to hospitals.

She needn't have worried on either count. By the time the Ellises arrived, Travis had improved enough to give a wide-eyed Tommy a much-expunged version of the shooting.

Carlo, thankfully, remained present when the police returned to take Travis's statement. Callie, Dawn, Joe and the Ellises retreated to the lounge during the process, which Kate guessed was considerably sped up by the prince's presence. When she tried later to express her appreciation for all Carlo had done, however, the prince merely shrugged.

"No thanks are necessary, Caterina. As I told you, I would be monkey bait were it not for your husband. Joe and I must go now, but we will return tomorrow. Also, I've reserved a hotel room for you and Callie, as she tells me she will stay in Bologna with you. And Dawn, if she…"

"Hold on." Brian strode into the room, trailed by Joe, Callie and Dawn, who had a close hold on Tommy. "I just got a call from our on-site rep. The NATO Evaluation Committee completed their review of the last three sortie results. They agree we've exceeded all test parameters. We've been green-lighted."

Carlo whooped and thumped his thigh with a fist. Travis's reaction was every bit as jubilant, if not quite as physical. Even Joe's habitually stony face broke into a satisfied grin.

"What does 'green-lighted' mean?" Dawn wanted to know.

"It means the mod Carlo and Travis and their crews have been testing did everything we advertised it would and more. EAS will go into full-scale development as soon as I get home."

"So you're finished at Aviano?"

"Pretty much." Brian gave his son's head a happy knuckle. "We'll fly back to the States next week, bud."

"But first we'll go to Rome 'n' see the Coliseum, right?"

"Right.

Tommy's whoop was much louder than the prince's and brought a nurse scurrying to check out the disturbance. After Carlo explained the situation in fluid Italian, she checked Travis's monitors and left with a gentle reminder that this *was* a hospital.

"The test crews will now disperse, as well," Carlo informed Dawn. "Mine will return to our base at Furbara, outside Rome. You must extend your stay and allow me to show you that most beautiful of all cities. You and Callie, of course."

"Of course," Callie murmured with a wry smile, but Dawn's glance went to Tommy before she answered.

"You're such a sweetie, Carlo, but I'm not sure what my plans are at this point. How about I contact you when I work them out?"

"Of course." The prince's dark eyes turned to Joe. "Our contract was for the duration of this special project, so I suppose you and your team will leave now, too."

"As soon as we get you back to Furbara and your own security detail takes over," he confirmed.

Kate couldn't help wondering why Carlo's personal security detail needed reactivating but knew better than to ask. The reason was no doubt shrouded by the same veil that had been draped over the rest of their highly classified project.

"Well, then," the prince proclaimed, "we must get

together a last time in Rome. All of us, yes? Assuming Travis is well enough to travel before we go our separate ways."

"I'll be well enough."

After everyone departed and the hospital had settled into the half-light of night, Kate shook out the sheets and blanket the nursing staff had thoughtfully provided. Frowning, Travis watched her tuck the sheets around the cushions of the reclining chair in the corner of his room.

"I still think you should have taken Carlo up on his offer of a hotel room for you and Callie."

"No way that was going to happen. Besides, Callie needed to drive back to Venice with Brian and Dawn to pack her things. We'll talk about a hotel room when she comes back down on the train tomorrow."

The chair made up, she edged it closer to his bed. Travis looked as though he wanted to continue arguing the point until she kicked off her shoes, curled up on the chair and slid her hand through the bed rails. His fingers twined with hers. For some moments the only sounds were the beep of the monitors and the occasional squeak of rubber soles in the hall.

Kate knew he had to be hurting, but he'd refused anything stronger than a mild painkiller. He'd also insisted the charge nurse use her handy-dandy portable computer to show him his electronic hospital record. He could read and interpret most of the numbers—temperature, pulse and respiratory rate, systolic blood pressure, oxygen saturation—but the surgical and postoperative notes required translation.

He rested more easily now, confident the wound wasn't disabling. She didn't want to burst his bubble but had to be honest.

"Dr. Bennati said the bullet went through your bra-chial...um..."

"Brachial plexus."

"Right. You could have nerve damage."

"I could. Don't think so, though."

She bit back a protest as he raised his injured arm a few cautious inches and lowered it just as carefully.

"Still have some range of motion. That's a good sign."

Maybe, but the effort had carved deep grooves at the corners of his mouth.

"Don't push it, okay? Dr. Bennati ordered a neuro-logical consult. Let the experts do their thing."

"Nag, nag, nag."

"Ha! You want nagging, flyboy, you try getting out of bed before the docs and I say you can."

"I wouldn't have to, if you'd get in with me." His teasing grin faded, and he blew out a disgusted breath. "Helluva second honeymoon. I'd intended to do much better by you, Katydid."

"Are you kidding? Touring Italy in a red Ferrari? Gliding through Venetian canals in the moonlight? Curling up next to you in Saint Ursula's surgical ward? How much better can it get?"

"Oh, hell, the Ferrari. It's still parked at the bank."

"No, it's here. I gave Signore Gallo the keys and he had it delivered to the hospital."

"Gallo was here?"

"With Maximo. They showed up while you were still in surgery, both really devastated by the shooting. Evi-dently Signore Gallo's been trying to help the young thug you took down."

Kate shared what she knew, starting with the brief encounter with Gabriella in the ladies' room and ending with her son's failed attempts at rehab. Travis listened and made the appropriate noises at various points, but Kate could see the sad family tragedy didn't really engage him. What had, apparently, was Signore Gallo's interest in her career.

"He's taken quite a shine to you, Kate. Two meetings in less than a week. An elegant lunch. Putting you up for membership in that international association." The pillows whooshed air as he rested against them. His head angled, he looked at her through half-closed lids with eyes gone cool. "That should give your career a real boost."

Kate thought at first the pain had got to him. Just as quickly, she realized the problem wasn't physical.

Travis had jettisoned his military career for her. Correction, for them. Yet he'd walked out of the Cassa di Molino thinking she might take an appointment that would put her on a different continent at least once a quarter, possibly more often.

"Membership in the International Bankers' Association *could* give my career a boost," she agreed, "if I had any desire to accept it."

"You sounded pretty hyped about it this afternoon."

"I was surprised. And flattered," she admitted. "But as soon as I thought about it, I knew I wouldn't accept."

"Yet you told Gallo you'd think about it."

Whoa! Kate hadn't realized her starry-eyed reaction to the proposed nomination had cut so deep.

"The only reason I said I'd consider it was that I didn't want to throw what he considers a great honor back in his face."

She leaned against the bed rail, her hand still caught in Travis's.

"In fact, I've been thinking maybe I need to cut back

on my hours at the World Bank. Now that my husband's going to be hanging around the house a little more, I want some time with him. And with the baby I think we should start trying to make."

His lids lifted. The coolness melted, but the question that remained put a hurt in her heart.

"You sure about that, Kate? We've got a big change coming in our lives as it is. Think this is the right time to add another variable to the equation?"

"To hell with the equation. I'm done trying to calculate and assess and factor in every possibility in every situation."

"Good Lord! Did you feel that? I think the tectonic plates just shifted."

"I'm serious, dammit."

And she was. She was done with the uncertainty, the annoyance, the sheer stupidity of trying to reduce the unknown to a predetermined set of possibilities.

"No more spreadsheets," she promised fiercely. "No more eight-page itineraries or long lists of pros and cons. From now on we take every moment as it comes."

The smile was back, crinkling the tan lines at the corners of his eyes. "Oh, sweetheart, when we make a baby, we're going to need those spreadsheets and long lists. Especially if we have a Tommy the Terrible."

"Or a Tomasina the Terrible."

The prospect seemed to unman him, but he quickly recovered.

"Okay, I'm game. Let's go for it. But you'd better check and see if there's a lock on that door first."

"You idiot. I didn't mean we have to start working on the baby now."

"Why not?"

"Travis! You've been shot. And you're hooked up to all those monitors."

"So we give the nurses a thrill."

"Absolutely not." Her eyes misted, and a smile filled her heart. "But when we get you out of this bed, you're in for one helluva ride, flyboy!"

Chapter Fifteen

Kate, Travis, Callie and Dawn made the trip down from Bologna in comfort and luxury, courtesy of Carlo. Travis had his arm in a sling but had regained as much range of motion as he could manage without pulling stitches. The prognosis was for a full recovery, thank God.

The Ellises came in from Venice later that same afternoon. The prince had arranged accommodations for all of them at a five-star hotel on the Via Veneto, although all parties concerned insisted on paying for their rooms. That first evening they gathered for dinner at an outdoor restaurant highly recommended by the prince.

The following day was their last in Rome, and a surprised Kate was informed that Travis, Dawn and Callie had conspired to set the agenda. None of them would divulge all the details; they just told her to be ready to kick things off at 10:00 a.m. with a girls-only shopping expedition. She was ready as instructed but hated to leave Travis alone on the final day of their Roman holiday.

"Go," he insisted, his feet stretched out on a plush ottoman and the TV remote in hand. "ESPN is going to rebroadcast the UMass/UConn opening game of the season. I'll be fine."

"Fine, my ass," Dawn huffed. "You won't blink for the next three hours."

Which was pretty much what the doctor had ordered, Kate reminded herself. Still, she felt a little let down by his preference for football over a leisurely stroll through the gardens of the Villa Borghese or sitting in the sun on the Spanish Steps with a shared gelato.

"What about the others?" she asked as her friends shepherded her into a cab. "What's everyone doing today?"

"Brian's taking Tom to the Coliseum, Carlo's checking in at Furbara and Joe disappeared to take care of unspecified matters," Dawn related.

"I thought you wanted to take Tommy to the Coliseum."

"I did, but decided it would be better for them to have some guy time. I'll see enough of the kid when we get home."

"Come again?" Wedged in the cab's backseat between her two friends, Kate had to angle sideways to gape at a smug, smiling Dawn. "You're going to do it. Move in with the Ellises?"

"Just until Mrs. Wells is back on her feet."

"But…what about your job? Your apartment?"

"I emailed my boss and told him I'd be working from a remote location for a while. My apartment…" Her shoulders lifted in a careless shrug. "It'll still be there when I get back to Boston."

Kate slewed in the other direction. "Did you know about this?"

"Dawn discussed it with me this morning."

"And you think it's a good idea?"

A smile tugged at Callie's lips. "Better than jetting off to a resort in Marrakech for an indeterminate period, which is what Carlo is pressing her to do."

"Wow! Talk about choices."

Kate wanted to probe further, but the cab swerved onto a side street and rattled to a stop. She climbed out, then waited while Dawn paid the driver and Callie compared a handwritten address to that of the tiny boutique squeezed between a drugstore and a flower shop.

"This is the place," Callie confirmed.

Kate eyed the mannequin in the shop's narrow window dubiously. Bald and bent into a back-breaking contortion, it was draped in layers of violent color.

"You want to shop here?"

"We do," Dawn confirmed. "Carlo's cousin owns the shop."

"Of course."

"He says Stefania will have exactly what we're looking for."

"I'm not really looking for anything."

"Yes, you are. No way you're leaving Rome without one Italian designer original. Travis's orders," she added sternly when Kate started to protest. "Now come on and let Stefania show us her stuff."

Despite the tortured mannequin in the window, Stefania's stuff ran the gamut from ultra sleek to gorgeously soft and feminine. The elegant henna-haired shop owner had obviously been advised to expect them and had a selection waiting, all in Kate's size and chosen to match her coloring. Callie and Dawn settled into chairs while Kate performed a scene straight from *Pretty Woman*. Silks, linens, spandex, lace-trimmed leather… She modeled combinations in every color and fabric.

Cups of cappuccino appeared. Biscotti and almond fudge cookies *dis*appeared. Eyes narrowed, Stefania tapped a crimson-tipped nail against her cheek as her assistant adjusted the drape of a feather-trimmed tunic or repositioned a belt to ride lower on her customer's hips.

An hour later Kate had settled on a cloud-soft white silk dress with spaghetti straps and swirly hem cut on a sharp slant. A wide red leather belt, suitably adjusted to mirror the hem's angle, cost more than either the dress or the red-and-white polka-dot stilettos that Dawn insisted completed the look.

"Not quite," Callie said, smiling as she caught one side of Kate's hair back with a jaunty white fascinator à la the Duchess of Cambridge. "There. Perfect."

Kate twirled in the three-way mirror and had to agree. "Okay, I'm set. Now it's your turn."

"I don't need anything," Callie protested.

"Ha! That's what I said. But need it or not, I intend to buy something for you and Dawn. You've helped Travis and me so much these past few days. I…" She had to stop and swallow the lump that formed suddenly in her throat. "I don't know what I would have done without you."

"That's what friends are for," Dawn replied a little gruffly. "But if you insist on buying, I've been lusting after these wide-legged palazzo pants. And this blouse, Callie, is exactly the same shade of purple as your eyes."

They left the shop thirty minutes later. At Dawn's insistence, they wore their new finery to the next stop on the preplanned agenda. The busy salon was located on the Via Arcione and had also obviously been warned to expect them.

"Don't tell me," Kate said as the three women were whisked into chairs. "Carlo has another cousin in the beauty business."

"Nope. Joe recommended it."

Kate blinked. "As in big, strong, *silent* Joe Russo?"

"He's not so silent around our friend here," Dawn commented with a nod at Callie. "Don't know how she does it, but she always gets the male of the species talking."

"It's called listening," Callie said with unruffled calm. "Works every time."

Nails, toes and hair done, the three women exited the salon with their shopping bags and rumbling stomachs.

"I'm starved," Dawn announced. "Let's have lunch at some swanky restaurant."

Kate shook her newly washed and shiny hair. "Thanks, but I need to get back to the hotel and check on Travis."

"I bet he's so into that football game he doesn't even know you're gone."

"Probably, but I still want to head back."

"Okay but…"

"No *but*s, Dawn." Kate stepped to the curb to flag a cab. "I'm heading back."

"Could you give us five more minutes?"

The request came from Callie, who so rarely asked for favors that Kate dropped her arm.

"I guess. Why?"

"We're just around the corner from the Trevi Fountain. Your coin didn't go in last time. You can't leave Rome without another toss."

"You're right." Laughing, Kate hooked arms with her two friends. "Let's go do it."

The crowd at the tourist site was every bit as thick as it had been the first time they'd made the toss...except in one spot, Kate noted in surprise. Velvet ropes cleared a path down the steps, then right to the basin. And there, waiting at the fountain's rim, were four men. Four and a half, she amended as her startled gaze took in the boy grinning from ear to ear.

Travis wore his dress uniform, the sling fitted across his chest full of medals. Kate wondered for a dazed few seconds how he'd arranged to have it flown over from the States on such short notice. Then her glance shot to Carlo, whose dress uniform was even more resplendent. What looked like diamond-studded decorations filled a scarlet sash. And the hat tucked under his arm sported a matching plume!

Brian and Joe were in dark suits. Even Tommy wore a suit. Still stunned, Kate let her gaze drift from them to the avidly interested crowd to her two smiling friends.

"What is this?"

"It was Travis's idea," Callie said. "He told us he planned to ask you to renew your wedding vows while you were in Italy."

"We suggested the Trevi Fountain," Dawn continued with a grin. "Then sweetie pie Carlo stepped in to take charge, and here we are."

"And here we are," Kate echoed, touched and almost overwhelmed.

"Here, I'll take those."

Dawn grabbed the shopping bags and nudged Kate onto the velvet-roped path. She understood the new dress and shoes now, even the fascinator. She felt every bit as glamorous as the Duchess of Cambridge as she floated down the steps and glided toward her husband.

Hundreds of cell phone cameras clicked and whirred. Grinning kids in backpacks wedged close to tourists in fanny packs to get a shot of the star attraction. Kate caught comments in a half dozen languages, probably everyone asking who the heck she was.

Then the crowd and the chatter and the clicking faded, and there was only Travis stepping forward. She felt the strength in the hand he held out to her, heard the love in his murmured "Hello, Katydid."

And saw the promise of forever in his smile.

* * * * *

MILLS & BOON®

Desire™

PASSIONATE AND DRAMATIC LOVE STORIES

A sneak peek at next month's titles...

In stores from 10th March 2016:

- **Take Me, Cowboy** – Maisey Yates *and*
  His Baby Agenda – Katherine Garbera

- **A Surprise for the Sheikh** – Sarah M. Anderson *and*
  Reunited with the Rebel Billionaire – Catherine Mann

- **A Bargain with the Boss** – Barbara Dunlop *and*
  Secret Child, Royal Scandal – Cat Schield

Available at WHSmith, Tesco, Asda, Eason, Amazon and Apple

Just can't wait?
Buy our books online a month before they hit the shops!
visit www.millsandboon.co.uk

These books are also available in eBook format!

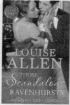

MILLS & BOON®

Why shop at millsandboon.co.uk?

Each year, thousands of romance readers find their perfect read at millsandboon.co.uk. That's because we're passionate about bringing you the very best romantic fiction. Here are some of the advantages of shopping at www.millsandboon.co.uk:

* **Get new books first**—you'll be able to buy your favourite books one month before they hit the shops

* **Get exclusive discounts**—you'll also be able to buy our specially created monthly collections, with up to 50% off the RRP

* **Find your favourite authors**—latest news, interviews and new releases for all your favourite authors and series on our website, plus ideas for what to try next

* **Join in**—once you've bought your favourite books, don't forget to register with us to rate, review and join in the discussions

Visit **www.millsandboon.co.uk**
for all this and more today!

Gemma gazed up at him. She couldn't mask the longing in her eyes—an emotion Tristan knew must be reflected in his own.

"I should go," she said in a low, broken voice. "People will notice we've left the room. There might be talk that the prince is too friendly with the party planner. It… it could get awkward." She went to turn from him.

Everything in Tristan that spoke of duty and denial and loyalty to his country urged him to let her walk away.

But something even more urgent warned him not to lose his one chance with this woman for whom he felt such a powerful connection. If he didn't say something to stop her, he knew he would never see her again.

He couldn't bear to let her go—no matter the consequences.

Tristan held out his hand to her. "Stay with me, Gemma," he said.